211A WEST 57TH STREET

211A WEST 57TH STREET

A novel

JAMES LAWSON

211A WEST 57TH STREET
A NOVEL

iUniverse books may be ordered through booksellers or by contacting:

iUniverse
1663 Liberty Drive
Bloomington, IN 47403
www.iuniverse.com
1-800-Authors (1-800-288-4677)

ISBN: 978-1-5320-7306-9 (sc)
ISBN: 978-1-5320-7307-6 (e)

Print information available on the last page.

iUniverse rev. date: 04/23/2019

Books by James Lawson

XXX

Disconnections

The American Book of the Dead

Crimes of the Unconscious

The Girl Watcher

The Madman's Kiss

The Fanatic

The Copley Chronicles

The Last Day of Peter Grenager

Forgeries of the Heart

The Reluctant God

Acid Rains of Fortune

Midway Through The Journey Of Our Life

Dedication and Acknowledgement

To my wife, Kathy, whose judgment, patience
and perseverance in rooting out errors large and
small was nothing short of miraculous.

1

Lobby, 89ᵗʰ Floor

O N THE "BILLIONAIRE'S ROW" of 57ᵗʰ Street in New York City, a new
building was erected that became an instant landmark and an
icon of wretched excess, a focus for the hatred and disgust of all
right-thinking people, and the envy and admiration of the others. It was
slightly taller than the pencil skyscrapers along the street, much wider
and somewhat bulbous, with wrap-around balconies of different shapes
branching out of many of the floors, including those at the very top of
the building. The building was capped by a glass dome that enclosed
what looked to the news helicopters like a tropical paradise, or at least
a projection of one.

What made the building even more intriguing was that, unlike the
other skyscrapers on the street, with their $100,000,000 penthouses,
the apartments were not on any realtor's list. There were no ads for the
building, no mailings, no brochures, no press reviews or public relations
announcements. The media speculated that the building, 211A W. 57ᵗʰ
Street, had been erected for a single family.

The young man knew nothing of this when he pushed through the
revolving door of the building, noting with some surprise that there was
no doorman at the entrance. He entered a veritable botanical garden,
with lush palms, sprays of bougainvillea and orchids, a fountain feeding
a pool stocked with goldfish, comfortable easy chairs, and on the walls
not covered with flowers and vines, children's art – great suns and wide
smiles, country houses with smoke swirling from chimneys, shaggy
trees and happy birds and animals. He was one of a stream of people
showing up for work at 8 in the morning.

He was greeted in the lobby by a slim, stylish woman in her late twenties. "How may I help you?" she said, with a charming smile.

He was new to the city and hadn't expected charm from its citizens. He had heard stories about how rude they were, how brusque and unwelcoming, and here was somebody who seemed genuinely nice. He wanted to ask her if she was from out of town but couldn't frame it in a way that wouldn't be insulting if she was from the city. "I answered the ad for the ornithologist's assistant …"

"You must be Ivan Anderson – we were expecting you." She held out her hand. "I'm Katie Moran."

Her hand was warm, almost hot, and he thought she must either have amazing circulation or she had warmed her hands as part of her duties as an official greeter, if that's what she was.

He returned her handshake with a sense of relief, perhaps at being welcomed to the big city, of finding a nurturing soul when he least expected it. "Do you work for Dr. Benjamin?" he asked.

She laughed. "I work for the building, or rather for the Nikkanen family, who own the building. Their children did the paintings on the wall."

She guided him over to a desk which held a large control panel manned by a slight Indian boy about Ivan's age, whose skin was as black as the darkest aborigine but whose features were entirely Caucasion. Ivan didn't think he had ever seen a male who was not merely handsome but beautiful, although he was no judge of these matters.

Katie introduced him as Isha and the boy nodded and smiled as Ivan reached for his wallet. "Do you need my I.D.?" he asked.

"That won't be necessary," said Isha. "We did a check on you when you applied for the job and now we have a photo scan that gives you access to the building."

"You don't need my address and cell?"

"You're staying with a friend, John Albright and his wife, Evie, at 100 East 32nd Street, Apartment 4B, until you can find a place of your own," said Isha.

"How on earth …"

"We're very efficient."

It was always unnerving to see Big Brother in action and Ivan shivered inwardly. What else did they know about him? Did they have access to his internet, for example, or his phone? Did they have a record of his impassioned snapchats with his girlfriend in Tucson?

"Right this way," said Katie, ushering him to a bank of elevators.

As they moved towards the elevators, another woman, who seemed to have come from nowhere, took Katie's place at the door. Katie waved to her.

"Hi Katie, hi Ivan," said the woman.

"How does she know me?" asked Ivan, startled at being addressed by name from a total stranger.

"The building knows you," said Katie.

"That's scary," said Ivan. "Or at least creepy."

Katie stopped and smiled at Ivan. "You have to get passed that. We only know what's written by you or about you, anything public. But do you really think you're so different privately, do you think your consciousness or sense of self is all that different from anybody else's? Is there anything truly individual about you?"

Ivan was completely taken aback by Katie's questions, even more by her intellect, which seemed way beyond a building receptionist. "I don't know ..." he started to say.

"Well, there are some things, of course," she said, breezily. "Come this way."

The elevator banks were a feast of color. On each door was a blowup of one of the children's paintings in the lobby, framed in different colors. You could take a "sun" elevator, or a "moon" or "bird" elevator, and so on. "I don't understand something," he said.

"I'm the doorwoman," she said, "but I like to think of myself as a philosopher. There are no jobs for philosophers outside of academia, so the building hires a lot of us as menial workers while we do our philosophizing and write our papers. Does that answer your question?"

Ivan smiled in response.

"Take the "smoke" elevator to the 89th Floor. Someone will be there to meet you."

"One more question," he said, as the elevator door opened. "Why am I here? I know that there's a zoo in Central Park that has an aviary and there's one at the Bronx Zoo, but why would an ornithologist's assistant apply here?"

"You don't know anything, do you?" Katie smiled, as the door closed.

The elevator, which operated by remote control, took Ivan's breath away. He felt glued to the floor as he watched the numbers speed by on the elevator screen. He arrived at the 89th Floor in what seemed like seconds. "Good luck," said Katie's cheery voice from a speaker above.

The door opened to a large reception area, with bird murals covering both the walls and the ceiling. It was like being enveloped by a forest.

What was even more startling was the receptionist sitting at her desk in the center of the room. She looked almost exactly like Katie downstairs. How could she have gotten here so fast?

"You must be Ivan Anderson," said the receptionist. Noticing his look of stupefaction, she added. "I'm her sister, three years younger. My name is Annie Moran, named after a famous tugboat."

"Are you a philosopher, too?"

"No, I'm a receptionist," said Annie. She indicated a bank of easy chairs. "Have a seat here. Dr. Benjamin has one appointment ahead of you."

"Another applicant?"

"No, you're the first today."

There was an array of ornithological and horticultural magazines and journals on a table in front of the easy chairs. Ivan was reaching for one when two men came out of another elevator. They were in civilian dress but obviously policemen.

"Go right in, detectives," said Annie. To Ivan she said, "They won't take more than 10 minutes, sorry for the wait."

"Did something happen?" asked Ivan.

Annie shrugged. "They don't tell me ..."

Ivan tried to concentrate on an issue of *The Auk*, an ornithological journal that he had read before, but he was consumed with curiosity about the building, why he was here, and the Moran sisters.

"Do you have other sisters who work for the building?" he said, lamely.

"You don't have to make conversation," she answered. "I have homework to keep me busy."

"What are you studying?"

4

"Quantum mechanics at the moment. It doesn't make any sense at all."

"I don't even know what that is."

"Physics?"

"I think I've heard of that," said Ivan.

"And no, I don't have other sisters working in the building. But I have one brother who interns in the IT center downstairs in the summers and during school breaks."

"The IT Center?"

"The computers that control all the systems in the building and the information stations and whatever. It connects everything to everything else."

Ivan had to beat down a sense of being overwhelmed by the scope of the building. "What kind of place is this? Some kind of government agency?"

"I think it's Doctor Nikkanen's town house."

The two detectives emerged from a door, shaking their heads. "Weird," said the taller one.

The other nodded, glanced at Annie appreciatively and turned back to his colleague. "What was that called again?"

"I got it in my notebook. Esmerda Woodie, something like that?"

Ivan jerked up. "Esmereldas Woodstar?" he said.

The officers eyed him suspiciously, as they eyed every male outside their profession. "Yeah, that sounds right," said the taller one.

"That's one of the rarest hummingbirds on earth," said Ivan, excitedly.

"That a fact?" said the detective, as the other rang for the elevator.

"They're from Ecuador and they're dying off. They've lost 95% of their habitat."

The detectives were clearly enthralled by the scope of Ivan's knowledge. "Good to know," said the shorter one.

"You can go in now," said Annie to Ivan.

Dr. Rand Benjamin was a large, genial Englishman in his 50's, who wore a cashmere sweater even though the temperature was 70°. His office was large and messy, with books and papers strewn about. One of the walls was a giant screen, split into individual images of birds, with an informational key beneath each one. Three of the images were blinking, several others were shimmering. All in all, there may have been a hundred bird images on the wall.

"Hallo, Mr. Anderson," said Dr. Benjamin, standing. "Glad you could come on such short notice." He reached out a large hand and shook Ivan's with enthusiasm.

"I just arrived in New York two days ago," said Ivan.

"From Tucson, Arizona."

"Yes."

"I've been there, fascinating place, the desert museum and all."

"That's where I worked …"

"Yes, I have your C.V. here. Rather decent regular zoo, by the way. Excellent anteaters."

"Yes, sir, they have three of them. And you can reach down and touch a rhinoceros."

"Like cardboard," said Dr. Benjamin. "I've done it." He looked at Ivan's C.V. "So, you've just graduated. B.S. in, what's this, 'ecology and evolutionary biology?'"

"Yes, sir."

"Did that include ornithology?"

"That was one of the electives."

Dr. Benjamin considered this for a moment, evidently disapproving of the elective status of the field, and gave an audible harrumph. "Well, that's not why you're here, of course."

Ivan waited while Dr. Benjamin read from his C.V. "You worked at the Desert Museum four years?"

"Full time during the summers and spring breaks, on weekends the rest of the year."

"All in the hummingbird aviary?"

"No, first in the regular aviary but the last two years with the hummingbirds. I also spent some of my free time at the Paton Hummingbird Center 50 miles east of Tucson."

"What species did you work with?"

"Well, Rufous of course, then some Costa's, Anna's, Broad-billed, Black-chinned, Calliope, Magnificent … I think that's it."

Dr. Benjamin nodded.

"And there was an Allen's in the regular aviary," Ivan added.

Dr. Benjamin smiled. "They can be pretty spectacular, with the orange throat. We don't have one at the moment."

"Excuse me, sir," said Ivan. "But when I was in the waiting room, two men came out talking about an Esmeraldas Woodstar. I don't think they knew what it was."

Dr. Benjamin looked alarmed. "What did they say?"

"They were just trying to remember the name."

"They're both idiots, but they might be useful. So, what did you do for the hummingbirds?"

"Everything, sir. Cleaning, feeding, waste disposal, air filtration, misting, bathing, lighting ..."

"What did they eat?"

"Nectar, fruit flies, aphids, fruit, beetles ..."

"Spiders?"

"They would, but we didn't put them out to be eaten. They used the webbing to build their nests."

"What kind of spiders?"

"*Metepeira arizonica*. They're the most common labyrinth spiders in the area."

Dr. Benjamin seemed pleased with Ivan's answers and gave a short Dickensian chuckle. "How would you like to work with a Leucistic?"

"Oh my god."

"Or a Purple-throated Mountain-Gem, or a Tufted Coquette, or a Fiery-throated ..."

"Oh my god ..."

"Or a Gould's Inca. And even an Esmeraldas Woodstar."

"That's not possible," said Ivan, truly excited and wondering where this was going. "Nobody has a Woodstar or a Leucistic."

"We do."

Ivan didn't understand. Did he work for the Bronx Zoo? Or was he opening a new aviary? "Where?" he asked.

"Upstairs."

2

Lobby, 15th Floor

ALICE JEYNES LEFT her children with her mother in the Bronx, took the subway to Columbus Circle and walked to the building slowly, in a state of depression. That she should be reduced to *this* gnawed at her. Once, she had been groomed as a model by Zora, the fashion agency. That was before she met Angel and had two of his kids. Once, she had walked a runaway at a Bergdorf show. Now, she changed diapers and spoon-fed squalling monsters.

She was still beautiful, she thought, but not *model* beautiful. She hadn't been able to take off all the weight from her first child, and then the second one finished the job of destroying her modeling career. She still had tawny skin and the oval face and startling eyes of what she thought were her Ethiopian ancestors, although, of course, they could have come from Somalia, or the Sudan or really anywhere in North or East Africa, who knows?

Now, she needed money and time away from her kids. She thought it didn't matter how low she had to stoop to make a living but she didn't think she'd have to stoop *this* low. She had answered ads for various jobs but she had no experience, no education, not even a high school degree, and no references.

She was met in the lobby by Katie Moran, who was startled by and possibly a bit jealous of her beauty and directed her to Isha, at his console.

"I'm here for the waitress job," she said.

"Do you have any I.D.?"

"No, I don't think so."

"A driver's license?"

"I don't drive."

Isha smiled. "That's okay, just raise your hand, palm upwards."

She didn't notice any images taken, beams of light or flashes of lasers but there must have been *something* because Isha looked at the screen and said, "So you gave up modeling for children."

"You can tell that from the palm of my hand?"

"It's an interesting palm," laughed Isha. "But your nose gives us even more information and your eyelids."

"You're kidding."

"Yes," said Isha. "And if you really want the waitress job, go to HR on the 15th Floor and ask for Chrystal McNabe." He pointed out the elevators.

What disconcerted Alice was that the elevator's button panel was blank, except for the 15th Floor. It seemed to know where she was going. She tried pressing some of the dark buttons but they didn't turn on. A monitor showed the floors as they passed. She wondered if the screen that showed the floor was actually a two-way monitor and she was being observed at all times.

At 15, the door opened to a colorful reception area which seemed Moroccan or Middle Eastern themed with walls of intense blues and greens, yellow tiles, benches and chairs with plush cushions, rugs with intricate patterns, lush shrubbery and exotic flowers. It seemed like a fairyland to Alice but she didn't have time to take it in, as a ruddy woman of about 30 approached her within seconds of her arrival and introduced herself as Chrystal McNabe.

"Let's go to the coffee shop," she said.

They went through a tiled archway into a dark old-fashioned cafe, dominated by a large, ancient espresso machine capped by a bronze eagle. The shop was almost full but they found a place and a waitress took their order.

"Do you do this for everyone who wants to be a waitress?" Alice asked.

"We do this for everyone who wants to become a part of the 211A family," said Chrystal.

"Is that what I want?" Alice was finding this attention disconcerting. She had expected applying at a diner with a pot-bellied cook leering at her before offering her a job at below minimum wage.

"I would think so," said Chrystal. "At the starting level, you'll make almost double the minimum wage, plus benefits."

"Health care and stuff?"

"Yes, health care and also a daycare center for Tony and Napheesa …"

"How do you know their names?"

"You put them down when you applied for welfare."

"Of course." They seem to have a complete dossier on her, Alice thought. This was truly creepy.

"We also have a school, where you could get your high school equivalency."

"In the building?"

"The 6th and 7th Floors," said Chrystal. "Let me spell it out for you. The food services division of the building includes a cafeteria, restaurants for workers and regular employees, dining rooms for scientists, artists and executives, a banquet hall, a dining room for the family and a dining area in the aviary, aside from coffee shops sprinkled throughout the building. You'd start at one of the restaurants and help out at banquets. If you do your job well, you'll be eligible for jobs in the more exclusive dining rooms."

This was too much to take in all at once. Alice felt uncomfortable; there had to be some sort of catch. Would she be signing up for some evil empire? She looked around and noticed that almost all of the tables were occupied by HR people talking to prospective employees, many of them shaking their heads. "Why me?" she asked.

Chrystal had been through this disbelief and sense of being overwhelmed time and time again, with almost every applicant. She had felt the same way herself, when she applied for the job at HR. She could understand the creepiness of the Big Brother atmosphere and the reluctance to commit oneself to an unknown and possibly evil employer. Her answer to "why me?" would probably make it worse.

"When you applied for the job, we did a check on you. We saw a tape of you walking the runway at Bergdorf three years ago and you seemed graceful and elegant."

"That was before children," said Alice.

"You're still graceful and elegant," said Chrystal. "The problem is Angel, the father of your children."

"He's out of my life."

"Good. He was a drug dealer and a lot worse. Does he still come around to see the children?"

"He sends them presents on Christmas and their birthdays but he doesn't visit."

"Good," said Chrystal. "Now for the job. Do you think you can handle taking orders from people and being rushed by the chefs and sometimes having guys hit on you and dealing with women's jealousy?"

"I'm used to it," said Alice. "Not a problem."

"Most people are pretty well behaved, but occasionally ..."

"Understood."

"When could you start?"

"Now."

Chrystal smiled. "Well, let's give it a try."

There were a few formalities they had to discuss, and Alice had to sign a few papers, but surprisingly few, compared to most jobs. Presumably, they had most of her information already. She was told to check in for a physical on the 4th Floor tomorrow morning at 8, then report to Irwin Mankowitz on the 6th Floor. Alice couldn't quite believe that she'd been hired, just like that.

"Do you want to enroll your kids in daycare?" asked Chrystal.

"Sure. What do I have to do?"

"Just bring them to the 11th Floor at 7:30 tomorrow."

They been talking for no more than five minutes and only when they were officially done did a waitress come over to take their order. They chatted while waiting for their coffees but the wait wasn't long. "So, any questions?" said Chrystal.

"A couple. You said there was a dining room for the family. What family?"

"The people who own the building. I've never seen them. Somebody told me there were five kids but I don't know any more."

"Has anybody seen them?"

"Lots of people – there's a staff of people who work up there. They take a separate elevator from everybody else."

When they were done, Alice asked if there was a restroom she could use before she left and Chrystal pointed to a door in the hallway. "I'll leave you here," she said.

The door didn't have a sign but opened automatically when Alice approached. Inside was a marble bathroom that you might find in a fancy hotel. A bathroom attendant, a sprawling woman in her 70's, welcomed Alice and told her she'd have a hot towel and some cologne waiting for her after she left the stall.

"How much is that going to cost me?" said Alice.

"Honey, if I had to live on tips, I'd be skin and bones. You don't pay for it."

The woman opened a drawer that displayed a wide selection of what looked like dildos. "Interested?" she said.

"What the fuck …"

"A lot of women get jittery talking to HR so this helps relieve the tension." Sure enough, she heard a slight, undefined grunt coming from a stall at the far end of the room.

"Does every bathroom in the place have this service?"

"No, this is just for the HR floor, as far as I know. But I don't know much."

"Thanks, but no thanks," said Alice, although she was intrigued.

3

61st Floor

HE TWO DETECTIVES from outside the building, Tim Follet and Jorge Ramos, accompanied the building manager, Aaron Houdi, the head of building security, Roanne Martin, and three members her staff from their headquarters on the 16th Floor to the office of the Head Butler on the 61st Floor.

Outside of the family itself, the Head Butler was in charge of the entire building, among many other duties. Although he had to consult with Dr. Nikkanen on the scientific, artistic and professional staff, and had little to do with the hospital or schools, he presided over the various departments that maintained and nourished the building – the farms, kitchens, dining areas, gyms, pools, stores, the daycare center, theaters, garages, the computer and HUAV systems, not to mention the domestic arrangements for the family and visitors. Ten department heads reported to him weekly.

His name was Mustafa Faoud, an Egyptian by birth. He graduated from the University of Alexandria in engineering and got an M.B.A. at the Wharton School of the University of Pennsylvania. He had worked for the family long before the building was erected, at the Nikkanen estate in Finland, at Nikkanen Industries in Helsinki and Hamburg, and at the Nikkanen Foundation in London. His wife, Aisha, was a botanist, working at one of the greenhouses on 74. At the moment, Faoud was in crisis mode.

His office was huge, befitting the CEO of a major enterprise, and ultra-modern, with spare lines and stark, Scandinavian furniture, a plain desk bristling with consoles, a conference area, its own kitchen and bathroom, a dining area, a small theater, and a bank of monitors. The one free wall was bare except for a single painting, a massive Rothko of two solid chunks of cobalt and burnt orange on a red background. Together with offices for secretaries and assistants, the Butler's office took up an entire floor of the building, nearly 10,000 square feet. From the immense windows, one could see parts of Queens, Brooklyn, the Bronx, and the panorama of the New York Harbor.

The two detectives and four members of the building's security department joined Dr. Benjamin, the director of the Aviary, the head custodian for the building, the chief of information technology, and several other officials around Faoud's desk. A large screen was set up nearby.

Faoud was in his 60's, with a muddy face that seemed to fold over itself with wrinkles and curves. He was invariably gracious, in the Egyptian manner, and could be charming and persuasive. But he was grim today as he displayed an image of a tiny hummingbird with a purple throat and blue/green body.

"This is an Esmeraldas Woodstar," said Faoud. "It is one of the smallest hummingbirds in the world, only slightly larger than a bumblebee. It is possibly the rarest hummingbird in the world. They live in Ecuador, where they are dying out as their environment shrinks. Dr. Benjamin tells me that as far as he knows, no aviary in the world has one, with one exception. We have two of them."

He pointed to the screen. "The reason you are here is because one of them, this one, is missing."

Most of the group from security and the building officials didn't quite know how to react to this. It was only a bird, albeit a rare one.

Faoud was secretly amused by their lack of reaction. "Let me give you an idea of why this is significant. A private collector in the Netherlands has offered us $5,000,000 for the pair, even though they might possibly die enroute. Not that we would consider selling them but, for clarity's sake, let's just say that two and a half million dollars has gone missing."

"Do you have insurance?" asked Tim Follet, one of the NYPD detectives.

Faoud glanced at Dr. Benjamin, who answered the question. "That's one of the reasons you're here, Detective Follet, so we can submit a stolen property claim or possibly a lost income claim, but we would never get anything like what the bird is worth."

"And you don't know if it was stolen," said Roanne Martin, the head of the building's security.

"No, only that it's missing," said Faoud.

"No ransom note?"

"Not yet."

"Is there a tracking device on the bird?" asked Detective Ramos.

"Unfortunately, the smallest tracking devices weigh as much as the bird," said Dr. Benjamin. "The Esmeraldas weighs a little over 2 grams, which is the weight of the smallest GPS. So the answer is *no*."

"Is it possible it died and you just haven't found it?" asked Detective Follet.

Faoud shrugged, with the implication that *anything* is possible.

Dr. Benjamin fielded the question. "We would have found it. It's also possible that somebody killed it or drugged it and took it out of the aviary in a pocket or purse, or stuffed it inside a shirt, but unlikely. We have tapes of everyone who enters and leaves the aviary 24/7. And X-rays of the contents of all bags, purses or pockets, for that matter. The tapes are available for you to study."

"Does the family know about this?" asked Roanne, who had been a police captain before she secured her pension and took the job with 211A. She was known as Captain Martin.

"Not yet." In general, Faoud had little to do with security on 16. Their job was mostly surveillance and when there was a real crime, like now, the NYC police were called in. They had occasionally been called upon to break up fights, eject unruly people or prevent unwelcome people from entering the building. They could verify credentials and almost every member of the department enjoyed spying on lovers. Only once had they been called upon to stop a rape in progress, which transpired in an elevator, when the prospective rapist pressed an emergency button, thinking (crazily) that this would render his actions invisible. There had been other thefts in the building but the thieves had been caught almost immediately, identified through videotapes and often caught in the act.

"Can we see the aviary?" asked Detective Ramos.

"We'll let you know when the aviary is available to be seen," said Faoud. "If the family or their guests are there, it's forbidden. But you'll be able to get in when it's free – there's a signal that lets you know if the family is there.

"Who has access to it aside from the family and their friends?"

Dr. Benjamin answered. "The aviary staff, ornithologists, gardeners, horticulturists, veterinarians, technicians who control the temperature and humidity, the sun roof and various environments, then there's the serving staff, waiters, chefs, bus boys, then cleaning people, maids, also some messengers – you have a complete list downstairs."

"What's our cover story?" asked Captain Martin.

"Unauthorized entry, of course," said Faoud. "That's serious enough to summon the city police but doesn't give away anything."

Faoud closed the meeting with the admonishment to keep the theft quiet. He knew the building people would but he was a little worried about Detectives Folly and Ramos. They had been vetted by Captain Martin and her group but they probably wouldn't lose their jobs if they blabbed. Still, they were needed. And their captain had been informed about an intruder.

Captain Martin was given charge of the operation, reporting to Dr. Benjamin, and the group dispersed.

4

6th Floor

THE MORAN SISTERS were having lunch in a restaurant on 6.

Usually, they took a quick bite at the cafeteria upstairs but every now and then they splurged on one of the boutique restaurants on 6, which included Indian, Chinese, Mexican, Italian, Japanese, Soul and a pizza stand, as well as a steakhouse. An after-hours pub, Finnegan's, was on 36 and the building's plush French restaurant, Genevieve, nicknamed Deux Cent Onze Ah, was on 62. Another group of upper scale dining rooms for the professional staff was on 63. Today, the Moran sisters treated themselves to the Trattoria del Marco, which served fairly decent Italian fare and reasonably priced pastas.

Rumors had been flying about the presence of outside police officers in the building. Katie had let them in, Annie had ushered them into Dr. Benjamin's office and heard one of them say, "weird" when they left. She was sure it had something to do with a rare hummingbird – she even knew the name, an Esmeraldas Woodstar – from the new ornithologist's assistant they had hired. She also knew Dr. Benjamin had a meeting on the 61st Floor, the Head Butler's office, which meant it was important.

"It not hard to see what's happened," said Katie. "One of the hummingbirds is dead, missing or stolen."

"A reasonable assumption," said Annie. "But I'm just the receptionist."

"Did you ask the pretty boy they just hired?"

"Ivan Anderson? He is pretty, isn't he? Do you want him?"

"He looks too innocent for a boytoy," laughed Katie. "You'd have to *talk* to him."

Chrystal McNabe stopped by their table. "Hey, morons," she said, an old joke that the Morans didn't dignify with a response. "Did you hear about the intruder?"

"We heard it was a dead hummingbird," said Annie.

"No, Debby in the hospital said somebody came in seriously injured, possibly a rape. They caught it on tape."

"How could it be *possibly* if they caught it on tape," said Katie.

"Good point. I'm just reporting what I hear."

Chrystal left with a shrug, as if to say, *who knows what goes on here?*

It was curious that in an environment where everything was videotaped, aside from the toilets, the dressing rooms and showers of the gyms and pools (although it was generally suspected that these were filmed as well), the private apartments of the residents (although everyone knew these were taped illegally) and the living quarters of the family (although there was conjecture about these as well), rumors could sweep through the building like wildfire. It was obvious that an intruder couldn't remain in the building for five seconds without being caught, yet the rumors persisted.

And there were endless rumors about everything. Faoud was a terrorist. The research labs on 57 and 58 were creating human clones. A nurse at the hospital on 2 was killing patients. The Message Center on 22 hired pedophiles. The forbidden floors (37-52) manufactured nerve gas. The farms on 75,76 and 77, or the restaurants on 6 and 7 were adding saltpeter to their crops or foods to suppress the libidos of the building's population. Or powdered walrus tusk to enhance them. It was also rumored that the IT Center on 8 spun out a steady stream of alternative facts, the more fanciful the better. (Powdered walrus tusk was the concoction of a bored programmer, it was said.)

There were plenty of facts to feed the rumors – affairs, thefts, undercover prostitution (one of the masseuses on 19 had actually advertised herself outside as a dominatrix), divorces, couplings, fights, births, deaths (there was a hospice on 59) – everything you might expect from a small universe within a big city.

The most constant rumors, of course, were about the family. Few people had seen them, although their presence in the building was pervasive. The family had their own entrance and their own elevator.

They even had a separate elevator that serviced only the floors they used, 78 to 90 and the Chapel on 60.

Most people knew that Dr. Nikkanen had a wife and children but didn't know how many children, or their names, since they weren't listed on any HR records. Dr. Nikkanen's first name was known to be Paavo, a Finnish name. What he was a doctor *of* was a matter of speculation – possibly medicine, possibly physics, or philosophy or business administration. There was universal agreement, based on owning the building, that he was fabulously wealthy, but he was not on the Forbes list of billionaires. He was not listed as an officer of any public company, and an intense search of Google turned up nothing. Neither Katie nor Annie (nor Chrystal or Isha, for that matter) had ever seen them. Knowingly, at least. The people that used the family entrance were taped on a separate system, one that was not in the building's data base or accessible to the regular building inspectors.

But rogue pictures had been taken of many of the people who used the family entrance. And even Katie and Annie, on their way home, had seen people coming and going – children with their parents, including several blind children, teenagers, well-heeled adults, elderly foreigners and business associates. It was easy to speculate that there were children and teenagers in the family, in addition to adults, young and old. Both Katie and Annie would eventually intersect with the family, but it was Alice Jeynes, the waitress from the Bronx, who saw them first.

5

90th Floor

VAN ANDERSON HAD been hired the day after he applied. He was exactly what Dr. Benjamin was looking for — someone who had experience with the nitty gritty of hummingbird care. Almost all of the C.V.'s that had crossed his desk had academic knowledge, one had studied them in the field and was conversant with their feeding and nesting habits, another had done a study of hummingbird predators and had claimed to have witnessed a praying mantis attack. But only Ivan knew how to clean up after them, how to encourage nest building and reproduction, how to spot signs of illness, how to discourage dangerous aggression.

What Dr. Benjamin liked most about Ivan was not his qualifications, however, but his enthusiasm. His excitement at the mention of a Leucistic hummingbird was thoroughly enjoyable. It would be fun having him as an assistant.

Although Ivan was officially hired, and had been vetted electronically when he applied, he still had to go through a day of physical exams, tests and authorizations, mostly at HR on 15, where he was met by Chrystal McNabe. Interviewing Ivan was something of a promotion for Chrystal, as she normally dealt with lower level hires, like Alice Jeynes, not professionals. There were different tests to administer and she had to be more careful about following the rules, especially as the entire interaction was taped and could be used as evidence of discrimination or other wrongdoings in court. The problem, if there was one, was that Ivan was so informal and relaxed that it was hard to keep to a formal interview.

"Is it Miss McCabe or Mrs. McCabe?" he asked, as they were walking to the same coffee shop where Chrystal had spoken to Alice.

"Does it matter?" asked Chrystal.

"I just want to know what to call you," said Ivan.

"Call me Chrystal. And welcome to 211A. I gather you've accepted Dr. Benjamin's offer."

"Are you kidding? It's a dream come true."

They arrived at the coffee shop and found a table. "I like your office," Ivan joked.

There were no lengthy forms to fill out, as she had most of the information she needed online, within minutes of the call that Ivan had been hired. But there was still a lot to discuss, starting with a salary that was more than Ivan expected. She gave him a folder about basic benefits, insurance, health, bonuses, hours, holidays, etc. and brought up the benefits unique to 211A.

"At your salary, you qualify for a lower income apartment, when one becomes available. You'd get a one-bedroom and they're way below what you'd pay outside. And since you're on the professional staff, you'll also have use of the gym and pool for professionals on 68 ..."

"What does that mean, for professionals?"

"There are gyms and pools for regular staff, like me or your cleaning lady, on 33, and another for professionals, scientists, doctors, ornithologist's assistants, like you, on 68, and another for the family, on 79."

"Who is this family I keep hearing about?"

"I don't know much about them. Dr. Nikkanen owns the place and he has a wife named Tuuli."

"What kind of a name is that?"

"They're Finnish but that's all I know about them. I've never seen them."

She told him about the building's medical and fitness programs, the lawyers he could consult, the restaurants throughout the building and the nightclub and casino on 65, the chapel and meditation rooms, the educational benefits if he wanted to go to graduate school and the convenience of having an I.D. chip implanted in his hand. "It's a simple procedure and it can be easily removed." She waved her hand, as if the surgery to remove the implant was of no account. "Lots of companies are doing it."

More and more, Ivan felt he was in some kind of dream world, that this wasn't happening. Yesterday, he was an ordinary person, camping out on his friend's couch, new to a great city, hoping for a job, chatting with his girlfriend back home, free of responsibilities, with enough money for a month of loafing. Now he was about to be outfitted with a subdermal implant that gave him access to endless resources, contained his profiles, medical records, location, unlocked his electronic devices, even turned on lights wherever he entered. He was becoming part of a vast enterprise that included his beloved hummingbirds. And he was being briefed by a redheaded woman who was becoming more and more attractive by the minute.

Chrystal was giving him the company spiel about the safety of the implant, how they had overcome the problems with infections, neurological damage, MRI incompatibility, tissue reactions and especially hacking by outside scanners, allowing a third-party to steal and use all the information on the chip, but she was also not unaware of Ivan's growing attraction. It wasn't a unique experience.

"Suppose I don't get the implant?" asked Ivan.

"No problem. It'll just make it a little harder to get around and pay for things. With the chip, you can pay for anything in the building, the restaurants or the pharmacy, whatever, you just have to wave your hand and it's taken out of your bank account. It's also hooked up to your credit card for outside purchases. The chip replaces all your cards."

Ivan was uneasy about the chip. He wondered if an integrated circuit device implanted under his skin could control him in some way. He remembered voicing the same concern to Katie Moran when she told him the building knew him (was it only yesterday morning?) She said he had to get passed that, but he wasn't convinced. Still, he was conflicted: he wanted to please this attractive woman, but wondered if she was using her beauty to force him into giving up his ... what was it ... *soul*?

Chrystal held out her hand and had him hold it so he could see her own implant, how small it was, how insignificant, and that gesture had him hooked. She didn't really know why she wanted him hooked – she wasn't really thinking of seducing him – but she liked the feeling that she had somehow overpowered him. She was surprised that Ivan hadn't put up more resistance to the idea. Perhaps he was just too innocent. The woman she'd seen yesterday for the waitress job, Alice Jeynes, had told her there was no fuckin' way in hell someone was going to stick something in her body. But Ivan shrugged it off, as if this was how jobs in the adult world operated. She sent him down to the clinic on 2 to get it done.

The procedure took five minutes. A nurse was waiting for him as he left the elevator and took him to a dark room off the waiting area, which seemed to be buzzing with sensors. The nurse studied a monitor and then swabbed Ivan's hand with alcohol and positioned it in a large machine that adjusted to the contour of his hand. He felt a slight prick in the space between his thumb and forefinger, and that was it.

"Okay, you've been stapled," said the nurse, with a hint of a smile, as if they'd just shared a secret. She rubbed the spot with what seemed like a soothing glue and patted it dry. "It'll itch for a day or two. Try not to scratch it too much."

"So I just wave this around in the air to buy stuff or go anywhere?"

"You'll catch on," said the nurse, and escorted him back to the elevator. "You're going to Dr. Benjamin's office on 89."

When Ivan returned to the 89th floor reception area, Annie Moran seemed like an old friend.

"You've been chipped?" she said.

"Did you get one, too?" he asked.

"Not at first, but eventually. It was just too convenient. Anyway, Dr. Benjamin's expecting you."

Ivan felt more like hanging out than starting his job immediately. He felt he needed a break from formalities, although in reality, he had experienced very little of them. "Is that your homework?" he asked, indicating the book on her desk.

"I have a test tonight."

"Where do you go?"

"Columbia."

"I think that's a good school," said Ivan, who wasn't sure if it was or not, or if he was thinking of the Columbia College in California or

Missouri. Wasn't there one in the Carolinas as well? He was a bit hazy on the world outside of Tucson, although his girlfriend, Kimberly, had gone to school in Phoenix, 500 miles to the north of Tucson.

"It thinks it is," said Annie.

Ivan was struggling with something to say but gave up and headed for the door leading to Dr. Benjamin's office. "Well, I'd better go," he said, and waved his hand at a, small pad on the door for admittance. Annie seemed amused.

Inside, he was greeted by Dr. Benjamin and then handed off to Dr. Fain, the man he'd be working with directly. Peter Fain was a pudgy, 30-year old rust-haired ornithologist from California, who was in charge of the upkeep of the aviary.

"I'm your boss," he said, cheerily. "Also, I'm gay but I don't think you are."

"No," said Ivan. "I have a girlfriend in Tucson."

"Too bad," said Fain. "But I'm not prejudiced, I'll show you around anyway."

He turned out to be fun to work for – friendly, enthusiastic and helpful, with a strong commitment to the gay lifestyle. He liked to view heterosexuality as an aberration that could be cured. He showed Ivan around the floor, the labs and holding pens, the sick bay, the equipment rooms and pantries, with stocks of bird feed, fruit flies and spiders, introducing Ivan to various people along the way. Ivan stopped at a cage to stare at a fanciful bird with a long beak, a frill of white feathers on its head and a long tail. "Is that a West African hornbill?" he asked.

"*Horizocerus albocristatus*, of the *Buerotidae* family," said Fain. "We're loaning this one to the Central Park Zoo to breed with the one they have. They're supposed to pick her up any time now."

Ivan had his own cubicle, with a computer hooked up to the building's net, with its huge databank of scientific articles and links to data banks throughout the world, as well as the regular Internet. "It'll take some getting used to," said Fain.

"When do I get to see the aviary?" asked Ivan.

"Right now."

They retraced their way through the maze of offices, cages, equipment rooms and pantries to a large service elevator at one end of the floor. "If you need to bring up something heavy, you'll use this. It only goes to three floors. We're going this way."

They turned a corner and entered an escalator that led up to a transparent door to a vestibule with large, heavy flaps barely containing a blast of heat and humidity. Ivan and Fain walked through the flaps into paradise.

The aviary was part of a tropical botanical garden, perhaps 90 feet high, capped with a transparent dome which (as Ivan later found out) was opened for short periods of time in the summer, replaced by a thin netting. A giant banana tree soared overhead, and there were moss-covered cypresses in the complex of waterways within the garden. Smaller trees, crisscrossed with vines, were festooned with flowers of all kinds, bougainvillea, orchids, columbine, various flowers that hummingbirds like, cardinals, fuchsia, delphinium, several varieties of trumpet flowers, as well as plants of all kinds, including huge green and purple elephant ears. On the far side of the aviary was a narrow ladder leading to what seemed like a precarious catwalk just beneath the top of the dome, presumably used for maintenance.

Equally as striking as the flood of colors was the noise – whistling, cackling, chirping, honking, warbling, an avian cacophony that Ivan found infinitely pleasing. There were birds everywhere.

"A Calliope!" he said, as a tiny hummingbird with a violet throat buzzed him at the moment they entered the aviary. They came to a walkway in the midst of a stream where a pair of scarlet ibises fished for insects. Ivan saw a spectacular bird with a metallic green/blue and copper breast and an iridescent mane sitting on a vine.

"What's that?" he asked.

"A Nicobar pigeon," said Fain. "And over there is a Fairy Bluebird."

The hummingbirds were everywhere, poking their bills into flowers or hovering about them. Ivan identified a Rufous from the Tucson museum but another he'd never seen before.

"A Fiery-throated *panterpe insignis*," said Fain.

The walkway ended in an octagonal Chinese pavilion with scarlet pillars and a jade-green tiled roof that splayed out from a single point at the top which sported a statue of a crane with its beak pointing upwards. Inside the pavilion were tables and chairs for dining in one area and a group of easy chairs around a coffee table in another.

"Can we get a coffee here?" asked Ivan.

"I'm afraid not," said Fain.

They walked down another path leading to a maintenance room where Fain began to instruct Ivan on his duties, which were similar to those he performed in the Sonoran Desert Museum, essentially making sure the hummingbirds were fed, healthy, well nested, reproductively active and happy. As no other birds in the aviary preyed on hummingbirds, they were relatively safe, but accidents happen, birds don't always look where they're flying, a virus could be lurking about or flecked off from the numerous humans working at the aviary. There were perhaps 15 people in blue smocks scurrying about the aviary on one errand or another.

A thin, freckled woman in her 40's approached them. "Any news on the Woodstar?" she asked Fain.

Fain shrugged no and introduced Ivan as the new hummingbird keeper.

"You're sorely needed," said the woman, whose name was Tess McAllister. "I've been pushing for a hummingbird person for a year. I'm into water birds myself, ibises, geese, too bad blue herons get stressed in places like this."

"He worked at the Sonoran Desert Museum in Tucson," said Fain. "In the hummingbird aviary."

"Oh well, that's the standard," said Tess. "But we have some hummers that they don't."

"I've noticed," said Ivan.

She turned back to Fain. "I think we should check out Carmine," she whispered. "He could steal a Woodstar."

"Just because he's Italian?"

"I *love* Italians. But Carmine's shifty, and I'm an almost infallible judge of character. I'd put my money on Carmine."

"I'm sure he'll be questioned," said Fain. "As you will."

"And you, too," said Tess, with a wink at Ivan.

A man came over to Fain. "Did you get the solution?" he asked.

"It's still on order," said Fain.

"We have three gallons left." He made a face and went off before Fain could introduce him to Ivan.

"Now *that* man is a piece of work," said Tess. "Weird but essentially okay. I've never been able to figure out his sexuality, if any."

"Did you want to?" asked Fain.

"Desperately," said Tess, walking off.

Fain was showing Ivan the hose system when the birds seemed to go quiet, some shutting down in mid chirp. Ivan could smell a slight aroma of some kind of perfume, perhaps lavender-based, accompanied by a slight whoosh like the sound of a white noise. The workers in the room dropped whatever they were doing and headed for the exits.

"What's happening?" asked Ivan.

"The family needs the room," said Fain, as they followed the crowd. "We have 5 minutes to leave."

As they left, Ivan could see a team of waiters, in light blue uniforms, coming with carts and table settings.

"The whole family is coming?"

"It could be all of them, or just one boy, it doesn't matter," said Fain. "Maybe Dr. Nikkanen wants to impress a guest. Maybe the girls are having a sleepover. We'll be notified when we can come back and do our jobs."

They joined the others downstairs, some going to the pens and labs, some headed for the coffee shop on the floor. Fain took Ivan to a changing room, where he could select a blue smock to put over his clothes when he worked.

"So the family can just kick us out at any time?" said Ivan.

"You have to be prepared to work irregular hours," said Fain. "There's even a small night shift here, when the aviary's dark and no one's using it, just in case. A lot of them are insect people – they seem to like the dark, although sometimes they don't show at all."

"Insect people?"

"They work on 88. It's an entomologist's dream world. That's where you'll get your spiders for the nests. I'll take you down there later."

"Entomologists?"

"And ichthyologists. That's where we get the fish for the ponds upstairs."

For some reason, this last piece of information put Ivan over the edge. "This is too much to take in all at once. It's giving me a headache."

"Don't worry, it'll get worse."

6

11th and 6th Floors

ALICE JEYNES DECIDED not to deposit her children at the daycare center right away. Her mother liked to be with the children, even though they were a pain and taxed her patience and strength to the hilt.

Still, Alice went up to 11, looked over the place and checked in with the director, who seemed solid and sympathetic. She signed up Tony and Naphessa for the following week. What she hadn't realized was that a small amount of her salary would be deducted for daycare, but it was so small, it didn't really hurt.

The center itself was essentially an indoor playground, with toys and blocks set up everywhere, a slide, a sandbox, swings, various animals on springs, furry teddy and panda bears, plush bunnies, Raggedy Anns and Andys, shelves of books, even a large doll house.

"Only the older children can play with this," said Mrs. Warner, the director. "We don't want little ones eating the furniture."

"What about older kids?" asked Alice.

"We have an afterschool section, a basketball court, a roller rink, desks and computers – ample resources for kids K-12, all staffed by professionals."

"Can I see my kids at lunch?" asked Alice.

"Yes, but we'd rather you didn't. Separation issues …"

"Yeah, I can see that. They'd scream their heads off when I leave."

"I hope not."

Alice realized she had said the wrong thing and tried to soften it. "I mean, some kids'd do that."

"We can't handle all kids," said Mrs. Warner. "Those with severe developmental or behavioral issues ..."

"Oh no, mine are fine, don't worry."

Alice arranged to bring them for an interview the following Monday, along with her mother, in case she had to take them back home. She thanked Mrs. Warner and left for her job on 6.

The restaurant, Tay's Kitchen, was considered one of the 6th Floor's "ethnic" restaurants, although it was a stretch to call soul food ethnic since it was quintessentially American, albeit African-American. Still, it was as popular as the Chinese, Indian, Mexican, Italian and Japanese restaurants on the floor, though not as popular as the instant pizza stand.

Alice was assigned to Tay's only because she was black, not for any particular skills or interest in food. The owner, Tay Reneau, was not happy. From the very first moment he saw Alice, he knew she was wrong for the job, that HR had made a mistake. She was way too beautiful, not nearly black enough, graceful but not particularly gracious, intrinsically lacking in *soul*. "Do you know anything about food, girl?" he asked.

"Don't call me *girl*, my name's Alice. And no, I don't know anything about food, except I think MacDonald's sucks and I wouldn't let my children near a Burger King."

"Well, that's a start," said Tay, amused. "What do you know about soul food?"

Alice had always found soul food fattening but didn't want to bring that up at the moment. "Fried chicken, corn pone, collard greens, Southern stuff – I've had it. My grandmother used to make that stuff."

"Was she from the South?"

"No, she was from New York, born and bred, but her grandparents came up from Louisiana, she told me."

"Why that's where I'm from," said Tay. "We could be cousins."

Alice decided she liked him. She was under no illusion that the job would be anything but drudgework, but she couldn't be choosy.

She was outfitted with a white shirt, black pants and a full-length red apron, with the name "Tay's" in white script and the motto, "down home good" in smaller letters below. There was a kitsch about it that appealed to Alice. It was so far removed from her former world of fashion that it was actually funny. She took a selfie to send to her friends.

The job required a day of training, learning the menu, the routines, the settings, the sales pitch and the like. She met the other waitresses and the chefs, including Tay's wife, Celine, a large, bosomy lady who seemed friendly but guarded. Everyone on the staff knew she didn't belong there, and she knew they knew. Still, she vowed to do her best.

"Could you get your voice a little more Southern," one of the waitresses said, confidentially. "A few *y'all's* wouldn't hurt."

"See what I can do," said Alice.

She assisted at lunch, which started around 11:30 and lasted until 2:30, and by the end of the period, she was caught up in the frantic pace of the place, with patrons waiting for tables and impatient customers. There were three shifts at Tay's and Alice was signed up for breakfast and lunch. She would arrive at the building at 6:00, consign Naphessa and Tony to daycare, and report for her shift at 6:30. *Breakfast* didn't have a stopping point so she was on duty continuously through lunch until 2:30.

Aside from the daycare center and the game areas, there was also an unsupervised playground on the same floor, where Alice would take the kids and sit around chatting with the other mothers. Gabby, a large woman who worked at the pharmacy on 21 confided in Alice as they each pushed their two children on a swing. "You better watch yourself, girl," she said.

"Why?"

"You never know what's gonna happen in this building. One dead and more to come."

"Who died?"

"They're not saying," said Gabby. "But just be careful."

Gabby, who weighed over 200 pounds, none of it muscle, turned out to be a leading exponent of any conspiracy swirling about the building.

This never failed to amuse Alice, who developed a fondness for Gabby, based in part on her entertainment value. The one area in which she was credible was the pharmacy, where she was basically a salesperson and definitely not a pharmacist.

"I know a few things about who takes what," she said, as they were transferring their children from the swings to the sandbox.

"Like what?" asked Alice.

"I know that Dr. Cavanaugh orders medications that cost almost $2,000 a pill. They must spend half a million in pills over the year."

"Who's Dr. Cavanaugh?"

"He's the doctor for the family. *The* family."

"So what are they for?"

"Well, that's the thing," said Gabby. "I don't know, and the pharmacist won't tell me. She's a real bitch."

"Did you look it up online?" asked Alice.

"Not there."

This is weird, like much of what she'd heard about the building, thought Alice. "Why won't she tell you, just bitchiness?"

"She's not allowed, she says. She'd be fired. I've worked with her for two years. Might think she'd let up a little."

"What's it called, this $2,000 pill?"

"Dafnopon. Ring a bell?"

"You're telling me that the family spends all that money on a pill that officially doesn't exist?"

Gabby nodded and raised an eyebrow to indicate *isn't that something else?*

"What do you think it's for?"

"I have no idea. Leprosy, maybe?"

Like many of Gabby's stories, this one couldn't be verified. Alice smiled politely and gathered up her children for the long ride home. The thought of renting an apartment in the building – the low-cost apartments on 24, 25, 26 and 28 – became something to look forward to, as they were cheaper and better than the dump she rented in the Bronx. They didn't come up that often, but it might be worth applying now. She'd have to take a look to see if they were big enough to fit her mother.

7

16th Floor

A CONFERENCE WAS IN progress in the day room of the building's police precinct on 16. It had been four days since the meeting in Faoud's office and the dazed security staff was making their first report to Captain Martin.

José Ramirez, a member of the security staff for the past three years, and now the senior security officer under Roanne Martin, summed up the results of their search of the videotapes: "nothing."

Captain Martin nodded for Ramirez to continue.

"We've viewed tapes of the aviary on 90, the labs and offices on 89, the aquariums, insect gardens, labs and offices on 88, the stairs and hallways between all the floors, the elevators, the kitchens and pantries on 86, the wait staff areas, the hallways on all the floors for the executives and professionals, the main lobby, the garages on the sublevels, on a hunch we even looked at the research labs on 57 and 58, from three days before the Esmeraldas was stolen to the day after. Nothing."

"What do you mean, nothing?" said Captain Martin.

"Nothing related to the disappearance of the Esmeraldas. We found lots of other stuff, as usual."

"Like."

"People necking in the hallway, people picking their noses, littering, smoking in the johns, a few people taking drugs ..."

"The blue fairy blowing his boyfriend in a broom closet on 88 ..." offered Dom Piccolo, a retired police officer working with Ramirez.

"If you're referring to Dr. Fain, change your language" said Captain Martin.

"We checked x-rays of purses and clothing going out of the aviary ..." Ramirez continued. "One of the ornithologists who lives on 70 sneaked out a plastic container of seed for his birds at home ...

"Who's that?"

"Dr. Fry. He does this every week. But we x-rayed the container, nothing but bird seed, and hummingbirds don't eat bird seed."

"Check him out anyway. What about lockers?"

"We need an okay from you to open people's lockers."

"Do it. Everyone signed the waiver when they started. What else?"

"Tess McAllister, the bird lady who works for Dr. Fain told him she thought Carmine Marino stole the Esmeraldas. We checked it out but didn't see anything suspicious with Marino."

"So where are we?" Captain Martin had pretty much delegated the investigation to Ramirez, keeping the two city cops at bay until they had more information to go on. Since Mr. Faoud was involved, she took this seriously but she had to convince herself that this was solvable.

Ramirez and Piccolo both shrugged.

"Well, if the lockers come up dry, that gives us one option," said Captain Martin.

"Bathrooms?" suggested Piccolo.

"I'm sure you've looked at those already, "said Captain Martin.

"You mean the family," said Ramirez.

Captain Martin nodded. "We'd need an okay from Faoud, and he'd need to ask permission from Dr. Nikkanen himself."

"Where are the family tapes? We don't have them here."

"No, I think Faoud has access to them. But we'd never get all the tapes, the private ones, just the ones in the aviary and the hallways and elevators. That may be enough."

"Do you really think that someone in the family had something to do with this?" asked Ramirez. "Why would they steal their own property?"

Captain Martin smiled at Ramirez. She often thought he'd be a good replacement for her when she retired. He was stable, thorough, thoughtful and had the diplomatic skills needed for the job. His only problem was that his credentials were light. He had a Marine background but he had never served as an M.P. or in a police department. Still, if he could solve this, that might be all the credential he needed. "Who knows why the family does anything?"

"The insurance?" offered Piccolo.

"Like they need it," said Ramirez.

8

36th Floor

KATIE MORAN HAD spent a year and a half on the waiting list for an apartment in the building but at the moment, she lived with her sister and brother in a large, ramshackle apartment at 115th Street, near Columbia University, where Annie studied physics, their brother, Billy, studied computer science, and where she had finished the course work for her Ph.D. They shared the apartment with a wealthy, wormlike student who greeted people with the peace symbol and two blazingly redheaded identical twin sisters who seemed to be enamored of the worm.

Katie's Ph.D. thesis was in part inspired by the worm, who was charismatically unattractive, and his relationship with the sisters, who slept in the same bed with him and presumably copulated en masse. The sisters had also flirted with Billy and Annie, although they seemed to sense that Katie herself was off limits, probably due to her great age (28). Her thesis discussed the attractiveness of ugliness and the aesthetics of immorality as part of the changing ethical environment. She had been working on the project for a year.

Most days, Katie and Annie ended their day with a workout at the gym on 33 or a yoga class. In the evenings, Annie and Billy went off to Columbia and Katie worked in the library on 81 when it wasn't in use by the family. Often, she was forced to transfer to the school library on 9. In the evenings, she might have a drink and bar food at Finnegan's, the pub on 36, or if she was feeling up to it, brave the disco, CBGBA's on 65, where she was all but guaranteed a partner for dance or sex, if she wanted it, and drugs, if she was interested, which was rare, and if the security police were feeling particularly negligent that night. She, and everyone else, was well aware that nothing anyone did at CBGBA's was secret, everything was being taped and it seemed no one cared. Fights, rapes and serious overdoses were another matter. The building police stepped in almost immediately. It was clear that security was tolerant about everything but serious injury or acts that might invite publicity or reflect too badly on the family.

Katie had been anxious to leave her apartment near Columbia for a number of reasons. She hated the worm and felt uncomfortable with his incestuous girlfriends, although she actually felt a mild frisson of attraction to them. Although the apartment was a good deal financially, the lease was in the worm's name and he could technically throw them out – not that he would – it was just an uncomfortable situation, living at someone else's whim.

Besides, the apartments in the building were an even better value. She had applied for a two-bedroom apartment, which she would share with her sister (her brother wanted to stay near Columbia). Unlike the apartment at 115th Street, the flats in the building were new, ultra-modern, well kept, with every convenience imaginable.

But the main reason had nothing to do with practicality. She was inexplicably drawn to the building. 211A provided a kind of comfort from the turbulent world outside (although there was plenty of turbulence within the building). She felt safe in the building and appreciated by her boss, Aaron Houdi, the building manager, and her associates. More than that, she felt a sense of personal freedom in the building that had nothing to do with her situation. Her sister shared the feeling.

"It's not like I'm a receptionist in an office building," said Annie, "although that's exactly what I am. But it feels different."

So it was with some elation that they got their notice on the building's server that an apartment on the 32nd floor had opened up and would be available for inspection next week. The cost was a little over half of what they paid at 115th Street but there was one catch: they had to remain employed by the building. If they left, voluntarily or involuntarily, they forfeited the apartment.

There was an agreement rather than a traditional lease that guaranteed them permanent occupancy, with raises in rent based on a variety of factors like inflation, utility and labor costs, the fortunes of the Nikkanen family finances and on a formula that only some people in IT could understand. Not even Katie's brother, who worked there part time, could figure it out.

There were also a host of benefits aside from the ones that came with working in the building, the membership in gyms and clubs and restaurants that were considerably less expensive than comparable restaurants outside. Living in the building gave you a better chance of renting a bigger apartment when the need arose, if one married or had children, for example, or got a better job within the building.

There were no rules on noise, since 211A was virtually soundproof, none on pets (except required checkups with the house vets), none on guests, parties, picture hangings, appliances, interior decoration, even on the removal of interior walls. There was a rule on foul odors emanating from an apartment, but no definition of "foul."

The downside was retirement or disability. There were jobs in the building for aging tenants but complete retirement meant giving up the apartment. Disability (except in the case of an accident for which the building was responsible) was punished by expulsion. Fortunately, most of the jobs in the building came with generous pensions, so no one was thrown on the street without resources.

Katie couldn't envision life beyond the building. She would finish her dissertation, get her Ph.D. and apply for post-docs or teaching jobs in the city, while still maintaining her greeting job in the lobby. Perhaps she would marry someone who worked in the science labs on 57 and 58, or even some of the mathematicians in IT on 8 – she couldn't imagine being with any of the ornithologists or botanists at the aviary or garden, or the entomologists and ichthyologists on 88 – they had a different sensibility than the physicists or chemists. Of course, there were doctors in the hospital on 2 and 3 that were possible, but she hadn't met one she liked, although she had once hooked up with a surgeon she met at CBGBA's. Actually, there were a world of possibilities for husbands in the building, and there was nothing in the building code that said she couldn't have more than one husband, although one of them wouldn't be recognized by law.

The thought of polyandry amused her, actually titillated her. She had occasionally had more than one boyfriend at the same time and she enjoyed the variety. But she could only officially marry one of them, probably in the chapel on 60. She could also marry a woman or a transsexual or hermaphrodite if she chose, and she kept that open as an option, but she simply wasn't attracted to them. Her sister, Annie, was more open about such things.

She speculated that she might have children, born in the building with the help of one of the building's midwives, take them to daycare on 11, educate them in the schools on 9 and 10, until they were old enough for outside school (the building's schools stopped at 8th Grade, except for night school for adults).

It was not that she didn't enjoy all the attractions of the city outside but the building was so convenient in every way. It was tantamount to living in a small city within a city. Perhaps it was intellectual laziness to limit herself to an earthly demi-paradise, but it was not like living in Disneyland – there were occupations and attractions of substance that one could devote oneself to without growing dumb with stupefaction.

On the day she received the notice of an available apartment, she celebrated with Annie and a group of friends at Finnegan's on 36. Aaron Houdi, the building manager and Katie's boss, dropped by to welcome her to full resident status. He had lived in the building since it opened four years ago and had moved to ever-larger apartments to accommodate a wife and child and another on the way. As a manager, of course, he lived on one of the floors reserved for executives, on 72. As the building manager, with a large office on 13, he was in charge of maintenance, repairs, reception, cleaning, security, elevators, storage and supply rooms, the garages on sublevels -1 and -2, the building controls on 6 and anything to do with the physical plant. He reported directly to Faoud. Some of his job overlapped with IT and the aviary, aquarium and insect gardens, the farms, the scientific labs and HR, and he had had to work out areas of responsibility with the heads of these departments. The idea of hiring academics as doorkeepers and receptionists had been his idea and Katie was one an example of its success. "I just wanted to say how happy I am that you and Annie are now with us all the time," he said to Katie, humorously.

"Yes, we've willingly fallen into the trap," said Katie.

"What trap?" asked one of her friends, who lived outside the building.

"She means she can't leave her job without losing the apartment," said Houdi.

"And our lives are circumscribed by the building," said Katie. "The building has its own values, its own morals, its own ethics …

"Like …"

"Beauty, science, the artwork everywhere, the flowers and greenery on every floor, a kind of fairy tale ambiance, like the idea of having hummingbirds hovering around you while you're having coffee. I've never done this, of course."

"I have," said Houdi, "and I have to admit, the effect is magical."

"That it exactly," said Annie. "The building casts a spell."

"But then you have CBGBA's," said Katie. "Which is orgiastic."

"Sex and hummingbirds, what more could you want?" said Houdi.

"Have you actually had coffee with the family?" asked a young intern at the hospital, who was ferociously attracted to Annie.

Houdi nodded.

"What are they like?"

"Private," said Houdi.

"That means he doesn't want to lose his job," said Katie.

"And every word we say here is on tape," said the intern.

Chrystal dropped by with the news that an arrest had been made in the bird theft. "The two cops were seen hustling someone out the building."

"In handcuffs?" asked Annie.

"Almost."

"How can you be almost in handcuffs?" asked Katie.

"What bird theft?" said Houdi. "It's a simple matter of unauthorized entry and nobody's been arrested yet."

Of course, nobody believed a word of this. After Houdi left, Chrystal noticed a new face at the bar. "Who's that?" she asked.

Ivan Anderson was drinking what looked like a ginger ale and speaking to no one, looking into his glass. He seemed forlorn.

"Our new assistant ornithologist."

"He looks so young," said Chrystal.

"He might have news," said the intern.

Katie called him over and introduced him around. He hadn't been as forlorn as he looked; he was on a break. The family had needed the aviary, he said, so he was waiting until they left. The implant in his hand would buzz when he could return.

"Tell us about the hummingbird," the intern said.

Ivan wouldn't say and everybody knew why. They searched his face for signs of complicity in a building secret but found only a kind of purposeful innocence. At last they gave up and made small talk, asking how he liked the city, was he looking for an apartment, was his girlfriend in Tucson coming to stay with him, etc.

"Actually, we don't have that kind of relationship," he said.

"What kind of relationship?" asked Annie.

His answer shocked everyone. "Moving in ... being intimate ... things like that ..."

"Like what?"

"Things like that."

"You mean no sex until marriage?" asked Katie.

Ivan was acutely embarrassed, which was fortunately relieved by a buzz in his hand.

After he left, Katie decided to seduce him, just for the fun of it, and because she truly despised celibacy.

9

86ᵗʰ and 87ᵗʰ Floors

ABOUT TWO WEEKS after she'd been hired, when she was just getting acclimatized to her job, Alice dropped her children off at daycare and reported for work.

"You've been reassigned," said Tay.

"What?"

"You did such a good job here, they want you for the family."

Alice was slightly stunned. She was just beginning to enjoy being an embodiment of Southern *soul* and had even made an attempt to flatten out her accent and countrify her manner. Her customers seemed to appreciate her play act and she almost made her salary in tips, which unfortunately went into a common pot. "How did I fuck up?" she asked Tay.

Tay was actually sorry to lose her but the call came down from on high. One of the family waiters had taken ill and they needed a replacement immediately. Why they picked Alice, he had no idea but her replacement at Tay's was on her way. "You didn't," he said. "Somebody up there likes you. Report to Mr. Lazarus on 86."

"This is a bummer," said Alice.

"No, it's a promotion, you'll get a lot more money. I'll be sorry to lose you."

When she left for the elevator, she felt she'd been fired, that somehow her *soul* routine had been defective, that its artificiality was too obvious – she'd been shunted off to the role of traditional waitress. As the elevator ascended, she wondered how the move would affect her children, if the hours would be different, if she could find enough time for them, or if her mother would have to take over again.

Much of the 86th Floor was a huge kitchen, devoted to the needs of the family. Aside from the head chef, Emile Lazarus, there were several sous-chefs, a sommelier who also worked at Geneviève's, a pastry chef who also baked for the executive dining rooms on 63, and a staff of waiters, busboys, dishwashers, cleaning ladies and launderers. Another part of the floor was an enormous pantry, including a vast meat locker and freezer that also supplied many of the restaurants in the building. The rest of the floor was a dining room for retainers of the family, attendants, assistants and maids, as well as the kitchen and wait staff. Secretaries, governesses and tutors ate in the dining rooms for professionals and executives on 63.

Emile Lazarus had learned his art by working his way up at several temples of cuisine in Paris and carried with him the snobbishness, arrogance and artistry those institutions instilled. He was technically in charge of all the kitchens and dining rooms in the building, excluding the ethnic restaurants and the steakhouse on 6, Finnegan's on 36 and the coffee houses scattered throughout the building, but including Genevieve's, the cafeteria on 7 and the wine cellar on subbasement -4. Given all his duties, his staff numbered nearly 100, some of whom were highly paid chefs themselves, recruited by Lazarus with great care. Lazarus himself had been lured to New York by Faoud.

When the elevator door opened on 86, Alice stepped out into what seemed like chaos, with people scurrying in every direction and shouting back and forth. She stopped one of the scurriers to ask directions to Mr. Lazarus and was pointed in a vague direction, somewhere in the neighborhood of a bank of ovens. Lazarus wasn't hard to locate. He was a large, overbearing figure, with a thin mustache, black hair slicked back with gel, the beginnings of a paunch and a commanding presence. When Alice approached him, he seemed to be talking to three people at once. She stood in front of him. "Yes?" he said.

"I'm Alice Jeynes, I've been assigned to you."

"Why?"

"You needed a waitress."

"You don't want me. You want Calhoun." He called out for Calhoun, who didn't seem to be in listening distance. "Where the hell is that fairy?" he said, with only the slightest trace of an accent.

In due time, a thin, clearly effeminate man approached Lazarus and was directed to Alice, who had been standing near a garbage compactor, getting more and more annoyed. "This is yours," said Lazarus to Calhoun.

At the first sight of Alice, Calhoun lit up, as if a prayer had been answered. "Ah," said Calhoun, "my angel."

"Fuck you," said Alice.

"Believe me, I've tried," said Calhoun. "I'm not flexible enough. I'm the head of the wait staff."

"I'm the new waitress," said Alice.

"Not yet, you aren't. You'll need a day of training. Maybe two."

Calhoun took Alice under his wing. He guided her through the maze of the kitchen and the pantry and showed her where she'd be eating with the lowlifes in the staff dining room. He had one of the regular waitresses, Heidi Grauber, another former model whom Alice thought she recognized, show her the family dining room and go over the place settings, the mechanics of service and the dining etiquette.

It was actually quite complicated. There were seven members of the immediate family and any of them might have invited guests, some at the last moment, so there might be as many as fifteen or twenty people at the table. They had to be prepared to add place settings and waiters as the occasion demanded.

"You'll meet the other waiters later on," said Heidi. "They won't hate you because you're beautiful – they were all models themselves."

"So that's why …"

"Yes, of course," said Heidi. "Weren't you at Zora?"

"For a while."

"I thought I'd seen you before. Didn't we do a runway at Bergdorf's?"

"That was before children," said Alice.

"That was before my accident," said Heidi. "Most of my body is scar tissue."

The family dining room was dominated by a massive table which seemed to be of solid oak but actually came apart and could be rearranged to suit the evening and the number of guests. On days when there were only seven, the table would be moved to the bank of windows, where everyone faced a magnificent view. Normally, however, there were guests, business associates of Dr. Nikkanen, family friends – three or four extra settings at the very least. Then the table would revert to its normal position by means of a track operated by the waiter in charge, usually Calhoun.

What was striking about the dining room, aside from its size and view, was that the walls were entirely bare. There were no paintings or decorations of any kind.

"That's because the walls and the ceiling are actually a screen. Every night there's a different projection. They might be dining in a forest, or in the South of France, or on an ocean liner at night, or along the Mississippi, or in space. Each member of the family gets to choose their night. Here, I'll show you."

Heidi took Alice to a control panel behind the door to the kitchen downstairs. She pressed a button and had Alice request a scene to the panel. "The South Bronx at midnight," said Alice.

Sure enough, the computer was up to the task and projected a 360° image of a neighborhood that Alice actually knew, a street scene with tenements and bodegas, storefront churches, and bars, with a ceiling projection of a moon trying to appear through a smoggy night.

"If you want a live show, it can do that, too," said Heidi.

They went over a few more details, then took an elevator to a coffee shop on 65, which also housed the nightclub and a small casino. Once they had settled at a table, Alice noticed a scar peeking out above Heidi's shirt and wondered if the uniforms they wore covered her enough to hide it.

"What are my hours?" asked Alice.

"You're definitely going to have to rearrange your schedule. I hear you have two children in daycare." Heidi explained that she would be working dinners and possibly lunches and, if she wanted to earn some extra money, breakfasts as well. If any of the staff fell ill, or needed a day off, Alice would be expected to fill in. If there was a banquet, which was rare, she'd be called upon to serve – that was in the banquet hall on 56.

"When do I see my kids?"

"Put them up for adoption."

They discussed uniforms, protocols, transportation – the special service, elevators and escalators between floors but they kept skirting around the topic that Alice wanted to learn most about.

"Alright, it's time I told you a little about the family," said Heidi. "That's the most difficult part of your job."

"Why?"

"They're difficult. Well, not Dr. Nikkanen – he's nice enough – at least he's polite – but the others …"

"What?" Alice smiled. She didn't know if Heidi was baiting her or having a joke at her expense.

"Mrs. Nikkanen will make you uncomfortable but won't give you trouble personally. But the kids will try to get to you. Not Silje, the eldest one, or Naziha, the adopted one, but the other three, especially Tero, the little one."

"Why would they bother with waiters?"

"They might not," said Heidi. "I just want to prepare you for anything."

"Like …"

"Racism, sexism, random insults, perversion, inappropriate requests, mind games, outright meanness – let's just say, some waiters and waitresses have fled from the room in tears. They'd consider that a victory."

"Impressive."

"On the other hand, we get double or triple what we'd be paid anywhere else, free gym, pool, massages, first crack at an apartment, financial advice, even more discounts at the theater, cinema, shops, restaurants … did you get your implant?"

"No, not yet," said Alice.

"You should," said Heidi. "If you forget your I.D. card, you're fucked."

Alice left her first day of training consumed with curiosity. She wanted a challenge in her life, at least one that was different from childrearing, which was often mind-bogglingly boring. She had already been measured for her uniform and a half-day of training to go before they'd let her be introduced at dinner and serve the dessert. She couldn't wait.

10

89th and 57th Floors

VAN HAD BEEN working in the aviary for three weeks in what was essentially a paradise for hummingbirds and those to care for them. He had learned to recognize species that were new to him, like the multi-colored Fiery-throated *Panterpe Insignis*, or the green iridescent Gould's Inca, or the startlingly white Leucistic Anna's which he never dreamed he'd see in this life. But as he worked with them, cared for them, cleaned up for them, he noticed something peculiar – so peculiar that he confided his concern to Dr. Fain.

"They're moving slower," Ivan said.

"All of them?" Fain asked.

"No, just the ones that nest near the pavilion, some of the Anna's, the Costa's and the Woodstar."

"How slower?"

"Compared to the other hummers in the aviary, their wings don't beat quite as fast, they seem to have trouble hovering, even the Anna's dives are slower than the ones who nest in a different area."

None of the former hummingbird keepers had noticed this and Fain wondered if this was just Ivan's misperception or this was a phenomenon that had only just surfaced. "Did you measure this?" he asked.

"No," said Ivan. "It's just something I noticed. I went back and forth from one area to another to see if I was imagining it or if there was some factor I hadn't noticed."

"Any food differences?"

"Yes," said Ivan. "There are a lot of cardinal flowers near the pavilion that aren't in other areas."

"They all love *lobelia*."

"Would I be allowed to pick one of the flowers and have it examined?"

"I suppose so," said Fain. "We'll have to ask Dr. Benjamin."

"One other question. When I was looking at one of the nests, I noticed some fibers that didn't look they came from sticks or plants. I know at the Desert Museum where I worked before, some of the birds would fly next to visitors and take threads from their sweaters, or even hair, and weave them into their nests. I wonder if that was possible here."

Fain hadn't heard about this. "So do you think this had something to do with the missing Woodstar?"

"Well, if the hummers are slower, they'd be easier to catch."

"Did you notice this with any other birds?"

"Frankly, I don't spend much time looking at the other birds," said Ivan. "I'm kind of focused that way."

"Anyway, I think we better discuss this with Dr. Benjamin. Good work, Ivan."

Early that evening while the aviary was being used by the family, they met with Dr. Benjamin in his messy office on 89. He was genuinely excited with Ivan's discovery. "If it's true, it could be the first clue we have to the mystery of the Woodstar.

"As I said, I haven't measured it — it would be pretty hard to in any case — but it's noticeable. At least to me."

"Dr. Fain, have you seen this for yourself?" asked Benjamin.

"I trust Ivan," said Fain. "But I'll check as well."

Benjamin thought for a moment. "I'll get Jerry to cut off a sample of the flower ..."

"Who's Jerry?"

"The head gardener — you've probably seen him around," said Fain.

"And do you think you could get a sample of the fiber inside the nest you saw?" asked Benjamin.

"I'll need tweezers."

"I think we can manage that," said Fain.

"It's in the nest of an Anna," said Ivan. "She'll be furious. And her mate will probably attack me."

"They're not scared of you?" asked Benjamin.

"Scared? He'll probably dive bomb me. I'll need a helmet."

The arrangements were made. Jerry, the head gardener, who was not in on the mystery, reluctantly clipped a flower from the *Lobelia Cardinalis*, which Fain and Ivan took to Dr. Mary Chen, the director of one of the chemistry laboratories on the 55th Floor. She was a diminutive woman, with a wide, flat face and a look that veered from severe to amused.

"I don't really have time for this," said Dr. Chen, "but your Dr. Benjamin can be very persuasive.

"We're very grateful," said Fain.

"He wanted to do this as a favor to Faoud but, as you probably know, we don't report to Faoud. We report directly to Dr. Nikkanen."

"Mr. Faoud appreciates this," said Fain.

"What sort of work do you do here?" asked Ivan.

"Private work," said Chen.

Ivan explained what they were looking for. Any kind of chemical inside the cardinal flower that might have the effect of a sedative or tranquillizer.

"Are there any cardinal flowers not near the pavilion?"

"Yes, on the other side of the aviary," said Fain.

"I'll need a clip from one of those as a comparison."

"Oh, shit, Jerry'll go crazy," said Fain.

Chen shrugged. "You say you have a fiber as well."

"Yes, here it is," said Ivan, taking out a glassine envelope with a thread he had taken from the Anna's nest, with a crazed hummingbird defending his territory in suicidal charges. Ivan had worn a helmet, goggles and thick padding to extract the thread.

Chen didn't open the envelope and seemed to look at the thread with disdain. "You don't want to know the chemical composition of the thread, you want to know where it came from, probably from the family or one of their guests. We're not a forensics lab so I can't help you there."

"Is there one in the building?"

"Do you mind telling me what's this for?" asked Chen, rather pugnaciously, Ivan thought.

"A change of behavior in some of the birds in the aviary," said Fain.

Chen understood. "I have no idea if we have a forensics lab in the building – we do basic research here. You'll probably need a police lab."

Fain didn't want to pursue the thread with Chen. It was agreed that Chen would have someone in her lab examine the flower and let them know about any soporific ingredient in the flower compared to a flower on the other side of the aviary. "How long will it take?" Fain asked Chen.

"A couple of weeks, I imagine. The chemists have a busy schedule."

Fain and Ivan simultaneously gulped, which Chen enjoyed. "Is there any way we can get it done sooner?"

"How much sooner?"

"Like tomorrow." Before Chen could protest, Fain added. "We're afraid for the health of the birds."

"You'll have it the day after."

The next morning, Fain and Ivan presented Benjamin with the thread and said they needed to trace it to garments worn by anyone who was in the pavilion on the day the Woodstar disappeared.

"Well, that's a big order," said Benjamin. "This will have to go through Faoud who will have to get permission from Dr. Nikkanen himself. I'll set up a meeting with Faoud as soon as you have the chemical analysis of the cardinal flower. We might as well do the flower and the thread at the same time."

The next morning, Fain called Dr. Chen. "Have you found something?"

"You'll never guess," said Dr. Chen.

11

87th Floor

THREE SIDES OF the wall had been set to dunes, palm trees and an endless ocean on a cloudy day, with an occasional seagull flying overhead. By the time the entrée had arrived, a gentle rain had broken out, to last throughout the dinner.

Heidi positioned Alice just inside the doorway to the dining room from where the dishes emerged, where she could see without being seen. She had already helped set up the table for seven in the nuclear family and two guests, one to be positioned on Dr. Nikkanen's right and the other next to his eldest daughter, Silje.

"What kind of a name is that?"

"Finnish. She's 16. I just want you to watch for most of the dinner tonight. If any of the adults want an espresso after dinner, or a cognac, you'll serve them. The kids won't want anything."

The family was supposed to appear at 7 o'clock and Alice fidgeted about impatiently. Calhoun and another waiter were already inside, ready to seat the family and their guests. They were wearing Chinese-style tunics in the light blue that seemed to be the official color of the building. Calhoun squirmed, as if he had to pee, and the other waiter seemed to be trying to calm him down. They stared out at the projection of an ocean as a cloud in the far distance seemed to draw nearer.

At last, the family appeared. Heidi introduced them as they took their places. Dr. Nikkanen was the first to appear, along with his guest. He was the blondest adult Alice had ever seen, almost but not quite an albino. His hair hung down on either side of his face, framing blond eyebrows and purple eyes (a common feature in albinos) and which could seem iridescent in the right light, and a blond mustache. He was

50, well built, with a slightly weather-beaten face and a look that could only be described as cruel. One could imagine him torturing heretics. Tonight, however, he seemed in a good mood, charming his guest, a robust man in his 60's with the air of a plutocrat.

Alice had barely recovered from Dr. Nikkanen when the rest of the family ambled in. The first was Naziha Hamdi, the adopted daughter, a short black-haired Tunisian, leading Silje, the eldest daughter, who rested her hand on Naziha's shoulder as she was guided to her seat.

"You didn't tell me she was blind," said Alice.

"Two of them are blind, the others have eye problems."

Silje was a strikingly beautiful girl of 16, tall, graceful, with the same platinum hair as her father and skin that seemed the definition of creamy. Her dinner guest, led to her seat by the waiter, was a dark, attractive girl from India, a classmate of Silje, also blind.

The oldest boy, Mika, filed in along with the others. Again, a strikingly handsome blond, with the lanky body of a 12-year old just beginning his growth spurt into adolescence. He moved tentatively, feeling his way along the table for assurance.

"He can see, but just barely," said Heidi. "I think he can distinguish shapes and colors but not much else."

Mika was leading in his 10-year old brother, Tero, who was also blond and beautiful but completely blind. In some ways, he was even more striking than the others. He had the spindly body of a child, but the cruel expression of his father and a quality that could only be called dissipation, if that could apply to a 10-year old. He projected the kind of purposeful lassitude that one might find in an addict. He also had glass eyes that glowed white in the dark.

Last to arrive was Minna, the 14-year old, who shared the exquisite looks of her sister, the same long, platinum hair and white skin, but whose eyes were entirely violet, not just the irises but the entire eye. From the way she took her place at the table, it was clear that she could see, but it must have been through a haze of violet. The effect was bizarre and alien, as if she had come from another planet.

Mrs. Nikkanen did not appear that evening. "Believe me, she's even more startling than the others," said Heidi. Also absent from the dinner was Dr. Nikkanen's mother, who lived in the building but preferred to take her meals by herself in her sitting room on 84, and Mrs. Nikkanen's parents, who also had an apartment in the building but were in France at the moment.

From where she was standing, Alice could hear the tenor but not the content of the conversations, a few snippets of language here and there, but little else. Dr. Nikkanen joked with his plutocratic guest and made him laugh but never managed more than a smile himself. Mika, the 12-year old, seemed to be making snide comments about something, which the girls pooh-poohed. Tero seemed to be spitting out invective but Alice wasn't sure if he was serious. She had the impression that Silje and her Indian guest were attracted to one another, but it was hard to decipher the gestures of blind people. Somehow, she felt that Naziha approved of the attraction, as if she was relieved that Silje had shifted the focus of her attention from herself to her Indian friend.

The food varied with the individual. The adults, and Naziha, were served cuisine that took some kind of ingenuity to prepare; Silje and her Indian friend preferred salads; the boys and Minna were given steaks and fries. Tero's steaks had been cut up into bite size pieces, which he ate with his fingers.

When they were done, a busboy collected the dishes and a waiter rolled a cart of desserts around the table explaining to the blind children what was there.

"Okay, you're up," said Heidi. A rolling cart of coffees and a selection of teas appeared at the serving elevator and Alice wheeled it into the room. Before she reached the table, Calhoun introduced her to the family. "This is your new waitress, Alice Jeynes, who has been trained by me and Heidi Grauber." Everyone turned in her direction, even those who couldn't see. Alice almost felt like a model again.

No one said a word as she pushed the cart to the head of the table, stopping at Dr. Nikkanen's guest. "May I offer you some coffee or tea?" said Alice, feeling abashed and angry that she was reduced to the status of a servant. Waiting at Tay's had a personal feel to it, a sense of fun and play acting. This was pure abasement and she wasn't sure she could keep her cool under the circumstances.

"I smell a negress," said Tero.

Prepped to expect remarks like this, Alice didn't miss a beat. "And if you'd like a cognac or Armagnac, I'll have the sommelier take your order."

"She smells like your Indian friend," said Mika to Silje.

"Not at all," said Silje. "Chitra has an Indian smell; the waitress has an African smell."

Silje beckoned in Alice's direction. "Come here, Alice."

Alice was amazed that the girl had caught her name. She excused herself from the plutocrat and stood next to Silje, who grasped her hand. Suddenly, she put one of Alice's fingers into her mouth and sucked on it. "Totally different taste from Indian," she said.

Alice pulled her finger out and returned to the plutocrat, without showing the slightest emotion. "Coffee, sir?"

"What does she look like?" asked Tero.

"She's beautiful," said Minna. "Tall, thin, I can't tell her coloring."

"Light skinned, like mine," said Naziha. "I think she may have been a model."

"Another one," sighed Mika.

Far from censoring his children for their rudeness, Dr. Nikkanen seemed to enjoy their banter at Alice's expense. He confided in his guest, "My children tend to be playful, especially with a new toy."

"Waitress," said Minna.

"Her name is Alice," said Silje.

"Why are you no longer a model? Did you get scarred in an accident like Heidi?"

Alice was pouring coffee and didn't respond.

"Why?" repeated Minna.

Alice poured cream into the plutocrat's coffee cup, held out the tongs for sugar and when the plutocrat nodded *no*, she turned to Minna and said, "Two children."

In the pause that followed, she served an espresso to Dr. Nikkanen, who stared at her fixedly, lowered his gaze to her body, returned to her face as if he was examining a prize horse or a rare emerald and turned to Calhoun, who was hovering nearby. "She'll do," he said.

12

61st Floor

A QUICK MEETING WAS called in Mustafa Faoud's office, attended by the same group as the last meeting, Tim Follet and Jorge Ramos of the NYPD, Aaron Houdi the building manager, Captain Roanne Martin and José Ramirez from security and Dr. Benjamin, with the addition of Ivan Anderson and Peter Fain of the aviary, and Mary Chen, the director of the chemistry lab on 54, and a chemist named Dev Chatterji.

As the official in charge of the investigation, Captain Martin made the opening statement to Faoud. "There's been a new development in the Woodstar case that we thought you should know about."

Faoud nodded. He hadn't expected new developments at all. He had assumed that the investigation would go nowhere, although he had to convince the family that steps had been taken to solve the mystery.

"It was based on a discovery by a new employee of Dr. Benjamin, Ivan Anderson, who takes care of the hummingbirds."

Ivan recounted his observation that the hummingbirds near the pavilion seemed to be moving more slowly than the birds farther away.

"Just the hummingbirds?" asked Faoud.

"Yes, and just the ones that feed on the cardinal flowers by the edge of the pavilion."

"That would include the Woodstar?"

"Yes, I've seen the Woodstar feeding from cardinal flowers all the time."

"Are these the only cardinal flowers in the aviary?"

Dr. Fain answered. "No, there are cardinal flowers all over the aviary and they didn't affect the birds anywhere but near the pavilion. So the logical conclusion was that somehow these flowers were different from the flowers everywhere else. When we brought this hypothesis to Dr. Benjamin, he got us permission to snip off flowers from both sections of the aviary and show them to Dr. Chen in the chemistry lab downstairs."

Dr. Chen took over. "As you probably know, each cardinal flower is a tube that points upwards. At the base of each tube is a pool of nectar that the hummers can reach with their beaks. Occasionally, insects fall into the nectar and the hummers eat those as well. As everyone knows, nectar is basically a sugar solution composed of sucrose, glucose and fructose, with a higher proportion of sucrose in flowers that hummers like."

Dr. Chatterji, the chemist who had accompanied Dr. Chen, a young, intense Indian whose mouth seemed curved in a permanent smile, interrupted. "Although sucrose is formed from the anomeric carbon atoms of glucose and fructose joined together." He looked around at everyone's utterly disinterested reaction. "Just thought I'd clarify that."

Dr. Chen continued. "Anyway, when we compared the nectar in the two samples, we found they didn't match. I'll let Dr. Chatterji take over from here."

"We extracted the nectar with capillary glass tubes and placed them on Whatman No. 1 chromatography paper."

"I don't think we need to go into that much detail," said Dr. Chen.

"Yes, you're right," said Dr. Chatterji. "We found a chemical in the flower near the pavilion that shouldn't be there. We found glycosides and flavonoids combined, as well as serotonin and maltol, harmane alkaloids and chrysin, all of which are present in passiflora incarnate, otherwise known as passion flowers."

"So?" said Detective Follet, who was already getting impatient.

"So an extract of passiflora can have a sedative effect. It could actually be used as a sleep aid."

"You're saying that if the hummingbirds fed on the flowers near the pavilion, they'd be sedated, and therefore slower," said Faoud.

"Exactly."

"So how did the passion flower extract get into the cardinal flower?"

Dr. Chen shrugged and looked over at Dr. Fain who looked over at Dr. Benjamin. Ivan answered. "There are passion flower vines not far from the pavilion and it's possible that some of the hummingbirds got some passion flower material on their beaks by accident in their search for food. But very unlikely. Hummingbirds don't feed on passion flowers and they would never mistake it for a cardinal. It's more likely that someone injected the cardinal flowers with passion flower extract or sprayed them with mist."

"Injected every flower?" asked Faoud.

"Well, many of them," said Ivan. "I know it sounds far-fetched ..."

"It does," said Faoud. "The whole thing sounds far-fetched to me. That somebody should spend time putting a sedative in flowers that hummingbirds use so they can slow them down enough to catch them ... that's what you're suggesting, isn't it?"

"Yes," said Ivan.

"Seems improbable at best. And who would have gone to that kind of trouble?"

"It would have to be someone in the family," said Ivan.

"We have tapes of everyone else," said Captain Martin.

Faoud turned to Captain Martin, whom he assumed would be eminently sensible, or at least practical. "So you subscribe to this fantasy?"

"It's the only clue we have so far."

"And I suppose you want me to convince Dr. Nikkanen to release the family tapes," said Faoud.

"Excuse me sir," interrupted Ivan. "I don't think we can call it a fantasy since we have definite proof that there is a sedative inside the flowers that doesn't belong there."

Faoud was not used to being contradicted. He eyed Ivan sharply for a moment and then relented, with a nod that could have signified almost anything. He rose, and everyone else rose with him. "Thank you, everyone, for coming. Keep up the investigation and let me know when you have anything more substantial."

"This is substantial ..." Ivan started to say but Fain led him out of the room.

Faoud held Dr. Benjamin back. He waited until everyone was out of the room before he spoke. "Rand, did it sound like I didn't believe the evidence?"

"A little," said Dr. Benjamin. "It's preposterous but it might be true."

"Did you get the impression that I didn't want the investigation to proceed?"

Dr. Benjamin shrugged, as if to say, maybe yes, maybe no.

"I'm worried about the outcome," said Faoud. "Suppose it turns out that one of the family stole the bird. It could be … uncomfortable …"

"To say the least."

Faoud sighed. "Oh well, let's see what happens. Are you and Fiona coming for dinner Sunday night?"

"Wouldn't miss it."

As Dr. Benjamin was on his way out, Faoud stopped him. "By the way, that Ivan Anderson boy is a real find. Is he any good with the birds?"

"He's remarkable," said Dr. Benjamin.

"Well, don't tell him I like him."

13

81st and 65th Floors

THE LIBRARY WAS housed in what was officially two floors of the building, although it really comprised one very high floor lined with books, with a balcony and ladder to provide access to the books higher up. The main room was modelled, somewhat loosely, on the main room of Bodleian Library at Oxford, with large, curved, multi-paned windows on two sides, but there the resemblance ended. It held, perhaps, 200,000 books, some old and valuable, some bound in leather, but mostly ordinary books, including paperbacks. Although there were books on every subject, it specialized in the sciences and history. There were online hookups to most of the world's libraries and little niches scattered about where one could plug in a computer and work in relative peace. Other niches had their own computers where you could plug in a flash drive or disk.

A full-time librarian with the imposing name of Sophie von Rennenkampff and several assistants kept the place in order and up-to-date, working continually to digitize the entire collection with the help of some part-time workers. Sophie was also nominally responsible for the school library on 9 and the medical and lending library in the hospital on 2, although these had full-time librarians of their own, and a lending library at the nursing home on 59 and several other small libraries throughout the building.

Sophie was 45, with long, gray hair pulled back against her head and remarkably fit. She had been a dancer in college and still kept up a barre in the studio on 14, as well as daily workouts and thrice-weekly yoga sessions in the gym for professionals on 68. She was also notoriously fickle in her romantic life, having gone through two husbands and more than several lovers, male and female, in varying degrees of perversity. At the moment, she was ferociously attracted to Katie, who used the library almost daily.

'I found the al-Farabi work you wanted," she said, in her low, library voice, handing Katie a flash drive.

"The al-madina al-fadila?" said Katie. "Who translated it?"

"Walzer."

"Thank you, Sophie," said Katie, with a look that melted Sophie's heart, as well as other parts of her anatomy.

"This is for your paper on ugliness?"

"Yes.

"Have coffee with me after you're done."

"No," said Katie.

"Do you want me to beg?"

"Yes."

Sophie looked around to see if any of her assistants were watching, then made a movement to get down on her knees.

"Okay," said Katie, with feigned embarrassment. It was a game they played frequently. Sophie had been trying to introduce Katie to the S & M world but could never get Katie to take it seriously.

The nearest coffee shop was on 88, but that was mainly for scientists; the one on 65 was connected with the nightclub and casino and wasn't open until 6; the one on 59 was connected with the nursing home and hospice and was filled with grieving relatives, so they went all the way down to 36, next to Finnegan's.

"Have the police been to see you yet?" asked Sophie.

"No, why?"

"That handsome Ramos boy from security."

"Ramirez."

"Yes. He wanted to know if anyone had asked for information about passion flowers."

"Passion flowers?" said Katie. "They're big and purple, aren't they?"

"They come in quite a few colors," said Sophie, "but they're all quite beautiful."

"Isn't there a passion flower ice cream?"

"Probably. But don't you find it odd that a security officer should be concerned with inquiries about passion flowers?"

"Very odd," said Katie.

"What do you make of it?" asked Sophie.

Katie sipped her coffee and stared at Sophie with an expression of mutual puzzlement. "Very odd," she repeated.

"Yes."

"It must have something to do with the missing hummingbird."

"I hadn't heard about that," said Sophie.

"I thought everyone had. It seems that one of the most valuable hummingbirds in the aviary upstairs is missing."

"What would that have to do with passion flowers?"

"I have no idea," said Katie. "But I know someone who might know."

"Who's that?"

"A 22-year old male virgin, whom I intend to deflower."

Sophie was delighted. "How wonderful! Can I help?"

Katie laughed and said she had to get back to the lobby. "By the way, did anyone ask about passion flowers?"

"That's privileged information."

"You mean somebody in the family asked about them," said Katie.

"I didn't say that."

They left the coffee shop arm in arm, well aware that everything they did and said had been filmed and recorded. Sophie whispered in Katie's ear. "Let's take this outside after work."

14

86th and 87th Floors

LICE WAS HAVING an early dinner in the staff dining room on 86 with Heidi, Calhoun, the rest of the wait and most of the kitchen staff, about 30 people all told. Normally, Emile Lazarus attended these dinners but he had been waylaid by a culinary emergency – a guinea hen had exploded on the rotisserie and seemed to have infected the other hens with some virulent-looking plasma.

As the group was eating heartily and chatting amiably, just as Alice was beginning to enjoy Calhoun's utterly unabashed gayness, a man in a gray suit appeared at the door. "Is there an Alice Jeynes here?"

Alice followed the man up the waiter's escalator that led to the main dining room. "What is this about?" asked Alice.

The man said nothing but pushed through the swinging doors into a bare theme-less dining room and through a French door at the far end. This led to an enormous living room, with magnificent views of the city on three sides. In between the windows were paintings that Alice didn't recognize but were probably famous and fabulously expensive. She thought one might be a Picasso she had seen at a modelling gig – at least somebody had said it was a Picasso, which didn't mean a lot to her except it was expensive.

The room was dominated by a massive fireplace in the middle of the room and, in another section, an equally massive piano, that seemed to have more keys than a regular piano. (It was, in fact, an Imperial Bosendorfer, with an extra octave in the base, colored ebony.)

There was sculpture everywhere and glass cases full of exquisite oriental and medieval European artifacts. Equally flamboyant were the flowers and plants that took up the rest of the space not devoted to art and rather grotesque furniture — chairs, sofas and tables of deep mahogany and walnut in twisted shapes, with eagles' claws and lions' feet, gargoyle, snake, bat and insect motifs, with plush cushions of burnt orange and deep purple, dark gold and somber emerald.

Alice had never seen or imagined a room like this, a room so colorful and oppressive at the same time. There was something unnatural about this room, Alice thought, something rank and evil, despite the brilliance of the paintings. She wasn't the type to be awed by her surroundings, no matter how evil or how magnificent. She followed the man across the room, nursing a righteous anger. By the time they had traversed the room, she had half a mind to quit the job and go home.

At the far end of the room was a narrow staircase, presumably leading up to the floor above. It was unlit and seemed to be made of some kind of hard wood, possibly amber. The man directed Alice to mount the stairs. "Go on up. She'll meet you at the top of the stairs," he said.

"Who?" asked Alice, but the man had left.

Alice entered the stairwell and noticed that the walls were not made of solid amber but of a mosaic of various panels of different shades of amber shaped in the form of what looked like a dragon, although Alice couldn't see its head in the darkness at the top of the stairs.

She mounted, barely noticing the wonders around her, until she saw a door opening at the top and a tall, menacing figure at the head of the stairway.

It was a svelte, Amazonian woman, dressed in black tights and a black smock, which offset her white face and long, platinum hair that splayed out around her shoulders. When Alice mounted a few more steps to approach her, she received a shock. The woman's face was not young but still beautiful, with an angry expression that seemed permanently etched in her features. But the shock was her eyes. They were entirely red, not just the irises, but the entire eye — the sclera were red, but not like paint, a translucent red which gave her glance the quality of a laser, penetrating whatever it set upon.

"The new waitress," she said.

"That's me," said Alice. "And you are ..."

"Tuuli Nikkanen, Dr. Nikkanen's handmaiden and the mother of his brood. You look like you're afraid of me, like everyone else," she said.

"I'm not," said Alice.

"You will be." She held out her hand. Perched in her palm was a medium-sized spider with thick, glossy black legs, spouting hairs, a bulbous body, a huge jaw region, six eyes spread across the head, and shiny black fangs. "When you serve my husband tonight, put this in his stew."

"What are you talking about?" said Alice.

"I want him terrified before he dies." She picked up the spider with her fingers and put it in a petri dish. "Here."

"You're out of your mind," said Alice, refusing the dish.

"Stupid girl," said Tuuli. "Here, I'll help you." She opened the petri dish, took out the spider and crushed it in her palm, holding the pulp out in her outstretched hand. "Take it."

To her credit, Alice didn't flinch. "Lady, I'll serve whatever they give me to serve but it won't be no spider, dead or alive."

Tuuli looked at the pulp for a moment and put it in a pocket of her smock. "You talk like something from the streets."

"I am something from the streets. I live in the Bronx."

"How unfortunate. Do you know what you just had me kill?"

"A spider?"

"A mouse spider from Australia, very venomous. We have quite a few of them upstairs."

"And I didn't have you kill it. You killed it on your own."

"Listen," said Tuuli. "Take the spider, freeze it and then grate it over his potatoes. He won't notice and it might kill him."

"I'm leaving now," said Alice.

"Nice to have met you," said Tuuli, turning around and disappearing through the doorway upstairs.

When Alice returned to the staff dining room, everyone stared at her, smiling, some shaking their heads.

"We should have warned you," said Calhoun. "Mrs. Nikkanen is completely batty. She really should be in an institution. What did she want from you?"

"Did she want you to poison her husband?" asked Heidi.

Alice nodded.

"She asked me the same thing. She blames him for making her eyes like that."

"Red?"

Henry Forbes, another ex-model turned waiter (for reasons that were not obvious to Alice) explained that her eyes were like infrared lenses. "She can actually see in the dark. That's why she roams around at night. You'll almost never see her for dinner."

"Where does she roam?"

"Everywhere," said Henry. "All over the building."

"But the place she likes the most is on 88," said Heidi. "The aquarium and especially the insect gardens."

Alice described how Tuuli held out the mouse spider and crushed it, which silenced the group briefly.

After a moment, Calhoun reflected. "I'm surprised they let her take one of those spiders – they're valuable."

"I'm sure they didn't let her," said Heidi.

"You'll have to report it," said Henry.

"Yes, I suppose so."

As expected, Tuuli didn't show up for dinner.

15

32nd Floor

KATIE AND ANNIE'S new apartment on 32 was ready. Most of their furniture they had ordered online, to be delivered on the same day. Their clothing, books, computers, CD's, stereo, memorabilia, a Moroccan rug, a few paintings and knick-knacks had been delivered to the cavernous loading docks on the 1st subbasement and moved up to 32 by the building's service staff. They had purchased new dishes, silverware, kitchenware, appliances and a large entertainment center, including a 65" TV, hooked up to the internet.

A large crowd of friends showed up to help them get everything in place, put up curtains, lay out carpets, assemble beds, set up a shower curtain, find the proper places for towels and sheets, and especially, party.

They ordered pizza for everyone and the Moran sisters had concocted their own version of artillery punch, which was essentially pure ethanol and fruit juice, to which they added rum, pineapples, champagne, vodka, bourbon and an olive. Henry, the waiter from 87, who had been Katie's lover for several days last year, characterized the punch as "insanely lethal."

The building was effectively sound-proofed so they could turn up the volume of the music to pre-deafening. At any given time, there were about forty people in the apartment, but this was a constantly revolving group of guests. There was as much dancing, drinking, smoking, talking and flirting as moving furniture. At one point in the evening, Katie realized they had left their garbage can at their old apartment near Columbia and they had completely forgotten to buy a vacuum cleaner, so they were not really prepared for the detritus of a party. Neighbors came to their rescue.

Ivan had been invited and showed up on the early side, in time for some of the heavier lifting, moving beds and chests, sofas and the entertainment center. He took a cup of punch out of politeness and winced when he tasted it. "What's in this stuff?"

"Fruit juice, with a little wine," said Katie. "It's good for you."

With Katie's encouragement, he drained the cup and almost instantly felt a buzz that should have warned him to stop immediately. He didn't. He danced with Katie and Chrystal, Annie and several other predatory women, and found his head spinning.

In between sips of the punch, he told anyone who would listen that his girlfriend, Kimberly, was coming from Tucson and did anyone know of a cheap hotel where she could stay? He had moved from his friend's apartment to a private room in a small apartment, which he shared with two other men and a couple, and was subletting for the summer.

A few sips later, he blurted out the story of someone putting passion flower extracts inside cardinal flowers to slow down the hummingbirds, which caused a sensation that Ivan failed to notice.

Henry added his story about the new waitress meeting Mrs. Nikkanen and it didn't take a forensic genius to surmise that Mrs. Nikkanen might have taken the Woodstar, even crushed it. Crystal was ready to go viral with the news and Annie planned to tell Dr. Benjamin the next day.

Sophie dropped by to help with the moving, hoping for a gesture of affection from Katie, lewd or otherwise. She settled for otherwise and only stayed a short time. It was a young person's party and way too loud for her taste. But she did leave knowing the reason behind the library search for information on passion flowers. She knew the query didn't come from Mrs. Nikkanen but was honor-bound not to reveal the true source.

Somehow, Ivan managed to totter to the bathroom, vomit, move to nearest bed, which happened to be Katie's, and pass out. He was still unconscious when the party dwindled out and by the time Chrystal left, on the arm of Isha Manekshaw, the console operator in the lobby, whom she hoped would be a pleasant diversion, or more, Ivan was still asleep on Katie's bed.

They left him to tidy up but got discouraged by the impossible mess and they were sleepy themselves. They tried to shake him awake but all they got were a few moans and the slurred words, "hannidy," which they assumed meant *let me be*.

"So what should we do with him?" asked Annie.

"Let him sleep, I guess," said Katie.

"On *your* bed?"

"I have an idea," said Katie.

They stripped him naked, appraised his body, which was slim and age-appropriate, fit but not especially muscular, and rated his genitals, which seemed disease-free and suitable for copulation, although it was hard to tell in their flaccid condition.

Since they hadn't made the bed, they just threw a cover over him and listened to him breathing, speculating on when he would start to snore, or wake up in horror and flee the apartment in a miasma of guilt.

"Do you want to sleep in my bed?" asked Annie. "He doesn't look very inviting."

"Drunk men rarely do. But I think I'll stay."

Predictably, he awoke around 5 in the morning with a terrible headache, slowly became aware of the naked woman beside him and realized that his whole moral edifice had been destroyed in a bout of drunken lust. He no longer deserved his girlfriend in Tucson. He would call her later on in the morning and tell her everything but he had no hope of being forgiven.

16

60th Floor

AFTER THE MOVING-IN party for Katie and Annie, Ivan had been faced with a moral crisis. He had a memory of being drunk, possibly blurting out the theft of the Woodstar but no memory whatsoever of what happened afterwards, until he woke up next to Katie in the morning. It took him a few moments to clear his head and slowly he realized that he was naked and the woman beside him, who he didn't recognize at first, was probably naked as well. She was mostly covered but one taut nipple appeared above the rim of the blanket and left the rest to Ivan's imagination.

Despite the pained fog in his brain, he leapt out of bed and retrieved his clothes, which were lying on the floor in a heap. He dressed in a flash, grabbed his shoes and socks and was about to flee when he was momentarily paralyzed by the glimpse of the nipple above the covers. "What have I done?" he thought, as he dashed out of the room, past the mess in the living room and out the door.

It was six in the morning, too late to go home and too early to go to work. He knew there was a 24/7 deli and a few coffee shops that might be open at this hour, but he preferred the cafeteria on the 7th Floor that would just be opening now and where he could sit in a far corner to collect his thoughts.

He was totally parched and surprisingly hungry. This was the first hangover of his life and he hadn't known what to expect, possibly thirst but not hunger. He ordered a large breakfast of pancakes and sausages, two orange juices and a large hot chocolate and took them to a farthest corner of the room.

He had no one to confide in about this. He was on his own. None of his acquaintances in the city or in the building had any sympathy for his point of view. He knew he was considered backward, prudish, hopelessly square and perhaps a religious freak. So be it. He simply did not believe in sex before marriage. His belief, and one that Kimberly shared, was that sex was for the procreation of children and was a serious activity, not to be taken lightly. The glut of sex in the media led inexorably to obsession and unhappiness, aside from spiritual degradation. That God had specifically required men to resist temptation was something he followed, although he would not impose it on others. He and his girlfriend and fellow celibate, Kimberly, occasionally kissed the way children kiss, experimentally, lingering slightly too long for friendship but not long enough to fire up desire. Well, perhaps just a bit. Like Kimberly, he was conflicted about God and the world, the Bible and science. It was even worse for Kimberly because she was a biology major and didn't believe in evolution, although she had to admit, heretically, that the evolutionists had a point, yet to be proven.

On premarital and recreational sex between adults, there was no question whatsoever. They had agreed to wait until marriage and Ivan had broken that vow. It was inconceivable not to tell Kimberly and she would never trust him again. His act was unforgiveable; their relationship was over. Arizona was three hours behind New York, so he could call her around noon.

Where did that leave *him*, a fornicator, a libertine? There was no way he could take back what he had done. There was no one to undo the fornication. Had he been a Catholic, he could have confessed his sin and be forgiven. But in his Baptist sect, it was not that simple. Only Jesus could forgive, not a go-between. Perhaps his pastor in Tucson could speed his prayer, or augment it, but only Jesus could forgive.

According to his own code of morality, he would have to marry Katie, but he knew she would laugh at him. For her, sleeping with a man – or woman – was like eating or drinking, a function, without moral overtones, without even emotion, perhaps. But he had to offer. And suppose she got pregnant? Would she even marry him then?

On the 60th Floor was a series of chapels, the largest of which was the one that the family used on Sundays and Christian holidays. On these days it was Evangelical Lutheran; on other days interdenominationally Protestant. The floor also boasted a separate Roman Catholic chapel, a small synagogue, a mosque with a fountain and footbath outside that was used for prayer five times a day, a small chapel to Shiva for Hindus, another centered around a bronze Buddha, lined with Tibetan and Chinese thangkas, a bare meditation room, used by Zen followers, mindfulness practitioners and unaffiliated meditators alike, and quarters for the resident chaplain, Rev. Jukka Pekonen, who was officially retired but kept on as long as he could perform the services.

The chapels were open 24/7 and welcomed all comers. In the seemingly secular world of the building, the services were surprisingly well attended, and most of the rooms were used at all hours of the day and night.

When Ivan arrived at the Protestant chapel, there were at least eight other worshippers around the room, praying or meditating. He took a pew in the rear, knelt at the kneeling bench under his seat – there were five to a pew – and tried to form a cohesive prayer for forgiveness.

But when he tried to conceptualize his sin, he had no memory of it. What he *could* remember was getting drunk and waking up. He had been stupid, he had blabbed about the Woodstar and the passion flower extract misted into the cardinal flowers, but getting drunk and being indiscrete could not be categorized as a *sin*. The sin was assumed – he had woken up naked next to a naked woman who was not his wife. Had he enjoyed himself? Had he succumbed to lust? There was no way of telling. That he was no longer a virgin was assumed but not experienced. If only there was a test for male virginity.

Could one pray for forgiveness for an *assumed* sin? He could pray for Jesus to guide him in deciding and he actually attempted this, but the fervor for forgiveness wasn't there. As he was half praying, half cogitating, an old man sat down next to him. "Can I help you?" he said.

He introduced himself as Father Pekonen, the resident chaplain for Protestants in the building. He was a small, wizened man of 83, with white hair and a kindly face. Ivan gratefully accepted his offer to consult with him in his office.

Father Pekonen's office was conventional, tending to dark woods and pastoral artwork, suitably book-lined, with a comfortable sitting area around a coffee table made from a block of oak, and a large, mahogany executive desk. It had a corporate feel that seemed at odds with the benign character of the pastor, who seemed acutely aware of the disconnect.

"Excuse this office," he said, ushering Ivan to an easy chair in the sitting area. "Was decorated before I came here and I haven't gotten around to change."

"Why, what's wrong with it?" said Ivan.

"Is too impersonal. Looks like a place where you make deals, rather than offer comfort and solace."

"I may want to make a deal with God," said Ivan.

"Ah, that's different," said Father Pekonen. "You seem to be in pain."

"Yes."

"I must tell you, I ordained as a minister in the Finnish Evangelical Lutheran Church. Can we work together?"

"I was brought up in the Tanque Verde Baptist Church in Tucson. It's very strict."

"Literal?"

"Yes."

"But we have Christianity in common."

Ivan explained that his girlfriend, Kimberly, and her family were members of his congregation, they had met in Sunday school, and their eventual union was warmly supported by both families. They were not formally engaged but it was understood that the formality was not far off. But now it was in jeopardy.

Ivan described his predicament with no little embarrassment. He knew that most people outside his church and family were more or less comfortable talking about sex but he wasn't. He never wanted to reach the point where he could discuss sexual matters as if they were ordinary, everyday topics. He simply wasn't brought up to be degenerate.

"Degenerate?"

"Yes, what I did with that woman downstairs (he had not named her) was degenerate."

"What you *assume* you did," said Father Pekonen, who was beginning to think he was dealing with someone who couldn't be dealt with.

"Whatever. I think maybe I should go back to Tucson. I'm not right for this city. I love my job but it's not worth throwing my life away."

"You are scared of what you'll become?"

Ivan hadn't thought of that. Perhaps he would sink into the moral abyss of New York City. His father had warned him about this. Both his parents were very concerned about the effect New York would have on him.

Father Pekonen had a meeting with some architects coming up and didn't want to waste too much time on a boy whose mind was clogged with superstition. "Let's not get into whether or not you should stay in the city. There's a perfectly simple way of determining whether you sinned or not."

"What?"

"Ask the woman you woke up next to."

Ivan cringed. "I couldn't."

"You were drunk and she put you to bed."

"But then why undress me and herself?"

"Forgive me for being indelicate but perhaps she hoped you would wake up."

That hadn't occurred to Ivan.

"Besides," continued Father Pekonen, "you are not spiritually responsible for what she might have done to you while you were unconscious, any more than if you were on the operating table under anesthesia. There is no sin involved in my denomination and I doubt very much in yours. According to your description, you did not wake up with lustful thoughts."

"No. I was horrified."

"Had you found her attractive before you passed out?"

Ivan had to admit he had. "But I had no intention of having sex with her."

Father Pekonen said nothing, which made Ivan think there was more to be said on the subject. "So there's no need to repent?"

"Of course there is," Father Pekonen counseled. "You must repent for getting so drunk you allowed yourself to be undressed and possibly manipulated. Doesn't Thessalonians tell us to abstain from all *appearance* of evil? You are responsible for letting yourself get in a situation where you *might* have sinned or it might *seem* like you have sinned. But I believe you are already suffering the penalty for your transgression."

Father Pekonen left for his meeting, wishing Ivan well, hoping he'd make the right choice.

Ivan remained in the office for a few minutes. He wasn't entirely relieved. He wasn't sure if he should confess his drunkenness to Kimberly without the incriminating details, which she might find suspect, to say the least. But not to confess meant keeping secrets from Kimberly – not the best way to start a marriage. It would always be on his mind and would interfere with their relationship. Eventually, his guilt would show and she'd ask him what was wrong. He'd have to blurt out that he'd slept with another woman, albeit unconsciously, and her love for him – so pure and unsullied – would be shattered forever.

Another problem: how could he face Katie again? He saw her almost every day when he came in for work and often several times a day, at the restaurant or at Finnegan's. Would she flash him a knowing smile? Would she smirk at him? He wasn't sure he could stand it.

Another thought struck him: perhaps she would want real sex this time or more sex if they had had some already. Perhaps she actually liked him, physically. How could he deal with that?

He left Father Pekonen's office, spent a few more minutes in the chapel, setting his mind in order, and left for work at the aviary.

17

61st Floor

USTAFA FAOUD WASN'T looking forward to another meeting so soon. It wasn't just that he found them tiresome (which he did) but he wasn't sure he wanted to pursue this investigation any further. He had felt it was his duty to pursue the theft of so valuable a bird, but he was afraid the answer wasn't going to be of his liking.

The group that gathered in Faoud's office included Alice, Heidi and Henry, as well as Ivan, Drs. Benjamin and Fain, the security team, Captain Martin and José Ramirez, and Dr. Aniashvili, the chief entomologist and director of the Insect Garden on the 88th Floor, but not the NYC police officers.

"Why are so many people here?" asked Faoud. The group had gathered around Faoud's desk, filling up the desk chairs and pulling more from the conference table at the other end of the office. The two comfortable easy chairs were taken by Dr. Benjamin and Dr. Aniashvili. Captain Martin preferred to stand.

"We have quite a story," said Captain Martin. "By now, we think we know who took the Woodstar but not the details."

"Well, that's something," said Faoud. "I don't think I'm going to like the discovery."

"Let me introduce you to Alice Jeynes," said Captain Martin. "She started work as a waitress for the family a few days ago."

Another model, Faoud thought. Dr. Nikkanen has a penchant for models but he never sleeps with them, as far as I know.

Alice described her encounter with Mrs. Nikkanen in detail, the presentation of the spider, squashing it and the request to sprinkle spider venom on Dr. Nikkanen's food to kill him.

"Did she actually tell you to kill him?" asked Faoud.

"She said put it in his stew and that she wanted him terrified before he died."

"Interesting."

Heidi took the floor and testified that Mrs. Nikkanen had also asked her to poison Dr. Nikkanen's food.

"With spider venom?" asked Faoud.

"No, she showed me a vial of powder that I refused to take."

When Heidi was finished, Henry backed up her story. He said Heidi had told him about Mrs. Nikkanen's request immediately after the interview. "When she returned to the dining room, she was shaking; she could barely serve."

Then Dr. Aniashvili spoke. He said that Mrs. Nikkanen was a frequent visitor to the insect garden. She often asked him about the spiders, especially the venomous ones. "I told her that the mouse spider's venom was as toxic as the Australian funnel-web spider and that the same antivenom worked for both."

"Do you ever see her handle one of the spiders?" asked Faoud.

"No, but I know she came to the Insect Garden at night, when nobody was around. It would have been easy for her to take one of the spiders."

"Why didn't the mouse spider bite her?"

"He was probably scared," said Dr. Aniashvili. "Mouse spiders aren't normally aggressive unless they think they can eat you. Most bites aren't particularly dangerous – they're what's known as *dry* bites, without venom."

"How valuable are they?"

"Not very. The Garden has six at the moment, well, five, now that Mrs. Nikkanen killed one. We get them from Australia. Scary looking buggers, though. I have one right here."

He brought out a large petri dish, meshed at the top, which contained a large, thick, hairy black spider with what looked like a flaming red heart on its head. It was truly the stuff of nightmares.

Everyone gathered around to look at it. "That's the ugliest thing I've ever seen," said Ramirez.

"Not to me," said Dr. Aniashvili. "I find it beautiful."

"Is this what Mrs. Nikkanen had in her hand?" Faoud asked Alice.

"No, it didn't have that red thing at the top."

"This is a male," said Dr. Aniashvili. "Females have all-black carapaces."

"How did you collect this one?" asked Faoud. "Did you use some kind of tongs for putting it into the petri dish?"

"No, I just picked it up with my fingers."

"So Mrs. Nikkanen could have done the same."

"It's easy, if you're not scared of them," said Dr. Aniashvili.

Faoud nodded and was about to ask another question when Dr. Aniashvili added, "Most people are scared of spiders like this but Mrs. Nikkanen isn't like most people. For one, she's crazy."

Faoud noted that almost everyone in the room nodded in agreement.

Captain Martin raised her hand to speak. "And someone who is crazy enough to squash a venomous spider in her hand is crazy enough to kill a hummingbird."

"But that's not evidence," said Faoud.

"No," Martin admitted.

Faoud sat back in his chair and surveyed the faces ranged around his desk. Everyone was waiting for him to decide something, whatever it was.

Captain Martin took the floor. "So what we have here are three criminal offenses. One, the theft of a toxic spider and a $2,000,000 hummingbird. Two, maliciously killing the spider, which is on the order of killing someone's dog, which could be a misdemeanor or a felony, depending on the amount of cruelty involved. And three, suborning an employee to kill her husband by poisoning him with an unnamed powder and a spider's venom, which is attempted murder and a Class A Felony."

"Probably Class B, if that." said Alice.

Everyone turned to look at her. How would a beautiful young waitress know about the finer points of the law?

"Planning to kill someone isn't necessarily Class A, even if you consider the spider a weapon." She looked around the room and saw everyone's surprised expressions. "I used to go out with a criminal," she said apologetically.

Faoud took out a black cigarette with a gold filter. "Would anybody mind?" When nobody protested, he lit the cigarette and blew out a satisfying puff of smoke. "They're called Sobranie Black Russians. Nobody knows what they're made of, not American tobacco, but not Turkish or Syrian either. My grandmother used to smoke them."

It was almost a shock to see anyone smoking inside a building these days but they had to admit, there was a certain elegance to the act that reminded Drs. Benjamin, Fain and Aniashvili of why they used to smoke.

Faoud took another puff, enjoying the reaction of the group, and gave his considered opinion: "Let's dispense with the theft and killing scenarios right off the bat. Mrs. Nikkanen, as Dr. Nikkanen's legal spouse, co-owns the hummingbird and the spider, so taking them can't be called stealing – you can't steal from yourself. It might make her husband angry and upset but it's probably not prosecutable. As to the killing of the spider, that's not a crime. You can kill your dog legally, as long as you do it humanely, so I can't imagine it's illegal to kill your spider unless it's extremely rare and valuable, which isn't the case in this instance. And since Mrs. Nikkanen squashed it in her hand, it died instantly, without pain. So she probably can't be prosecuted for aggravated cruelty.

"As to … what did you call it? … *suborning* an employee to kill her husband, that's a different story. I'll inform Dr. Nikkanen and see what he says. I doubt that he'll wish to get the police involved, and no one in this room should mention it to anyone. I hope that's understood."

Alice made a face, which Faoud caught immediately. "Yes, Miss Jeynes?"

Alice sighed, to give her time to choose her words. "Are we supposed to wait until someone actually poisons Dr. Nikkanen? She *asked* Heidi and me to kill him. She gave us the means to do it. I guess I can see why you might want to cover it up but shit, this is a real crime, you can't just ignore it."

"Did she offer you any money for killing Dr. Nikkanen?" asked Faoud.

"No."

He turned to Heidi. "Did she offer *you* any money, anything in return?"

"No," Heidi admitted.

"So she didn't hire you to kill Dr. Nikkanen, she just expressed a desire," said Faoud.

"Legal or not, she ought to be locked up," said Alice.

Faoud noticed a current of approval in the room.

"I mean, I'm just new here, so it won't make a big difference to me," said Alice. "But if Dr. Nikkanen gets bumped off, everyone in this building might be out on the streets." She shrugged as if to say *don't say I didn't warn you.*

Faoud smiled. "Good point, Miss Jeynes."

"What about the hummingbird?" asked Ivan.

Faoud looked over at his chief security officer. "Captain Martin, you said you found no direct evidence linking Mrs. Nikkanen with the Woodstar?"

"No, sir," said Captain Martin. "We know she's capable of doing it, she's probably smart enough to think of sedating the bird and she's crazy. But we don't have evidence."

Faoud sat back and took a long drag on his cigarette, letting it out in a series of short puffs. "She's certainly smart enough," he said. "She ran a Finnish Women's Sports Association before she married Dr. Nikkanen."

"I didn't know that," said Dr. Benjamin. "Was she an athlete?"

"Could be, I never asked," said Faoud. "She named her daughter, Minna, after a famous Finnish pole vaulter, so I suppose that was her sport."

The Sobranie Black Russian had produced an ash so long, it riveted everyone's attention. Faoud tapped it into a coffee cup on his desk. "Does anyone have anything else to say?" asked Faoud.

Several people seemed on the verge of saying something but no one spoke up.

"Very well, I'll inform Dr. Nikkanen about everything we talked about, the threats to his life, the spider, the hummingbird and the perceived state of Mrs. Nikkanen's mental health. Meanwhile, we keep searching for evidence tying Mrs. Nikkanen, or any other member of the family, to the hummingbird."

"All the others?" asked Dr. Benjamin.

"You must realize by now that most of the members of the family are disturbed in some way. They're all suspects."

"What do we do about the city police?" said Captain Martin.

"Let them keep searching for the hummingbird for now. Don't mention the death threats until I've talked with Dr. Nikkanen."

18

87th Floor

MRS. NIKKANEN SHOWED up for dinner the next night. Their guests, Senator and Mrs. Mitchell, had joined with them in the aviary, been dutifully impressed, and decided to brave a dinner with the whole family. It was Tuuli's turn to choose the setting and she selected a hillside village in Tuscany.

Tero, the 10-year old, made the introductions. "We're all subatomic particles," he said. "Pop is the Higgs Bosun, because he gives mass to matter."

"We had a hard time finding him," said Mika, the 12-year old. The Senator and his wife got the joke and smiled.

"Mom is the gluon," continued Tero. "Because she makes things cling to her. Silja is the graviton because she's brings things down to earth. Minna is the photon, because she brings light. Mika is the tachyon, because he's faster than light."

"I'm hypothetical," explained Mika. "I can't go slower than light."

Tero continued. "Naziha is the strange quark, because she's a strange quark."

"And you?" asked the Senator.

"The neutrino, because it's so small it can travel between everything else and changes as it goes. It's almost impossible to catch a neutrino."

"But it can be done," joked Dr. Nikkanen. "Bribery helps."

"You seem to have all the bases covered," said Senator Mitchell. "But don't think I'm going to fund another cyclotron."

The group laughed except for Tuuli.

Calhoun, Alice, Heidi and Henry brought out the dishes and were ogled by the guests for their beauty. Henry invariably flirted with the female guests and was occasionally rewarded later on.

The conversation was ordinary, with comments on a baseball team which the blind members of the party couldn't share. When it was clear that no one at the table had any interest in sports, Senator Mitchell switched the conversation to the arts, but realized too late that that was inappropriate as well. It was hard to talk to a family that was half blind. It was Tero who brought the conversation to an interesting point.

"Why can't we eat the birds in the aviary?" he asked. "We wouldn't have to have chicken or duck all the time." He looked in Mika's direction and received a raised eyebrow, which could have been alarm.

"You don't eat duck anyway," said Minna.

"No, but I bet I'd like peacocks or pygmy geese."

"What about it?" said Dr. Nikkanen to the Senator and his wife. "Shall we serve you fawn-breasted bowerbirds next time? Or golden breasted starlings? We could do it."

"We'll stick with the chicken," said Mrs. Mitchell, who lobbied for a food company that wanted to remove all regulations on the humane treatment of animals.

"We wouldn't know anyway," said Silje. "Unless it was cooked whole and we could feel what it looked like. It would just be chicken with a different flavor."

"Minna or Mika could tell us," said Tero. "They can see a little."

"I can only see in one color," said Minna.

"And I never know what I'm seeing," said Mika.

"I could show you," said Naziha. "But I don't know all the birds."

"I have an idea," said Tero, excitedly. "Naz, you catch one and we'll give it to Lazarus to cook up."

"Dr. Benjamin wouldn't like that," said Minna.

"So what? He works for us, doesn't he?" said Tero. "He could help."

"Enough, children," said Dr. Nikkanen. "We've gone to considerable trouble to collect these birds and we have one of the finest private aviaries in the world. It's not a food farm."

"Don't we have food farms downstairs?" said Tero.

"We have three floors of farms and another of greenhouses," said Dr. Nikkanen. "But these are for crops, like the vegetables you're eating right now. "We don't have space for animals, like chickens and cows."

"Why don't we throw out the fish and the insects on 88 and put in some cows and pigs?" said Tero.

"Because then I'd have to eat you," said Tuuli, speaking for the first time, without a trace of humor. Tuuli had greeted the Senator and his wife with a stony sigh and a seemingly malignant glare that would have frightened the visitors if they hadn't been forewarned. Given with what they had heard about Tuuli, they wouldn't have put it past her to eat one of her children, like the spiders she loved.

"Let's eat Naziha, with couscous and apricots," said Tero.

"I'll eat chopped Tero with ketchup," answered Naziha.

"Nobody's eating anybody," laughed Dr. Nikkanen. "Calhoun, what's for dessert?"

The conversation was not lost on Alice, Heidi and Henry, who conjectured simultaneously that the Woodstar was not merely stolen but could have been eaten, and that anyone in the family was capable of it.

19

85th Floor

THE 85TH FLOOR was a complex of large areas devoted entirely to Paavo and Tuuli Nikkanen and split into two areas. The living area was dominated by an enormous master bedroom, with striking views of the Empire State Building, the New York Harbor, the Statue of Liberty and an expanse of New Jersey. There were sitting rooms for both husband and wife, dressing rooms with cavernous closets, bathrooms, a hot tub, and a sauna. The working area took up more than half of the floor and had a small office for Tuuli, which she rarely used, and Dr. Nikkanen's office suite which included separate rooms for his secretaries and assistants.

The corner office was entirely Finnish in design, with wide, open spaces, floor-to-ceiling windows overlooking Central Park and beyond, Marimekko-type fabrics, and a wide desk of Finnish pine. What was not Finnish was a large Rothko painting, the second in the building, a Barnet Newman and, inexplicably, an ornate landscape from a medieval Book of Hours that invited one to lose oneself in its lush fields and forests where unicorns might emerge at any moment.

Usually, Faoud met with Paavo once a week to keep him updated on the state of the building, the various projects going on, personnel changes, finances, and pure gossip – births, deaths, romances, scandals and the like. For one reason or another, they hadn't met for nearly a month and Faoud had lots of news to convey.

He started, predictably, with the death threats. Paavo shrugged them off.

"There's a difference this time," said Faoud.

"Oh?" Clearly the subject bored him.

"It's public. She asked two of your table waitresses to poison you."

"At the same time?" asked Paavo, amused.

Faoud described how Tuuli had approached Heidi and Alice, recounted as much as he could remember, and rather deliciously recalled the spider crushing incident. All this was of great interest and little concern for Paavo, but what bothered him was that everyone in the building knew about it. "I suppose they think I should call in the police or have her committed to a mental institution."

"I suppose the latter would be the most reasonable solution."

"You know I can't do that, Mustafa," said Paavo. "She'd blab about things she shouldn't blab about."

"True."

Paavo accepted one of Faoud's Sobranie gold-tipped Black Russian cigarettes, leaned forward for a light and sat back, inhaling deeply with great pleasure. "This is what a cigarette should be. Silja and Minna don't want me to smoke so I've given up the habit around them. But I *do* look forward to our meetings together."

"Otherwise they'd be boring," Faoud laughed.

"Quite," said Paavo, smiling. "But I don't mean to make light of Tuuli's threats. She's wanted to kill me for years, ever since the disaster. She blames me for all the family's eye problems."

"Well, she has a point."

Paavo nodded. "I suppose so. Do you think she'll succeed?"

Faoud had considered this and shook his head. "If she hasn't by now, she's probably not serious. On the other hand, she's also insane."

"Which means she could get away with it."

"Not just that," said Faoud. "At the moment, she's roaming around the building in the middle of the night, stealing spiders from the insect garden, trying to recruit accomplices for your murder, doing God knows what with the night guards, causing your children great distress and embarrassment ..."

"So what do you suggest we do about it? Lock her up?"

Faoud paused for a moment before saying, "Yes."

Paavo was astonished. "What?"

"We have a floor free."

"43, I know."

"We could set her up with an elegant apartment, servants, nurses on call day and night, gigolos if necessary, and the right drugs to help her relax. As you know, I've always liked Tuuli, but she's not the same person since the accident. I'm afraid of what she might do to herself, and the children, and you."

"She'll go even crazier."

"We could start by insisting she get the sub-dermal implant, so we can know where she is at all times."

"She's already refused that," said Paavo.

"May I suggest something illegal and immoral?" said Faoud. "In place of locking her up."

"By all means."

"Drug her and place the transponder inside her body cavity in a way that wouldn't break the skin or leave any tell-tale mark. She wouldn't know it was there. Of course, she couldn't use it as a credit card, or pay groceries with it, it wouldn't be useful for *her*, but we'd know where she was, how fast or slow she was moving, her heartbeat and other vitals. We could keep track of her emotional state by monitoring her hormones ..."

"Do we have the capability to trigger hormonal secretions?"

"Not yet," said Faoud.

Paavo shrugged. "I suppose we could do that by drugging her food, the way she wanted to drug mine. At any rate, I prefer using the transponder to locking her up in some palatial mental ward. It'd have a bad effect on the children. Arrange it. What's next?"

With a significant pause, Faoud broke the news about the Esmeraldas Woodstar theft. Paavo was shocked. He knew how rare the Woodstar was, how valuable, how important it was to have a Woodstar in his aviary. It was the pride of his hummingbird collection, along with the Leucistic, and it made his aviary the envy of the hummingbird world.

"And you think Tuuli took it?" asked Paavo.

"Captain Martin and her team seem to think so; I'm not sure. The whole family is suspect, including you, Paavo. We've gone through all the tapes for everyone who had anything to do with the aviary and now we need the family tapes."

"No," said Paavo in a tone that left not the slightest opening for debate.

"Very well, we'll search in other ways," said Faoud. "We did find an interesting clue." He described how the new keeper of the hummingbirds, a boy who had worked at the Desert Museum in Tucson, had noticed a discrepancy in energy in the birds who fed on the cardinal flowers near the pavilion and that Dr. Chen, the director of the chemical lab, had posited the existence of passion flower extract in the blossoms that the hummingbirds feed on. "This would slow them down enough to catch them."

"Now *that's* a clue," said Paavo.

"We're pursuing it. At the moment, Sophie at the library is looking for anyone who might have inquired about passion flowers, which involves a massive online search."

"How many people know about this?"

For insurance purposes, we had to inform the city police, so the theft is public. Aside from that, everyone in the building knows about it. Dr. Fain first reported the absence of the bird to Dr. Benjamin, who called in Captain Martin and her team. A search was conducted. Gradually, more and more people were involved. Ivan Anderson, the boy who cares for the birds, Dr. Chen, Dr. Aniashvili of the Insect Garden, Sophie in the library, now even the receptionists and door people. The gossip has intensified, so the theft is becoming more difficult to investigate. We don't even know if the Woodstar is dead or alive."

"No ransom notes."

"Nothing."

"Nothing to connect it with our product?"

Faoud shook his head.

Paavo had finished his Sobranie Black Russian and accepted another. "That new waitress, Alice, seems sharp. Do you think we could recruit her as a kind of spy?"

"She needs money."

"Good. I'm thinking she might get close to the children, especially Mika and Tero."

"I'll tell her to keep her ears open," said Faoud.

"Give her the option of flirting."

"She *is* beautiful, isn't she?" said Faoud. "Shall we move on to new products?"

20

Lobby, The Forbidden Floors - 37 to 52

KATIE WAS INSATIABLY curious. She reveled in the gossip of the building, the stories, the secrets, the personalities. She was attuned to the various projects going on in the laboratories on 54-56, mostly basic, theoretical research. She knew about the various collections of plants and animals, including the aviary, the aquariums and insect gardens. She was amused by the various scandals that seem to crop up constantly, mostly sexual but sometimes financial or even criminal.

She was so keenly aware of the life of the family that she felt she knew them, although she had never actually met them. She had heard talk of Mrs. Nikkanen's insanity and her desire to enact revenge on her husband for the blindness of her children, although she didn't know the details of the incident.

Of course, she knew about as much about the theft of the hummingbird as anyone closely connected to the incident. Her friend, Sophie, whom she kept on a string of sexual potential, also kept her apprised of the search for passion flower information. She had listened carefully to Ivan's drunken revelations at her apartment moving-in party and was aware of his visit to Father Pekonen through a friend who worked at the chapel.

What she did not know was what happened on the sixteen floors between 37 and 52. Her implant gave her access to almost every other floor, except those reserved for the family, but 37-52 were forbidden to her, a complete mystery. If she pressed 37 in the elevator, there was no response. Once, she had gotten off at the mostly unused ballroom on

53 and tried to walk down, but the door wouldn't respond to her pass. She had tried to walk up from Finnegan's on 36 with the same result.

At her post in the lobby, she tried to befriend the workers who she knew had access to the forbidden floors. There was nothing to distinguish them from ordinary people except their access. Most arrived at 8 or 9 in the morning and left at 5 or 6. Most seemed to be factory workers but there were clearly some scientists and executives among them. She had actually asked one of the factory types what they did up there. He was a heavy-set man in his 40's, with a military crew cut and teeth that literally glistered when he opened his mouth.

"We don't do much," he replied, flippantly. "This 'n that."

What was astonishing was that within 15 minutes, her boss, Aaron Houdi, came down to question her about the conversation. He seemed satisfied with her answer but cautioned her to rein in her curiosity on the subject. Floors 37-52 were off-limits for speculation.

"Understood," said Katie. "But what do you think is really there?"

Houdi sighed. "I don't know, Katie, maybe some kind of government thing, top secret – we're not supposed to ask about it."

"Understood."

"… if you want to keep your job, your apartment and your head …

"I get it."

With her appetite for revelation whetted even further, she wondered if her brother, Billy, working part time in the IT section on 6, could lend a hand. He had been a major hacker in high school, to whom the school's finances and grade system was child's play. He and his friends regularly broke into government systems for fun and if anybody could figure out what was happening on 37-52, he could.

Except that he couldn't. "It's a whole different system," he said, over drinks at Finnegan's. "Whatever's going on there isn't accessible to the Internet. They have their own personnel records, separate from the rest of the building. I'm assuming they have their own Intranet."

"But surely you could hack into it," said Katie.

"I could try," said Billy. "What's in it for me?"

Katie tried to think of a sufficient bribe but Billy came up with one immediately. "Introduce me to that model who used to work at Tay's."

"Alice? She's ten years older than you, with two children."

"Great."

Katie agreed, without knowing quite how to arrange it. The next day, a noticeably grayer Billy came back with the results of his hack.

"I've been up all night on this. It's really bizarre," he said. "Usually, I can reach a gate which can be opened by a password. It could be constant, or constantly changing, or controlled by a feature of the gatekeepers, or *something*. But I can't even reach a gate for what's on those floors."

"Did you try a military address."

"Of course. I tried the Finnish military as well, cause Dr. Nikkanen is Finnish. I tried terrorist addresses, Russian and North Korean connections, drug trafficking connections …"

"How on earth do you know about drug connections?"

"Elementary," said Billy. "They're not really secret. I tried a lot of the criminal sites. I also checked the architectural records of the building, the construction permits, any paperwork I could find. Then I looked into Dr. Nikkanen's history, to see if I could get some clues. Even his school records in Finland."

"You read Finnish?"

"I have an app," said Billy.

"What about the accident, when some of his children went blind?"

"I don't know. Wasn't that before they built the building?"

"I think so," said Katie. "I just wondered if there was a connection."

"I'll check it out. Do I still get to meet Alice?"

"Sure. I just have to figure out an excuse."

During a break, Katie went to visit Sophie in the library. "Can we meet outside somewhere?" she asked. "Everything we say here is being taped."

"Sounds interesting," said Sophie. They arranged to meet at a bar on 9th Avenue after work.

Obviously, Sophie hoped the meeting was about sex but she wasn't surprised or too disappointed when Katie brought up the subject of Floors 37–52.

"Why do you want to know?" asked Sophie.

"Because everyone wants me *not* to know."

"That's a good enough reason," said Sophie. "But I haven't the slightest idea what goes on there."

Katie told her about what she had learned so far (i.e. nothing) and the dead ends her brother had encountered. But what interested Sophie more was the visit from Aaron Houdi. "That means there's something to hide," she concluded.

"Exactly."

"Have you checked the elevator shafts and the garage?" asked Sophie.

"No. Why should I?"

So far, Sophie had not been successful in seducing Katie and introducing her to any of her more colorful eccentricities, but hope perseveres and she took this opportunity to take Katie's fingers in her hand and rub the tips, almost absentmindedly, knowing that Katie was waiting for her to explain herself. "Have your brother see if there is a separate elevator shaft from those floors to somewhere in the garages."

"On Sublevels –1 and –2."

"Or maybe elsewhere. Perhaps they're making something that has to be transported and the only way to do that is through an egress, probably a garage. You might station yourself near the elevator that goes to these floors."

"Excellent suggestion," said Katie. "But what if it's a C.I.A. black site?"

"They have to get the prisoners in and out."

"Perhaps they burn the bodies after they've gotten whatever information they want. That's the American way these days."

"I wouldn't put it past us," said Sophie. She took Katie's fingers and held them up to her mouth. "May I?"

"Dream on."

21

Lobby, 86th and 87th Floors, Alice's apartment

A FEW DAYS AFTER Faoud's conversation with Dr. Nikkanen, Alice was approached by José Ramirez, the security officer second in command to Captain Martin, who had received direct orders from Faoud. When Ramirez told her that Mr. Faoud had requested she keep an eye on the Nikkanen kids, especially Mika and Tero, her response was instantaneous. "Why should I?"

Ramirez expected hesitation but not resistance. They were outside the staff dining room on 86. Alice had recognized Ramirez from their meeting with Faoud a week ago but just barely. He was the one who thought the mouse spider was the ugliest thing he'd ever seen, but hadn't said anything after that. He was also quite handsome, Alice noticed.

"It's a direct request from Mr. Faoud," said Ramirez.

"Do I get any more money?"

"They haven't told me."

"What does 'keep an eye on' mean?" asked Alice.

"Shit, I don't know. I'm just delivering the message."

Alice should have been pleased that Faoud had singled her out for an assignment of some importance, dealing with the family, but what she felt was irritated. As if I don't have enough to do – serving two meals a day, taking care of my two children and trying to have a life. And now this exasperatingly vague commission with no tangible rewards.

"Listen ..." she said, "...what's your name?"

"José."

"José, get back to me tonight with exactly what I'm supposed to do and exactly what I get for it. I'm sure you know how to reach me and where I am at any given moment."

That evening, after serving dinner, as Alice was leaving for home (her mother had picked up the kids from daycare, fed them and put them to bed), Ramirez was waiting for her in the lobby.

"Miss Jeynes."

"You can call me Alice. And I'm calling you José."

"I apologize for not having all the details before ..."

"*None* of the details."

"Right. Captain Martin just wanted to give you a heads-up before we went any further."

Alice decided she liked Ramirez; she was actually attracted to him, even though he was a security officer, which was the next thing to being a cop. But despite the attraction, she wasn't going to let herself be used. "I haven't said I'd be interested yet."

Ramirez shrugged it off. "I've been authorized to offer you a 3-bedroom apartment in the building – not huge but bigger than what you're living in now ..."

"You know how big my apartment is?"

"I do my homework."

Alice was impressed. "Go on."

"It's on 25, one of our low-income housing floors – I can show it to you now, if you like. It's a little more than half the rent of your present apartment."

Alice shrugged, without indicating interest.

"You'll get a slight raise in salary and bonuses for any pertinent information. You'll have access to the family sections of the building, in addition to what you have now."

"And what do I have to do?" asked Alice.

"Find out who took the hummingbird. Dr. Nikkanen wouldn't give us access to the family tapes, but he agreed to let you sort of insinuate yourself with the kids and poke around."

"Can you be vaguer?"

"Shit, I don't know. You wanna get a drink somewhere?"

"You're wearing a ring," said Alice.

"Separated."

"Bullshit."

Ramirez managed a weak smile. "So do you want to see the apartment?"

Alice wasn't in the mood to be propositioned by a cop in an empty apartment, although he was certainly desirable and looked strong, healthy and potent. Still, she didn't want to get mixed up with somebody on the level of her former boyfriend, anyone on the criminal-cop spectrum, which she supposed would include judges, correction and parole officers, criminal lawyers, social workers, psychologists, court officials, anyone who might have had the slightest contact with the father of her children. Much as she would have liked to have a little uncomplicated sex (if there was such a thing), she declined Ramirez' offer to view the apartment.

"I gotta get back to my mom and my kids," she said.

Ramirez smiled resignedly. "So you wanna take the job?"

"I'll think about it," said Alice as she went to leave the building. "But tell me one thing. You and the whole security team couldn't find who took the hummingbird, nobody who works in the aviary could find out, the city police couldn't find out, none of the scientists could find out, Faoud couldn't find out, nobody in the building could find out – what makes you think that I can find out?"

Ramirez shrugged. "Worth a try."

Back home, Alice discussed the offer with her mother, Marpessa, who had once been as glamorous as Alice before men, pregnancies, poverty, drugs, alcohol and age had washed away her beauty and most of her will to live.

"This is a trap," said Alice. "They give us an apartment that they can take away if I don't do what they say."

"What do they want you to do?"

"I don't know exactly. Infiltrate the family, be a spy."

"So?"

Marpessa was not entirely sober but alert enough to tend a child awakening from a bad dream. Now that Alice was home and on duty, she felt she could switch from wine to Ambien laced with gin, her favorite bedtime cocktail.

"So?" was an interesting response, thought Alice. "Really, what did it matter if she discovered something incriminating about the family.

What would they do, kill her? The best they could do was fire her and take away her apartment and the daycare. She'd be no worse off than she was before they hired her.

"And it'd be nice to be out of this shithole for a while," said Marpessa.

So it was decided that Alice, Marpessa and little Napheesa and Tony would move to 211A West 57th Street, Napheesa would be enrolled in the building's nursery school on 9, Marpessa would consider joining the Senior Center on 59, with its own pool and gym for seniors, and Alice would add spying to her job as waitressing. However, she drew the line at getting an implant.

22

87th Floor

FOR TWO WEEKS in the summer, the Nikkanen children were sent to camp, which they hated, except for Naziha, who had opted for an all-girls camp and loved it. Silje and Tero went to specialized camps for the blind, Minna and Mika were sent to a cocd camp and couldn't stand it, as they were considered *freaks*. Naziha stayed an extra week but the others were more than glad to get home after two weeks. They had summer homework from their various schools and were anxious to get started on that.

A few days after their return from camp, at a dinner in the Himalayas (Mika's choice), Alice, Heidi, Henry and Calhoun were on duty serving haute cuisine to the senior Nikkanens and their guests, an army general and his wife, and to Silje and her guest, and ordinary food to the other children. Tuuli was sane that evening and kept up a running conversation with the general's wife on military versus civilian childcare.

Once again, Silje had invited her blind Indian classmate, Chitra, for dinner and a sleepover, and Tero wondered if they were a couple.

"I've seen them touch," said Mika.

"Of course we touch; we're blind," said Silje.

"Don't be obscene," said Minna. "It's perfectly innocent."

"That's not what I've seen," said Mika.

"I've heard them making out," said Tero.

"Don't be ridiculous," said Silje.

"I think you're a dyke," said Tero.

"You don't even know what that is," said Minna. "And anyway, so what if she was?"

"She licks black pussy," said Mika to Tero.

"Is her friend black?" asked Tero.

"Indian, same thing."

Alice happened to be serving spaghetti to the two boys at the time and, leaning between them both, whispered, "Listen, you little fuckers, behave yourselves or I'll knock the shit out of you." She smiled, doled out their food and went back to her station at the entrance to the dining room.

Mika and Tero were stunned. Nobody had ever spoken to them like that before. Their governesses and tutors had disciplined them, the caregivers and helpers chided them and generally tolerated their abuse, but never, never had they been threatened. And why? Who was this waitress?

After dinner, instead of doing their homework or retiring to the playrooms on 80, where they usually spent the evening reading, playing games, watching TV (Mika) or listening to music or audio books (Tero), they went to 84, which housed the children's bedrooms and apartments for Paavo's mother, Tuuli's parents and the children's helpers.

Mika's bedroom was large, papered with sports figures, movie stars and the usual detritus of a 12-year old boy. Mika's room had no distinguishing features that might indicate an interest, a hobby, a future, a distinct personality. His computer was large and loaded with games. His attended a private school on the Upper West Side of Manhattan and, although his eyesight wouldn't permit him to go out for competitive sports, he enjoyed intramural wrestling and sang in the school chorus until recently, when his voice started to change.

Mika led Tero into his room and placed him on his bed. Tero slid to the floor, which he preferred. They said nothing for a moment. They didn't know how to compute what they had just heard. "Can she do that?" Mika said, finally.

"Knock the shit out of us?"

"Yes."

"You can see her, I can't," said Tero. "Does she look like she can knock the shit out of us?"

"I don't know. She's tall, skinny, black, I hear she was a model, she doesn't look that tough but she could be."

They eventually agreed that Alice was physically capable of beating them in a fight because she was bigger and an adult. They weren't sure what "knocking the shit" out of them meant. Was that a punch to the stomach or the intestines that would literally cause poo or whatever was inside to come out? Or was it symbolic, a generally all-purpose beating? Mika favored the literal shit being knocked out; Tero thought it could be both.

The question was *why* should she want to beat them? Just for teasing Silje? Well, perhaps they had gone a bit too far on the lesbian bit but what business was it of the waitress? Why would *she* step in?

"We should tell Dad," said Mika.

"I think Dad put her up to it," said Tero. Mika seemed skeptical but Tero argued that the waitress wouldn't have dared to threaten them on her own — she'd be fired on the spot — she had to have the backing of their father, as a way to control us without having to step in himself.

"That's crazy," said Mika, who nevertheless believed it. A question remained: "Why does Dad want to control us? Are we really out of control?"

"Because that's what dads do," Tero reasoned.

"Does he know something?" asked Mika.

Tero shrugged. "Let's wait and see. Meanwhile, what do we do about this waitress?"

23

89th and 36th Floors

VAN HAD DECIDED to postpone his confession to Kimberly. She was supposed to be coming to New York in less than a week, and he still hadn't found her a place to stay. She had texted to remind him several times but he couldn't get himself to concentrate on it. He really didn't want her to come until he had worked out his emotions over having slept with Katie, chastely or carnally.

His indecision naturally affected his work. Not that he failed to perform his day-to-day duties with the hummingbirds, cleaning, feeding, watering, monitoring, inspecting, keeping strict records of each hummingbird's health, activities and general welfare, but his enthusiasm had begun to wane. The hummingbirds themselves remained mesmerizing and miraculous, but the duties connected with them seemed slightly more onerous.

One thing he had accomplished: replacing the cardinal flowers near the pavilion, working with one of the resident horticulturists, Sally Ames, a middle-aged depressive with flaming red hair and uneven teeth. At first, they thought they might detoxify the cardinal flowers, flushing out the passion flower extract with mist or air. But that seemed to affect the nectar and kill the miniscule bugs that lived inside the flowers. The hummingbirds grew anxious trying to find a suitable flower to feed on. After only a short time, it was obvious that the flowers would have to be replaced.

Within a day, a shipment arrived from a nursery in Connecticut and Sally replanted the entire section. The hummingbirds buzzed around confusedly for a moment, but then fed voraciously. Ivan and Sally watched them in awe as they hovered at the mouth of a flower, wings beating faster than the eye could see.

By this time, Ivan knew or recognized almost all of the people working at the aviary, the ornithologists, the horticulturists, the veterinarians, the maintenance people, even the inspectors for the city and state. Often, there were visitors, many from other aviaries and botanical gardens around the world, usually guided by Dr. Benjamin or Dr. Jerry Lefkowitz, the head gardener, a title as uninformative as Faoud's "head butler," as he was responsible for all the landscaping in the building, the floral themes on every floor, the pools and fountains, the greenhouses on 74, as well as the flora in the aviary. He also served as a consultant for the farms on 75-77. Lefkowitz was massive, with a gray goatee, a high voice and a genuine, 14-carat twinkle in his eyes. He was in love with flora of every kind and worked indefatigably on their behalf. He had come over to inspect Sally's new cardinal flowers.

"Good job, Sally," he said. "We were lucky Connecticut had them at the right stage; the ones in our nursery aren't ready yet."

He turned to Ivan. "Are your hummingbirds happy?"

"At the moment, yes," said Ivan.

"No clues on the missing one?"

"Other than the passion flower extract, only suspicions."

"Odd thing, that," said Lefkowitz. "I would think that the hummingbirds wouldn't feed at a flower with an unfamiliar smell, like a cardinal with passion flower extract inside."

"Yes, I guess that's true," said Ivan.

"And if they didn't feed, they wouldn't feel the effects of the extract. They wouldn't be slower."

Ivan hadn't thought of that. "But they *were* noticeably slower," he said. "I didn't test it, but I could tell."

"Oh, I don't doubt that," said Lefkowitz. "But the cause may not have been passion flower extract. It could be some drug that had a similar chemical composition to passion flower but lacked the smell. It could also have been something in the air, released when the hummingbirds were near the pavilion."

"But that would have slowed down the other birds as well, and I didn't notice that."

"Well then," said Lefkowitz. "Perhaps you should have the chemists look for another sedative that mimics passion flower."

Of course, Ivan thought. This was a revelation. The passion flower theory was too pat, too easy, ridiculous on the face of it. It was something he should have debunked himself. What Dr. Chen and the other chemists had found was not passion flower but something else, perhaps something unknown.

He discussed it with Dr. Benjamin later that afternoon. He was sympathetic. "Well, what you say makes sense," he said. "But I don't know how Dr. Chen is going to take being wrong."

"I was hoping you could help me with that," said Ivan.

24

Sub-basement -1

THE BUILDING HAD two floors of garages below the lobby level. Sub-basement -2 was for cars and passenger vans only. It was where people who commuted to the building parked for the day (Section A), where people liable to be working nights parked (Section B), where visitors parked (Section C) and where the residents had their long-term parking spaces (Section D). The family had two separate mini-garages, accessible from an unmarked entrance on the street to an elevator which let out directly onto an area next to Dr. Nikkanen's office (85) and to the floor for the living and dining rooms (87).

Sub-basement -1 was the transportation hub of the building, mostly a series of loading docks. This was where the trucks came to deliver food for the restaurants and grocery stores, equipment and supplies for the building, where the moving vans loaded and unloaded, the linens collected and delivered, where mail and packages were delivered to the post office and then to the apartments, where the Brink's trucks delivered money to the bank on 20. Huge garbage trucks came every morning to cart away the trash.

Plants and birds on their way to the aviary, pharmaceuticals destined for the hospital and clinics and pharmacies were unloaded on this floor. A ramp to the left of the entrance led directly to the emergency room of the hospital on 2, where there was parking for several ambulances. Some docks could accommodate 53-foot semis, others were for small delivery vans; there were separate docks for USPS, UPS, FedEx and other delivery services.

A series of specialized freight elevators were located at various parts of the garage. A hospital elevator only stopped at 2 and 3. Another, for storage and wine, emergency supplies, HUAV systems equipment, only stopped at Sub-basements -3, -4 and -5.

Most went to all floors, except for the family floors, which required special access.

The garages were active 24 hours a day and were a maelstrom of teamsters, crane and forklift operators, checkers, traffic coordinators, inspectors and purposeful workers on tight schedules. It was always noisy and the air was foul, despite the fans and filters meant to tamp down or detoxify the pollution.

Katie was on speaking terms with most of the attendants on -2 and on nodding terms with others in the parking garage. But she had little reason to know the people in charge of the freight garage, since they came in through a different entrance, by-passing the lobby.

She had met a few of them when she moved into the building and supervised the unloading of her furniture from her old apartment. And she made a point of chatting up the manager of the garage when she had a chance, waiting for her furniture to arrive.

Joe Barash had been a long-distance truck driver, a stevedore on the docks of Newark, Gulfport and Long Beach, a Navy Seabee, and a dispatcher for a cargo company before he had the brilliant idea of signing up for a year-long program in facilities management at Cornell online. Armed with an Executive Certificate, he could apply for supervisory positions and landed the job as manager of 211A's garage and cargo operations. It was a complicated job and required a staff that was not hired by the building's HR department and did not report to the building's general manager, Aaron Houdi. He used the building's computer, accounting, bookkeeping and financial services and, of course, the security and medical services when necessary, but he was a separate entity from the normal building hierarchy and officially reported directly to Faoud (although he usually dealt with one of Faoud's assistants.)

He amused Katie on first sight but she wasn't certain if she was attracted to him. He was certainly striking, with a shock of black hair, a constant stubble, the physique of a bodybuilder who liked his beer, and a Seabee tattoo on his right arm. He was 46, twice divorced, with children in other cities, and a penchant for prostitutes, simply because they were cheaper and easier than wives or girlfriends. Katie had met him for the first time when she moved in, but she had seen him at Finnegan's once after that. It was fairly late, he was at the bar, winding down, and noticing Katie across the room, gave her a grin of recognition. She was with a group of people but found time to wander over to say hello.

"Haven't seen you here before," she said. "I thought you just hung out in the garage."

"Usually the casino but just not in the mood tonight."

"What are you in the mood for?" asked Katie.

"Beer."

Katie spent 15 minutes flirting with him and finally got an invitation to tour the facilities downstairs, which was what she was after. She would probably have to have sex with him somewhere in the inner recesses of the garage, but he was attractive in a rough trade way and it probably wouldn't last very long since he was a busy man.

She showed up for the tour during her lunch break, bringing down sandwiches and a thermos of coffee for both of them. The garage was in full swing when she arrived and Joe had to be paged.

While she waited for him in the office, at least ten trucks showed up and were directed to their loading dock, or to an area where they could wait for a loading dock. Most were refrigerator trucks delivering food to the various restaurants in the building. A huge moving van was having trouble with the paperwork when Joe arrived. One of his assistants showed him the order slip and Joe spoke to the driver. "You're three hours early; the tenant in 67G isn't ready yet." There was no place to park on the street so Joe directed him to a waiting area at the far end of the garage where he could park his van, get some lunch and wait for his loading time.

A giant Mitsubishi Fuso was waiting in the entrance and let out a belch of diesel smoke instead of honking impatiently. A cargo director examined his papers.

"I brought you some lunch," said Katie.

Joe looked at the turkey sandwiches and smiled. "Thanks, but I'm vegan," he said.

"Who would've thought?" said Katie.

Joe took her into the office and showed her the computer programs they used for tracking and reporting. "We can track a shipment from its starting point to its destination and everywhere in between. We know exactly where everything is at all times. Now that moving van that just came in..." He brought up a video of the truck, his interchange with the driver, the truck's progress to the waiting area in the rear of the garage and details about the driver and his assistant mover, the exact items being moved, including their degree of fragility, how long the loading was going to take, insurance, safety, and a long series of numbers and acronyms that were too detailed to explain. "Now I'll take you to the bay where this new truck is unloading."

They wandered through the garage while Joe commented on the various docks and explained the hydraulic dock levelers and locks, the cranes and forklifts and the various elevators they used.

As they walked further into the interior, they were passed by a small van from a bakery delivering bread and pastries to the cafeteria on 7 or to the cheaper restaurants on 6 (the more expensive restaurants, like Genevieve's on 62, baked their own, as did the family kitchen.)

"At my entrance, we deal with the takeout people," said Katie, "Or the guy who delivers baguettes by bicycle."

A deep blast alerted them to the presence of a massive semi crossing their path. "She's just delivered a new MRI machine to the hospital."

"She?"

"Yeah, you don't get many women driving a semi. Times are changing."

"I hope so."

The garage was lit reasonably brightly but seemed darker and darker the more they walked. She was aware that they were in what she thought of as the bowels of the garage, and the thought that he could kidnap her and stash her in one of the trucks flashed through her mind. She was waiting for a pass, perhaps some crudity, or arched compliment, as the prelude to a seduction, or even a rape, but none came. He was invariably polite and informative. He showed her the mechanics of unloading, the cranes and moving equipment; he introduced her to forklift operators and freight inspectors; they watched a team of workers unloading treadmills for one of the gyms into one of the giant freight elevators that could have accommodated a small house.

It occurred to her that it would be difficult to stage a rape even this far into the garage, at least during the day. Unlike a parking garage, there were workers in every area of the space and a scream or its echo would carry throughout the garage unless momentarily drowned out by the roar of a semi in first gear. She wasn't going to be raped today, she felt, although she might be invited into the depths of an idle 18-wheeler – fortunately there were none in sight at the moment.

As they neared what seemed like the far end of the garage, where they could see the moving van parked, they came across a group of tanker trucks, standing idle in their bays. They were shorter than gasoline trucks but thicker, with an array of tubes and gauges on the outside. What was even more unusual about them was that they had no markings on them whatsoever, not even the name of the manufacturer. When they neared the trucks, she noticed that their license plates had retracted into slots beneath the bumpers.

"What are these?" she asked.

"Medical supplies I think," he answered.

"You *think*."

"Medical supplies," he said firmly.

"But I thought the elevator to the hospital was back where they were delivering the MRI."

"It's not to the hospital," said Joe. "It's some kind of project the scientists are working on. I don't know much about it."

"So are these tankers delivering or picking up?" asked Katie.

"I'll have to check the computer."

Katie noted the number *17* over the entrance to the elevator but said nothing as they walked by, heading back to the entrance. Her suspicions were aroused to the fullest, especially as Joe wouldn't answer a straight-forward question.

"Don't those kinds of trucks carry hazardous materials?" she asked.

"What kind of trucks?"

"The ones we just saw."

"They could carry water, or orange juice," he said, shrugging.

"Or 8,000 gallons of shampoo?" she quipped.

He laughed and they returned to the entrance. She was relieved that nothing had happened and disappointed that he hadn't tried. There were no sparks whatsoever, but she could sense that he was deliberately stifling them, as if she had been sent to inspect him and make a report to the management. Perhaps it was her questions about the unmarked tanker trucks – no, he was that way before that. She thanked him for the tour in a way that seemed formal and stilted.

"You up for a drink at Finnegan's this evening?" she said at last, not entirely seriously.

"Can't this evening," he said.

"Some other time maybe."

She shook his hand and headed for the exit, but stopped herself and turned back. "Joe?" she said.

"Yeah?"

"What gives?"

Joe laughed and it was evident he understood their suppression of chemical attraction completely. "I'm not gay, if that's what you were wondering."

Katie waited.

"Romance doesn't work out for me. I only do prostitutes."

Katie snorted. It wasn't the first time she'd heard this. "I'll let you know when I'm hard up for money," she said, and left.

Up in the lobby, few minutes later, she had Isha check out the elevator system in the building on his console. Elevator 17 only stopped at floors 37 through 49, the forbidden floors.

25

84th Floor

ALICE HAD BEEN given access to all the floors used by the family, except 85, the master bedroom and Dr. Nikkanen's office, with its mini-garage.

The day after she had threatened Mika and Tero, she still had no idea how to approach them, even though she had access to their floors. Her threat had been a spur-of-the-moment impulse and she was not sure how they had taken it.

She served dinner as usual and noticed that Mika and Tero were unusually subdued in her presence. She speculated that they wouldn't put up with being subdued for long and they were contemplating ways to get her replaced before she could make good on her threat. For some reason, she didn't think they'd bring up her threat with their father. But "we don't like her" wasn't reason enough for their father to discharge her; it could be suspicious. They'd have to manufacture some criminal act to accuse her of, perhaps something sexual. She knew she didn't have much time to do whatever she was going to do.

She had noticed that Mika and Tero enjoyed a particularly gooey mocha cake, which she had served them two nights ago and had the kitchen make one that she could take to them tonight. After serving dinner, after everyone had left the table, she waited half an hour and took the cake up to the 84th Floor, which opened up to what first looked like a garden but was actually a study area, surrounded by bedrooms for the children, and apartments for their helpers, Paavo's mother and Tuuli's parents.

When she emerged from the elevator, she saw a man she didn't know, middle-aged and bookish, sitting with Silje in front of a computer with an attachment that printed out strips of paper. She was answering questions posed by the computer but stopped when Alice entered.

The middle-aged man looked up. "Who are you?" he asked.

Silje turned to her. "She's Alice, our waitress," she said, presumably smelling her.

"I didn't think the wait staff was allowed up here," said the man.

"They aren't," said Silje. She turned to Alice. "What *are* you doing up here?"

"I was nasty to Mika and Tero the other day," said Alice. "I brought them a cake to apologize."

Silje considered this with some skepticism. "They're in Tero's room, third door on the left," she said. "But who gave you access to this floor?"

"Mr. Faoud wanted me to get to know you all."

"Me, too?"

"All your father's kids. The cake seemed like a good way to start."

Silje turned to her companion with a confused expression.

"I'm John Parr, one of Silje's tutors, by the way," said the middle-aged man.

"Nice to meet you."

"I don't understand," said Silje. "Nobody's ever been allowed up here without a personal invitation from one of the family. Faoud can't invite anybody he chooses …"

"I guess he had the okay from your father," said Alice.

Silje shrugged. "I heard what you said to Mika and Tero," she said. "They deserved it."

"You think so?"

"They're brats, especially Tero."

Silje clearly wanted to say more but stopped herself. She turned back to her tutor and told him to continue.

"What's the machine?" asked Alice.

"It prints out the spoken word into braille, so Silje can review it," said Parr.

"Some machine," said Alice.

Silje and Parr nodded and went back to their work. Alice felt summarily dismissed. And also defeated. She hadn't established any connection with Silje other than a negative one, as an interloper.

Alice knocked at the third door on the left and received no reply. On the second knock, somebody (she thought Tero) replied angrily, "Wait a minute."

She heard some kind of scrambling inside. Perhaps they were getting dressed or hiding something. Finally, Tero called through the door, "Come back tomorrow. Or never."

"I have mocha cake," said Alice.

There was a pause. Then Tero said, "Shove it up your ass, Minna."

"I'm not Minna."

The door opened slightly. Mika stared at her in surprise and whispered to Tero, "It's the monster."

The word didn't compute. Alice had heard herself called *the model, beauty, black beauty, skinny, littletit, bones, runway nigger, Afrocunt,* and any number of names, admiring or disparaging, but never *monster.* Were they referring to her *height?* she wondered. But she wasn't huge, six feet in heels. Maybe this was how young people referred to the older generation – to a 10 and 12-year old, she was large, perhaps forbidding, even scary, but not a *monster.* That couldn't be *her.*

"Listen, I was rude to you the other day and I just wanted to say I'm sorry."

"And you have a cake?" said Mika.

"Well, you guys seemed to like the mocha cake we had a few nights ago."

The two boys held a brief, whispered conference. "Leave it outside," said Tero.

"Don't be ridiculous," said Alice. "I just want to talk to you. I'm not going to hurt you."

"That's not what you said before."

"Did you really think I was going to hit you?"

"You weren't?"

"Of course not. That was just talk."

"Hold on a minute," said Tero. Alice could hear them whispering hurriedly and then sounds of footsteps.

"Okay, you can come in now," said Tero.

Alice held the mocha cake in one hand, pushed open the door with the other and was hit by a hard plastic hammer from a children's tool box, delivered by Mika standing on a chair. The hammer hit Alice squarely on the forehead and knocked her to the floor, unconscious.

When she awoke, she was on a hospital gurney in the ER on the 2nd floor, with a massive headache and a small bump in the middle of her forehead.

26

55th and 36th Floors

KIMBERLY, IVAN'S TUCSON girlfriend, was due to arrive in four days and had been texting him regularly about a place to stay. He replied that he'd been looking and hadn't found anything but in reality he hadn't been looking at all. He kept putting it off until he had spoken with Katie.

The difficulty was, he was avoiding Katie. He could have easily gone down to the lobby, or hung out at Finnegan's, or even shown up at her apartment after work, but he couldn't bring himself to confront her.

The other difficulty was, he wasn't sure he was looking forward to seeing Kimberly at all. At least not in the charged atmosphere of the building. In his mind, he had relegated her to a quiet Eden where there were no complications, where everything was straight-forward and aboveboard. Although Tucson had its share of minorities (mostly Hispanic) and a burgeoning art scene, and the university was as diverse as any university, his own life had been bounded by people just like him, Christian, church-going, Republicans rooted in an Eisenhower ethos, suspicious of *isms* and extremes. After a few months in the building, the Kimberly he was almost engaged to seemed curiously spiceless, a distant representation of the things he was supposed to believe in, like God and Country. He kept putting off looking for an appropriate hotel or hostel.

In the meantime, he had been called into a strange meeting by Dr. Benjamin which was convened at the end of the day in a small conference room on 55, the floor which housed the chemistry labs, presided over by Mary Chen.

In the meeting were Drs. Benjamin and Fain, from the aviary, Drs. Chen and Chatterji from the chemistry labs and two men and a woman who were never introduced. From the questions they asked, they appeared to be doctors or scientists of some sort and they seemed to control the meeting. One had a notebook computer open and took down whatever was said.

An older man, florid and somewhat sickly, addressed Ivan. "You said you noticed the hummingbirds near the pavilion behaving differently. Could you tell us about this?"

Ivan was flustered. "Excuse me, who are you?"

The man stared at him and took a moment to make up his mind about answering. "A bird lover, like yourself. Dr. Chen and Dr. Benjamin can vouch for me."

Chen and Benjamin nodded.

"So tell me," the man continued. "What exactly did you see?"

"Why does this feel like an inquisition?" asked Ivan.

The man apologized and said they just wanted to get at the facts. There were some things they didn't understand.

Ivan mentally shrugged and told him what he had told everyone else, that the hummingbirds seemed to fly more slowly.

"Slower in what direction? Moving forward, backward?"

"Both."

"Was their ability to hover in the air compromised?"

Nobody had asked that question before and he seemed to call up a new memory. "Now that you mention it, there was a difference. They didn't hover as long as before."

"They grew tired?"

"Possibly," said Ivan. "But they just didn't spend as much time in the air."

"When they hovered, did the angle at which they stayed in the air change?"

The man pressed for more and more details, which Ivan answered as best he could. Then the woman took over. She was in her 40's, attractive, somewhat Teutonic, with a smile that seemed utterly insincere. She asked him a series of questions about the aviary itself, in particular about the cardinal flowers, did he sense any odor emanating from the flowers.

"Cardinal flowers don't have any particular odor," said Ivan. "And hummingbirds can't smell anyway."

"That's why I'm asking," said the woman. "Did you smell anything?"

"I don't think so."

"Surely the foliage in the vicinity must give off some aroma," she said.

Ivan could see what she was getting at. "Of course, but I didn't notice any difference in the aroma when the hummingbirds got slower."

Then she wanted to know about any changes in his own behavior since the hummingbirds got slower. He said he didn't know of any.

The third investigator, a man Ivan's age, was typing nonstop on his computer.

"You got drunk and spent the night at the Moran sisters on Friday, July 21, well after you noticed the birds getting slower," the woman continued, rather matter-of-factly. "Then, you went to the chapel and spoke with Father Pekonen. Is this normal behavior on your part?"

Although he should have known better, Ivan was still surprised at the level of surveillance in the building. Everything he did was public. "No, not at all," he said. "Never."

"Wouldn't that imply that after you noticed the birds flying slower, your behavior changed?"

"It's from working in this building I think," he said. "I don't think it was something in the air."

"Nevertheless, you got drunk for the first time, slept with one or two women for the first time – we're not that intrusive – and spent 20 minutes with a minister who was not of your denomination. Is that correct?"

Ivan nodded that it was.

"We'll need to take your blood," she said, abruptly. "You're expected at the office of Dr. Chandra on 4 immediately after this meeting. She'll be giving you a complete physical and compare it with the one you had when you took this job."

Before he was dismissed, Ivan felt he had to mention his talk with Dr. Lefkowitz, the head gardener, who thought that the sedative in the cardinal flowers was not from passion flowers."

"We know all about your conversation with Dr. Lefkowitz," said the woman, abruptly (it seemed like everything she said was abrupt). "We interviewed him this morning. Thank you, Mr. Anderson. We trust you'll keep this meeting to yourself."

On the way to his physical, Ivan couldn't help thinking that the disappearance of the Woodstar had a greater import than a simple theft. There was clearly something going on that he didn't understand. Who were these three people who interviewed him? Why didn't they give their names? What was all the secrecy about? Their interest in his behavior must mean that there was something more potent than a sedative effect involved. It was all very strange.

The physical was slightly more rigorous than the one he took when he started working in the building. Aside from blood work, a urine sample and a DNA swab, they gave him a breathalyzer test and took samples of his skin, his fingernails and his hair.

After the exam, he went back to work and finished up so exhausted that Dr. Benjamin took charge of him. "You need a drink," he said.

I never want to have a drink again, Ivan thought, but allowed himself to be guided to Finnegan's and order a ginger ale.

"What was that all about?" he asked Dr. Benjamin.

"This building has many secrets," he answered.

"So you *know* why they asked me those questions?" said Ivan.

"No," said Dr. Benjamin. "But they gave me the same inquisition a few days ago. All I know is that they were authorized by Faoud himself."

After a time to wind down, Benjamin left for dinner with his family on 73 and Ivan remained at the bar, nursing his ginger ale. He was about to give up on the evening when a woman plopped herself down on the next stool him and said, "Hey."

It was Katie, giving him what he thought was a knowing smile, although it may have been completely innocent, if anything Katie did was innocent. "Hey," he replied.

"Did you ever find a hotel for your girlfriend?" she asked.

The question took him by complete surprise. It was a shock that she could so blithely ask about his girlfriend as if nothing had happened between them. He didn't know what to say other than shake his head.

"Well, Annie's going on vacation next week so I'll have a bedroom free. She can stay with me."

"That's not possible," he said.

"Oh?" she said, again with what seemed like total innocence. "Why not?"

'You know."

Katie started up and was about to comment when the bartender asked for her order. "Stoli on the rocks," she said and turned to Ivan with a look of amusement. "Oh, *that*," she said. 'What do you think happened?"

"I don't know."

"No, you don't," she said, with what might have been a show of irritation although Ivan couldn't be sure. She turned away from him and watched the bartender pour a jigger of vodka into a small glass of ice and hand it over to her. She took a sip and turned to face Ivan who was waiting impatiently for some kind of closure.

"In the first place, you were drunk and passed out and we were nice enough to let you stay until you sobered up. In the second place, you were lying on my bed and we didn't think we could drag you to the sofa so we left you where you were."

"But my clothes ..."

"You had thrown up and they had vomit on them, it was really disgusting. So we took them off, threw a cover on you and let you sleep it off."

"That's it?"

"What else? Did you think I took advantage of you?"

"But you were ... you didn't have any clothing on."

"That's how I sleep."

This was too much to compute all at once. It didn't make sense. A naked man and naked woman in bed side by side was categorically a sin, wasn't it? But if they didn't touch ... well, Kimberly would never believe they didn't touch; it wasn't possible.

"Tell you what," said Katie. "If your girlfriend stays with me, I promise I won't take advantage of her either. You can both remain in a state of primordial innocence, like Adam and Eve before the apple. How long would she want to stay?"

"A week."

"Perfect. When would she arrive?"

"Monday afternoon."

She downed her vodka and slipped off the stool. "Sounds good."

Ivan wanted to object but couldn't think of a reason that wouldn't embarrass him. He felt he should thank her as well but the words wouldn't come out. He was wondering if Katie would try to seduce Kimberly, if not physically then mentally, but he couldn't express the thought.

Katie seemed to understand his hesitance and the lack of a thank you. "You can pay for the drink," she said, and left.

27

84th and 2nd Floors

RONICALLY, THE NIKKANEN children's appreciation of Alice really began with Mika's attack on the "monster." When Mika's plastic hammer knocked her to the floor outside Tero's room, Mika was terrified.

"What's happened?" said Tero, hearing a whack and a thud.

"I think I just killed her," said Mika.

"Was there really a cake?" asked Tero.

By that time, John, Silje's tutor, had cried out and explained to Silje that the waitress was on the floor. Minna came out of her room and knelt beside Alice, feeling her pulse. She tapped her implant and said, "111," which was the building's emergency number. "They'll be here in a minute."

"Is she dead?" asked Mika.

"She's alive, no thanks to you," said Minna.

By the time the building EMTs arrived, everyone on the floor was in the study area, including Minna and caretakers for the totally blind children, Silje and Tero. Mika and Minna accompanied the paramedics to the emergency room and stayed with Alice until she returned to consciousness.

Meanwhile, Silje continued her lesson with John, and Tero shared the cake with Omar Rikanen, Tero's 29-year old caregiver, who lived in an apartment near Tero's room and was on call with a tap from Tero's implant.

Naturally, the incident drew them together emotionally but they still wanted to know what Alice was doing in their study on the bedroom floor. "We thought you had come to beat us up," said Mika.

"Mr. Faoud told me to come up to make friends," said Alice.

"But why?" asked Minna. "We all have contacts with the outside world. We all go to school, even Silje and Tero."

"He was hoping I could find out about the hummingbird."

"What hummingbird?" asked Minna.

As they talked in the ER, while Alice was rapidly recovering, the story of the Nikkanen children gradually emerged. The "accident" had happened five years ago, as the foundations were being laid for 211A West 57th Street. Minna and Mika took turns telling the story to Alice as they waited for her to be discharged.

Their official residence was in Finland, although the girls went to school in Switzerland and Dr. Nikkanen spent much of his time traveling. The boys were educated in Helsinki but spent part of the year in various countries, including England and the U.S.A. That Christmas, they all gathered at the Nikkanen country estate five miles West of Oulu, a small city in central Finland, just South of the Lapp country, essentially in the middle of nowhere. Dr. Nikkanen was known to own property on the Luppojoki River in Puolanka, which was a few miles West of their country place, but no one else in the family had ever seen it. Tuuli assumed it was a secret laboratory but Paavo insisted it was basically an abandoned hunting shack.

Tuuli and the boys arrived from Helsinki two days before Christmas; the girls arrived from Switzerland the next day. Dr. Nikkanen was late for dinner on Christmas Eve and then in a highly disturbed state. He wouldn't say what was wrong but couldn't eat the ham and picked at the beetroot salad, leaving the table for the bathroom several times in the midst of the meal. Later on, a servant told Tuuli that Paavo had visited the hunting shack earlier that day.

What happened next was mysterious. Over the course of the dinner, everyone in the house got sick in varying degrees, including the servants, the cook, the cook's helper, and the housemaids. Paavo was well enough to call a doctor in Oulu, who advised them to get to the emergency room of the University Hospital as soon as possible.

"No one here is well enough to drive," said Paavo.

Within the hour, a team of ambulances was dispatched, staffed by disgruntled paramedics taken from their Christmas dinner, which in Finland is celebrated Christmas Eve.

The cook, a Nikkanen retainer for 20 years, died in the ambulance on the way to Oulu but was brought back to life by the paramedics. Silje lost her sight in the ambulance, without feeling any of the nausea that affected most of the others. She blinked and her sight was gone. Tero, who was five at the time, reached the hospital feeling merely queasy. He was given a sedative, slept till the morning and woke up blind. He was sure he was dreaming and couldn't wake up. Eventually, he grew more and more hysterical and insisted he was in the middle of a nightmare for nearly a week.

Of the others, one of the servants was blinded, Tuuli, Minna and Mika exhibited their eye deformities within hours of reaching the hospital. Paavo, the cook's assistant and the family chauffeur were endlessly nauseous but recovered without any eye problems. Only Naziha, who had been adopted from a Tunisian orphanage 10 years before, was completely unaffected.

The doctors could explain none of this, but not for lack of trying. Some thought it was a virus, some thought poison, the symptoms indicated a variety of diagnoses. The paramedics had the presence of mind to bring back the food from the Christmas dinner, which was tested for every known pathogen they could think of. Tuuli and Minna's eye discolorations were literally unheard of and the fragmentation of Mika's sight could possibly be explained through neurological anomalies, but these were not present in any of the others.

The hospital called in the national health institute to test the Nikkanen estate but before their inspectors even started out from Helsinki, word came down from the police in Puolanka that a fire had broken out at the Nikkanen estate. The place had burnt down to its foundations. Oddly enough, a shack on the Luppojoki River in Puolanka had suffered the same fate.

"So who burned down the houses?" Alice asked.

"They blamed lightning," said Minna.

"How did your father manage that?" asked Alice.

"Didn't you know he could control the weather?"

Alice nodded and smiled. Dr. Nikkanen *did* seem to be all-powerful in many ways. From what she could tell waiting on him at dinner, his word was respected more than any father she knew of – most of the ones she had known were either deadbeats or non-existent, like her own.

"After the accident, were there any personality changes?" Alice wanted to know.

The others laughed. "*Were* there?" said Mika.

"Tero was the worst," said Minna. "He was a sweet kid before the accident. Now he's a monster. I don't know if it was going blind or whatever made him blind."

"Probably both," added Mika, who was clearly uncomfortable with this conversation.

"No, the worst was our mother," said Minna. "She went from being a formidable woman to the crazy ghoul she is today." The others nodded in agreement.

"What about Silje?" asked Alice.

A nurse came by and discharged Alice before they could answer the question. "Go home, you need to get some rest," she said. "Do you live nearby?"

"I'm moving to the building in a couple of weeks," Alice said. "But now I live in the Bronx."

"You can stay with us," said Minna.

"Do, that'd be great," said Mika.

There was no question now that she'd been accepted by the kids. "I'd really like to, but I have kids at home. They wake up during the night and my mother needs her sleep."

On the way home, she reflected that the ice had been broken. A victory of sorts had been achieved, as Alice now became an intimate of the children except for Tero and Silje. It was the first step in solving the mystery of the hummingbird, if that was really what she was supposed to solve.

28

90th Floor

IVAN WAS WORKING late in the aviary. Kimberly was coming the next day – staying with Katie despite Ivan's better instincts – and he wanted to get everything in order before her arrival, basically to make sure the hummingbirds were happy. He knew the Tufted Coquettes had mated and the female was about to build her nest for the eggs, so he had to have plant fibers and spider webbing available.

He had watched their courtship ritual with fascination. The male, a spectacular creature, one of the smallest hummingbirds, with a brilliant red crest on his head and speckles of iridescent green, began dancing above the female, flying backwards and forwards, circling closely and then backing away from the jabs of the female until she finally let him approach.

He noted that the Woodstar was feeding at full speed among the cardinal flowers, and one Rufus appeared to be ill but not ill enough to let himself be easily caught.

It was close to nine at night and the aviary was empty of people except for Ivan. Dr. Benjamin had left hours ago and Dr. Fain and Tess had left by six. The family hadn't used it today, so there were no busboys clearing away dishes or maids cleaning up.

Aside from the lights of the city, which created a soft, luminous ceiling for the aviary, there were dim lights situated throughout the room so there was never a feeling of total darkness, which would have upset the birds, although there were patches of darkness where many of the birds congregated.

It was Ivan's favorite time in the aviary, when most of the birds had gathered together in trees and only a few flitted about looking for family or a comfortable perch. An unearthly stillness reigned, with no calls or screeches to interrupt the quiet, just the occasional flutter of wings and a barely audible undercurrent of machine hum.

He was musing about whether the white Leucistic hummingbirds would mate in November and he'd be able to see the male dive bomb from the top of the roof to the ground as part of the ritual, when he heard a voice behind him.

"What are you doing here, boy?"

He started at the sound and turned around. The sight of Tuuli, with her platinum hair splayed out around her shoulders and fierce laser eyes was enough to startle anyone. She was wearing a camouflage sleeveless body suit and had the air of a creature that was about to pounce.

"I said what are you doing here, boy?"

"I work here," said Ivan.

"I know that, but the aviary is closed at this hour. Only the family can be here."

Ivan had never seen eyes like Tuuli's. But her hostility was even more startling. "I'm sorry. I'll leave."

"I didn't say leave," said Tuuli. "I may need you."

Ivan was confused. He assumed this woman was Dr. Nikkanen's wife and he had heard talk that she was crazy and possibly dangerous. What could she possibly need him for? He was about to ask her why but fell silent under her gaze, which had grown more intense.

"I know you," she said.

"How could you possibly …"

"You're Ivan the Virgin," she said. "The hummingbird keeper."

Ivan the Virgin? Where did *that* come from? How could she have known? He had an intense urge to run out of the room when Tuuli held out her arm. "Can you see where they put the implant?"

"What?"

She held out the other arm, twisted it in front of him and then pointed to her hand, at the joint between her thumb and forefinger. "This is where they usually put it, but I don't see anything. Do you?"

Ivan gazed at the hand she proffered and then at her arm, which seemed chiseled by years of working out in a gym. "I don't see anything."

She took away her arm. "No, they probably put it in my butt when I was asleep. Or up my cunt."

"I can still see where they put mine," said Ivan, holding out his hand and pointing to the flesh between his thumb and forefinger. "Are you sure they implanted anything at all in you?"

"Oh, they tagged me alright. If you don't agree to it, they do it in your sleep, or drug you first. That's how they operate."

"Who's *they*?" asked Ivan. "Don't you and your husband *own* the building?"

She ignored the question. "Listen, we have to get out of here. Something awful is going on in this building."

"I don't understand."

"Where do you live? I know it's not in the building."

"Way West on 54th."

"Take me there until I can find a place to stay."

Was she serious? Ivan wondered. "It's a tiny room in an apartment I share with three other people."

"I don't care about the fucking details. I can share your bed or sleep on the floor. Let's go."

Ivan was completely flustered at that point. He could imagine Kimberly finding out he was living with or sleeping with a crazy woman with laser eyes. "Can't you just leave on your own?"

"Ah, that's how I know about the implant. I can't get out of the building on my own. But if you're with me, maybe I can."

Ivan wanted to impress upon Mrs. Nikkanen that she could definitely not stay with him. How could he stop her from following him, he wondered? Could he just run away as soon as they left the building? Could he say, "No," and still keep his job? And would she pay any attention to a flat-out refusal?

While Ivan was dithering about this, Tuuli grabbed his arm and said, "Move!"

They entered the elevator that Ivan normally took to go to the lobby, or Finnegan's, or the restaurants on 6, or any of the other floors he was eligible to access. He pressed "lobby" and waited for the door to close.

Nothing happened.

"I knew it," said Tuuli. "Try 85, my bedroom."

Again, nothing happened but when Tuuli pushed the button, the elevator responded immediately. The door opened and Tuuli said, "Try 79, the family pool."

"I don't have access to that."

"Try it anyway."

Ivan tried and the elevator remained open. Tuuli tried and the elevator responded."

They tried various combinations and the results were always the same: if Tuuli had access to the floor, only she could make the elevator obey; if Ivan had access, only he could press the button.

"What if I had to go to the hospital," said Tuuli. She pressed "2."

A panel near the control buttons displayed a message, accompanied by a voice. "If this is a medical emergency, please press the button on the left and you will be met by a response team."

"What if I had a doctor's appointment?" said Tuuli. "What if I had to get a cast removed?" She answered herself. "I guess I'd always be met by someone."

"But suppose you were," said Ivan. "Couldn't you just send them away and walk out?"

"Let's go to the ballroom on 53, no, wait, I have access to the bank."

Ivan was surprised that Tuuli had access to so few floors. When she pressed the button for the bank on 20, the panel and voice reminded her that she needed authorization from the building manager and please press the button on the left to speak to his office. When Ivan pressed the button for the bank, he received no response, although he had been to the bank several times in the past and had no trouble whatsoever.

When they were refused admission to the post office on 22, they gave up. The lowest floor they could access was the ballroom on 53 and they made for the stairway. By law, the stairway could not be blocked on any floor but that didn't mean they could gain entry to any of the floors. A sign told them they could be admitted to a floor on 36 (Finnegan's Pub) but the door was locked. When they knocked on the door, there was no answer.

On the way down from 53, Ivan asked, "What did you mean: something awful is going on in this building?"

Tuuli seemed amused. "Have you noticed any changes in your personality since you started working in this building?"

"No," said Ivan, but then he remembered getting drunk at Katie's apartment and passing out on her bed. "Well, perhaps."

Tuuli gave a knowing grunt and they continued all the way down to the lobby. Again, by law, this could not be locked and it wasn't. José Ramirez and Dom Piccolo from Security were waiting for them at the bottom of the stairs.

"Will you come this way, Mrs. Nikkanen?" said José, indicating a hidden door next to the exit to the lobby.

"I knew it," said Tuuli. "You've been watching us the whole time."

José turned to Ivan. "You may go," he said, and Piccolo opened the door to the lobby. "We'd appreciate it if you didn't talk about this," said José. Ivan wanted to offer a word of sympathy to Mrs. Nikkanen, or at least say goodbye, but she was no longer looking in his direction and seemed in a fog of disgust.

Ivan emerged from the stairwell into the lobby while Katie was on duty. She was more than surprised to see him, seemingly slinking out of the building still wearing the blue work smock he wore in the aviary. "What are you doing here?" she asked.

"Just exploring," said Ivan.

"You're a terrible liar," said Katie. "I'm going to have to tell Kimberly about this."

29

81st Floor

"SO YOU HUNG out in the garage," said Sophie.

"I did," said Katie.

"And was it enlightening?"

"It was."

Sunday evening, Katie had gone to the library ostensibly to work on her thesis – she had a conference with her mentor at Columbia coming up in a week and felt pressured to work – but actually to review all that they had learned over the past two weeks. And tangentially, to flirt with Sophie. Katie did not consider herself a lesbian, although her few experiments in that direction were not too awful, but she didn't sense that Sophie wanted an affair that included love and romance. She was into something more perverse – bondage, S&M, something along the fetish continuum. Katie was slightly titillated by the possibilities but not enough to actually encourage Sophie. Sophie would make her move, or not, and their friendship would remain. Meanwhile, there was the building to think about.

"I believe they're making some kind of toxic liquid on the forbidden floors," said Katie.

"Or gas."

"I suppose that's possible. The trucks I saw looked like gasoline trucks – shorter but thicker – but I suppose they could be used for gas – I don't know the difference."

"Why do you think it's toxic?"

"The secrecy," said Katie. "If those floors are forbidden, if no one is able to go there, or even talk about what goes on there, there must be something to hide. Something either illegal or classified by the government."

211A West 57th Street

"That's a stretch," said Sophie. "There are industrial secrets that a company might want to keep secret from their competitors – new products, new technology."

"That's true," said Katie, although she hadn't even considered this. "But stacked up against the other odd things going on, it makes me just a little suspicious. What did you find out?"

"Not much," said Sophie. "Nikkanen went to Helsinki for undergraduate and got his masters and doctorate from the University of Turko."

"Where the hell is that?"

"Southwest Finland, about 100 miles West of Helsinki. He got his degree in chemistry but I couldn't find his Ph.D. thesis."

"Chemistry, huh?"

"That doesn't prove he's making toxic gas."

"That doesn't prove he isn't," said Katie. "Doesn't it strike you as odd that Mrs. Nikkanen and all the children went blind or almost blind at the same time?"

"Christmas Eve, 2012. I have all the newspaper articles from the accident, mostly in the Oulu *Kaleva*."

"The what?"

"The newspaper in Oulu, a small city in Finland where they were taken for treatment. It's just South of the Lapp country. I've sent the links to your email."

Katie and Sophie were in a little office off the main reading room, just large enough for Sophie and her computer, a few books and one chair. They had pulled in a second chair from outside so Katie could see the pictures from the Oulu articles, which included formal photographs of the family before the accident.

"My God, they're so beautiful," said Katie.

"They still are," said Sophie. "Probably the most beautiful family I've ever seen, *physically*."

"This is the first time I've seen them," said Katie.

They reviewed the article and then Sophie took a deep breath and dropped what could be a bombshell. "In other news, what slowed down the hummingbirds in the aviary was not passion flower extract."

"What was it?"

"Nobody knows. Perhaps the same chemical that blinded the family."

"But whatever blinded the family and leaked into the cardinal flowers to sedate the hummingbirds could be whatever they're making on the forbidden floors."

Sophie gave a wry smile, "Y'never know."

"What about Nikkanen's company?" asked Katie.

"What company?"

Katie started. "His source of income?"

"What source?" said Sophie. "He has no company, no source of income, he has no money in any public bank and no investments that I could find. The paychecks he makes out to his employees, including us, aren't from any recognized financial institution but from him personally, through his own unincorporated bank."

"But he takes out withholding, social security ..."

"Yes, and the checks are deposited in whatever bank you want, or in your account in the building's bank. That gets reported to the government, but not the source of the money."

"So it's all undercover," said Katie.

"So it would seem."

They looked at each other and smiled. "How very bizarre," said Katie. "What about in Finland?"

Fortunately, Sophie had a Finnish translation ap. There was a record from 1996 of a Paavo Nikkanen as an employee of a company called Oy Woiloski Ab, which specialized in industrial and medical gas.

"What's that?"

"Well, the oxygen you get in hospitals, or anesthetic gas, or liquid nitrogen to freeze things or sulfur dioxide as a food preservative, or propane for cooking, or argon for welding – it's a huge field."

"This is beginning to add up," said Katie. "How long did he work for a company that makes gasses?"

"After 1996, he disappears. There is no record of him anywhere until Christmas Eve, 2012."

"*Very* interesting," said Katie, standing up, without giving Sophie a chance to act on her inclinations. "Well, I'm off to prepare for the Virgin Mary."

"The Christian girlfriend?"

"She's staying with me for a week. I hope that's enough time to corrupt her."

30

32ⁿᵈ Floor

KIMBERLY AYERS ARRIVED at LaGuardia at 8PM, carrying a large backpack, which contained all the clothing and toiletries she felt she would need for a week in the big city.

Ivan didn't recognize her at first. There were two women her age and size coming out the exit ramp. He hadn't remembered her frame being quite so robust, although she seemed fit and energetic. He thought she might have cut her hair – it was shorter than he remembered and quite irregular – probably cut by a friend. It was somewhere between light brown or dark blond, depending on the light. She was not exactly pretty but not exactly plain either. Although she was only 22, she seemed like an older woman, imitating her age.

Ivan greeted her with a chaste kiss and was about to spring for a taxi but Kimberly wouldn't hear of it. "We can take the Q70 bus to Roosevelt Avenue and catch the F train directly to 57th Street, I've looked it up. That way it costs only $5.50 for the two of us."

Ivan tried to explain that the bus and train route might end up taking three hours, or the whole night, but Kimberly had consulted the schedules in advance and had timed their trip to an hour and a half, including 15 minutes waiting for the F to arrive, and walking from the F to the building.

They had more than enough time to chat in the three and a half hours it took them to reach the building. Kimberly talked about the impossible flight from Tucson to New York with a layover in Chicago that took so long she thought they'd never leave. "But I'm here, praise the Lord."

She wanted Ivan to know that the whole congregation prayed that he wouldn't be corrupted by the big city. She was hoping her visit would mitigate the damage that had already been done.

"What damage?" asked Ivan.

"I don't know yet," she answered. "But wanting to spend a fortune for a taxi gives us *some* indication."

Ivan was unnerved. He never remembered her like this. Was she really this judgmental? Was she really this Christian? Was she really this awful? "You're kidding," he said.

She smiled. "Yes."

"The congregation didn't pray for my salvation from the city?"

"You idiot," she said, taking his hand. "The congregation has better things to pray for."

Ivan was so relieved he impulsively kissed Kimberly in the line waiting for the bus, which, of course, turned out to be the wrong line and meant another half hour waiting in the right one. They held hands most of the way into town, catching up on the news from home, friends, the church, which had an extensive missionary program in Africa. "I often thought we might spend some time there after we were married," she said. "Joan and Hartley are in Cameroon right now and Joan says the people are quite receptive."

"Lots of birds I bet," said Ivan.

"You'd go crazy."

She was fascinated by Ivan's tales of the building, the hummingbird theft, the people, the endless rumors about the family, the whole saga of a world within a world. "The woman you'll be staying with is doing her Ph.D. in philosophy while working as one of the doormen."

"Is she nice?"

"It's hard to say. She was nice enough to offer you a place to stay, but she's not what you'd call godly."

"She not Jewish …"

"Jews can be godly."

"I forgot – of course they can. Have you seen any of those funny ones with the hats?"

"Hasidic Jews? They're on 47th Street, the diamond markets. I'll take you to see them. But I think your hostess comes from an Irish family, so that'd be Catholic – not that you'd ever know."

They arrived at the building around 11:30 and Kimberly had to be vetted by the security and given a visitor's pass for the week she would be staying, which entitled her to the restaurants, the cafeteria, the supermarket, the deli, the gym and swimming pool for non-professional non-family, the night club, casino, Finnegan's, the laundry, bank and post office, the cinema, the hospital and emergency services, as well as access to Katie's floor. She was dutifully impressed.

Katie was just about to go to bed when they arrived. Ivan had called to alert her to the late hour, but Katie had an early meeting with her mentor the next morning before reporting to the building. She had written out a note for Kimberly, made Annie's bed, set out towels and was indulging in an Armagnac before turning in.

"Welcome," she said, greeting the couple at the door. Although one look at Kimberly told her they would not be best friends forever, Katie was friendly, gracious and exuded warmth. They refused her offer of Armagnac but accepted Peppermint tea, which Katie always had on hand for guests.

"You're welcome to spend the night," she said to Ivan, "with Kimberly or on the couch, whatever."

Ivan had a horror of spending another night in Katie's apartment, even with Kimberly. "No, I'd better be getting home," he said. He arranged to meet his girlfriend for breakfast at the cafeteria and left without kissing her, partially out of embarrassment but also because the thought of kissing Kimberly in front of Katie made him distinctly uncomfortable.

As the door closed, Kimberly seemed to relax and told Katie to go to bed. "It's only 9 o'clock my time so we can catch up in the morning."

Katie nodded and said she'd be out early. Actually, she was interested in chatting with Kimberly. "So you guys met at church?"

"We grew up together, same nursery school, same Sunday school."

"And when did you get engaged?" She noticed that Kimberly wasn't wearing a ring.

Kimberly laughed. "Well, we're not officially engaged – really, I don't know what an official engagement is – but we're planning to be married soon, we don't know when exactly."

This was curious. Katie thought she might give up an hour's sleep to explore a completely different species of human, a woman who believed in the old ways, chastity, prudence, godliness. Kimberly might as well be an Amish or Mormon fundamentalist, some exotic extremity of Christian.

She seemed normal enough, as Katie showed her around the apartment, the bathroom, the kitchen, the washer/dryer, whatever Katie was free to use during her visit. "How long have you been going with Ivan?" Katie asked, off-handedly.

"From birth," said Kimberly. "Our mothers were pregnant around the same time and when we were born, they decided we were meant for each other."

"You're kidding."

"A little, yes," said Kimberly, smiling. "But from the time we were little, our parents assumed, since we went to the same church and shared the same values, and since we were both mentally, physically and morally healthy, we would eventually mate and produce more of the same."

Katie was surprised at Kimberly's irony. Clearly, she wasn't as pure a Christian as she was supposed to be. "You sound like you don't exactly go along with this."

"Why not?" said Kimberly. "Ivan's completely acceptable on all fronts and I'm not about to go to bars or go online in the hope of meeting the love of my life."

"So Ivan is the fallback?"

"Ivan is good enough. I don't want a parade of freaks."

This was startling, coming from Kimberly, the vaunted girlfriend. "So you've never even kissed another man," asked Katie, "or woman."

"I didn't say that."

"But you're still a virgin."

"Technically."

"What does that mean?"

Kimberly shrugged. "There are lots of things you can do and still remain a virgin."

Katie was shocked. "Does Ivan know about this?"

"I'd appreciate it if you wouldn't mention it."

Now that Katie knew that Kimberly was human, perhaps even a kindred spirit except for the church rigmarole and the romantic resignation, they could sit and drink their brandies and peppermint tea and chat about their lives and jobs and the world in general.

It was another hour before they went to bed. In the morning, when Katie was about to leave for work, she opened Annie's bedroom door to check on her new houseguest. Kimberly was unconscious, ashen, breathing with a labored rasp and bathed in sweat.

31

84th Floor

ALICE HAD BEFRIENDED Minna, Mika and Naziha, now back from camp, and had a joking relationship with them. She could also be relied upon to bring extra dessert from dinner, which gave her a limited entrée to Tero and none whatsoever to Silje.

Both Tero and Silje had caretakers who helped them navigate the world. Tero's main caretaker, Omar Rikanen, was, as his name would suggest, part Egyptian and part Finnish and had been with Tero since the accident. Alice tried to sound him out but he was uncommunicative. Tero could summon him by tapping his implant and Omar would seem to slink out of his room and be ready for service, whatever that might be. Tero berated him constantly and Omar bore it silently but Alice had the impression he was husbanding his anger to slaughter Tero one day. What was interesting to Alice was that he had a girlfriend who worked on the forbidden floors.

Silje's main caretaker was an ethereal young woman named Apollonia Bax, the granddaughter of a famous British composer. She knew no Finnish, spoke with a barely audible upper-class British accent, and had only been hired since they moved into the building. It was hard to tell what was going on between Silje and Apollonia. Tero and Mika insisted Silje was gay and was sleeping not only with Apollonia but also her blind Indian classmate, Chitra, her adopted sister, Naziha, and several others, virtually anybody else who asked her. "Try feeling her up," said Mika. "See how far you get."

"Don't be disgusting," said Alice.

"It's true," said Mika. "At least it could be true."

"Nonsense."

One evening, as Silje was being tutored by John, Alice sat next to Mika while they were watching TV in the common room and asked him outright. "What do you really think happened to the hummingbird? And don't say 'what hummingbird?'"

"Mom crushed it."

"That was a spider."

"Oh yeah, I forgot. Why is it so important?"

"All comes down to money," said Alice. "It's a valuable bird."

"How valuable?"

"I don't know – millions," said Alice, not really knowing how much.

"Holy shit." The figure impressed Mika enough to let down his guard.

"I bet Tero knows something."

"*You* don't?"

"I never know anything."

Alice didn't want to push it farther, for fear of losing Mika as a source of information, but she resolved to pursue Tero more closely.

Her opportunity came later that evening when Tero emerged from his room and felt his way along a rail that had been set up to help the blind children navigate around the room. He held what looked like an abacus and scurried to Silje's part of the floor. He called out to her. "I can't get this fucking thing to work."

"What's that, no-eyes?" said John, Silje's tutor.

"Fuckin' Cranmer's Abacus."

"It's an abacus for the blind," said Silje to John. "I used one before we graduated to the talking calculators."

"I can show you," she said to Tero.

Since Tero had left his door open, Alice nonchalantly popped into Tero's room. She expected to find a typical 10-year old's room but, of course, that was impossible. Tero wouldn't be able to see most of the toys and playthings that normal children had. There were no sports heroes on the wall, no team or circus pennants, the floor was not littered with games or clothing. It was arranged so that Tero would not stumble over anything in the middle of the room. There was a long desk for Tero's computer and printer, which could print in braille, an iPod and several other machines that were a mystery to Alice. A bookshelf held books in braille, an unsculpted ball of clay, braille playing cards, dominoes with raised dots and a collection of shells in one jar and toothpicks in another. What a curious thing to collect, Alice thought. But then, they were tactile and she could see that there was a wide variety. On a separate table stood a plastic replica of a ferocious praying mantis, triple life-sized, about to pounce. An electronic piano took up the rest of the play area.

She was about to examine the room further when Tero returned unexpectedly. "I can smell you," he said.

"I didn't know you played the piano," said Alice.

"It's not just a piano – look at the buttons."

There was a full panel of electronic instruments, including a harpsicord, chimes, horns, winds, brass, a xylophone and even something called percussion.

"Do you play all of these?"

"Yeah. What were you doing in my room?"

"I just noticed the piano," said Alice.

"Get out," said Tero.

"Can I hear you play?" asked Alice, looking for some excuse to stay in the room.

"No."

"So you don't really play," said Alice, "that's just bullshit."

Much to Alice's surprise, the tactic worked. "If I play you one thing, will you get out?" said Tero. When Alice assented, he said, "Close the fucking door."

Tero walked over to the piano without hesitation and unhooked the earphones attached to it, so his playing could be heard. He turned on the piano, pressed the button for the piano sound and positioned his hands without feeling his way.

He played a Bach two-part invention that seemed simple at first but actually contained a world of nuances. Alice had never willingly listened to classical music before, and had never even heard of Bach, but she could tell that he was playing with a sensitivity that belied his age and temperament. It was actually quite beautiful, she thought, and her opinion of Tero was utterly overthrown.

"That was fantastic," said Alice, sincerely.

"Fuck you, get out," Tero answered.

As she left, she thought she might steal something, maybe to create a talking point, or to see if he noticed. She might justify it as taking a souvenir of the evening. She hesitated between the jar of shells and the jar of toothpicks on the shelf and finally took the toothpick jar.

Tero didn't notice, or at least he never said anything.

32

2nd Floor

KATIE CALLED IVAN from the hospital on 2. By the time he hurried to the building from his apartment, Kimberly was already in quarantine; he wasn't allowed to see her.

"But how is she?" he asked the doctor.

The doctor, who was supposedly in charge, shrugged. "Who knows? It's out of my hands."

"What do you mean *out of my hands?*"

"Some other doctors have taken over the case."

"I don't understand."

"Neither do I," said the doctor. He explained that he was the attending physician on call in the emergency room when the building EMT brought Kimberly down from Katie's apartment. He had examined her and noted no obvious causes for her condition. He thought it might be some sort of allergic reaction to something. He ordered a full blood workup but in the meantime, gave her oxygen and started her on an intravenous drip while he figured out what was wrong with her. Her eyes were mostly closed but when they opened, he noticed a very faint blue tint in the sclera that seemed unusual.

Dr. Cavanaugh, the family's PC, happened to be in the hospital at the time and somehow heard about an emergency patient with an unusual symptom. Within minutes, Dr. Chance, the head of the hospital, came in with three people the doctor didn't know.

"Were they two men and a woman, an older man?" asked Ivan.

"Why, have you seen them before?"

"Yes. So what happened?"

The doctor explained that Kimberly had been transferred to a ward at the far end of the hospital and put in strict quarantine. They didn't tell the doctor what they suspected and he didn't have access to the ward.

Ivan thanked the doctor and walked down to the ward. The entrance was closed and wouldn't open with his implant. He pressed a buzzer and eventually an attendant spoke to him through an electronically enhanced grill.

"What can I do for you?" the voice asked.

"My name is Ivan Anderson, I work in the building. You have my girlfriend in there."

"Name?"

"Kimberly Ayers."

"Hold on."

Ivan paced outside the door for what seemed like ten minutes, although it may have been less. Eventually, he scrunched down in the hallway and leaned against the wall.

The voice returned but the door remained closed. "She's alive, in quarantine."

"With what?"

"They didn't tell me," said the voice. "But I guess it's serious."

"Could you tell her I was trying to see her?"

"She's unconscious. But I'll ask the doctors to tell her when she wakes up."

"*Doctors* plural?"

"That's all I can tell you," said the voice, seemingly irritated. "Come back tomorrow."

Ivan left the hospital and reported to work at the aviary. When Dr. Benjamin came up, Ivan told him about Kimberly and what had happened to her. "Is there any way I can see her?" he asked.

"I'll check," said Dr. Benjamin.

A few hours later, Ivan had his answer. "From what I could find out, your girlfriend has what they think is a highly contagious virus that could infect the whole building," said Dr. Benjamin.

"I know that," said Ivan.

"Evidently, the quarantine is so tight that not even Mr. Faoud could see her. They don't want to take any chances."

"Don't they have protective clothing, like what they use against plague or Ebola?"

Dr. Benjamin shrugged. He had nothing more to add.

That evening, Ivan sat by himself at the bar in Finnegan's, nursing a beer, ruminating on a plan to break into the ward and rescue Kimberly.

33

25th, 86th and 90th Floors

THE ORDER MUST have been facilitated by forces on high, but a low-income apartment had suddenly opened up on the 25th Floor and Alice was, miraculously, first on the list.

It was the largest apartment Alice and her mother had ever rented, with a bedroom each for Alice, her mother and the children. It had appliances that Alice had never before encountered, such as a trash compactor and a dishwasher. Alice went over the bare space in a daze. *If this is a low-income rental, what's a middle-income rental like?* she wondered.

They could move in anytime but Alice wasn't sure she wanted to keep the ratty furniture from her old apartment, which exhibited complete indifference to décor, taste or even minimal attractiveness. Fortunately, the building provided a consultant decorator, who could suggest interior arrangements and find the best prices.

As she wandered about her new apartment, someone knocked on the outer door. "It's open," she called.

She returned to the living room and saw Omar, Tero's caretaker, in the front entrance. Although she had met him before, he was still startling. He had a handsome Arabian face topped by a mop of curly red hair, which made him look freakish and potentially dangerous, helped by a naturally ferocious expression. His body was short, thin and muscular and gave the impression of having been toned in some dojo or fighter's gym. He wasted no time on his mission. "Miss Jeynes, you have something that doesn't belong to you."

"And what would that be?" said Alice.

"The jar you took from Tero's room."

Alice had known this was coming. She had taken it on a pure whim and couldn't see what difference it would make, or even if Tero would notice the theft. Still, although the jar's contents seemed insignificant, she didn't want to give in to Omar and return them. She didn't like Omar's attitude.

"Get the fuck out of here," she said.

Omar was unphased. "Not before you tell me where I can get the jar back. I can go to your home in the Bronx, if you've got it there, or maybe it's in your locker up on 86. Tero wants it back."

"Tero can stuff it up his ass."

Omar considered his response and controlled his natural instinct to belt her one. "We have it on tape," he said, calmly. "I can show it to security and you'll be thrown out on your ear. Or you can hand it over."

Alice couldn't take the chance that he was bluffing. She *knew* almost everything was taped but she wasn't sure that applied to the family quarters. "Where will you be in two hours?" she asked.

"Up on 84."

"If I can find it, and I don't say I can, I'll bring it up to you."

"Why don't I come with you now?"

"Why don't you go fuck yourself?"

Omar showed a glimpse of a smile. "If you're not up in my room in two hours, don't bother to move into this apartment."

"All for a jar of toothpicks?"

"So you *did* take the jar."

"Get out of here. I'll see you in two hours."

After Omar left, albeit reluctantly and with many reservations, Alice waited until she was sure he was off the floor, then took an elevator to Finnegan's on 36. She waited a few minutes, then took another elevator to 84, where she had her waitress outfit and the jar in a locker. She tried for the elevator which would take her to the aviary but didn't have access, as she had never served at the pavilion. She grabbed one of the pavilion waiters and pleaded with him to take her to the aviary, agreeing to take over one of his shifts, if she could get access. Finally, she was able to enter the aviary.

Almost immediately, she was accosted by Tess McAllister, the thin, freckled woman whose specialty was water birds. "Can I help you?" she said, caustically.

"I have to see Ivan right away," said Alice. "I work in the dining room downstairs."

"How did you get in here?"

"It's urgent."

Tess examined Alice, up and down, and decided that she represented no immediate harm to the birds or the environment. It took another moment for her to access how much trouble she'd be in if she didn't report Alice to security. Fortunately, she spotted Ivan nearby.

"He's over there," she said.

Alice had met Ivan in Faoud's office, waited on him once at Tay's and nodded to him a few times in the cafeteria. He was known as the hummingbird man and she had heard the rumor that he was a virgin by choice. Perhaps because of that, or perhaps by his general manner, she felt he was trustworthy. She went up to him, reintroduced herself, and showed him the jar of toothpicks.

"I'm operating on a hunch," she said. "Do you have any idea what these are?"

Ivan opened the jar and examined each of the toothpicks, shaking his head and eventually breathing hard. "This can't be," he said.

"What?"

"I have to show this to Dr. Benjamin."

"What is it?"

"Come with me," said Ivan.

They went downstairs directly to Dr. Benjamin's office. Ivan opened the jar and laid out all the "toothpicks" on his desk. They were of different sizes, mostly black but some gray and off-white. Some were slightly curved, some straight.

"Where did you get these?" asked Dr. Benjamin.

"Tero's room," said Alice. "Omar, his caretaker, wants them back right away."

"I'm sure he does," said Dr. Benjamin.

"I guess they're not toothpicks," said Alice.

Ivan and Dr. Benjamin studied them. "Can you tell which are the Woodstars?" asked Dr. Benjamin.

"It could be these two," said Ivan. "But they could also be an Anna's, or a Rufus."

"Are you saying these are hummingbird beaks?" asked Alice.

"Almost certainly," said Dr. Benjamin.

"I thought their beaks were hollow, like straws," said Alice.

"No, they have an upper and lower beak, encasing the tongue, which is what laps up the nectar from flowers."

"So they're all from different hummingbirds?"

"It looks like it," said Dr. Benjamin.

"Holy shit," said Alice.

"Exactly," said Dr. Benjamin.

"Are any of the other hummers missing?" asked Ivan.

Dr. Benjamin had to confess he didn't know. Ivan's predecessor had left suddenly without providing an up-to-date account of the hummingbird population. Even now, Dr. Benjamin wasn't sure how many hummingbirds were in the aviary, much less if any were missing. It was possible that Wilmar, Ivan predecessor, had taken some of them and given them to Tero, or that someone else had captured the birds for Tero – there was no way of telling. "How many hummingbirds do we have now?" he asked Ivan.

"Forty-eight, when I started," said Ivan. "Since then, one has died, two have hatched, both Rufous, and several have laid eggs."

"Is there any chance that Tero's beaks could have come from birds that have died? Say, as a gift from Wilmar?"

"Of course, that's the most likely explanation," said Ivan. "But would he have taken the Woodstar with him when he left? He must have known how valuable it was. And why would Tero want the beaks – souvenirs?"

"To be explored," said Dr. Benjamin.

"What do we do next?" asked Alice.

"Measure and photograph the beaks, try to determine what hummingbirds they're from and give them back to Omar. Meanwhile, I'll call Captain Martin in security and let her know what's happening."

Two hours later, Alice took the jar back to Omar on 84. "Sorry," she said, without explanation.

34

Lobby and 2nd Floor

WHEN KATIE HAD a moment from greeting visitors in the lobby, she got a chance to speak with Isha, at his console. "So what's going on?" she asked.

"I was going to ask you the same thing," said Isha.

"People are going to an empty floor."

"I guess 43 is no longer empty," said Isha.

"I checked downstairs with Joe Barash and he said they're loading a lot of construction material and hospital furniture onto one of the forbidden floors. It must be significant, cause he's usually not that talkative."

"Hospital furniture?" said Isha.

"That's what he thought," said Katie. "He wasn't allowed to see the unloading, but the truck was from Selby Supplies, which makes hospital beds."

"Curious," said Isha. "I'll do some checking."

"One other thing," said Katie. "A lot of grim-looking people are going to see Mr. Faoud. Do you have I.D.'s on them?"

"They're from Washington," said Isha. "Department of Agriculture."

"Agriculture?" said Katie, incredulous.

"That's what shows on their I.D.'s."

"What do you think?"

"They don't look like farmers to me."

"So their I.D.'s have been doctored," said Alice.

"Not necessarily," said Isha. "The Department of Agriculture is a big place."

Katie had to break off to greet another grim-looking man in a dark suit who had an appointment with Mr. Faoud.

Meanwhile, Captain Martin had been briefed on Tero's beaks and rather than confronting Tero and Omar, decided to study tapes of Omar, especially his relationship with his girlfriend, Chloe Day.

Omar and Chloe met publicly at Finnegan's, various restaurants on 6, sometimes in the cafeteria on 7, sometimes at the pool and sauna on 33, and privately in the family game room on 80. There were no accessible tapes of the game room itself but they were seen entering and leaving the room late at night, presumably to make love.

Captain Martin wasn't sure what she was looking for, aside from some reference to the hummingbird beaks. She was as curious as everyone about the forbidden floors and as much in the dark. Viewing tapes was excruciating and Captain Martin assigned two men to back her up.

One thing was clear and one thing repeated over and over again. Omar hated Tero. He referred to Tero as "that little fucker," "the shithead," "the devil" and even "the blind bastard."

"So why do you work for him," Chloe asked, in the cafeteria.

"For the same reason I like *you* – masochism."

There were telling references. "Did you find out?" he asked, as they met for a hasty cappuccino at the 15th Floor coffee shop. "It'll work," she answered. "When can you get it?" "I have it with me."

But they never said what "it" was, perhaps aware that the coffee shop was not safe. Perhaps they were referring to the chemical that sedated the hummingbirds near the pavilion, perhaps not.

A conversation from two days ago seemed significant. Omar wanted to see Chloe that evening but she said she couldn't. "Things are crazy down here," she said. "I might not be able to get away for a while."

"You're that busy?"

"Frantic."

"Deadlines?"

"Something else, I can't tell you."

There was no way Captain Martin and her cohorts could listen in on all the tapes. And as of yesterday, she was shorthanded. One of her security officers had suddenly taken sick and was in the hospital. When she went down to visit him, she was told that he was in quarantine and couldn't be seen at the moment.

"I'm the head of security for the building and I'm going to see him whether you like it or not," she told the attendant.

"I'll get a doctor," said the attendant.

The doctor who responded was the head of the hospital, Sam Chance, who took Captain Martin by the arm and led her to a consultation room. This kind of familiarity was so unusual that Captain Martin knew something big was up. They sat at a table in a room that had last been used by a doctor telling a couple about the death of the husband's father. Dr. Chance offered coffee, which Captain Martin refused.

"Listen Roanne, something's going on here that I can't talk about," said Dr. Chance.

"Sam, I should know about it, even if no one's supposed to talk about it," said Roanne.

Chance took a moment to digest this and eventually nodded. "There seems to be an epidemic of something. We don't know what it is just yet but the quarantine ward is so full we have to find more space."

"On 43?" Roanne suggested.

Sam threw up his hands. "I'm out of the loop."

"How can you be out of the loop – you're head of the hospital?"

"I'm *just* head of the hospital," said Sam, with a shrug.

35

81ˢᵗ Floor

ALICE HAD ONCE had a photo shoot outside of the New York Public Library on 5ᵗʰ Avenue, and she had been required to visit the school library as a child, which was a relatively safe place to neck when she was a teen, but she had never entered a real library. Her visit to the 81ˢᵗ Floor, part of her general access to family floors, was revelatory. She didn't think there could be a room this large in a skyscraper aside from the aviary.

"How many books in this library?" she asked Sophie.

"Including periodicals?

"What's periodicals?" asked Alice.

"Magazines. We also have videos, microfilms, data banks, photo banks, podcasts, scientific and academic journals and access to almost every major library in the world."

"How many books?"

"As of this morning, 198,462. How can I help you?"

Alice nodded, impressed and somewhat charmed by this attractive and somewhat flirtatious librarian.

"This is going to sound weird …"

"Try me."

"I want to know about hummingbird beaks."

Sophie laughed. "Like those on an Esmeraldas Woodstar, for example?"

"You know about that?" said Alice, surprised.

"Doesn't everybody?"

Solely on intuition, Alice decided to trust Sophie. She told her the whole story about being recruited to get close to the Nikkanen children, slipping into Tero's bedroom, the books in braille, the unsculpted ball of clay, the triple life-sized replica of the ferocious praying mantis on a table, the jar of shells, and the second jar of toothpicks, which turned out to be hummingbird beaks.

"Why would Tero collect beaks?" mused Sophie.

"Same thing I asked Dr. Benjamin. He didn't know but now I'm thinking maybe he didn't want the beaks at all, maybe the beaks are just a record of the birds he killed."

"He's blind, so somebody must have killed them for him."

"Omar, who else?" said Alice.

"But why would Tero want to have the birds killed?"

"To prove he could do it," said Alice, without hesitation. "Maybe it gives him a sense of power."

"Tell me more about Tero."

What had impressed Alice most was Tero's proficiency on the piano — there was romance in the notion of the bitter, blind pianist. What impressed Sophie most was the plastic replica of a ferocious praying mantis on a table in Tero's room.

"I got a request about praying mantises last year," said Sophie. "It was so odd that I remembered it. Hold on."

She spent a few minutes at her computer, nodding to let Alice know she was on to something. Finally, she said, "Aha!" and turned the computer around to Alice could see it. It was an article on the feeding habits of praying mantises.

"Who requested it?"

"Omar," said Sophie.

"What's in the article?"

"I haven't read it but I will now. Let's look at it together."

Sophie and Alice sat side by side, aware and, in Alice's case, wary of the delights of proximity, while Sophie downloaded the article. They read it with little interest until they scrolled down to a video of a praying mantis at dinner.

"Holy shit," said both of them at the same time.

"This could explain everything," said Alice.

36

———————————————

Lobby and 7th Floor

ON MONDAY, AT 9 AM, a colonel, two captains and a malevolent civilian showed up at the lobby and announced their appointment with a Dr. Nordheim on the 41st Floor. Katie, her curiosity and imagination ignited and thrilled at the potential for gossip, guided them to Isha's console.

"Is this a surprise visit?" she asked the civilian. "We had no record of an appointment."

"You wouldn't," said the man.

"We need to see your I.D.'s," said Isha.

As they took out their identification, Katie noticed a shoulder badge on the uniforms of the soldiers that plainly identified them as part of the army chemical corps, with a distinctive insignia of two gold beakers crossed within a blue hexagon.

She had just shown them to the "Tree" elevator when five women in nurse's uniforms showed up and also asked for Dr. Nordheim.

"Are you going to the hospital on 2?" asked Katie of a large, fleshy woman who might have been the head nurse.

"If that's where Dr. Nordheim is," said the woman.

"No, he's on 41," said Katie. "Take the elevator with a green tree on it."

Shortly afterwards, Ivan showed up for work. "Something's happening here," said Katie in an undertone.

"So everybody tells me," answered Ivan.

"Where are you having lunch?"

"I thought the cafeteria," said Ivan.

"Good, we'll meet at the farthest corner we find at … noon?"

"12:30."

"I'm going to invite some other people who might help."

The group that met in the cafeteria that afternoon was larger than Katie had anticipated. She had invited Sophie, of course, and José Ramirez from Security, who had recommended that they include Alice, who had a direct connection with the family. Katie had also invited Alan Graff, an attending physician at the ER on 2, with whom she had had a brief affair two years ago.

Somehow the cafeteria, the most public room in the building, seemed the most private place to hold a meeting on sensitive topics. They brought their trays to a corner table near a group of rabid sports fans and another of complaining HUAC service people.

"They can hear every word we say anyway," said José.

"Not that we're dealing drugs or plotting a coup," said Katie.

"Just gathering information."

First they discussed Dr. Nordheim, since both the military and the nurses had asked for him. Sophie had looked him up but found nothing. "He's even more elusive than Dr. Nikkanen. He seems to have graduated from nowhere, had no jobs, no publications, no background at all."

"Perhaps that's not his real name," José suggested.

Ivan told them about his encounter with Mrs. Nikkanen, her dire pronouncement that something awful is going on here and her efforts to escape from the building. José Ramirez admitted that they had to sedate her when she emerged from the stairway into the lobby, a detail that Ivan hadn't known about and that he found incredibly disturbing.

Alice talked about the hummingbird beaks and her suspicion that Tero had killed the birds with the help of Omar.

Sophie added a bizarre note. "Alice said Tero had a replica of a praying mantis in his room. Omar had requested information on praying mantises six months before. When we looked it up, we saw an image that was truly eerie: a praying mantis had captured a hummingbird and was eating its brain."

"Yuk," said Katie.

"It's not unusual," said Ivan. "Mantises are common predators of hummingbirds and they seem to like feasting on their brains."

"That doesn't prove that Tero killed the birds," José pointed out.

"But that's not the something awful that's going on here," said Ivan. "It's what's happened to my girlfriend, why I can't see her."

"They may be connected," said Katie.

Alan Groff, the doctor from the ER on 2, weighed in. "I don't know about any hummingbirds," he said. "This is the first I've heard of it. But I can tell you, something awful is happening in the hospital right now. We have an epidemic of a disease we haven't seen before."

This was exactly what everyone had expected. Alan explained that new cases were coming in daily and that the overflow had gone to a new space on 43.

"Any idea what it is?" asked Sophie.

"We know it's not a bacterium," he answered. "And we don't think it's a common virus."

"What else is there?" asked Katie.

"Poison," said Ivan.

Alan admitted that was a possibility. The disease manifested itself in blindness or eye problems, malaise and bizarre behavior.

"Like killing hummingbirds," said Alice.

Alan admitted that was possible although none of the patients he saw exhibited violent tendencies.

"Have you seen Mrs. Nikkanen's eyes?" said Ivan.

Alan said that he'd never seen Mrs. Nikkanen at all but he wouldn't be surprised if her eyes were blank or completely unfocused or red or violet or even orange or purple. "We're seeing eye conditions that we've never seen before. And yes, there's a mental component but that may be an aftereffect of losing their normal vision."

"Do you recognize a patient named Kimberly Ayers?" asked Ivan. "22, 5'6", short dark blond hair, athletic build ..."

"Sorry," said Alan.

The group was silent for a few moments, digesting the information they had gathered from their different perspectives. Then Sophie asked the obvious question: "So what do we do next?"

"Faoud?" said Ivan.

"He may be part of the problem," said Katie.

They discussed other people they could enlist. Captain Martin, Dr. Benjamin, Dr. Chance, the NYC police, the media. All were on the table when Ivan said, "What if Mrs. Nikkanen isn't crazy?"

"She crushed a spider right in front of my eyes," said Alice.

"But she may know things that nobody else knows about."

"How can you reach her?" Katie asked Ivan.

"*I* can," said Alice. "I have access to all her floors."

"Meanwhile, I have another idea," said Katie, and the group agreed to meet the day after next.

37

Lobby and 43rd Floor

KATIE KNEW THE ins and outs of the building and could access all the floors except 37 to 56, the forbidden floors, and three of the family floors. Theoretically, she could visit the aviary at any time or the insect garden, or the playrooms for the children on 80, or the farms and greenhouses on 74-77. Not even Captain Martin and the security staff could visit 37-56. Only Isha and the other console operators, Dr. Nikkanen and possibly Faoud had access to the entire building and control of the "Tree" elevator that went to 43. Isha, therefore, was Katie's only hope.

"You realize I could be fired for letting you in there," said Isha.

"It could be a mistake."

"They have records of everyone who goes to those floors. They'll have a video of you in the elevator."

"Is there a way of getting me to the 43rd Floor without you being implicated?"

"Of course," said Isha. "There are three of us on the console 24 hours a day and two alternates. You can implicate one of *them*, although I don't think they'll go for it."

Katie began to feel a desperation that she hadn't known was there. "Do you know what's going on up there? There's an epidemic that's threatening to spread throughout the building. It seemed to have hit suddenly, with a force that almost wiped out some of the restaurants and services. One of Katie's alternates in the lobby had it, as did one of Isha's replacements. It hit some of the teachers in the school, doctors in the hospital, perhaps 10% of the janitorial staff, several scientists in the labs on 39 and 40, workers on the farms and gyms. It struck randomly, regardless of age, sex, ethnicity or state of health, although, oddly enough, no one in the Senior Center and nursing home on 59 was stricken.

"They've constructed a whole new hospital floor to take care of the overflow," Katie told Isha, who didn't really need to be reminded. "Did I tell you about Ivan Anderson's girlfriend?"

"Not yet."

"She was staying at my apartment and got sick the first night. The EMT's took her and now they won't tell anyone where she is or even if she's alive. They won't even tell the doctors in the regular hospital what's going on."

"And you're going to stop them?" asked Isha, casually.

"Yes."

Isha stared at something on his console for a moment. "You know, I'm getting married."

"You're kidding. To who?"

"Who do you think?"

"Chrystal?"

Isha nodded.

"But you just met her at my house warming party."

"Weird, isn't it?" said Isha. "How much time do you need on 43?"

"Maybe 15 minutes at most. When my shift is done at 6."

"Be at the "Tree" elevator at 6."

"Why are you doing this?" asked Katie.

"Because Chrystal went blind. She's in there somewhere."

It was a little tricky, but it worked out. The evening shift showed up on time but Isha asked his replacement to give him an extra 20 minutes, as he had to work on something. Katie spent a minute on small talk with her replacement before heading for the "Tree" elevator.

As the elevator closed behind her, Katie had an unheard-of rush of claustrophobia. "Isha, can you hear me?"

"Yes."

"Is there something in the air in this elevator?"

"Not that I know of. You'll be there in 15 seconds."

Katie wasn't sure what she was expecting. Perhaps just a reception area leading to a treatment room and rows of wards. Certainly, a well-ordered hospital environment, doctors on rounds, attended by interns, nurses with carts of equipment, a few ambulatory patients shuffling along the halls in robes and gowns, joking at the nurse's station, a volunteer wheeling a book cart. On the other hand, since this was a quarantine ward, perhaps there would be a kind of eerie silence, as in the presence of a divine plague, punctuated by the muted tones of hospital codes.

What she opened the door to was its opposite: pandemonium. Even before the elevator opened, she heard a general roar and men shouting. When the elevator slid open, two men and a woman piled in, blocking Katie's exit.

"Close the door," one man shouted to Katie. His eyes had an orange tint. "We have to get out of here."

The woman was blind and the other man squinted, as if trying to focus.

Another man, with the red eyes of Mrs. Nikkanen, pushed into the elevator.

Katie could see people milling about haphazardly.

"Close the fucking door!" the orange-eyed man shouted.

There was a "close" button on the panel but Katie had no intention of pushing it. Before she could respond to the man, a group of soldiers, in camouflage and face masks, ploughed into the elevator, grabbed the fleeing patients and half-pulled, half-pushed them into the corridor. One of them started to drag Katie out of the elevator.

"Not a patient," she shouted. "I'm here to see Dr. Nordheim."

The soldier looked at her eyes and, without releasing her, changed his grip and guided her through a crowd of people who seemed to be milling about with no purpose other than general restlessness.

"What's happening here," Katie asked the soldier, who had a corporal's stripes on his arm.

"We can't keep them in bed, can we?" he said, keeping hold of Katie's arm as he navigated around a group of soldiers dragging two struggling men along the corridor.

"They won't stay where we put them," he said. "We only have so many rooms we can lock."

"This is chaos," said Katie.

"Tell me about it," said the corporal. "We're about 200% over capacity."

He guided her to a large office space, spare to the point of sterility, more of a storeroom, with unopened boxes stacked up haphazardly, an empty metal bookshelf, no file cabinets, a makeshift desk with a laptop and no phone. "He's around somewhere," said the corporal. "I'll see if I can find him and tell him you're here. What time is your appointment?"

Katie knew she couldn't tell him she didn't have one. "I'm five minutes late," she said, sitting on one of the unopened boxes.

She waited what seemed like half an hour before a slight, bedraggled man of about 50 came in. Half his face was hidden in a mask and when Katie stood up to greet him, he pulled down the mask and motioned for her to sit down. He had a lined face, short graying hair and looked exhausted. "I'm sorry, I didn't remember our appointment," he said.

"You're Dr. Gunther Nordheim," said Katie.

"No," he said. "I'm Goran Vulin, I work for Dr. Nordheim. I run the emergency ER. And you're …"

"Katie Moran, I'm the gatekeeper for the building."

"I've seen you. Should you be here at all?"

"Do you have a young woman named Kimberly Ayes in here? She would have arrived two or three days ago."

"That's privileged information."

"What about Chrystal McNabe, in HR?"

"That's also privileged," said Dr. Vulin.

"Then consider me one of the privileged."

He sat on one of the boxes and nodded his head without looking at her. "Chrystal McNabe and Kimberly Ayes are definitely on this floor. You'll have plenty of time to find them."

"What do you mean?"

"You haven't been wearing a mask; you might be infected. I can't let you leave."

"You're kidding."

"You also came here without proper authorization and you've seen things you're not supposed to see. And by the way, your cell phone won't work here."

"You can't keep this place a secret," said Katie.

He pursed his lips for a moment and then called out the door. "Millie!"

A large, muscular woman of 45 or so entered. She had thick black hair that looked like it had taken years to straighten and wore mirror sunglasses that one might associate with Mississippi state troopers. "Millie, this is Katie Moran," said Dr. Vulin. "She may have been infected. Can we find her a bed somewhere?"

Millie spoke with a Jamaican accent. "You know we got no beds, Dr. Vulin."

"Where can we put her?"

"I'll find something," said Millie.

"Put her in one of the locked wards. We can't let her leave."

"We have to get her checked in first. I'll take care of it."

Millie had her hand on Katie's shoulder when she faced Dr. Vulin. "You can't keep me locked up. People know I'm here."

"I don't care if they do. You've been exposed to a virus and if you were let out, you might become a danger to others. Millie, take her away – I don't have time for this."

As Millie led her away, Katie wondered if the elevator door down the hall was still open. She might make a run for it. But, of course, the soldiers would stop her, if Millie called out. Then she noticed something unusual about Millie.

"You're not wearing a mask," she said.

"I already got the bug," said Millie. She raised her sunglasses. The whites of her eyes were an iridescent violet, like Minna Nikkanen's, only darker.

"I'm sorry," said Katie. "Did that come on all of a sudden?"

"No, I was knocked out for a while. When I woke up, I had this condition. Least I'm not blind."

"Like Chrystal McNabe?"

"You know her?"

"She's marrying a friend of mine."

Millie shook her head. "I don't know. She's in bad shape."

"Blind?"

"Blind and the fever hasn't gone away. She's in the ICU."

It was hard to imagine someone as vital and gossipy as Chrystal being in danger. It seemed an affront to reality. "What about Kimberly Ayes?"

"She recovered. She's around somewhere, helping out."

The crowd had thinned out somewhat. They passed several blind men and women being led by nurses, perhaps to give them some exercise. Katie recognized one. "Tay?" she said.

Tay Reneau, the owner of Tay's Soul Restaurant on 6 where Alice had waitressed when she first came to the building, turned at the sound of Katie's voice. "Who's that?" He looked old and desperate, dressed in a short hospital gown that looked frayed and dirty.

"Katie Moran, from the lobby."

"Tell Celine I here."

"Your wife doesn't know you're here?"

"She know I go to the hospital but don't know where I am now. They won't let her see me. Don't tell her I blind. Tell her I good."

"I'll try, Tay," said Katie. It was shocking to see him; it was shocking to see all of them. This was so much worse than she imagined. Millie continued leading her by the shoulder down the hall.

"And what about *you*?" Katie asked Millie. "Are you going to recover?"

"I don't think so."

"How bad is it?"

They were passing the door to one of the stairwells leading to the lobby. "I'll tell you how bad, Miss Moran," said Millie. "If you were to press 2378 on that panel next to the door and go on through, I probably wouldn't be able to stop you."

"If I go, he'll know it was you."

"He's so stressed, he won't even know you're missing."

"Thanks, Millie. I'll be back."

"I hope you will."

Katie pressed the buttons and bolted through the door to the stairwell.

38

86th and 90th Floors

T HAT EVENING, ALICE served dinner to the family as usual. It was Silje's turn to set the tone and she chose a Monet's garden motif with weeping willows, water lilies and fields of flowers in full bloom. The guests of honor were a Swedish plutocrat and her fashionable husband, a Brearley classmate of Minna, who wore a dark blue hajib with the Nike swoosh on one side of it, and most unusual of all, a friend of Tero from a playgroup of blind children that he attended twice a week.

Mrs. Nikkanen was there, which was unusual these days. But she had gone to university with the plutocrat and it would be considered unforgiveable if she wasn't there. Unfortunately, that would mean it would be quite late, after dinner, drinks and required socializing, before Alice could speak to her.

It wasn't until she was serving expresso, during a joke by the Swedish plutocrat, that she was able to whisper, "Can I speak to you after dinner?" She had no idea if Tuuli agreed or even heard her, or if she had been overheard by anyone, but she had to assume that they would meet later on.

By ten o'clock, the children had retired to their rooms, the adults were in the living room, lingering over cognacs, and Alice was preparing to leave for the night. She was in the locker room on 86, had changed out of her uniform into her street clothes, and said goodnight to Heidi (Henry had agreed to stay until the end of the evening and the plutocratic Swedes had left.) She was headed to the elevator when the door to the stairwell opened and Tuuli beckoned her inside.

Again, as always, there was something terrifying about Tuuli. Not just the laser eyes but the fury in her manner. Even Alice, who was afraid of almost nothing, was taken aback by Tuuli's intensity. "You wanted to see me. I'm here," she said.

Alice really didn't know what she wanted to ask. She was essentially fishing for information. She was at a loss for a question but she had to ask something. "Do you know what's going on here?" she said.

"Tell me."

"You told Ivan that something awful was going on here."

"Who's Ivan?"

"The boy who works with the hummingbirds ..."

"The virgin."

"What did you mean by something awful?" asked Alice.

"Come with me." Tuuli took Alice's hand and led her up the stairs. At the door to the living room and dining room, where Alice expected to stop, Tuuli kept to the stairs.

"Where are we going?"

"To see something awful," said Tuuli, tightening her grip on Alice's hand.

The next floor, 88, was the only circular floor in the building. It held the aquariums and insect gardens, in which Tuuli had been known to wander, picking out insects for destruction.

"You're going to show me another spider so I can poison your husband," said Alice.

"No."

"Was that a joke before?"

"Yes. Come."

They continued up to 89 with its maze of labs, holding pens and sick bays, as well as offices for Dr. Benjamin and other scientists. Tuuli stopped to catch her breath.

"Is this about the epidemic?" Alice asked.

Tuuli let go of Alice's hand. "What epidemic?"

"You didn't know?"

"They keep me on ... what do you call it ... a tight leash."

Alice explained everything she had heard from Alan Graff, the doctor in the ER, which replicated Tuuli's own visual and mental disorders and those of her children. Tuuli listened carefully, nodding, smiling and shaking her head, as if savoring a fond memory. "Well, it was only a matter of time," she commented.

"What do you mean?"

"Where do you think my husband's fortune comes from? He thinks he's doing good. He's making nuclear bombs obsolete, doing away with war machines, soldiers, tanks, cannon, all the horrors of modern war. Don't kill your enemy – blind him. We're all – what do you call it – collateral damage – in the service of good."

She took Alice's hand again and they ascended the steps to the heavy flaps leading to the aviary. "There's also an escalator but they turn it off at night," said Tuuli.

As they entered the aviary, Alice involuntarily gasped. If the place was paradise during the day, it was even more enchanted at night. The lights of the city, coming through the dome, somehow softened the air, and the great trees and giant leaves were dark, abstract shapes that could hide mythical night creatures and dangerous illusions.

Most of the birds were asleep but not all. There was the occasional squawk, a sudden, unexpected call, a rustling in the bushes, accompanied by the gurgling of a brook, the rush of a mini waterfall and the hum of machinery, imperceptible except if you were listening for it.

There was supposed to be a minimal night staff, checking in from time to time, but they were nowhere in evidence. Tuuli and Alice had the fairyland to themselves and their voices were a shock, like breaking into a dream.

"You've waited on my husband at dinner," said Tuuli. "He seems reasonable, well-adjusted, intelligent, humorous, paternal ..."

"He's not?"

"He's obsessed. He doesn't care if we live or die. It's not even the money anymore, it's the task that his scientists have set for themselves, a kind of absolute power."

"We all suspected that."

"Who's 'we all?'"

Alice hesitated with her answer. She didn't want to name names or get anyone in trouble.

Tuuli interrupted her thought. "That's alright, don't tell me. They have tapes of everything you've said. If there's a conspiracy, they already know about it."

Tuuli still held Alice's hand and guided her towards the pavilion. She couldn't gauge Tuuli''s mood or intention. Is she going to make a pass at me? Alice wondered. And what would happen if she refused?

But then, Tuuli seemed anything but amorous. She didn't exactly pull her towards the pavilion but walked with her as if there was no other destination.

They reached the group of easy chairs in the outer part of the pavilion and here, Tuuli let go of Alice's hand. "Wait here," she said.

"Where are you going?"

"To put a stop to it." She made sure Alice was seated, gave her an odd expression that Alice couldn't interpret, her red eyes flashing, then turned and walked away.

"I don't understand," called Alice.

"To make him listen to me."

She walked to one end of the aviary, to the narrow ladder that led to the catwalk under the roof. When she started climbing, Alice rose and hurried after her, not sure of Tuuli's intention but suspecting the worst.

Tuuli climbed the ladder with difficulty, halting every now and then to catch her breath but never looking down, ascending with sheer determination.

It was a long way up and by the time she was halfway to the roof, Alice had reached the bottom of the ladder. "What are you doing?" she called. Should she climb up after her? Could she stop her if she did? Did she really want to fight a crazy woman 50 feet in the air?

Tuuli kept climbing and Alice followed, despite herself. Maybe she could talk some sense into her if she was physically closer. There was little chance of catching up to her before she reached the catwalk but she might get within persuasion distance.

Alice had never been afraid of heights, so scaling the ladder didn't bother her. She could look down and appreciate the wonders of the aviary as she moved. Looking up, she saw Tuuli pause for breath once more and she could decrease the distance between them. Tuuli noticed, perhaps for the first time. "I told you to wait," she said sharply.

"I have no intention of waiting," Alice replied.

This made Tuuli climb even faster until she reached the catwalk and ran out into the middle, 85 feet above the ground, protected by a low metal railing on either side.

She leaned over the railing and shouted something in Finnish that sounded like a roar and made Alice's blood curdle and the birds awaken. But she didn't jump.

Suddenly, the lights went on in the aviary. Captain Martin, José Rodriquez and several other members of the security team rushed inside.

The birds let out a collective roar and went crazy, flying back and forth in panic, screeching and honking as if pursued by some huge ravenous pterodactyl.

Captain Martin tried calling but her voice was lost in the avian frenzy.

Faoud appeared, followed by Aaron Houdi, the building manager, and then Sam Chance, the head of the hospital, and several other doctors, who in the general mania, could only stare in silence as Tuuli leaned over the railing and screamed, "Bring him here!"

By now, Alice had reached the catwalk but thought better of approaching Tuuli. "Mrs. Nikkanen …" she called.

Tuuli ignored her. Seeing the crowd milling about below and the birds beginning to lower their volume, if not the wildness of their flight, she yelled again, "Bring him here!" This set off the birds again.

"Someone's gone to get him," Faoud shouted back, hoping Tuuli could hear him.

They waited. Alice stood at one end of the catwalk, feeling useless and unsettled. There was really nothing she could do but she felt she had to remain where she was rather than climb down the ladder.

The birds were further disturbed by a noise behind a large service door that Alice hadn't noticed. The door opened and there emerged a massive hydraulic crane with a railed platform that could telescope up to the roof so the dome could be cleaned or repaired.

"I'm just coming up to talk with you," said Faoud, walking towards the crane.

"Where is he?" said Tuuli.

"I've sent someone to get him. He should be here any moment."

"Then stay down there until he comes."

They waited for what seemed like forever. There was now a crowd in the aviary, looking up. A security guard came up to Faoud and said if he could climb up to where Alice was, he could probably throw a rope around Tuuli and hold her until the crane could get there – he'd worked as a cowpuncher in Texas. Another man said he was an expert marksman and offered to shoot her with an anesthetic. Faoud considered the last proposal, thought of the endless complications and shook his head.

Tuuli paced back and forth along the catwalk, paying no attention to Alice. Faoud tried to converse with her but she ignored him as well. She was angry and ferocious and one could see her laser eyes from the ground below.

A man came into the aviary, ran up to Faoud and spoke to him in a whisper. Faoud looked startled and called up. "Tuuli, wait."

"You have five minutes," said Tuuli.

Faoud ran out of the aviary with the man and Captain Martin tried to take up the slack. "Mrs. Nikkanen, can we get you anything while we wait? Tea, a drink?"

Tuuli didn't bother to respond.

Two minutes later, Faoud reappeared, seemingly shaken. He walked to the crane and was about to enter the platform when Tuuli said, "No."

"It's better if I talk to you in private."

"What did he say?" asked Tuuli, almost imperiously.

"Can I ..." He indicated the crane.

"No. What did he say?"

Faoud paused and took a deep breath. "He won't come," he said.

"Very well," said Tuuli and flung herself over the railing, dropping without a sound to a short stone bridge 85 feet below and landing with an audible thud before a stunned audience.

The birds panicked once again, zigzagging back and forth chaotically, bumping into one another and knocking some of the smaller birds out of the air. The humans covered their bodies from the onslaught of the birds and closed their ears to the deafening cacophony. No one noticed Alice climbing down the stairs, being hit by one bird after another, finally ending up flat on the ground, bloodied but alive.

Tuuli lay broken on the stone bridge, bleeding into the pond below.

39

3rd Floor

A T THIS POINT, in the normal ways of things, the police would have been called in, a medical examiner, a coroner; an inquest would have been held and Alice would be a key witness to Tuuli's desperate measure. The reasons behind it would come out, of course, and the whole operation on the forbidden floors would be exposed.

Except that Tuuli was not dead. Her body was smashed beyond repair, unrecognizable, permanently unconscious, but she was still breathing. Dr. Chance had rushed over to her body and called his emergency team to the aviary. They took her down to a private ICU set up on the 3rd floor.

As this was happening, Faoud had a brief consultation with Captain Martin and then called Alice over for an explanation. "So exactly what happened?" he said, calmly, seemingly not in the least disturbed by Tuuli's leap from the catwalk.

Alice selectively described what had transpired between them. She knew they had her whisper at dinner on tape, so she couldn't pretend she didn't initiate the contact. She admitted she had heard about the epidemic and wanted to hear what Mrs. Nikkanen could tell her. What she omitted was what Tuuli had said about her husband seeking absolute power, replacing killing people with blinding them. No doubt this was taped as well but Alice wanted to talk with Katie and the group before the tape was reviewed by security. "She wanted Dr. Nikkanen to pay attention to her," she said.

"For what?" said Faoud.

"To stop what he was doing."

"Which was."

"Whatever caused the epidemic."

"How do you know about this?"

"Everyone knows about it by now."

This stopped Faoud. He nodded thoughtfully and appeared to be considering possibilities. His face seemed muddier and more wrinkled than usual. Then his expression changed, as if hit by an emotion he hadn't expected. "I liked Tuuli," he said.

Alice waited, struck by his sadness.

"She wasn't always crazy, you know. She was a strong woman, an athlete, the head of a sports association in Finland."

"Before the accident."

"Yes. And when Silje went blind, and Tero, and she could still see, it unhinged her."

He snapped out of his reverie. "I can't tell you to say nothing about this – it's all over the building by now. But don't fan the flames with conspiracy theories. I have to talk to Dr. Nikkanen and we have to figure out what to do about it."

"Why wouldn't he come to see her?" asked Alice.

"Only he knows why," said Faoud. "Maybe he wanted her to jump."

Alice went to the children first to see if she could be of any comfort. It was two in the morning and they were probably asleep but when she arrived there, Silje and her caretaker, Apollonia, Minna and her friend from Brearley, Mika, Naziha, Tero, his caretaker, Omar, and his friend from the blind playgroup, had all left for the ICU on 3.

Alice found them there surrounding the bed of their mother. Technically, only two visitors were allowed in an ICU room at a time, but no one had the heart or nerve to stop them from crowding around the inert form of their mother, hooked up to a ventilator, her face covered in bandages to spare her family the sight of her broken face.

No attempt was made to set her bones, as almost every bone in her body was shattered and she wasn't expected to live more than a few days, if that.

Minna and Mika stared at her clinically while Naziha described the scene to Silje and Tero. What with the sounds of the ventilator, almost banging the air into Tuuli's lungs, the constant beeps of the various monitors and the undertones of doctors, nurses and aides, the ambient murmurs of a hospital, it was actually quite noisy in the ICU.

"Do you think she can hear us?" asked Minna.

"What do you want to say to her?" asked Tero.

"Just that I hope she gets better."

"Do you?"

"Of course, you idiot." None of the children was in tears. They seemed not merely interested or curious but mesmerized by the mechanics surrounding an inert body who might or might not be their mother.

"Suppose it's someone completely different," said Minna's friend from Brearley.

"We'd never know," said Minna.

"Do you think she feels pain?" asked Naziha.

"How?" said Silje.

"There's a drug I read about called curare, which paralyzes the body but not the senses, so you can feel pain but can't express it. They use it during operations but sometimes a patient wakes up in the middle of it and can't tell the doctors about it."

"It's like torture," said Mika.

"Yes, exactly," said Naziha.

"It's no fun if they don't scream," said Tero.

No one would dignify that with a response.

When Alice came in, they all wanted to know exactly what had happened and how it happened and if what they had heard was true.

Alice wasn't sure how much she should reveal. Faoud had hadn't forbidden her to talk about it but she knew he would be uncomfortable if she revealed too much – especially Tuuli's acknowledged reason for jumping – to call attention to her husband's activities and put a stop to them. Of course all that was on tape. She assumed the children hadn't seen it.

Answering Tero's immediate question, she answered, "Yes, I saw her jump. I called out to her but she wouldn't listen to me."

"Did she give a reason?" asked Minna. "We heard it was because father wouldn't see her."

"Yes, that's right," said Alice.

"But why?" asked Minna.

"You already know why," said Naziha.

"Because he won't talk about the chemicals he's developing?"

"He can't," said Omar. "It's probably in his contract."

"That's not the reason," said Tero.

"What is?" asked Omar.

"Because he wanted mom to die."

The other children automatically objected but then Tero turned to Alice and asked her what she thought.

"It's confusing," said Alice. "At one point, she said she wanted *him* to die, but then she said she was joking."

"And where is he?" said Mika. "Why isn't he here?"

"He *is*," said a voice. Paavo walked in, followed by Faoud, Dr. Chance and a thin, guarded man in his 50's, with the ideal poker face, expressionless, giving away nothing. Neither Alice, nor any of the children, had seen him before. Paavi called him "Whit" but didn't introduce him.

Paavo acknowledged the children, hugging them each in turn, gave Alice a nod and then stood in front of the bed. Dr. Chance came over to his side.

"What's the prognosis?" said Paavo.

"She could go at any moment. Her brain waves are flat, there's nothing there."

"How long can you keep her alive?"

"On the machine?"

"Yes."

"Probably indefinitely," said Dr. Chance, clearly uncomfortable with the question and his answer.

"Whit?" Paavo glanced at the guarded man, who turned out to be one of Paavo's lawyers.

"She's still alive, being treated at an accredited hospital, doesn't pose a problem."

"And if she dies?"

"Problem."

"Why?"

"Exposure," said Whit.

"Ah," said Paavo, understanding.

Silje had her guardian, Apollonia, escort her over to her father. "Dad, why didn't you come to her?"

Paavo seemed put off by the question. He had so many other considerations to think about that it came out of the blue. He struggled for an answer for a moment, then put his hand on Silje's shoulder. "Ah, Silje, there was no way of telling if your mother was serious."

"True," said Silje.

"She had what you'd call a flair for the dramatic."

"Yes."

Tero added, "She wasn't what you'd call motherly."

"She used to be," said Minna.

"She wasn't sane," said Naziha.

"Then why wasn't she treated?" said Tero, with a kind of false indignation.

"Children," said Paavo. "your mother is complicated. She won't be *treated* by anybody, she makes gestures, she stages productions, sometimes she *seems* crazy but that's for show. When she threatened to jump from the catwalk if I didn't come, she knew I wouldn't come, she never expected me to show up."

"So she was going to jump anyway?" asked Mika.

"I suspect she slipped," said Paavo. "She lost her balance and couldn't pull back."

Alice knew for a fact this wasn't true but didn't feel she could say anything.

Paavo gestured for the children to approach him and whispered. "She can hear every word we say." He placed a finger over his mouth and then waved everyone out of the room. The children took one last look at the mummy who might have been their mother and followed their father and his minions out of the room.

Whit lingered by Paavo. "Nice touch," he said.

"What?"

"Lost her balance."

"I thought so," said Paavo, under his breath.

Alice accompanied the children up to the 84th floor, just to be there if anyone wanted to talk. As it turned out, she spent the entire night.

Just before she left, at 5 in the morning, Tero beckoned her into his bedroom, shooing away Omar. His friend from the blind playgroup was asleep in on the floor next to Tero's bed and they whispered so as not to awaken him.

"I wanted to tell you before anybody else. Something's happening with my eyes."

"Something new?"

"Of course, idiot," said Tero.

"This doesn't mean you can see."

"Yes. I can see black."

Alice didn't understand. "Isn't that what every blind person sees?"

"No," said Tero. "Normally, when I open my eyes, I see nothing. Now I'm seeing black. There's a difference."

"Since when?"

"Just around the time you started serving dinner. I don't know if that's a coincidence."

"It must be – I haven't done anything. So is what you see solid black or does it respond to light?"

"It definitely responds to light. It changes all the time."

Alice was astounded by the news. "This is really major ..."

"Just thought you should know," said Tero.

40

7th Floor

NEWS OF TUULI'S leap from the catwalk spread throughout the building within hours that night and dominated conversations the next day. It was presumed she was dead but the wall of secrecy they had clamped around the ICU was breached almost immediately. There were rumors that she was in a makeshift morgue or that her body was being kept alive for useable body parts. The epidemic was known but not its extent, as almost everyone had a friend or associate who had taken sick and not returned from the hospital.

The day after Tuuli's "incident," the group gathered in the cafeteria on 7 to debrief everyone on what they had learned. Alice repeated the events of last night, which had now surfaced on the building intranet, but included the scene at the ICU (which hadn't) and her night with the children.

"There were no tears," she said. "They considered her dead – the body in the ICU was not a living human being – but they didn't seem to mourn her."

"That's odd," said Sophie. "She *was* their mother, although I gather not a very good one."

"No, that wasn't it," said Alice. "I don't think they're capable of mourning, something with the disease maybe."

"Isn't there one who doesn't have it?" asked Katie.

"Naziha," said Alice. "The adopted one. I don't understand her but she seems connected with Silje somehow – not just because they're the same age but in some other way."

"Sexual?" Katie suggested.

Alice shrugged. "Maybe from a long time ago."

Katie described her visit to 43, the pandemonium she experienced, and confirmed the presence of Chrystal and Kimberly, although she hadn't actually seen them. "From what I heard, Chrystal is blind and Kimberly is okay, although they seem to be keeping her prisoner. I barely escaped myself."

Alan Graff, the doctor from 2, reported what he had heard: that they were expanding the quarantine section to the 44th Floor, which had been used as a storage area.

"What did they store there?"

"No one knows, but I'm worried that what was there might infect the people they put there."

"They can't keep this a secret forever," said Katie. "Sooner or later ..."

"And if *you* could escape, others can escape," said Sophie.

"They already have," said José.

Everyone was immediately rivetted. This could be a significant development. "We're all ears," said Katie.

"Somehow, a group of patients got access to the stairs and fled before they could be stopped. We saw them on our monitors at security. My colleague, Dom, and I took the elevator to meet them at the bottom but a group of soldiers had gotten there ahead of us. There was a captain who told me, 'we'll handle this.'"

"Holy shit," said Katie. "That was quick."

"Tell me about it," said José. He turned to Ivan. "I think your friend, Kimberly, was among them. I recognized her from the tape we had when she first arrived here."

"How was she?" asked Ivan.

"She seemed okay, whoever she was. None of the patients was completely blind, although some of them had only peripheral vision, or laser eyes, or ultra violet eyes."

"Like Minna," Alice commented.

"So what happened to them?" asked Sophie.

"They were herded into a bus," said José. "Except for one guy who tried to run and was zapped by a stinger in his hand."

"This is so surreal," said Sophie, who, like everyone except Alice, became acutely aware of the implants in their hands.

"I got the license plate of the bus. I'll check it out when I go upstairs."

"We should call the police," said Alan.

"They'll find them, take down their stories and do nothing," said José. "They probably won't even check."

"Paid off, probably." said Alice.

"No." Katie shook her head. "This is a government thing. I'm willing to bet the police have been told to keep their hands off."

A pall settled on the group as the various disclosures began to sink in. An epidemic out of control, a kidnapping, a government conspiracy, a secret lab making dangerous chemicals, and they felt powerless to do anything about it. "Could there be anything else?" Sophie muttered.

"Yes," said Ivan.

The group waited patiently, and with some dread, for the next revelation.

"Another hummingbird is missing. A Calliope."

41

69th Floor

SOPHIE HAD BECOME tired of pursuing Katie. It might happen, it might not, but she didn't want to jeopardize their friendship by constantly harassing her with lascivious innuendos or outright propositions. Once she had accepted this, she availed herself of a building service that few of its residents knew about.

The gym for non-family professionals on 68 had several legitimate massage therapists on staff and others on call, who would offer their services at the gym or, for an extra fee, in the apartments of their clients. What most residents did not knew was that the gym was also the source of illegitimate services who could be viewed on the internet and summoned by name through the gym.

Sophie choose a small, spare woman named Gay, perhaps 33-35 with a haunted face and a scar running down her cheek. There was something so bizarre about her that Sophie was captivated, at least with her online profile.

Gay did not disappoint in any way. She was enthusiastic about whatever sexual eccentricity Sophie fancied and added nuances of her own. The sexual part of the evening was a complete success but the more interesting part came afterwards.

Gay followed the Paleo diet rigorously and refused Sophie's offer of wine or beer. Although red wine was permissible in small amounts, Gay felt that any alcohol was bad for her. She passed on Sophie's peanuts (they're legumes, not nuts) and settled for carrot sticks and green tea.

As might be expected, she was vehemently opposed to modern medicine and followed herbal remedies for every ailment. "Doctors make you sicker," she said. "They want to stick needles in you and make you pay through the nose for it."

"Surely, you're not against immunization," said Sophie, more as a tease than a serious question.

"The stories about autism, they're true," Gay replied.

"No, they're not."

Gay stared at Sophie as if she were some poor, deluded innocent. "Check out noprick.com for the proof. That's the story you won't get from the New England Journal of Medicine."

"Noprick?"

"I have your email," said Gay. "I'll send you the link."

"What about drugs?"

"Using hallucinogens is almost universal among indigenous people. For paleos, peyote is permissible but not LSD or cocaine, or anything that's *processed*."

"Marijuana?"

"As long as it's straight from the farm."

Since they were talking about supposedly serious topics, Sophie felt the need to put on a robe and tie it at the waist. Gay felt no such inhibition. She sat cross-legged on the bed, naked, and proceeded to lecture Sophie on the benefits of what she called "botanical" medicine for almost every ailment.

"Cancer?" asked Sophie.

"Depends on the type," said Gay. "Ginger as an overall, sutherlandia, pau d'arco, red clover … there are many others. But the best thing is to detoxify yourself first. You must have heard of Gerson therapy."

"No."

"The idea of flooding your body with natural nutrients, mainly fruits and vegetables …"

"What about heart disease?"

"Doctors don't understand heart disease," said Gay. "Flaxseed, garlic, hawthorn and good sex can do more for you than any of their drugs." She reached over and put in hand inside Sophie's robe, which made Sophie infinitely more receptive to anything Gay had to say.

"I've got to educate you, girl," said Gay. "Gokshura for sex – it works 99% of the time. Organ meats are the most concentrated source of almost every nutrient there is, as long as they're grass-fed meats. I'm talking liver, kidneys, brains, heart ..."

Sophie stopped responding to Gay's fingers. "Brains? What are they good for?"

"Memory, diabetes, birth defects, some kinds of blindness ..."

"What kind of brains?" Sophie asked sharply.

"Lamb, goats, anything grass-fed."

"Birds?"

Gay had to search her memory for a moment. "Yes, I think I've read that the brains of some birds can cure disease-caused blindness. I mean, not if somebody poked a stick in your eye ..."

"Can you remember what birds?"

Gay laughed. "Well, this is going to sound weird but I remember hearing something about peacock brains, nightingale tongues and hummingbirds drowned in cognac. Very poetic, don't you think?"

"I've heard of ortolans, little birds drowned in Armagnac and eaten whole. The peacock brains and nightingale tongues come from a play by George Bernard Shaw. Where on earth did you hear all of this?" Sophie asked, controlling her excitement.

Gay shrugged. "I have no idea. When you get into nutrition, you pick up a lot of stuff."

Sophie took Gay's hand away from her robe. "Do you think you could find out for me? I'd make it worth your while."

Gay took a moment to ponder *worth your while*. "I can try," she said.

42

Lobby and 32nd Floor

A WEEK AFTER TUULI'S fall, Aaron Houdi, the building manager, Katie and Isha's boss, told them what to expect. "The army has taken over security for the building. They'll be stationed on the 45th and 46th Floors."

"What about Captain Martin and her team?" asked Katie.

"They'll be around but they'll report to the army. The thing is, we have to make it look as normal as possible. The soldiers will enter and leave in the middle of the night by way of the service garage. They will have access only to the forbidden floors, so you won't see them in the Lobby or in any of the restaurants."

"I saw a colonel and two captains yesterday," said Katie.

"A few high-ranking officers may come in through the Lobby but that will be the exception," said Houdi.

"All going to 45 or 46?" asked Isha.

"No, they may meet with Dr. Nikkanen or Mr. Faoud as well."

"Aaron, we all know what's going on," said Katie. "There's a full-blown epidemic caused by a chemical they're making up there. So tell us, are they going to close down the lab up there and dump the chemicals somewhere?"

Houdi shrugged.

"And what about the patients?" Katie continued. "Are they just going to keep them up there in quarantine or move them somewhere else, like with the ones who escaped?"

"Houdi shrugged again. "I have no idea," he said.

"Aaron, they can't keep this a secret for long. The patients have friends and family who'll want to see them, it'll be in the papers, it'll be all over the internet ..."

"The building has it all under control," said Houdi.

"No, they don't," said Katie. "I've been up there and it's chaos. People who can barely see are running around trying to get out. There's going to be fighting and possibly killing."

"You've been there?"

Katie recounted her experience on the 43rd Floor but left out any reference to Millie, the nurse who had helped her escape. She liked Houdi but didn't trust him with the information. He was weak enough to be exploited by someone with power. He was also clearly out of the loop.

When Houdi had left, she phoned Joe Barash in the lower garage, who already knew about the army.

"Yeah, I've been briefed, but thanks anyway."

"Has the military showed up?"

"They're here already. And I've got help managing the garage."

"Help?"

"A Sergeant First Class. Seems to know a lot about garage management."

Katie let this sink in for a moment. "You up for a beer tonight?"

Barash paused for a moment, considering. "Finnegan's at 6?"

"6:30."

"You're on."

After a beer or two, Katie and Joe ended up in Katie's apartment on 32. Annie had returned home from her vacation and didn't seem surprised to see her sister with a man she didn't recognize. He seemed nice enough, if a bit old.

Katie and Joe wasted no time on chitchat and went into Katie's room to copulate while Annie watched TV with a jigger of Tullamore Dew and went to bed light-headed.

It wasn't exactly copulation – it was closer than that. But it wasn't exactly making love either – there were no emotions in play. It was more mutual enjoyment, happy lust.

"I thought you only went with prostitutes," said Katie, during a break.

Joe reached over for his pants, pulled out a wallet and deposited a $50 bill on the end table by the bed.

"That's all I get, a 50?" said Annie, amused.

"How much do you normally charge?" asked Joe.

Katie had never considered this but she felt she was at least as skilled as a high-priced escort. "1,000 a trick and 3,000 for the night," she said.

"That's exactly what I charge," said Joe, turning back to enfold Katie.

They fell asleep somewhere around 3 in the morning and when they awoke, a violet fuzz had descended on Joe's eyes and he could barely see.

43

90th Floor and Ivan's apartment

DESPITE KIMBERLY'S SICKNESS and abduction, despite the tragedy of Mrs. Nikkanen, whose body still lay at the point of death in the ICU on 3, despite the widening epidemic and the rampant unease that had spread throughout the building, Ivan still had a job to do. The hummingbirds still had to be fed, cleaned, their water changed, their waste removed, the materials for nest building made available.

The loss of a calliope, with its magenta wings and splash of violet about its neck, the smallest bird in North America, seemed to be a disaster he should have been able to prevent but couldn't. He was fairly certain that Omar had taken it for Tero, but there was no way he could prove this or prevent it happening again.

He was at a loss as to how to protect his hummingbirds. The building surveillance cameras were turned off when family entered the aviary and he had no access to the family tapes. The only thing he could think of was confronting Omar directly, which he could do through Alice, who had direct access.

It was unsettling to work in the aviary the day after Mrs. Nikkanen's fall. The blood and bits of flesh had been cleaned up but some birds and insects canvassed that spot along the stone bridge for nourishment. The aura of tragedy was still palpable and permeated everyone who worked in the aviary.

There were a few workers who were no longer there — Tess McAllister, the woman who specialized in water birds, had succumbed to the epidemic two days before and remained incommunicado on the forbidden floors. One of the cleanup ladies was also missing but, on the whole, the aviary remained relatively unscathed. Perhaps replacing the contaminated cardinal flowers had something to do with it.

The abduction of Kimberly and the other escapees by soldiers in the lobby, coupled with Ivan's fevered moments with Mrs. Nikkanen trying to escape the building, had convinced Ivan to go public with the epidemic. The question was how and when. He didn't feel compelled to tell the group about it because they might change his mind.

When his shift was over, instead of going to Finnegan's or one of the restaurants, he went directly to his apartment on West 54th Street, an ungentrified tenement he shared with three other tenants. All were Christians, a condition he had specified when he had searched for an apartment, although they included a Mormon couple living in sin and a sour, defrocked minister who worked in a print shop and lived on spaghetti and meatballs from a can. There was no camaraderie among them and he passed them with a nod and went to his room.

He felt slightly more private here than he did at the building but he knew that as long as he had the transponder buried in his hand, real privacy was impossible.

There was so much going on in the building that it was hard to know who to call first. Public Health about the epidemic. The police or the F.B.I. about the kidnappings. The newspapers about both of these and the suicide attempt of Mrs. Nikkanen.

A thought stopped him. Although Kimberly was supposed to have gotten ill, rushed to the hospital, recovered, escaped, been caught and herded into a bus, he hadn't actually seen any of this. Katie had told him about it. He knew about the epidemic through her and Alan Graff at the hospital. He knew about Mrs. Nikkanen's fall through Alice – he hadn't witnessed any of this himself. Anything he might say would be hearsay.

He could tell someone about Mrs. Nikkanen's approaching him and their escape attempt but that was hardly a public health or police matter and not much of a story for the media. If he went online about it, his accusations would certainly be monitored, possibly censored or erased and would brand him as treasonous to the building, at the cost of his job and possibly his life. Anything online was toxic.

That left anonymous calls, without corroborating details, basically crank calls. He didn't think any reputable newspaper or TV station would pay any attention to a crank call. That left disreputable sources, like the tabloids you see at supermarket checkout counters or vitriolic pamphlets or conspiracy rants.

The other consideration was the implant in his hand. Was that a listening device as well as a credit and access card? Could it modify his behavior? Was it a direct line to the security office? Was it recording his treasonous brain waves as he produced them?

He decided he didn't care. No matter what the consequences, he had to do something to let the world know what was going on in the building. He had to do something to find Kimberly. It took him a while to find a public health number he could call, and when he reached it, he got the loud whine of a fax machine. He called the federal number, the city number and finally the state number. At last, he got a human being on the line.

"I want to report an epidemic," he said.

The voice on the line was bureaucratic. "Our office is closed now. Is this an emergency?"

"Yes."

"Then dial 911."

Ivan hung up. After taking a moment to shrug off his annoyance, he dialed the emergency number. To a calm, composed and barely concerned listener, he repeated, "I want to report an epidemic."

To the listener, this wasn't exactly pressing news. "May I have your name and the location of the epidemic?"

"I won't give you my name but the epidemic is at 211A West 57th Street."

"Is that in Manhattan or Queens?"

"Manhattan."

"One moment, sir."

There was a click, the line went dead for a moment and then another man, with a high, friendly voice, came on the line.

"Are you still there?" he said.

"Yes."

"Is this about an epidemic at 211A West 57th Street?"

"Yes."

"Oh, we know all about that one," said the man, cheerily. "It's not a problem. But thank you for calling."

44

85th Floor

THE MEETING WAS held in Dr. Nikkanen's office on 85. In attendance were Dr. Nikkanen and Faoud, Dr. Nordheim of the secret laboratories and factories of the forbidden floors, Colonel Benedict Allen, director of the army's chemical, biological, radiological and nuclear section, Colonel Paul Dupont, director of the army's chemical material command, Lt. General Hiram Wolcott, representing the department of the army and John Farago, one of the anonymous high-level functionaries of the Department of Defense, whom Katie had tagged as "malevolent" when he first showed up to visit Dr. Nordheim. There were several other onlookers, both civilian and military, who took no part in the discussion.

They were not gathered around Dr. Nikkanen's desk but in a separate conference area in one section of the room, at a round table that would equalize the participants. It was 10 in the morning of a clear, cloudless autumn day and from the windows one could see the Hudson River, the palisades of New Jersey, the George Washington Bridge and beyond.

"The ideal solution would be to incinerate the entire building and everything in it," said John Farago, facetiously, to a slight undercurrent of amusement from the others.

"I hope you have an alternative," said Faoud, to lighten up the mood, which he accomplished. People who never smiled were smiling.

"The alternative would be empty the building, isolate the residents at some army facility until we can determine if they're infected or contagious, and fumigate the entire place," said Farago.

"We could accommodate them at our facility in Missouri," said Colonel Dupont.

"Them?" said Faoud. "We have hundreds, maybe thousands of people coming and going every day. There are day workers, night workers, truck drivers, cleaning crews, restaurant workers, the hospital staff, the farmers, the gym people, the daycare staff, people who can't be isolated and moved to some facility in Missouri."

"Point taken," said Colonel Dupont.

In a moment of silence, General Wolcott sat up higher in his seat and leaned forward. "I think we can all agree that the contract is terminated."

Paavo took issue with that immediately. "We've been supplying you with chemicals and gases for a decade. This problem has cropped up before and we've dealt with it."

"Not on this scale," said the general.

"Up until this month, we've delivered exactly what we've promised, on time and within budget. This problem comes from experiments that have been going on for years, with your approval and in full knowledge of the consequences."

The general backtracked. "I don't mean to say we wouldn't abide by the financial aspects of the contract ..."

"I don't see how that's possible, general," said Colonel Allen. "The payments depend partly on delivering the materiel. Research and development are a percentage of manufacturing and transportation."

"Well then." General Wolcott spoke directly to Paavo. "Can you contain the problem while still delivering the goods?"

"Without question," said Paavo. "But what I want to emphasize is the tremendous benefit of this research. The possibility of winning a victory over our enemies without killing, without bombing and widespread destruction, without firing a shot, could fundamentally change the nature of warfare."

"Am I missing something?" Farago interrupted. "There's still an epidemic to be dealt with, and it's not going away. As I understand it, you now have 3 floors devoted to patients suffering from major eye problems and related conditions."

"Some can be released," said Dr. Nordheim. "And we've already made plans to move the others to an army facility."

"What about the ones who tried to escape?" asked Faoud.

"They're in a secure nursing home in New Jersey," said Colonel Allen. "We can transfer them to any facility you designate."

"How are they doing?" asked Faoud.

"Most tried to escape again. One succeeded. The others are under guard."

"Out of curiosity, was it the girl from Arizona?"

"I'll have to check," said Colonel Allen. "I think so."

"This is interesting but beside the point," said Farago. "How do we make sure this never happens again?"

"I can answer that," said Dr. Nordheim. "We think we've been able to isolate a substance that might cure these attacks or prevent them from growing worse."

"You think?" said Farago, with some hostility.

Dr. Nordheim was prepared for this. "It's tested positively but we don't know if we can make enough of it just yet. Then there's the problem of FDA approvals …"

"We can handle that," said the general.

"You don't need it for emergencies anyway." said Farago. "Where do you get this substance?"

"It comes from a very unusual source," said Dr. Nordheim.

"What's that?"

"You're not going to believe it."

"Try me."

"Hummingbird brains."

"I don't believe it."

45

25th Floor

ALICE WAS CONFLICTED about moving into her new apartment on 25. On the one hand, it was far nicer and cheaper than her old apartment in the Bronx. It had three bedrooms, kitchen appliances that she could only have dreamed about, a great view and a feeling of freshness and cleanliness. It was immensely convenient, an elevator away from schools, daycare, medical care, shopping and entertainment. It even had a consultant to help decorate her apartment since she had no interest in bringing her decrepit furniture to her new place.

On the other hand, there was the epidemic, the craziness, the possibility that the whole building would implode and they would be turned out on the streets, the presence of the army and being at the whim of an eccentric billionaire, who liked her at the moment but could shift on a dime. Also, she couldn't imagine being a waitress for the rest of her life and had no idea what role she could play in the building if she gave up her job. Her tenancy in the apartment was entirely dependent on a menial job that she didn't like.

When she rethought it, it seemed likely that she could get another job in the building, if it came to that. There were other waitress jobs, jobs in childcare, reception, ushering, even farming, although admittedly that would be torture. There was a list of jobs on the building intranet and she could qualify for a few of them. She might be able to use her connection with the Nikkanens to help.

In the end, she decided to take the apartment and begin the arduous process of moving in. To her surprise, shock almost, everybody wanted to help. Not just Katie and Ivan and the people from the cafeteria, but Heidi and Henry from the dining room, and even Minna, Mika and

Naziha from the Nikkanen family, who didn't do any of the heavy labor but made critical decisions on the placement of furniture and pictures.

It had the aura of a wedding. People brought things – dishes, silverware, appliances, place mats, tablecloths, quilts and the like. Alice was not merely grateful; she was touched. She didn't think anything that white people could do for her would reach her emotionally. But, when all the work was done, when everyone had left, and she sat across her new dining table with her mother and children, she found herself on the verge of tears. She couldn't detect any taint of patronization in everyone's gifts or demeanor. They all seemed genuine, even the Nikkanen children, who generally thought of themselves as above the rest of the world. The visit of the Nikkanens was also the first time that Katie and Ivan had seen them. They were duly impressed.

She didn't want to admit to this, but it was almost like having a real family, people who seemed to care about her, who would listen to her and not judge her. Of course, no real families were like this – it was more of a pop ideal of a real family. But still, Alice felt uncharacteristically warm.

The following day held a major surprise. It was midafternoon, after she had picked up her kids from daycare and was having a relatively quiet moment with them and her mother, and before she was due to wait on the family. The doorbell rang, which was still somewhat startling as she had never had a doorbell in the Bronx. Rather a buzzer that sometimes worked and more often not.

She opened the door to Omar and assumed he had something cruel or onerous in mind. But peeking out behind him was Tero, who was actually smiling. "You're a shape!" he said, excitedly. "I can see a shape!"

Alice was delighted. "A few weeks ago, all you could see was black."

It must have something to do with the hummingbird beaks, she thought. She wondered if Silje's sight was improving as well, without eating brains.

Tero merely wanted to *sense* Alice's new apartment, to take in its aromas and air, its noises and *feels*. He was introduced to Alice's mother, Marpessa, and to Tony and Napheesa, who allowed Tero to touch their heads and faces, their arms and shoulders, even down their bodies to their feet. They thought it was funny although Marpessa had different ideas.

"You're all negroes," said Tero. "The smell is very different from Indians from India."

"I suppose it is," said Marpessa, coldly.

"What's wrong?" said Tero. "We all have smells. I smell like a Finn."

Marpessa chuckled. "I don't know. I've never smelled a Finn before."

Omar said nothing, just oozed hostility. He had never liked Alice, liked her mother and children about the same and wanted to get out of the apartment as soon as possible.

Tero and Alice chatted briefly and amicably. Alice wondered whether Silje's vision was changing, if she saw *shapes*. "No idea," said Tero. "You'll have to ask her."

As they were leaving, Tero casually mentioned that something big was happening.

"What's that?"

"I think they're moving out all the patients."

Alice was shocked. Tay was in there, Chrystal, Joe from the garage, Gabby from daycare and the playground, numerous acquaintances were in there. "To where?" she asked.

Tero shrugged. "Your guess is as good as mine."

46

Sub-basement -1 and 36th Floor

THE NEXT DAY, a few survivors trickled out of the quarantine units on the forbidden floors. After an initial period of fuzziness, Joe Barash was left with nothing worse than a violet tint to his eyes. The other patients they released had similar conditions – discolorations, astigmatism, acute sensitivity to light, shadows around objects, floaties, minor blocks – but none of them debilitating enough to remain in quarantine. Chrystal McCabe had not emerged, nor had Tay from the soul restaurant, or Tess McAllister from the aviary.

Instead of going home to shower or rest, Joe went directly to the garage to reclaim his position as manager of the depot. The army sergeant who was supposed to have taken over had been pretty much overwhelmed by the job and was relieved, if not glad, to have Joe back. Joe's own staff had been capable enough to keep the garage working but were pleased to have the promise of normalcy returning. They were also fascinated by Joe's violet eyes.

The sergeant remained in charge of the military floors and demanded priority in loading and unloading, traffic and the perks of his personnel. Joe felt the sergeant was a disciplined assistant manager but not quite up to the job of running the whole show. But Joe had no say in the sergeant's command that all surveillance be suspended for the area of the garage operated by the military, that is everything coming and going to the forbidden floors. Once that was established, they got along. Joe took back running the garage.

On a break, he called Katie and left a message that he'd been released, had returned to the garage and wanted to see her that evening.

Amidst the normal chaos of trucks coming and going, goods loading and unloading, he noticed that the chemical container trucks in the area controlled by the army had been parked far away from the loading docks. In their place were vehicles that looked like a cross between ambulances and buses. They were bus-sized, loaded only from the rear, like ambulances, and painted a military olive. They were also without windows, except in the cab, which was separated from the rear of the vehicle by a steel mesh, like a prison van. Again, like the chemical trucks, the license plates were retracted until the vehicles had actually left the garage.

On his first evening of freedom, Joe watched three of the vehicles leaving, obviously loaded with some kind of cargo, whether equipment or people he couldn't tell at first. Although there was no surveillance permitted in the military areas, he had cameras trained on the trucks as they were leaving the garage and then it was clear that there were people inside.

Later that evening, he reconnected with Katie, not in her apartment but at Finnegan's on 36. "I think I'm a carrier," Katie explained. "You're the second person to get sick in my apartment."

Joe described the buses leaving the garage and they both assumed that the three quarantine floors were being emptied. "Where are they taking them?" Katie wondered.

"I put trackers on the buses leaving the garage," said Joe. "We'll soon find out."

There were a few other odd-eyed survivors in the coffee shop and they came over to Katie and Joe's table, since everyone knew Katie and most of them recognized Joe from quarantine.

One of them, with violet eyes like Joe's, wasn't technically a patient, but Dr. Vulin's right-hand woman Millie, who had let Katie out of the hospital.

"I see you got out okay," she said to Katie.

"Thanks to you."

"So what's happening up there?" asked one of the survivors. "We thought you'd stay with Vulin."

"He fired me," said Millie. "The soldiers told him what I was doing, letting people go and all. So I'll see if I can get work in the regular hospital. Meanwhile, everybody's leaving."

"They can't contain the epidemic?" asked Katie.

"They don't even know if it's a regular epidemic. It doesn't seem to be contagious, least not transmitted person to person. May be a reaction to some chemical in the air but they won't talk about it."

"So what will happen when everybody's out of there?"

"Nobody knows," said Millie. "I guess they'll fumigate the place."

Joe got a call on his cell. "They're in New Jersey," he announced. "In or around Fort Dix."

"The army base?" asked Millie.

"Used to be," said Joe. "Then it became a prison, then something else. I don't know what it is now."

"There's bound to be a hospital or a clinic on base," said a survivor.

After a moment of silence, Katie voiced what was on everybody's minds at that moment. "So is it time to leave this place?"

There was a chorus of hmms and maybes.

47

90th Floor

VAN GOT A call from Kimberly the next day, while on duty at the aviary.

She was back in Tucson. She had escaped from what she thought was a nursing home in New Jersey, which had been emptied of residents. The staff was entirely military.

Everybody that had been captured with her had tried to escape at one time or another, and she was very surprised to hear that she was the only one who succeeded.

"I got out of there as fast as I could," she said. "They took our cells but they didn't take our wallets."

"They let you keep your I.D. and credit cards?"

"I don't know they were thinking about it. Everything was in such a rush." She sounded breathless, as if she was still caught in the rush to escape.

"Can they trace this call?" she wanted to know. "Are they going to come after me?"

"Yes, they can trace this call," said Ivan. "And maybe they'll come after you, especially if you try to explain what happened to anybody."

Kimberly hmphed. "Of course I'm going to explain what happened to me. I'm writing it up right now and I'll post it as soon as I'm done, with a copy to the *Star*."

"I tried it from here and they blocked me," said Ivan.

"You don't understand computers," said Kimberly. "I can get around their blocks."

"Since when?"

"There's a lot of things you don't know about me," she said.

195

She didn't elaborate but asked about Katie and a few people she had met in the hospital whom Ivan didn't know. She talked about her parents (who were fine), his parents (who were fine), the church (still functioning) and several friends in common (who were fine).

As their conversation was winding down, Ivan asked if they were still a couple.

"Not if you keep working where you are. I'm not coming back."

"The whole place may come crashing down anyway," said Ivan.

"Let me know when it does."

48

61st Floor

DESPITE THE MASS move of patients from the forbidden floors to the hospital at Fort Dix, the epidemic didn't stop or even waver. New patients included Katie's sister, Annie, Faoud's wife, Aisha, Peter Fain, Ivan's boss, two security officers, Henry, the ex-model waiter, and Aaron Houdi, Katie's boss.

They were kept in the hospital quarantine section on 3 until it could be determined whether they had recovered enough to be released or had to be transferred to Fort Dix. The quarantine sections of the forbidden floors were closed. The process of fumigating them was pending until they could isolate what it was they were supposed to fumigate. They had their chemistry labs on 39 and 40 working around the clock to identify the source of the epidemic. They had a clue to ameliorating the symptoms in some chemical connected with hummingbirds but not the source of the infection.

Meanwhile, Floors 43, 44 and 45 were enclosed in a wall of foam meant to contain the unidentified pathogen, although it could clearly pass through walls and floors and possibly foam as well.

Faoud called Dr. Benjamin into his office to discuss the hummingbird situation. "Evidently, people have been stealing hummingbirds for months now, probably the people from downstairs. How many are missing, do you know?"

"There were 12 beaks in Tero's room."

"Out of how many?"

"Ivan Anderson tells me there are about 50 total. The Woodstar was taken the day he arrived and since then there are two more missing. That doesn't mean they were stolen, just that Ivan can't find them."

"Presumably stolen."

"By somebody who didn't know how valuable they could be."

"It possible they weren't taken for money," said Faoud. "More for experimentation. Our researchers seem to think their brains might be the key to curing the eye epidemic. And they're going to need more hummingbirds — they haven't specified the type, just a steady stream of them."

"We have some of the rarest hummers in the world, some that no other aviary in America has. The Woodstar we have left may be worth two million. The Leucastic pair could be as much or more."

"Yes, well we don't need those, but we may have to sacrifice some of the others. Can we get more?"

Dr. Benjamin sighed. He hated to see even a small part of the aviary depleted. "We're part of a network that spots the ones we want, or even those we don't know we want, and tries to capture them."

"What about ordinary hummingbirds? Are there dime-a-dozen birds we can get to supply the demand downstairs?"

"I suppose so. How many do they want?"

"They'd like 50 to start," said Faoud.

"Fifty! My God!"

Faoud waited a few moments for Dr. Benjamin to settle down. "Can you do it?"

Dr. Benjamin nodded. "When?"

"ASAP."

As he was leaving, Dr. Benjamin stopped. "So what was Tero doing with the birds? And who gave him the beaks?"

"Questions we should answer," said Faoud.

49

87th, 84th and 16th Floors

ALICE AND HEIDI served dinner as usual. They were handicapped by the absence of Henry, who was one of the patients taken to Fort Dix, and Horace Calhoun, the head waiter and Alice and Heidi's boss, who was taken ill but refused medical treatment and partially recovered within a few days. He still suffered from frequent flashes in his eyes and poor balance, so his usefulness as a waiter was limited to supervision.

What made it harder was the presence of the grandparents, who had returned from their time abroad. Paavo's mother, Sanni, was 82, in peak physical condition, and much more upbeat and friendlier than one would expect from knowing Paavo. Tuuli's parents, Pirkko and Jari Niinisto, 75 and 80 respectively, were much more restrained than their daughter, mostly silent and uncommunicative. They had been content to remain in France until Tuuli's accident. Now, Pirkko spent much of her time at Tuuli's bedside while Jari went to one movie after another. Their apartments were on 84, the same floor as their grandchildren and their guardians but on the other side of the building.

The theme for the evening was chosen by Silje, who unlike Tero, lived in total darkness, without even seeing "black." She opted for soft rain in the forest, which had an audio component so it was something she could hear and sense, at least in her imagination.

"How is she today?" Paavo asked Tuuli's mother. They spoke in English, for the sake of the staff and Naziha, whose Finnish had lapsed during her time in New York.

"The same," sighed Pirkko. "Not really alive."

"She should be dead," said her husband, Jari. He turned to Paavo. "Why are you keeping her like this?"

"The doctors think there's a chance," Paavo lied.

"There's always a chance," said Tero, out of the blue, to the surprise of all. This kind of optimism was so unusual in Tero that most of the table thought he was being sarcastic.

"Tero, *please*," said Minna.

"I'm not kidding. If I can see shapes now, why couldn't Mom get better?"

"And why can you see shapes now?" asked Paavo's mother, Sanni.

"Improved diet," said Tero.

"You eat the same diet as all of us," said Minna.

"He has his snacks," said Mika.

"And what would they be?" asked Minna.

"Bird shit," said Tero.

The conversation veered to other topics but Tero's answer wasn't lost on Alice. In the curious way that information got transmitted within the building, Sophie relayed the information she had gotten from Gay to Katie, who told Isha, who told someone in the cafeteria, who told Alice about hummingbird brains as a cure for blindness.

"That's ridiculous," said Alice to the anonymous *someone*.

"And furthermore, Sophie found out that praying mantises catch hummingbirds and eat their brains."

"So?"

"Have you ever seen a blind praying mantis?"

"Ah, concrete proof," said Alice.

After dinner and cleanup, Alice paid a visit to the 84th Floor, where the kids were allegedly doing their homework. Alice knocked on Tero's door, identified herself and was told to get lost. She took this as an invitation to enter and walked inside. Tero was at the piano, with his fingers at a sheet of braille music, a musical notation for the blind similar to literary braille but with its own syntax and conventions.

He stopped when Alice entered the room.

"Bird shit?" said Alice.

"That's what I said."

"Don't you mean bird brains?"

"Get out of here," said Tero, who didn't seem too annoyed.

"By the way, thanks for coming to see me when I moved in," said Alice.

"Omar made me do it."

"Yeah, right," said Alice, and left. She just wanted to register her skepticism of Tero's *birdshit* answer, not to push him to reveal more.

When she left Tero, she approached Mika, who was playing a video game next to his study materials in the common room. "Bird shit?" she asked again.

Mika smiled. He was 12, on the cusp of 13 and, like his siblings, the essence of blondness. His eyes were cloudy and the pupils were at odd angles so one was never quite sure what he was looking at. Still, he attended a regular, all-boys private school on the Upper West Side and participated in sports that didn't require athletic vision, like swimming or track (although even there he was handicapped by his lack of peripheral vision). He had reached the age where he had attached pinups to the walls of his room, mostly punk stars or multi-pierced goth girls in horrendous makeup whom he was hoping to meet someday. He smiled at Alice's mention of bird shit and admitted, "well, not exactly."

"So what does he snack on? Bird brains?"

"Not exactly," admitted Mika.

"So *what*?"

Mika hesitated. "Omar can tell you."

"Omar hates me," said Alice. "He won't tell me anything."

"Omar hates everybody," said Mika.

They talked a little more, of nothing in particular. But he seemed to enjoy her presence a little more than was comfortable. She didn't want to spend too much time with Mika as he was beginning to show signs of being attracted to her. It was nothing that he said, but what he almost said, his body language. For an adolescent, there is no such thing as an innocent flirtation. She removed herself as quickly as possible and took the elevator down to 16, which was the building's internal police precinct, hoping to speak with Captain Martin.

It was late and Roanne wasn't there. Two of her staff had succumbed to the epidemic and the only officer on duty was a large, pleasant woman who looked like a fitness instructor but was actually a math whiz moonlighting as a security guard while she studied for her Ph.D. "What can I do for you?" she asked, with a slight accent that might have been Jamaican.

"Oh, nothing," said Alice. "I was just hoping Captain Martin was around."

"Anything I can help you with?"

"I just wanted to give her some information" said Alice.

"My shift is over at 8 in the morning when Captain Martin comes in. Is there something I can tell her?"

"Just that I think I've solved the hummingbird case," said Alice.

50

89th and 90th Floors

ALICE HAD NO chance to communicate with Captain Martin, as she had other things on her agenda. A notice came the next morning to clear the building. They were going to fumigate not just the forbidden floors but the entire building. This was an enormous undertaking and the apartments, offices, restaurants, spas, gyms, shops, etc., were to be cleared in stages, starting with the forbidden floors and then the floors on either end of those floors, which included assisted living facilities for retirees and, unfortunately, Finnegan's. The fumigating agent was the creation of a chemical lab on 55 and developed by a manufacturing facility on 52. As far as anyone knew, it was some form of a gas.

Not every floor was included. The exceptions were Floors 88 to 90, the aviary and the aquarium and insect garden. These were to be sealed off to prevent the disinfectant from harming the birds, fish and insects and their food and environment. It was simply too great and too dangerous an enterprise to remove the flora and fauna of the building to other homes. There was always the possibility that everything might die but then again everything might survive, good as new. That did not include all the plants, flowers and trees that decorated most floors of the building. They were expected to die. An agonizing decision was made to spare the farms, the nursery and greenhouses on 74-77, which grew most of the vegetables for the building. If the initial fumigation for the other parts of the building didn't work, these would be sacrificed as well.

As for people, they had several choices. Some were given hotel accommodations in the city, graded by their rank in the building's hierarchy. Group homes were set up in Long Island, New Jersey and

Connecticut, many of which were catered by the building's restaurant staff. Hospital patients were transferred to Fort Dix. Seniors in assisted living or the nursing home were transferred to similar homes in New Jersey. Or, if they preferred, the residents could find their own homes or stay with relatives.

Katie wasn't scheduled for another month – she was allotted a room at a boutique hotel on 55th Street. Annie, of course, was presumably at Fort Dix. Katie was determined to visit her and, if possible, rescue her.

Alice and her mother and children were scheduled for a suite at a Marriott in midtown, not as nice as their new apartment in the building but miles above their old place in the Bronx. This was a mark of privilege, as most of the other people in low income apartments were in group homes in the suburbs.

The library would be unusable for a week and Sophie, as a professional, was given a small suite at the Plaza. The family had an entire floor at the Carlyle.

The fumigations were not supposed to be long. Residents would be inconvenienced for about a week. The schools and daycare center a few days longer, just to be certain they were completely purified. The supermarket and deli on 27 would not be fully stocked for about a week and a half. By that time, the restaurants should be back in business, the gyms and pools would be open and the building close to normal.

They had decided it was pointless to fumigate the garages and subbasements which housed the HUAV systems, storage area and the emergency shelters but then changed their minds. The garages would be sealed off for three days. Joe took a vacation in Las Vegas, winning, losing all he won and a little more, sampling the prostitutes and none the worse for wear.

There was no way an operation this size could be kept from the press. The official story was an outbreak of influenza that they were doing their best to contain within the building. Since reporters had seen the buses leaving he building, *The Post* played it up as "FLU FLIGHT." *The Times* and *News* buried it on an inside page, *CNN* aired a favorable story and interviewed Faoud, who said that the building's management was determined to act responsibly and make sure they'd nipped the infection in the bud. Several reporters had traced the sufferers to the hospital at Fort Dix but they bought the story of a necessary quarantine.

For the people in the building, who knew the flu explanation was nonsense, the question was: what were they fumigating against? Had they even identified the virus that was causing blindness and damaged eyes? Was the fumigating agent just a general, all-purpose disinfectant that they hoped would do the job? Was it specific to anything at all? Or had they actually discovered something?

Ivan experienced almost no changes from his daily routine. The hummingbirds still had to be fed, watered, protected and cared for. He still had to make nectar for hummingbird stations, supply insects for food and spider webs for nest building. He still had to make sure they were healthy, that mothers didn't abandon their nests, that their eggs were intact.

It was still a miracle to see them darting about, hovering in midair, their wings beating faster than he could see, feeding voraciously and constantly. It was astonishing to see their courtship rituals, males divebombing and performing intricate aerial maneuvers. It was fascinating to see them stop on a perch to copulate, or shut down in the evening, sleeping on a perch or hanging upside down on a branch. Ivan was still fascinated with the way they caught the light, flashing glints of emerald, sapphire, ruby, amethyst, even a dazzling, metallic rust.

He thought perhaps he was happiest watching the hummers all by himself, without having to think about his future, his past, Kimberly, his new friends in New York, or the ominous tidings from the building.

Watching a purple-throated Mountain-Gem was a totally immersive experience, complete in itself, blotting out everything but itself, an incontrovertible proof of the existence of God.

He was in his cubicle on the floor below, checking supplies on his computer, when he came across a very odd invoice that had been cc'd to him and that he probably wasn't supposed to see. Evidently somebody had ordered 50 unspecified hummingbirds from a breeder in Pennsylvania and paid $1,000 apiece for them. This was truly bizarre. He knew they hadn't been delivered to the aviary. He checked with the building's post office, message and delivery center on 22 and even called the manager of the commercial garage, a man called Joe Barash, whom he didn't know, who confirmed that no shipment of birds had been delivered to the building in his garage. Since the invoice didn't specify which hummingbirds had been delivered, he assumed they were Ruby-throated or Rufus, which would have been common in Pennsylvania and the least expensive. Also, he knew that it was illegal to buy hummingbirds without a mound of permits and paperwork, none of which was in evidence here.

Since he could find no answer to his inquiries, he ended up consulting Dr. Benjamin, who seemed older to him these days, clearly worried about the state of the building and traumatized by Tuuli's fall and the epidemic, which had depleted some of his staff.

Dr. Benjamin was puzzled. No one was supposed to know about the 50 hummingbirds. How had Ivan been copied on an invoice that was supposed to be top secret? How much could he reveal? For that matter, how much did he know?

"They're not for the aviary," he said, tentatively.

"I know that," said Ivan. "The invoice said they'd be delivered to some lab in New Jersey."

"Dr. Benjamin blew out imaginary smoke. "Yes, they've moved the research labs on 54 and 55 to the Generation Labs in the north of the state."

"I understand about the epidemic, and the need to move the chemicals they're working on, but why hummingbirds?"

"Their brains," said Dr. Benjamin. "Hummingbird brains may contain a substance that retards or even cures the blindness."

"Are they serious?" said Ivan. "How are hummingbird brains any different from regular bird brains, pigeons or sparrows?"

"I have no idea. But evidently they've found something and need the birds for their research."

"So they're going to kill 50 hummingbirds."

"I have no idea what they're going to do with them," said Dr. Benjamin. "But I imagine they'll want to extract material from their brains, which could have unfortunate side effects."

"Will they go after the birds in the aviary?"

"I won't let them."

"How will you stop them?"

Dr. Benjamin had been pondering this very question, with no solution in sight, other than quitting in protest. "How would you like my job?" he said, finally.

Ivan had also been debating whether to tell Dr. Benjamin about his attempt to bring in the press. Seeing how impotent his boss was in the face of all that was happening, he decided to come clean, aware that this could get him fired. He described his attempt to contact both the police and the press and how they seemed to have clamped down on all information about the epidemic and chemical operations within the building.

"It's called *National Security* and they can justify anything they want with that term."

"So what do we do?"

"Just do your job," said Dr. Benjamin, without much force. "We'll think of something."

51

16th Floor

ROANNE MARTIN HAD been a police officer in Massachusetts and New York for 25 years and retired, at the age of 48, as captain of a hectic but not overly dangerous precinct in Queens. Her present job, as head of security for 211A West 57th Street, was meant as a low-key sinecure where she could breeze through her remaining years in relative peace and quiet, with a few arrests to break the boredom.

She had not expected a mass epidemic, an uneasy and at times angry population, a military takeover, chaos in the hospital wards, forced transportation, and now a mass displacement of the entire population of the building, including sections she had no control over and couldn't help or protect.

With her perpetually understaffed department further weakened by the epidemic: there was no way she could cope with the demands of her job. Arranging for the evacuation of the building she would gladly have left to the military, except they wouldn't accept it. Aaron Houdi, the building manager, was in quarantine at Fort Dix and he had never gotten around to hiring an assistant manager, so a lot of the work of overseeing the building devolved on Captain Martin.

On top of this, the residents of the building were so freaked out that the bars and restaurants, the casino and the nightclub on 65, and especially Finnegan's, had been scenes of minor brawls and rampant drunkenness. The laundry services for the building had been hit particularly hard by the epidemic and the waiting time for clean towels and linens had frayed everyone's nerves, so there was actually an epidemic of stealing clean linens. The cleaning staff had been hit by the epidemic, so there were long waits for maid service, which further ruffled people's composure.

With all this going on, Alice's message to Captain Martin that she had solved the hummingbird theft didn't seem that important anymore. It was not high on her list of priorities, despite the value of the theft. Still, she was intrigued enough to contact Alice and have her come to the station the next day.

Roanne had been fully aware of Alice's special place in the building hierarchy, her relationship with Dr. Nikkanen and his children and with Faoud. She had a full dossier and album of tapes of Alice's jobs with Tay and the family, of her children in daycare, of her apartment and Omar's menacing visit on her first day. And, of course, Alice was famous throughout the building as the intimate of Mrs. Nikkanen's suicide.

Alice had started working out at the gym for non-family non-professionals on 33 and came down in her gym clothes: a black, skin-tight Capri and a striped tank top, which seemed almost too informal for a police station. "This is going to sound crazy," Alice started.

"I'm all ears."

"And it might not hold up in court."

"OK."

"But this is the story." She put it succinctly. Either Tero or Omar had discovered that hummingbird brains could counteract some of the effects of whatever had blinded Tero. Omar's girlfriend, Chloe, who worked in one of the forbidden labs, had developed (or had someone else develop) a chemical that could be in injected or sprayed into the flowers that hummingbird feed on to slow them down. When the birds were drowsy, Omar was able to catch them and feed their brains to Tero. Since Omar couldn't tell one hummingbird from another, he didn't realize that the Woodstar was particularly valuable – it was just another hummingbird. And Tero couldn't see what he was eating anyway.

"You're right, that *is* crazy," said Captain Martin.

"And it's working," said Alice. "Tero's eyesight seems to be getting better."

"That's even crazier." Captain Martin and Alice shared an amused glance. "Any proof?"

"No," said Alice. "I just thought you should know what to look for."

Captain Martin nodded, smiled and seemed to reflect for a moment. She was interrupted by an image on one of the monitors in a bank against the wall and held up a finger to Alice that she'd be right back. She flipped a switch and spoke into a microphone. "Abel, 57-07 in progress on 17." A voice responded, "I'm on it" and Captain Martin redirected her attention to Alice. "Suppose we got proof, suppose we got a full confession on tape, what then?"

"We bring in the city cops, have Omar and his girlfriend thrown in jail and send Tero to a reform school."

"*That's* gonna happen," said Captain Martin.

"Faoud asked me to find out who took the Woodstar. I've found out. Do you think he needs proof that will hold up in court?"

"No, proof that will satisfy Dr. Nikkanen. He'll take it from there."

"So how do we get proof?"

"Are you willing to wear a wire?" asked Captain Martin.

Wearing a wire – Captain Martin couldn't have come up with anything more repugnant. Everything in Alice background, with the exception of her relatively brief time modeling, ran against cooperating with the police, essentially ratting out her friends. The police were the enemy.

But this was different. She liked Captain Martin. She had come to her voluntarily, with a solution to a theft. She had been treated kindly by the building. There didn't seem to be any innate prejudice among the powers that be. She had become rather attached to the children, although she hadn't been able to reach Silje. But she definitely wanted to bash Omar.

So she agreed.

52

Fort Dix

I T WAS IMPOSSIBLE to transfer a hundred patients from a hospital in New York City to a remote asylum in the hinterlands of New Jersey without an outcry from spouses and children, parents and friends. They had been denied access to them in the city, for reasons that were more or less understandable, but transporting them to the country seemed suspicious, more than that, underhanded, criminal, something the Nazis would do to the Jews.

At the Fort Dix location, Dr. Nordheim was again in charge, officially, but there was an army colonel as co-director who made sure there was no repeat of the chaos in the quarantine sections of the building.

As a result, friends and relatives of the patients were permitted to visit only at designated times.

Katie went to see her sister two weeks before she was required to leave her apartment on the 32nd Floor and move into the 55th Street boutique hotel, where she had been given a small suite with a TV in every room, including the bathroom.

Her brother, Billy, whose internship in the IT Center on 8 was in abeyance at the moment, rented a car for the trip to New Jersey. Katie, who had lived in the city for most of her life, didn't have a driver's license and never felt she needed one, but to Billy, obtaining a license was a requirement of masculinity. A man without a license was somehow neutered.

They arrived at the gate to Fort Dix, were checked off a list by a guard and directed to the hospital, a large, unattractive building obviously designed by an army architect, with a no-frills ethos and an army budget. There was a large lawn in front, and it was still warm enough for patients and relatives to sit on the Adirondack chairs provided for them. The patients wore white robes and displayed a wide variety of eye disorders, from discoloration to fractures within the eyeball to total blindness. Although the visitors wore masks, Katie could tell one them was Faoud, visiting his wife, Aisha.

After they had checked in and were given their masks, they expected Annie to be brought out to them, so they could picnic on the lawn – they had brought a fully-stocked picnic basket along with them. Instead, a male nurse, with a grave demeanor, led them down a long hall to a quarantine ward. They passed through the ward until they came to an ICU unit, with 6 beds enclosed in thick partitions, bristling with machinery. The nurse on duty led them to Annie's chamber.

Annie was lying of the bed, intubated, hooked up to a lung machine which gasped with every artificial breath, and to various feeding and delivery tubes. She was mercifully unconscious. "What's going on?" asked Katie. "I thought people just had eye problems."

"She does," said the nurse. "She's blind."

"But …"

"The doctor will talk to you."

After 10 minutes of staring at an inert body, Katie and Billy were on the verge of springing Annie from her prison when a doctor ambled into the room. He was a tall, lanky, sandy-haired man with a laconic manner and a cowboy accent. "She got an infection," he said.

"That's it – she got an infection?" said Katie, incredulously.

"Essentially, yeah," said the doctor.

Both Katie and Billy were tempted to belt him one. Sensing this, which was not too difficult, the doctor tried to elaborate, in a bored, off-hand manner. "We got her pumped full of antibiotics and she seems to be responding, might be able to take her off the breathing tube pretty soon."

"And her eyesight?"

"It's as if someone shot out her eyes," said the doctor. "No activity in the optic nerves at all."

"No chance of recovery?" asked Billy.

The doctor shrugged. "We're operating in the dark here, no idea what's causing this – that goes for everybody here."

"I notice our sister is the only patient in the ICU," said Katie.

"Yeah, she's the worst at the moment."

"Has anyone died?"

"Some have been taken away," said the doctor. "I don't know if they're dead or alive."

"Can we transfer our sister to a hospital in the city?"

"You can try, but nobody's succeeded."

Finally, Billy had had enough. "So what are you doing here?"

"Marking time, m'boy, marking time."

53

The Forbidden Floors (37 to 52), 36th Floor, The Pierre and The Fuller ICU Center

WITH BREATHTAKING SPEED, Floors 37 to 52 had been emptied of people, furniture and equipment. The assembly lines on 50-52, mostly a single, open floor on 50 with offices and inspection stations on the higher levels, had been dismantled and carted away. The storage tanks on 44 and 45 had been emptied into tanker trucks and dispersed to their new location. The testing facilities on 47-49, the research laboratories on 39-41, the packaging machines on 37-38 had all been carried off. Where the overflow from the hospital had been housed on 43, nothing remained, not even a loose needle or a paper clip.

It had been a military operation, overseen by officers and NCO's, but carried out by workers who did not seem to be regular soldiers. Joe Barash saw them entering the garage and loading the equipment and described the scene to Katie at Finnegan's after work. "I don't think they're soldiers on duty at all," he said.

"So what are they?"

"My guess is prisoners, military prisoners. They don't have insignia, they don't goof off the way regular soldiers do, they don't joke around, they don't take breaks, they don't interact with anyone else in the garage, not even a nod or a wave. And they're working 24 hours a day. I assume they work in shifts but I get the feeling they're long shifts, like 14 or 15-hour days.

"Slave labor."

They had been drinking at the bar, which Joe preferred over tables, when the bartender, came over to them.

"Last call," he said.

214

Katie looked at her watch, which registered only 10 pm, the time when Finnegan's was just beginning to liven up. "What do you mean?" she asked.

"We're closing down," said the bartender. "I've given you a few extra minutes but that's it."

"Would've been nice if you gave us some notice," said Joe.

"It's on the door," said the bartender. "It's on every table. And we sent everyone an email."

Joe nodded. "So when are we going to see you again."

"They say it's just for a week or two, starting tomorrow. But who knows?"

"Yeah, I've got to be out of my place by next week," said Katie.

"I don't think they're doing the garage," said Joe. "Least I haven't got any notice."

"So what'll it be?" asked the bartender.

"Why don't we finish up with a single malt scotch?" said Katie.

"Glenlivit, Glenfiddich, Laphroaig or Macallan?"

"How much?" asked Joe.

"On the house," said the bartender.

"That sounds like you're closing for good," said Joe.

"Who knows?" said the bartender.

Gradually, the building was cleaned out, except for the top 3 floors, the farms and greenhouses on 74-77 and the garages and sublevel building systems, storage areas and the huge mihrab-like vault on the lowest level.

For the people who still reported to work, like Katie and Ivan, it could be lonely, as the cafeteria and restaurants, the gyms and pools, the casino, the cinemas and coffee shops were all closed.

As the family had relocated to a suite at the Carlyle, served by room service, Alice had no waitressing duties, but she still visited the children when she could, when she wasn't taking care of her own children. Fortunately, the building had opened a playground/daycare center on West 49th Street to handle the children of the building.

Teams of fumigators in Level A lime-green protective suits entered the building with huge drums of toxic gas. Katie greeted them at the door, Isha checked their I.D. and directed them to the appropriate floor. Faoud had decided that they should start with the forbidden floors, which would remain untouchable the longest, and then move on to the hospital, the nursing home and hospice. Then, the cafeteria and a few restaurants would open on a limited basis, the supermarket would start stocking up and the building would resemble a habitable environment before the residents started returning.

Faoud himself had moved to the Carlyle but kept his office at the building until the day before it was to be fumigated. Fortunately, his wife, Aisha, had left the hospital at Fort Dix with a mild violet hue in her eyeballs and joined him at the Carlyle.

For Ivan, the days were getting lonelier. Although only two of his co-workers, including Dr. Fain, his immediate boss, had succumbed to the virus, and another had left for a nature reserve on the West Coast, the aviary seemed deserted. There were no visitors now, the family was gone, there were no guests to admire the birds or flowers and no one who worked there could ignore the sense of being on the periphery of contamination, as if a nuclear device had been set off in the building below and the zone of radiation stopped just below their feet.

He was in touch with Kimberly most days but they had little to say to one another. She had found basically grunt work at the university's biology department, bearing the disapproval of her parents and her church, neither of which provided her with an alternative. He sensed that she was moving away from the church, spiritually if not physically. More and more Ivan felt that her *aura* had changed. When she related that Gene and Laura, two of their fellow parishioners, whom they had socialized with occasionally, had gone to proselytize in Cameroon, Ivan felt a tinge of disapproval in her voice, a sense of hopelessness and almost irritation. It was nothing she said, but the tone of her voice, or rather a hint of a tone.

As to their coming engagement, nuptials and life forever after, till death do them part, nothing was said. It was neither mentioned nor alluded to and Ivan had the distinct feeling that it was on some far back burner that might never light. It wasn't just Kimberly. He wasn't in the mood for it either.

Most of his co-workers at the aviary had lived in the building, so they were now in various apartments and hotels around midtown, except for the cleaning people and other nonprofessionals, who were mostly in Queens. So whatever camaraderie had flourished before was temporarily suspended. Dr. Benjamin and his wife, Fiona, had been given a suite at the Pierre and invited Ivan to dine with them at Perrine, the hotel's main restaurant, which was not on the spectrum of New York's culinary scene but served solid, respectable food, if not cuisine. They discussed hummingbird brains and the pall that had settled over the aviary in the absence of visitors. Ivan had the impression that Dr. Benjamin was depressed, not quite enough to leave the building immediately but ready to open his options.

Unfortunately, Dr. Benjamin had nothing substantive to say about hummingbird brains. Yes, he had supplied 50 hummingbirds to a new laboratory in New Jersey, but he had received no feedback from them. The lab had no name, no obvious connection with Dr. Nikkanen or the building, nothing more than a P.O. Box, not even an address. The Pennsylvania suppliers of the hummingbirds had been instructed to transfer the birds to another truck at a rural crossroads and leave.

When he talked to Faoud about the fate of the birds, he was cautioned not to inquire further. "It's a government thing," Faoud had said.

Mrs. Nikkanen had not been taken to the Fort Dix hospital with the rest of the patients. She was placed in the Fuller Center, a private hospital on the Upper East Side which specialized in hopeless cases. It was essentially a private ICU with one nurse for every three patients at every hour of the day and night. Two doctors checked in three times a day and once during the night. At the moment, the center accommodated ten living corpses.

As visitors were allowed anytime in any number, the whole Nikkanen clan except Silje and Tero spent part of their day there. Jari, Tuuli's mother, seemed to have planned her life around her visits. She frequently spent most of the day sitting by her daughter's side, staring at her for signs of life.

The most surprising visitor came only at night, usually between midnight and 3 in the morning, remaining at Tuuli's bedside for several hours. Dr. Nikkanen knew the night nurses by name. He was frequently there for the doctor's midnight rounds and showed no reaction when the doctor told him once again that there was no change, no hope for the better and that she was, for all practical purposes, dead.

"Can the bandages be removed from her face?" Paavo asked the doctor.

The doctor consulted his notes. "Well, her nose is broken, her eye sockets are smashed in, her teeth are gone, her chin ..."

"Can these be repaired?"

The doctor was taken aback by the idea, perhaps by the sheer magnitude of the restoration. "Well, I suppose, with plastic surgery ..."

"See to it," said Paavo. "Let me know when you're ready."

54

85th and 84th Floors and the Fuller Center

T HE FUMIGATION OF the building proceeded more rapidly than anyone had expected. For the most part, it met the deadline of Monday, November 13 and to the exhaustion of Joe, the garage workers and movers, everybody had either moved back or were in the process. The grocery stores were partially stocked, the cafeteria, Finnegan's and Genevieve's, Tay's (without Tay) and the ethnic restaurants were back in operation, the coffee shops were serving and the school, the daycare center, the gyms and the labs not connected with the government contract were beginning to function.

The exceptions were the hospital, the nursing home and hospice, whose patients had been transferred to the facilities at Fort Dix, which was still a hardship for visitors. The hospital on 2 and 3 had a token staff to deal with accidents and emergencies not connected with the virus.

Only the 16 forbidden floors remained empty and uninhabitable for the moment. The fumigation of these floors had been a lengthy process of cleaning and recleaning, scalding and purifying every centimeter of surface and air. When it was certain that nothing could live in the atmosphere they had created, they fumigated all over again. When the rest of the building reopened, no one had decided what to do with the floors. It was possible that Dr. Nikkanen had another project in mind that didn't including poisoning multitudes.

November 13 was also notable for another reason. It was the day a team of plastic surgeons and dentists repaired the face of Tuuli Nikkanen. It had taken several weeks to assemble the team, which included surgeons flown from France and India, to decide on the techniques they would use, to quantify endless images of Tuuli at various stages of her adult life, to plan every detail of the operation, who would do what, where and when. It was decided to repair not just her face but her entire skull and parts of her neck on either side of her breathing tube. Images of the projected restorations were presented to Dr. Nikkanen for his approval. Was the nose right? The lips? The scalp? The only thing they didn't correct were the laser eyes. Perhaps an eye surgeon could have replaced her eyes with ordinary ones but Paavo wanted to keep the tainted originals.

An undertaker used to prettifying corpses for viewing at a funeral would have probably sufficed, but Paavo wanted a more professional job. Actually, he had considered restoring her entire body but, when he thought about it, he wanted her body at age 24, when they had first met at a party in Helsinki, but that would require a more drastic reconstruction and he would know the result was artifice and not Tuuli.

On the day of Tuuli's surgery, rather than wait around in the hospital for results he couldn't possibly see, Paavo spent the day at his office, which, along with the master bedroom, dressing rooms, a sauna, several other offices and a mini-garage, took up the whole of the 85th Floor. Even though there were secretaries and assistants in the other offices, the place felt lonely, almost uninhabited. He thought of a French movie where one of the characters had an apartment so large that his girlfriend navigated it on roller skates. *That's what I need — roller skates*, he thought.

A meeting was scheduled in an hour and, since he had been briefed on the salient details, he decided to visit his eldest daughter on the floor below. There had been a teacher's conference in Silje's school, the Haley School, a private school for children who were both blind or visually impaired and gifted, which was also attended by Tero, and so Silje had the day off.

The 84th Floor was usually a busy place, since it housed his children, their caretakers, his mother and Tuuli's parents, and included a large study area, which also served as a living room. When Paavo arrived. Silje was in the open area with Apollonia, her caretaker, wearing glasses and pointing to the pages in a book.

"Hi, Daddy," she said, as soon as Paavo entered the area from a stairway between the floors.

"How ..."

"I could smell you," she said. "Everyone has a distinctive odor and I know yours by heart, even though it's changed over the years."

"Really ..."

"It might be the food," she said. "You ate more fish before we came to New York."

"Were you reading?" asked Paavo.

"It's the glasses. There's a camera on one side and when you point to an image or writing, it takes a picture and reads what it sees through a speaker in the camera."

"Remarkable," he said, and touched her shoulder. "Let's go to your room."

There was something different about Silje today, he thought. He was used to seeing her as a prototypical ethereal blind girl, soft and mythic, who might whisper prophecies or incantations, someone not of this world. But he really had very little contact with her. She might have changed, or not be that way at all.

Silje's room was stark, almost severe, with no ornamental decorations, but stocked with machines of all kinds, a large, braille computer, an audio system, a braille printer and several other machines that Paavo couldn't fathom. She had shelves of books in braille and an automated system for locating them. Her bed was a queen-sized futon and it suddenly occurred to Paavo that if she had a sleepover, they certainly shared the one futon. Perhaps Tero's vulgar innuendos were right after all. The dominating feature of the room wasn't the machines or the bed but two full-sized harps in the center. Paavo remembered her taking harp lessons before her blindness but didn't know she had continued playing.

They sat on cushions over a thick Moroccan carpet. It took them a while to adjust to the floor and to being in the presence of one another. "How long as it been since we talked together?" he said in Finnish.

"I don't think we ever talked together," she answered. "You spoke as a father talking to a daughter, which is not the same as talking together."

He smiled. "Like what are you studying in school these days?"

She returned his smile.

"So what are you studying in school these days?"

"Chemistry, physics, mathematics, poetry, history and economics."

"In high school?"

"You didn't come here to ask me about my studies," she said.

Paavo looked at his daughter and liked what he saw. Aside from her ethereal beauty, she was alert, intelligent and straight-forward, not at all like a mythic oracle. It made it easier to say what he'd come to say. "Silje, what with your mother incapacitated and our business threatened, it occurred to me ..."

"It occurred to you that if anything happened to you, I'd be next in line to inherit the company."

Paavo hadn't expected her to think so clearly. *"If* you wanted. You could share it with your siblings, or buy them out, or just give it over to Faoud to make all the decisions. Or someone else if you choose. Even without the company, you'll all be very rich."

"I do," she said.

"What?"

"I do want to run the company. The only one I might share it with is Tero, who's the sharpest of all of us. But, of course, he's only 10 years old."

"And also blind."

"He's beginning to see patterns now. I think the hummingbird extracts are doing him good."

"You know about that?"

"Of course."

"Do the others know about it?"

"Rumors have been filtering through for a while. We don't know the details."

Paavo had never really thought of his children as people rather than adjuncts of his family. He knew them as *children*, a beloved but subhuman state that he could nod to benignly, brag about, supervise, demand respect and limited obedience from, but never really *see*. He also thought of them as victims of his experiments, which he could simultaneously capitalize on and forget. But now, looking at a blind, beautiful woman of almost 17, he had to face the fact that she was possibly more capable than he had dreamed. "What else do you know?" he asked.

Silje hesitated. She could sense that a lot was of riding on her answer. "I know that your contract with the government is in trouble because of the virus."

"How do you know that I have a contract with the government. Your mother?"

"Some from her, some from research, some I figured out myself."

"Go on."

"Even if you lost the contract, you still have industrial gasses and medical gasses, which have nothing to do with what went on downstairs."

Paavo interrupted her. "I want to continue this discussion with Faoud tomorrow. When do you have school?"

"8:30 to 4."

"5 o'clock in my office."

55

The Carlyle

WHILE THE FAMILY was at the Carlyle, Alice was able to visit fairly frequently, for the boys were bored to distraction and the girls appreciated anyone from the real world. She debated whether to wear the wire Captain Martin had outfitted for her and eventually rejected it. Wearing it to betray children who more or less trusted her seemed more than a little despicable. She would have to find her proof by other means.

She made herself useful and somewhat entertaining, organizing a checkers tournament with Mika, Minna and Naziha, which Naziha won hands down. Just as they were about to wrap up for the day, Tero came by and asked if he could play.

"You need eyes, you idiot," said Mika.

"No, I don't," said Tero.

"You don't even know the game."

"Then teach it to me."

Alice and Naziha described the board, giving each square a letter and number, and explained the game. "I think I have it," said Tero.

Tero started as white and played well for a while but lost concentration in the middle of the game. He tried again, playing black and actually gave Mika a run for his money. On the third try, as white, he beat Minna.

"I could see it in my mind," he explained.

"Could you see any of it with your eyes?" asked Alice.

"I could see the vague shape of a board but no details. I had to close my eyes to play the game."

"Remarkable," said Alice. "And you haven't had a hummingbird brain in how long?"

Tero might be only 10 but he was too smart to fall for Alice's rather blatant probe. "Since the last time you got laid by my father."

Alice laughed. "Okay, I'll drop the subject. I was just wondering why you had that praying mantis statue in your room at home. They eat hummingbird brains."

"Fancy that."

"Someone told me that some chemical in hummingbird brains might improve sight, so I was just wondering ..." said Alice, wishing she'd worn her wire.

"I'll have to try it," said Tero, still toying with Alice.

Alice smiled and went off to chat with Minna, skirting, as much as possible, the lascivious gaze of Mika.

The blind children's' caretakers, Omar and Apollonia, were in evidence, but Alice had never been able to relate to either of them. As she was leaving, already at the elevator, Omar came over to her and held up a hand to pause her before she pressed the button. "Before you go ..." he said, in a hushed voice.

Alice was surprised. Omar seemed actually civil. "Yes?"

"You know my girlfriend, Chloe?"

"I've heard of her."

"She was in the research lab on 39."

"Okay."

"I can't reach her," he said. "The whole lab moved somewhere and they're not accepting calls. I don't even know where she is."

"New Jersey."

"Do you have an address?"

"No," said Alice.

Omar took a breath. It was obvious that he hated asking for help. "Well, could you find out?"

"Why should I? You've always been pretty much of a shit to me."

"Information," he said, taking no pains to sound pleasant or accommodating. "If you give me the information I want, I'll give you the information you want."

Next time, she'd be wearing a wire, she thought. She would clearly have to go through Faoud on this, if he wanted her to complete her mission of solving the Woodstar theft. "What's her full name?" she asked.

"Chloe Day."

"I'll see what I can do."

56

61ˢᵗ Floor

I N THE TIME between Alice's meeting with Omar at the Carlyle and the return of the building to near normal, Alice made several attempts to discover the whereabouts of Chloe Day. Since she feared an emphatic *no* from Faoud, which would jeopardize any further attempts, she solicited various friends in the building to see if anyone had a clue to where the forbidden floors had been relocated.

Katie was no help at all. She had been to the hospital at Fort Dix and assumed that the forbidden labs were somewhere in the area, but that was only a guess. She consulted Joe, who had been monitoring the trucks leaving the dock and noticing that they had returned to pick up more people and equipment after half a day, so it could be assumed that the new labs weren't all that far away, possibly upstate New York, New Jersey or Connecticut. That was useful information but not enough to help Omar find his girlfriend.

Isha, Sophie and Captain Martin were blind alleys and she tried to sound out the kids, but they knew nothing, except for Silje, who was unapproachable. Only Ivan had a tip worth pursuing. He knew a shipment of live hummingbirds had been delivered to a place called Generation Labs in northern New Jersey. Of course, there was no Generation Labs listed in any phonebook or business directory, except a web marketing firm in Utah, whose representative had never heard of a company with their name in New Jersey. She had Katie enlist her brother, Billy, in the search and he checked for large-scale building or remodeling permits in the area but these were mostly legitimate businesses, malls, factories that could be identified and confirmed.

What Billy was looking for was under the radar. Presumably, the scientists and workers involved in the government project weren't prisoners. Like the patients at Fort Dix, they had spouses and relatives who would want to get in touch with them and presumably they had some means of contacting them. They wouldn't use Facebook or Twitter or any of the easily traceable social media. There must be some sort of private channel that couldn't be accessed by the general public. But why hadn't Chloe Day used it? Why should she be completely incommunicado?

Billy had friends who were dedicated hackers and they managed to pinpoint a stream of communication coming from the Northwest corner of New Jersey, not far from where New Jersey, New York and Pennsylvania meet, just South of a town called Matamorus, Pennsylvania, near the northern edge of High Point State Park, a ski resort. The communications were on a government frequency known to the hackers but they couldn't penetrate it, unless they could find somebody they had contacted. If someone was trying to contact Omar, they could trace that to its source. But Omar had insisted that he hadn't heard anything from Chloe since the move. So perhaps she was not attempting to contact him. Or couldn't. Or wouldn't.

Eventually, Alice felt armed with enough information to approach Faoud. He wasn't easy to reach as he seemed to spend much of his time away from the building, sometimes for days at a time. His wife, Aisha, despite major eye problems, had returned to work at the greenhouse and nurseries on 74 and when Faoud wasn't travelling, he wanted to spend as much time as possible with her.

Fortunately, she asked for a meeting at exactly the right time, between trips and obligations, less than a week after her initial request. When she entered Faoud's office, she was struck by how much older he looked. She knew he was in his early 50's but he could have been 70. The furrows in his brows had deepened and the bags beneath his eyes enlarged. Still, he brightened up when she entered and seemed glad to see her.

She explained that she had solved the hummingbird thefts but she couldn't prove it without Omar, and Omar's cooperation was dependent on finding Chloe.

"You know I can't tell you that," he said.

"You don't have to," said Alice. "I'm pretty sure I know where the labs and everything moved to."

"Really?"

"Not the address but the latitude and longitude, so it wouldn't be hard to find."

"Impressive," said Faoud, with a hint of a smile.

"What I don't know is why the people who moved, the scientists and workers, have been kept incommunicado from the rest of the world. Omar hasn't heard from her, hasn't been able to reach her and is worried sick. As much as someone like him could have an emotion."

"You don't like him."

"I think he's a complete shit but he knows what happened to the Woodstar."

"Is he a bad companion for Tero?"

"He hates Tero. But he does his job."

"Well, that's quite interesting. You know, you've become quite a valuable asset. You might be up for a premature raise."

Why was he changing the subject? Alice thought. "Well, I wouldn't turn it down but that still doesn't explain why Omar can't reach his girlfriend."

"The answer is, he *can*."

"What?"

"All she has to do is send him the password and they can communicate all they want. What's striking is that she *hasn't* sent him the password."

"I don't understand ..."

"The labs may have relocated from the building but the people who work there are free to come and go as they please. Some of them actually commute to the location; others have taken homes and apartments nearby. Chloe could even visit Omar if she wanted."

This took Alice completely by surprise. The *secret location* probably wasn't even a secret. And the people who worked there weren't prisoners or slaves. The whole thing had been blown out of proportion. She almost felt sorry for Omar. "I'm 'fraid Omar's not gonna like this," she said.

"I'm afraid not. But maybe he'll tell you about the Woodstar anyway."

57

61st Floor

FAOUD HAD REASON to look older. There were troubles in the Nikkanen empire that would have exhausted anyone. First and foremost were the ominous signs coming from Paavo Nikkanen himself. He lived in constant expectation of imminent death. While this is a more or less common symptom of ordinary anxiety, the *sine que non* of panic attacks, it was striking coming from a man of Paavo's character. The difference was he didn't fear death, there was no particular emotion connected with it, it was just an expectation, an inconvenient fact.

Faoud had worked for Paavo for 20 years, rising through the ranks of the Cairo office to become Chief Operating Officer of the whole Nikkanen company, public and private, and now Head Butler, a title that Faoud thoroughly enjoyed for its deceptiveness. In that time, they had become friends, their wives had taken to one another, although between an Egyptian and a Finn, there was a certain cultural reserve, and they maintained a four-way attraction, never consummated or even acknowledged, but definitely there. With Tuuli essentially dead, and Paavo contemplating death, Faoud felt bleak and unmoored. It was so sad to lose friends, not to mention an employer and possibly a job.

This particular anxiety ratcheted up after last Tuesday's meeting with Paavo and Silje. It looked like Paavo was grooming Silje for his job if anything happened to him. True, Silje was the eldest child and one of the heirs to the Nikkanen fortune. But to turn the company over to a blind teenager seemed the height of folly. In terms of experience and competence, the job probably should have gone to him, but blood trumps competence every time. He accepted that but with grave forebodings.

For the time being, the decision was only apparent. At the meeting, nothing was mentioned about Silje taking over the company, presumably being tutored by Faoud. It started out as a strategy meeting, more an exchange of dreams, how the company should proceed in the future. What surprised – actually amazed – Faoud was how much Silje knew about the company, including markets and processes that she wasn't supposed to know about. Could Paavo have been confiding in her all along? Faoud wondered.

Silje foresaw, in a soft, delicate, almost seductive voice, that their contract with the government would be cancelled and that the future of the company would rely on their industrial gases, of which they had a minute share of the market. She outlined a plan to enlarge those markets and suggested ways to use their capacities for converting toxic gases to non-lethal uses. Paavo took issue with this. He claimed the whole point of his gas was that it wasn't lethal, just debilitating. Silje was not at all put off by her father's objection but deflected it in a way that won Faoud's admiration.

"Whether it's lethal or debilitating, it's still considered a war crime," she said. "Which is why we've been conducting our operations in secret. But if the same chemical elements were merely the fallout of a conventional bomb, it wouldn't be a crime. Just something to explore."

Faoud noted that she didn't contradict her father or denigrate the validity of his vision but merely offered a possible alternative, which, if enacted, would move the company in a completely new direction.

Her tone was so mild and her manner so unaffected that it was hard to believe she could articulate a sound corporate strategy.

By the end of the meeting, nothing had been decided, nothing had even been planned, but it was clear that this was a test of Silje's corporate character and that she had passed with flying colors. Faoud felt less insecure about the future of the company, but not secure either. Silje was still 16, almost 17, not yet in possession of a high school diploma, and blind. He hoped Paavo had years remaining.

There were a host of other worries. Aside from the patients at Fort Dix and the empty floors of the building, he had reports from 30 offices to digest, some of which would need immediate action from him, Paavo or various other officers of the company. Probably the most time consuming was recruiting. HR would suffice for the lower levels, but top executives within the company would need his approval and sometimes Paavo's. Not a day went by when he wasn't interviewing someone somewhere.

At the local level, HR was lining up candidates to replace Aaron Houdi, the building manager, who was still at Fort Dix and had indicated that he did not expect to return. Replacing him would be difficult – someone with management skills fluent with the details of laundry, leases, cleanup, security, tenants, plumbing, the restaurants, gyms, endless permits, HUAC systems, electricians, able to field complaints with aplomb and respond to emergencies immediately. When he thought of all the talented people who worked at the building – people like Katie, Isha, Joe in the garage, Sophie, Captain Martin, dozens of others – no one came to mind. He would have to act soon – too many details were piling up in the slow return to normalcy. Aaron's assistant, Heejoo Kim, a short, stocky, 38-year old woman who was always smiling, was filling in while they searched for a replacement.

While the toxic gasses were still being produced in the building and distributed to various government installations, Faoud was kept out of the loop by executive fiat, even though he'd helped develop those gasses in Finland and elsewhere. Paavo didn't want him involved as long as they were in the building, possibly because Faoud could plead ignorance to any suspect activities in the building. But since the strategy meeting with the military, and now that the operation had been transferred to Generation Labs, he'd been brought in to coordinate the activities in New Jersey with the rest of the world.

He didn't quite know what that was supposed to mean – *coordinate*. It had been left to his discretion how much information from New Jersey could be shared with the rest of the Nikkanen companies, but it was tricky, as much of the information was classified but not all. Whatever he did, however, he would now keep Silje informed and had arranged an unhackable link with her computer and phone.

58

84th Floor

FTER SERVING DINNER on Sunday, Alice paid a visit to the children's floor. She had meant to meet with Omar and actually saw him guiding Tero to his bedroom from the common room, which was unusual because Tero could easily do it on his own. Alice and Omar acknowledged one another and were about to talk when Apollonia Bax came out and summoned Alice to Silje's room.

This was a first. Silje had never evinced any interest in Alice, aside from appreciating her efforts with her siblings and her comforting presence at difficult times, like their mother's accident.

Apollonia was somewhat of a mystery to the family. She rarely interacted with anyone other than Silje. At mealtimes, she ushered Silje into the dining room but took her meals in the common room on 84. She was English, spoke with an upper-class accent and seemed to have no friends, other than Silje. Tero was sure they were lovers but then he suspected Silje of being lovers with every woman. He imagined threesomes with Naziha.

"Why does she want to see me?" Alice asked.

"Curiosity, I suppose," said Apollonia, in a soft, distant voice.

"The curiosity is mutual," said Alice, opening the door to Silje's room.

"She's here," said Apollonia to Silje. "Shall I go?"

"No, stay," said Silje.

Alice had never been in Silje's room and was impressed by the size and starkness of the room, as fully equipped as Tero's. She was surprised to see the two harps in the center, among the machines and bedroom furniture.

"Hi," said Alice.

"Hi."

"I didn't know you played."

"We both do," said Silje. "That's why there are two harps."

"Do you ever play with Tero?"

"Not yet. It's difficult with both of us being blind. I play with Polly."

"Polly?"

"She's the only person in the world who calls me that," said Apollonia.

"She studied at the Royal College of Music."

"Is that supposed to mean something to me?" said Alice.

"You're supposed to be impressed," said Apollonia.

"Is that why I'm here?" asked Alice, a little more abruptly than she would have liked.

"Exactly why *are* you here?" asked Silje, equally as abrupt.

Alice realized there was more to this meeting than curiosity but she had no idea what it was. Possibly an interview for something. "It was Faoud's idea," she said.

"Yes, I know," said Silje. "He wanted to get an unbiased opinion on what was going on with us, especially what Tero knows about the Esmeralda Woodstar." Her tone was matter-of-fact, with no trace of hostility or suspicion.

"That about covers it."

"And what have you learned?"

Alice decided she trusted Silje. There was more to her than she suspected – she was definitely not where Alice supposed she was: in the clouds – and it would be useless to hide anything from her. "I believe Tero got Omar to catch hummingbirds so he could extract their brains. He had heard that hummingbird brains could cure his blindness."

Silje smiled and motioned Alice to sit down beside them on the cushions in a seating nook. It was difficult not to be dazzled by the surface of Silje, all that beauty and blondness packaged in a slender, dancer's body. But what struck Alice more was Silje's grace, her unassertive manner, the kindness of her glance, the softness of her voice. When they were seated, she took Alice's hand and said, "Thank you so much for opening up about that. I appreciate it. Now, let's talk about what else you've discovered."

Slowly, she led Alice into sharing her feelings about the rest of the family. She agreed with Alice's glowing assessment of Tero as a genius and laughed at Alice's brief description of Mika as one who had hit puberty head-on. "And what do they think of me?" asked Silje.

"I don't know about Minna and Naziha, but the boys think you're a lesbian."

"With who?"

"You, for one," said Alice, nodding to Apollonia. "But Tero thinks you also sleep with your Indian friend, possibly Naziha, possibly others. He thinks you're totally promiscuous. Wishful thinking if you ask me."

"Interesting," said Silje, revealing nothing.

She steered the conversation to the building, the virus, various people she had befriended, the theories about the toxic chemical, her father and mother. "Do you think she was insane?"

"Well, asking me to kill her husband, crushing a venomous spider in her hand and throwing herself off a walkway 90 feet in the air doesn't seem especially sane," said Alice.

"Those are actions. Do you think she was insane?"

Alice thought about this a moment. She realized she was being tested on her insight, on being able to see beneath a surface. True, Tuuli's actions were *crazy* but it was a studied craziness. At no point did she seem out of control. Crushing a spider to make a point, or even throwing herself off a walkway as an act of protest, was excessive, unbalanced perhaps, but with full knowledge of their effects. Her mind was *there* and she was in direct command of it. "No," she answered. "She was sane."

Silje nodded and seemed to come to a decision, which she didn't reveal. Gracefully, she let Alice know that the interview was over for the time being and thanked her for being so straightforward.

She had spent nearly an hour with Silje and Apollonia. When she left, Omar was waiting outside. Evidently, he'd been waiting for nearly that long.

"Well?" he said, as soon as Alice emerged.

59

84th Floor

LTHOUGH ALICE HAD come to the 84th Floor specifically to speak to Omar, his presence immediately after her interview with Silje threw her off momentarily. She wasn't prepared to deliver bad news to Omar and endure his disappointment and hostility. Still, there he was, right outside Silje's door. There was no avoiding him.

"Let's go to your room," she said.

Omar's room was adjacent to Tero's, so he could be on call at a moment's notice. It was almost like an antechamber to Tero's area, though somewhat larger and had a door connecting the two rooms.

Alice didn't know what she expected Omar's room to be like, but she wasn't prepared for austerity. It felt like a monk's cell, although it did have a window, a closet and an adjoining bathroom. But everything about the room was bleak – a single bed, table and chair, no bookshelves, no equipment, no TV or stereo, no decorations – the walls were bare, a single, white shade covered the window. The one thing she never expected to see was a prayer rug, rolled up against the wall. "Do you pray?" she asked.

"That's none of your business," he answered.

Alice shrugged. "Could I bring you something to brighten up your room?" she said. "A plant to put on your windowsill?"

There was no response.

"Something to make the place a little more cheerful? This room is death warmed over."

"That's the way I like it," he said.

He gestured for her to sit on the chair, while he sat on the edge of the bed, leaning towards her. He seemed uncharacteristically nervous. "Did you find out anything?" he said.

"Yes."

"Where is Chloe?'"

"Generation Labs, just South of Matamorus, a small town in Pennsylvania."

"Where the fuck is that?"

"In the northwest corner of the state, near where New Jersey, New York and Pennsylvania meet, just above High Point State Park."

"Do you have the address?"

"There isn't one. It doesn't seem to be in a town, just in the middle of nowhere, on the Jersey side of the border with Pennsylvania."

"Wait a minute." He went to a drawer in his desk and took out a pad and pencil. "Tell me again."

She repeated the area details, spelled out M-A-T-A-M-O-R-U-S, and asked if he had a laptop or smart phone so she could show him the location. He gave her his phone; she punched in the area and showed him the approximate location on Google Maps.

"How do I get there?"

She realized that Omar was living in an alternate world, without a clue about the modern world. His only service to Tero must have been his eyes, not his opinions or advice. "You rent a car," she said. "Do you have a license?"

Again, he shook his head.

"I'll give you the information you want if you drive me there," he said.

"I don't have a license either."

"I have some friends; they'll take me. We'll need a plan."

"Why?" asked Alice. What on earth was he thinking?

"We need to break her out of there."

Alice wanted to laugh but thought better of it. She had always thought Omar was a seriously disturbed man but now she was sure. "She's not being held prisoner."

"She can't get out, can she?"

"Anytime she wants. Most of the people who work there live nearby. There are no walls or guards. It's a laboratory."

"Then why hasn't she contacted me? Why can't I reach her?"

"You can. She just has to send you her number or email and give you the new passwords."

Omar went blank for a moment, unable to process this information. "Say that again."

"If Chloe wants to reach you, she can call you on the phone or email you. If she wants you to reach her, she has to give you a password for the new laboratory in New Jersey."

Again, Omar went blank to process this explanation. "Then why hasn't she sent me the password?"

"That I can't tell you."

They spent a few moments in what could be called pregnant silence. Omar stood up, his face darkening, then turning blank again. "Does that mean she doesn't want to reach me?"

Alice shrugged. "Could be."

He began pacing the floor. "This doesn't make sense," he muttered. Then he breathed out something in what she guessed was Arabic that sounded bitter.

"What does that mean?"

He turned on her. "It means get the fuck out of my room."

"You promised me information."

"I said get the fuck out of my room."

Alice stood up, not the least bit intimidated by Omar's anger. "I can see why she doesn't want to contact you," she said, and left the room.

60

85th Floor

ON TUESDAY AT 2, Paavo held a meeting in his office on 85. In attendance were Faoud, Gunther Nordheim, who headed the toxic project, Mary Chen, head of the chemical lab on 54, Sam Chance, head of the hospital on 2 and 3, Eamon (Whit) Whitaker, Paavo's personal lawyer, Ron Avery, head of Global Human Resources, Heejoo Kim, the woman who was temporarily in charge of the building until they could find a replacement for Alan Houdi, several serious officials that no one knew except that they were important and not Americans, and Silje, guided by Apollonia.

They were seated at the round table in the conference section of his office, nursing their coffee, tea or water, presumably having had lunch. It was gray outside and threatening to rain. New Jersey was visible only in outline and the George Washington Bridge not at all. The group was surrounded in gray until Paavo pushed a button and switched on the overhead lights, which made everyone blink.

Paavo indicated Silje. "Most of you know my daughter, Silje. She'll be part of every meeting from now on. She went blind from the experiments we conducted in Finland 5 years ago. The woman with her is Apollonia Bax, whose function is to be Silje's eyes."

Several people muttered *hello* or *good afternoon* in Silje's direction, not expecting her to recognize their voices. "Please go around the table and introduce yourselves so I'll be able to place a voice with a person," said Silje, in a voice that was strikingly composed, almost commanding. The effect was stunning. Everyone expected a blind teenager, slight and celestial, to listen in silence, to absorb the meeting instead of participating. Yet she had used her blindness to initiate the

239

proceedings. She thanked everyone for the introductions and nodded to her father.

"Most of you know some of what this meeting is about," Paavo started. "Without beating about the bush, we have to prepare to lose our contract with the government."

"Is that certain?" asked a man with a foreign accent, possibly Scandinavian.

"It's certain but not official," said Paavo. "We've had to stop research on Agent 1498 ..."

"What's that?" asked Dr. Chen.

"I'm sorry, Mary, we've had to keep you out of the loop on that," said Paavo. "That's the latest version of a gas we've been working on for the past 10 years, first in Finland, then here."

"I assumed that's what it was. I didn't know the name."

Betraying no emotion, Paavo told the meeting that the project he'd been working on for the past decade had come to an end. The gas was uncontrollable. "We thought we'd capped a lid on it after the disaster to my family but our precautions obviously didn't work."

Generation Labs in New Jersey would be closing down. Of the teams of scientists who had been working on the project, some would be let go, some would take early retirement, but most would be returning to 211A and reassigned to other projects, working for Dr. Chen or Dr. Nordheim. The people involved in manufacturing and marketing the products would return to 211A to work on other projects.

"What other projects?" asked a handsome, well-dressed woman who had flown in from Amsterdam for this meeting.

Gunther Nordheim responded. "Medical gases – purified air, instrument air, oxygen, carbon dioxide, nitrogen, various types of anesthetics ... we'll have a full medical department."

"We have that in Finland," said Silje. Nobody expected her to speak at the meeting. Nobody considered her a factor in the Nikkanen enterprises. How much did she know? How deeply had she been briefed? How much had her father trusted her, behind people's backs? This was their first glimpse of a new Nikkanen mind. "We have that in France, Hungary, Denmark, Germany, the Netherlands and a dozen other countries," said Silje. "We even have a medical gases factory in Nevada. What are you not telling us?"

Dr. Nordheim was not prepared to answer her. He looked at Paavo for permission to reveal more. It was not given.

"Different gases," he said. "To fill out our offerings."

To Silje and most of the other participants at the meeting, this was a highly unsatisfactory answer. She turned to Paavo. "What is the purpose of this meeting, Father?"

Paavo seemed pleased with the question. "Just to give everyone an overview of what's happening, not to go into details."

If Silje had working eyes, she would have rolled them. "Has the virus broken out at Generation Labs?" she asked.

"Yes," said Paavo. "Three people have been infected. "They're in the hospital on 3."

"Not Fort Dix?"

Sam Chance, director of the hospital on 2 and 3, answered the question. "We're moving the people from Fort Dix to here. Most of them don't need a hospital at this point, although a few are still in the ICU."

"What about the ones that are completely blind?"

"We'll take care of them here or wherever their families want."

The group was silent for a moment, pondering the significance of that answer, financially, morally and legally. Then Faoud asked a question to both Paavo and Dr. Nordheim. "We know that research is going on about a possible cure for the virus – Dr. Benjamin at the aviary supplied birds for the experiments – is there any progress on that front?"

Dr. Nordheim sighed and then shrugged. "Not much," he admitted. "We're working on the cure but we haven't figured out the cause."

Silje interrupted. "My younger brother, Tero, who was completely blinded by the virus at the same time as I was, seems to be improving. Have you consulted him?"

Faoud answered. "Alice has a theory that may be helpful."

"Who's Alice," asked Dr. Nordheim.

"A woman I recruited to be a companion to Dr. Nikkanen's children, except for Silje. A woman who works for you is aware of this."

"Who?"

"Chloe Day."

"She's in the hospital downstairs, fully blind at the moment."

Discussion of the virus was a diversion from the main purpose of the meeting but it let people take a break and refill their drinks. When they returned to the table, Paavo took over.

He had prepared a new corporate structure for the company, with Directors for various divisions in Europe, Asia/Pacific, North and South America, and the Middle East/Africa, most of whom were at the meeting. There were various worldwide directors – finance, worldwide marketing, general counsel, communications, engineering, research, IT, and so on, and a new Chief Operating Officer, Hans von Bissingen, an Austrian aristocrat who had just been recruited from Siemens and had not yet reported for work. These were listed on a chart projected on a screen and on a paper that Whit handed out around the table, which elicited obvious expressions of approval, dismay and surprise. Under the Directors and global officers were the national presidents who were too numerous for the chart and were unknown outside their division.

At the top of this far-flung enterprise was Paavo, of course, as Chairman, and Faoud, as Chief Executive Officer (as well as Head Butler, a title he preferred but which was not listed in the chart). The major surprise on the chart was the inclusion of Silje in a direct line from Paavo but not connected with any other officer. Her name was on the same level as Faoud but isolated, undefined, somewhere in the corporate ether.

The woman from Amsterdam, who had been named head of the European Division, picked up on this immediately. "May I ask, what is Miss Nikkanen's title?"

"Heir," said Paavo, silencing any further discussion.

(This also served to remind them that Nikkanen was a private company, owned by one person and not beholden to stockholders or a board of directors.)

The meeting continued with a working lunch and brief presentations from Faoud, Dr. Nordheim and from the directors of the five divisions, which consisted basically of introductions and general projections. The purpose seemed more social than informational.

When the meeting was over, close to 4, and everyone had filed out of the room, to reconvene that evening for a feast at Genevieve's on 62, the building's fanciest restaurant (at which Alice and Heidi were serving this evening), only Paavo, Faoud and Silje remained. Faoud was exhausted – he found large meetings incredibly tiresome. Silje was fresh, alert and seemed somewhat excited by the proceedings. But Paavo was in a strange, distracted state, as if the whole meeting and the people involved were a diversion from something more important.

Silje broke through. "One thing has been on my mind," she said.

"What's that, Kani?" This was a Finnish nickname that Paavo had initiated when Silje was 2. It meant "rabbit."

"All our other factories and labs are located far away from urban areas, which makes sense because we're dealing with dangerous chemicals. But for the most toxic of all our products, one that had gotten out of control once and could again, you chose the center of New York City, one of the most densely populated areas in the world."

"The very same question I asked 5 years ago," said Faoud.

Paavo smiled and shook his head, as if the answer should have been obvious. "Only Tuuli understood."

When this clearly perplexed Silje and Faoud, he gave another, small, distant smile. "See you at dinner."

61

60th Floor

IVAN HAD TAKEN to using the interdenominational chapel on 60 almost daily. On Sundays, he attended the service and took communion from Father Pekonen. He felt the ritual and prayers kept his head straight during the heady days of the virus, the sickening and blinding of so many friends, including Kimberly, and the general sense of malaise everyone felt in the building.

He had felt particularly unsettled the day before most of the people in the aviary were about to break for Thanksgiving. Dr. Benjamin and his family had already left for Vermont. Peter Fain, who had fully recovered from the virus, and his latest boyfriend, were headed for Provincetown on Cape Cod. Tess McAllister, who had also recovered but with a sand-colored tint in her eyes, was taking the time off but wasn't telling anyone where she was going. Ivan and a few other ornithologist's assistants were holding down the fort.

That evening, after work, he called his parents to confirm that he couldn't be home for the holidays. He tried Kimberly but only reached her voicemail. He was having dinner by himself in the cafeteria when she returned the call.

Shortly after speaking with her, he went to the chapel and sat in the pew, trying to digest what had just happened. Fortunately, Dr. Pekonen happened to pass by and noticed Ivan looking suspiciously shell-shocked. They retired to Dr. Pekonen's office and took seats in the plush easy chairs around the oak coffee table.

"What happened?" asked Dr. Pekonen. "Perhaps something to do with your job?"

Ivan smiled at this, since both knew it was something entirely different. But it broke the ice.

"Your fiancé," said Father Pekonen.

Ivan nodded.

"She was the one who visited you and got the virus. Is she still in the hospital?"

"No, she's home in Tucson now. It's a long story."

"I have time."

Ivan recounted Kimberly's attempted escape from the quarantine ward on 43, her abduction to a house in New Jersey and her eventual escape and return home. He recounted how Kimberly had told him she was going to go public with the story of the virus and that she would never return to New York under any circumstances. If they got married, she would never live in New York. So as long as I held my job in the aviary, we would never be a couple.

"All this is meaningless background, of course," said Ivan.

"Why meaningless?"

"Because she turned out to be an entirely different person from the girl I was engaged to, or almost engaged to."

Dr. Pekonen waited, remembering how disturbed Ivan had been when they first met, how horrified he was when he thought he had betrayed Kimberly, how he had gotten drunk at a party for the first time, passed out and awakened next to a naked woman, how they had discussed the ethical consequences of an assumed but not confirmed betrayal. When Ivan didn't elaborate, Dr. Pekonen spoke up. "From what you told me before, you had both vowed to remain chaste until marriage. Have you broken that vow?"

"No."

"Has *she*?"

"Worse."

Dr. Pekonen raised his eyes. He didn't share Ivan's views on the importance of chastity. But from Ivan's perspective, what could be worse than his fiancé's renunciation of their vows? "How so?"

Ivan couldn't understand why he was having so much trouble talking about it. The story was so unlikely, so preposterous that to blurt it out in public would almost seem to burst its validity. Nevertheless, he persevered. "Her parents kicked her out. She's sharing a little apartment in downtown Tucson."

Father Pekonen waited for details.

"She broke from the church. She's not going anymore."

"Alright."

"She said we had never been engaged and we won't be. She was tired of that game. She was tired of being manipulated by gibberish."

"Is that how she put it?"

"Yes."

Well put, Father Pikonen thought. *If misguided.* "So the bride who had been chosen by both sets of parents lost her faith and bolted," he said.

"No, that's not it. Or only part of it."

"What?"

Ivan seemed unusually reluctant to respond and actually spent a few moments debating whether to answer at all. "She was cold over the phone. I think she told me just to get under my skin."

"Told you what?"

"I really don't like to talk about things like that. I don't understand how a person can be one thing all her life … I don't see how a person can live by one set of principles … and then all of a sudden reject them … for no reason."

"One can lose one's faith in an instant. And get it back just as quickly."

"She rejected God, she rejected her church, she rejected her family, she rejected everything she lived for, everything *we* lived for."

Father Pekonen waited for the real reason for Ivan's shock to be revealed. He didn't think it was her loss of faith.

"We've never *ever* talked about bodily functions," Ivan went on. "But just now she told me she missed her period. I didn't know what that meant at first."

"It meant she could be pregnant," said Dr. Pekonen, who had not expected this development. "Did she take a test?"

"Yes."

"And?"

"She said it showed positive but those tests aren't always reliable. So she's going to a doctor next week."

"I'm sorry, Ivan. I know she meant a lot to you."

"It's like my future going up in flames."

"One part of it perhaps. But it's just as well you didn't get married. Imagine having this renunciation after you were married and had a child. By the way, who's the father?"

"That's the worst of it. She doesn't know."

62

3rd Floor and the Moran apartment

FOR THE MORAN family, this was the best Thanksgiving of all. Their daughter, Annie, had been taken off the ICU at Fort Dix, breathing on her own, and transferred to the hospital on 3. Within a few days, she could sit up, eat solid food and, more importantly she could see a sliver of light. What were the whites of her eyes were almost black, except for a band across both eyes, which allowed her a slim range of vision. But vision, nonetheless. On November 23, she was discharged from the hospital, just in time for the Thanksgiving weekend with her family.

Annie, Katie and Billy's parents lived on the Lower East Side within a few blocks of where their ancestors had lived when they first came to America in 1870. Peggy and Mike Moran lived in the neighborhood out of principle. They believed in the working man and the nobility of the proletariat. Both Mike and Peggy's grandparents had been communists in the 30's, their parents had been active in union and city politics and, although both Mike and Peggy had graduated from C.C.N.Y. and held professional jobs, they felt the Lower East Side was where they belonged.

As soon as Annie had been transferred out of the building to Fort Dix, and visitors were finally allowed, either Mike or Peggy had been out to see her on a daily basis, even when there was nothing to see but a body hooked up to tubes.

Their apartment on the Lower East Side was in a gentrified tenement and fairly spacious, taking up two floors of a building that looked run-down from the outside. They had actually bought the building in the 60's and slowly renovated it, taking two floors for themselves. The rest they refused to rent – the very thought of being *landlords* was viscerally abhorrent to them – but donated the floors to the Democratic Party, to use as they saw fit.

Every year from the time they were old enough to leave the nest, all three children returned for Thanksgiving dinner, to dine with their friends and relatives in what invariably turned out to be a huge feast and a monster pain. The relatives didn't always get along, there were old grudges in new guises, husbands and wives new to the family sometimes felt alienated by the boisterous ways of an Irish family in a celebratory mood, and there was way too much drinking.

The latest guest truly didn't belong and felt continually on the defensive throughout the whole dinner. Ivan had been invited at the last minute by Katie, who had heard about Kimberly and felt sorry for Ivan, especially having to spend Thanksgiving alone. Ivan surprised himself by accepting. He certainly didn't want to be pitied. He was fully prepared to deal with loneliness, but he had gradually gotten to like Katie and was no longer embarrassed by the incident in her apartment, so he allowed himself to be persuaded.

He was introduced around as the "hummingbird man" and everyone he spoke to was surprised that hummingbird aviaries actually existed.

"Yes, aside from ours, which is not specific to hummers, there are big, exclusive aviaries in Tucson and San Diego, smaller ones in Florida and Texas, Washington D.C. ... I read that Boston bred some Costas ..." The patience of his listeners was usually exhausted by that time.

The guests were more interested in the building, but Katie had the most interesting gossip on that front. "The scoop is, the blind daughter is taking over the building, maybe the whole company."

"How old is she?" asked a guest.

"16."

"Where did you hear this?" asked Annie, who was just beginning to get back in the building loop.

"There was a big international meeting," Katie explained. "All the top brass from the various Nikkanen companies around the world. And Silje, the blind daughter, had been invited to attend, according to Isha.

"That doesn't mean she's taking over anything," said Annie.

"True, but then Alice told me that Silje had interviewed her."

"For what?"

"Alice didn't know. But it was definitely an interview and she said that Silje was sharp, sharper than she'd ever expected."

"That's not proof of anything."

"No," said Katie. "But she also said that sometimes Dr. Nikkanen didn't show up for dinner, and when he did, he was distracted and didn't care about anything. His mother is back and his wife's parents are back and he almost didn't interact with them at all, even less with the kids. Alice said that Silje seemed to be the one everybody looked to."

"All hearsay."

"Yes."

Katie's father, Mike, cornered Ivan after the dinner. He'd had quite a bit to drink and recommended Tullamore Dew to Ivan. "It's like mother's milk to me."

"What is it?" asked Ivan.

"What, never heard of Tullamore Dew? Where've you been around all your life?"

"My parents don't drink."

This seemed to shock Mike, who was red-cheeked from the afternoon's excesses. "In Gaelic we call it *Uisce Beatha*, water of life."

"Whiskey?"

"*Irish* Whiskey, comes in a crock, a little more complex than Jameson I find."

"I've never tried whiskey. I like beer though."

Mike nodded, as if this was important information. "Well now, the great Irish beer is Guinness, of course, but I prefer some of the heavy Belgian brews, like Corsendonk."

"I've never tried those," said Ivan, wondering where this conversation was going, if anywhere.

"Katie tells me you're a practicing Christian," said Mike, abruptly changing the subject.

Ivan was fairly certain Katie's father would bring up the subject of his virginity, it seemed to have gone viral. "Yes, I am."

"I'm a practicing atheist myself, raised my kids to the faith."

Now he's going to try to convert me, thought Ivan. He'll tell me how silly my religion is, how unreasonable, how cruel – he'll probably bring up the Crusades or the Inquisition – that's what everybody does. But Katie's father surprised him.

"But I admire people like you. Katie tells me you're a good person, kind-hearted, with a real love for your birds, for doing right by people, for being good even when your religion tells you to be bad."

"My religion never tells me that."

"Stoning adulterers, or people who work on the Sabbath, selling your children into slavery, smashing the heads of the children of your enemies against the stones …"

"Yes, that's in the Bible, but not in my religion," said Ivan.

Mike smiled. "A good answer. I hear you need a girlfriend."

It had been only two days since his conversation with Kimberly. "Is it all over the internet now?" he said, disbelievingly.

"Well, you're too good for Katie, and too young anyway, but you might be right for Annie. She's a good person, bright, attractive, and she can see out of slits in her eyes."

Ivan had no idea what to make of this. Was he offering Annie to him? For marriage? For something else. He decided to make light of it.

"But she's named after a tugboat."

Mike laughed. "I admit, that's a problem. But she likes you."

This was a total surprise. True, he had seen her almost every day on his way to work, before the virus. And they had enjoyed a nice banter. But it had never gone farther than this. He had never even thought about it. "She likes me?"

"She's attracted to you. And you're the kind of person who wouldn't be put off by her eyes."

"That's true, but …"

"And one other thing: she loves hummingbirds, can't get enough of them. You're perfect."

63

84th Floor

ON THE MONDAY after Thanksgiving, Dr. Nikkanen called everyone in to the common room of 84, including his mother, his wife's parents, all the children and their caretakers, Faoud and several other people who were known to be close to Tuuli, like Dr. Aniashvili, the director of the insect garden, and Dr. Cavanaugh, the family doctor. An ancient, beloved former cleaning lady was there in a wheelchair, along with an even older Finnish lady, and several current domestics. For reasons that eluded her, Alice was also invited.

The room was packed, the elders sat on chairs, the rest on the floor. This was the first time a group like this had ever assembled, but it was not hard to see it was devoted to Tuuli. "Is she dead already?" asked Mika, who had wriggled next to Alice. She shrugged and inched away from him.

"I hope so," said Minna. "I hate to see her lying there, half dead half alive."

"99% dead, 1% alive," said Tero.

Silje was not sitting on a floor with the other children but in a chair next to Faoud, a juxtaposition that did not go unnoticed. "Why is Silje up there?" asked Naziha to no one in particular.

"She's been promoted," said Tero.

"From what to what?"

"Child to adult."

Apollonia stood behind Silje, with her hands on the back of Silje's chair, sometimes on her shoulder, whispering the identities of everyone in the room. When she didn't know one, Faoud chipped in. "That's Helvi Malkki, remember her?"

"Mom's nurse back in Finland? I didn't know she was still alive."

"She's very old now. We'll talk to her after."

There was a buzz in the room as everyone waited for the entrance of Dr. Nikkanen, who was already 15 minutes late.

Omar sidled up to Alice and whispered in her ear. "I have to see you later."

"Have you seen Chloe?"

"Yes."

"How is she?"

"Eyes like Minna, violet, a little darker, but okay."

Even before Dr. Nikkanen entered the room, the buzz softened and stilled, as if people could sense his incipient presence. He came in through the elevator, accompanied by a gray-haired, lightly bearded man, probably in his 60's, who was dressed in a beautifully tailored suit but looked sloppy nonetheless. Paavo himself was dressed casually, in an open sports shirt, jacket and beige pants, but looked gaunt, possibly ill. He gestured for the gray-haired man to take the seat in front of the group. He remained standing.

Paavo started by introducing his guest. "This is Dr. Stavros Lountoura, the director of the Fuller Center on East 61st Street."

The man half rose from his seat and nodded.

"As most of you know, this is a private ICU center, where my wife is on life support, thanks to a breathing tube in her neck, a feeding tube in her arm and another tube to keep her hydrated. So many of her bones were broken in her fall from the top of the aviary that I didn't think it worthwhile to reset them. Since then, I've had a change of heart and had many of them reset, so her body looks more or less normal. There are attendants at the Center who massage her limbs so they don't become atrophied."

This made most of the audience uncomfortable and there was much shifting of position. Why was he going into these details? many of them wondered.

"When she fell, she landed on her front and her face was badly disfigured, her nose and eye sockets crushed, her teeth knocked out and her chin pulverized. Since then, I've had a team of surgeons and dentists reconstructing her face, with very positive results."

By now, most of the audience was aghast, if not sickened. *Was he enjoying this*, thought Alice.

"Many of you have visited her, in various stages. But you never really saw my wife. You saw a form in bandages, a lump that breathed, with tubes sticking out of it.

"The doctors have told me there's no hope. She will never wake up, she will never breath on her own, she will never walk or talk or have any sentient life, she's functionally brain dead. This is not just the opinion of a few doctors but a certainty from every doctor who's examined her. She's beyond miracles. She can't hear us or sense us. There's nothing to resurrect."

At this point, everyone knew what to expect.

"So I've decided to pull the plug. There's no point drawing this out any longer. I'm doing it on December 4th so you have one week to visit her and pay your last respects. Family can visit anytime but everyone else should make arrangements with Dr. Lountoura here."

Paavo hesitated for a moment, which gave several people time to stand up and raise their hands.

"I'm not taking any questions," he said, and abruptly left the room. A moment later, Faoud and Silje, guided by Apollonia, followed after him.

64

84th Floor

T HE AUDIENCE WAS stunned and took time to dissipate, although many of its members lived on the same floor. There was talk of relief and sadness, of fond recollections of a distant time and amazed memories of Tuuli in the year before her death.

Pirkko Niinisto, Tuuli's mother, who had spent part of almost every day by Tuuli's side at the ICU Center, remembered her daughter as a young teenager in Turko. "She was quite the athlete, that's what she lived for."

"What was her sport?" asked Mika.

"Pole vaulting," said Pirkko. "Which takes the strength of a weightlifter and the agility of a gymnast."

"She named me after a pole vaulter," said Minna.

"Yes, the national champion at the time," said Pirkko. "But Tuuli was also an organizer and an advocate for the athletes at the university. Which is where she met Paavo."

Pirkko was a youthful 75 and had been an athlete herself. She had the slim figure of a woman half her age but wrinkles that were age-appropriate. Her formerly blond hair had slowly lightened to gray but her eyebrows and lashes retained their blond tint. By any accounts, she was a handsome woman and what Tuuli might have been. "She was such a beautiful girl," she said, "but not like Silje and you, Minna. Harder, with sharper features, more angular, but like you and Silje, gorgeous. She had many admirers."

"Lovers?" asked Tero.

"Don't be vulgar," she snapped, but with a smile.

Around the room, others were reminiscing and Pirkko, her husband and Paavo's mother gravitated to Helvi Malkki, Tuuli's nurse in Finland, who spoke minimal English and felt somewhat uncomfortable in the society of her wealthy American *family.*

Eventually, Omar escorted Tero to his room and came out to look for Alice, who was reminiscing with George Aniashvili, the director of the insect garden, about the spider incident.

She introduced him to Omar and the three of them chatted for a while, although Omar was pretty much of a monosyllabic chatterer. Finally, Dr. Aniashvili drifted off and Alice took Omar to a corner of the common room, where they could talk without being overheard.

"You've found Chloe," said Alice. "What do you have for me?"

"I gave my word not to tell."

Alice rolled her eyes. "Does that mean anything to you?"

"It does when my job depends on it."

"You also promised to give me some fucking information."

"Calm down," said Omar. "I'm getting to it."

"I'm calm." She shouldn't have expected that Omar would be trustworthy.

"Tomorrow night, around 10 o'clock, have someone come to the aviary, maybe that kid who takes care of the hummingbirds ..."

"Ivan?"

"Whatever his name is. He should stay out of sight. We'll be right outside the pavilion. He can bring binocs but he can't take a picture with a flash or a loud click. Nobody must know he's there."

"Why? What's gonna happen?"

"I can't tell you that. Just have someone there at 10, maybe a quarter to. Well hidden."

"So why can't I go myself?"

"It needs to be somebody who has access to the aviary and an excuse to be there, just in case."

"Is that the only window of opportunity? Tomorrow night at 10?"

Omar exhaled in disgust. "I'm doing you a big fucking favor."

"Okay, I'll try to get someone."

"That hummingbird man would be perfect."

"He might not do it. He's got morals."

"I'll leave that up to you."

65

89th Floor

EARLIER THAT DAY, the Monday after Thanksgiving, Ivan showed up for work on the 89th Floor and was pleased to see that Annie was at the receptionist's desk. She was cheerful as ever but it was strange to see her black eyes, with a light band across them which allowed her to peer out, like looking through a slat in a shade.

"You're back," said Ivan, who hadn't seen her since his conversation with her father on Thanksgiving.

"Thank God," said Annie. "I was going crazy doing nothing."

"Do you remember most of it? You were in the ICU for quite a while."

"I don't remember that part of it, but afterwards. By the way, my father thinks I should marry you and have your babies."

Ivan laughed. "Yes, I got that impression, too."

"He thinks my eyes make it impossible to catch someone who doesn't work in the building and isn't used to eyes like mine. He may have a point."

"I don't think so. You're really very attractive anyway."

Annie hmphed. "*Very attractive.* Is that a compliment or an insult?"

Ivan was confused for a moment and then said, "Neither, I'm just stating a fact."

Annie laughed. "Alright, I'll let you buy me a drink at Finnegan's tonight. I don't think we'll mesh – we're on opposite sides of the moral spectrum. But at least we can tell my father we tried."

Ivan seemed to go along with it, by his lack of expression.

"And by the way, Dr. Benjamin wants to see you."

Over the year, Ivan had established a friendly relationship with Dr. Benjamin and entered his office without trepidation. He was curious, however, about the fate of his hummingbirds, if he was to be required to sacrifice one in the interests of science, or perhaps find an outlet for the wholesale sacrifice of anonymous hummers.

Dr. Benjamin was as jovial as ever and extended a fat hand. "Pretty wild these days, eh?"

Ivan noticed that the screen behind his desk, which documented every bird in the aviary, had 6 sections blinking, two more than usual. Dr. Benjamin noticed him looking and explained, "Two of our Scarlet Ibises died, our Keel-billed Toucan, *Ramphastos sulfuratus*, two of our parrots and our Fawn-breasted Bowerbird, *Chlamydera cerviniventris*. Such a shame."

"From the virus?"

"No, none of our birds have been affected by that. Just nature taking its course. We'll try to replace them."

"I imagine that won't be easy with the Toucan and the Bowerbird."

Dr. Benjamin chuckled. "We can get them online. Not a problem if you know where to look. Anyway, that's not why you're here."

"If you'd like to know the status of the hummingbirds, I can have a report on your desk by tomorrow morning."

"I'm sure they're in good hands. How much do you know about the other birds in the aviary?"

Ivan had tried to stay abreast of what was there but his devotion to the hummingbirds was, if not exclusive, at least single-minded. "Not much," he said.

Dr. Benjamin nodded. "As you know, Dr. Fain, your immediate superior, is not returning after he finishes recuperating from the virus. He's going to the National Aviary in Pittsburgh."

Ivan hadn't seen Dr. Fain for nearly a month, so he wasn't surprised. "That's a great aviary but I'll miss him."

"Tess McAllister is filling in for him while we find a replacement. You'll report to her for the time being, although I think that'll be just a formality."

"Is she fully recovered?" asked Ivan.

"She got the fever but not the eye problems," said Dr. Benjamin.

"Her specialty is water birds. I don't think she knows that much about hummers," said Ivan, who could envision having to educate Tess, or rather Dr. McAllister, on every aspect of hummingbird peculiarity.

"That not why I asked you here. What I'd like to know is if you're interested in a career in ornithology."

"*Am* I? That's my dream."

"Good. I'd like you to learn about all the birds in the aviary, not just the hummers. I'd like you to get an advanced degree in ornithology from some college in the area – I think Fordham has a program, C.C.N.Y., maybe Columbia, N.Y.U., although I don't know if they all have night programs – you'll still be working here. Actually, I hear you can get a degree online – you'll have to check it out.

Ivan was about to comment but Dr. Benjamin interrupted him. "Not to worry, the building will pay for it. No, you don't have to thank me." Dr. Benjamin seemed to be enjoying himself. It was always fun to be the bearer of good news. "And I think you'll find a little extra in your paycheck. Now you can thank me."

"Thank you."

Ivan went to work that day wondering how Tess would take to his new assignment but it turned out she knew about it already and was happy about it. "My specialty was water birds, yours is hummingbirds, so we'll learn about the others together."

Since she had taken Dr. Fain's place during his illness, and only spent a few days in the hospital herself, she had a head start on the entire aviary population and had reams of information, links and articles Ivan could consult.

After he had finished his hummingbird duties, he spent most of the day wandering around, sometimes with Tess, sometimes with others, identifying the birds, noting their behavior and seeing how they were cared for by the other ornithologists and assistants.

At the end of the day, he cleaned up on the floor below, and found Annie waiting for him at Dr. Benjamin's reception area. As most workers in the building dressed casually (except for the domestics, who wore the building blue), Annie was in tight slacks and a man's shirt, opened just enough to show a suggestion of a white bra. Ivan found it overly provocative (as it was meant to be) but said nothing.

As they were heading for Finnegan's on 36, Alice was on her way to the same place. She had assumed Ivan would be in the aviary or in his cubicle on the floor below but rather than make a trip for nothing, went down to the lobby and had Isha locate him. Since everyone who had an implant could be located immediately, she knew Ivan was in the elevator and had gotten off at 36. As she entered the elevator, she reflected that she was so glad she hadn't gotten an implant and couldn't be located unless she wanted it. Of course, that wasn't strictly true, as there were cameras everywhere throughout the building, but at least she could get away from them if she felt like it.

Annie and Ivan took a table in the back and ordered drinks, which came with peanuts and snack food, with chicken wings, mini-pizzas and shrimp handed out by a traveling waitress.

They made small talk for the first few minutes, commenting on the slight changes in the décor after the bar had reopened. Neither had the slightest inkling that they might be compatible but that made it easier to talk.

"You said before that we were on opposite sides of the moral spectrum," said Ivan. "What did you mean by that?"

The question amused Annie. "Shouldn't that be obvious?"

"Not to me."

"Well, to start. You're a virgin and I'm not. You're saved and I'm fallen."

"That doesn't mean you can't be saved," said Ivan, smiling because he knew he wouldn't be taken seriously.

"It's not just that I'm sexual," said Annie, "I'm bisexual, trisexual, actually polysexual, since New York recognizes 31 different sexes and I'd probably fuck all of them. I'm into things you'd find disgusting and degrading – oral, anal, various fetishes, practices you'd find too heretical to even think about. I know my sister wanted to deflower you for fun, but I'd eat you up. I'd go after your soul."

"But aside from that," said Ivan, laughing.

"There's more," said Annie, also laughing. "I can't stand religion, any religion, not just yours. I find it ridiculous, Jesus means as much to me as a dishrag, the Bible has some pretty stories most of which never happened, and the god of Israel – don't get me started on that."

"What about hummingbirds? Your father said you liked them."

"He told me to say I liked hummingbirds so you'd be interested in me and we'd get married and have babies."

"I admit, that's a shock. So you *don't* like hummingbirds?"

"They're cute, yes, I like them, but I prefer vultures."

Ivan realized that most of what Annie said, if not all of it, was just to tease him, and he found it enjoyable. "So it doesn't look like we're totally compatible."

"On the other hand, I like you."

"More than vultures?"

"I don't know, I suppose it depends on the vulture."

They chatted amiably for another few minutes. To Ivan's surprise, Annie was not studying to be a physicist, she was an undergraduate at Columbia, having taken a few years off after high school to follow a boyfriend to Ireland and Greece. Ivan talked about expanding his role in the aviary and going to grad school. It was at this point that Alice came into the room and broke up the date.

She pulled over a chair to Annie and Ivan's table and seated herself. "Sorry to break up your little romance," she said, "but we have a hummingbird emergency."

66

89th and 90th Floors

I T WASN'T HARD to convince Ivan to hide out in the aviary that night, once Alice explained that he could solve the mystery of the Esmeraldas Woodstar.

Alice explained to him that he might see another hummingbird being captured by Omar and the absolute necessity of keeping quiet and doing nothing to stop it. She expected Omar to pierce its skull with some kind of implement and feed its brain to Tero.

"That is unbelievably disgusting," said Ivan.

"Yes, it is. But if Tero believes its brain can restore his sight ..."

Ivan nodded that he understood.

"And it seems to be working," said Alice. "His sight is undeniably getting better."

"Yes, that's why Dr. Benjamin imported 50 hummingbirds for research on their brains."

"I didn't know that."

They discussed the details of tonight's intelligence gathering. Did Ivan have a cell phone? Was it charged? Did he know how to take videos? Did he know how to work the zoom feature? Since there were no longer any drugged flowers, where would he be likely to find a hummingbird? For that matter, did hummingbirds sleep?

"Yes, they sleep," said Ivan. "There are several nests near the pavilion. He could go after a Broad-Billed or a Tufted Coquette. I just hope he doesn't grab one of the Leucistics – they're so rare and they're within reach."

"And what if he did?" asked Alice. "Could you keep quiet and just video it?"

"I hope so."

They discussed where Ivan might hide, how near he'd have to be, did he have any black clothes, anything with a hood?

"I have an idea," said Ivan. "Why don't you come with me? If anything goes wrong with my phone, we'd have a backup from yours."

"I don't have a reason to be there – it might alert security. I have to serve dinner anyway."

It was 7 o'clock. Alice went off to serve dinner to the family while Ivan rushed home to get dressed. He had black jeans and a black turtleneck but he only had one hoodie and that was olive. Then he remembered a detachable hood from his black winter parka. He grabbed that and hurried back to prepare.

It was almost 8 when he arrived back at his office on 89. He checked his phone and practiced taking videos. Then he plugged it in to charge it and turned to the phone Alice had lent him. It was a later model than Ivan's but seemed to work the same way. He practiced with her video ap and then plugged it in to be fully charged.

It was nearly 9 by the time the cleaning crew had left the aviary. He could hear them speaking some Slavic language, Polish perhaps or Serbian or Croatian, as they replaced their equipment. He was on nodding terms with them, as he often spent late evenings in the aviary, but he didn't want to be seen by them tonight. They didn't use the lockers and changing rooms but they always spent some time in the bathrooms.

It was another 20 minutes before the last of them left the floor and by then both phones registered 100% charged and he was ready to leave.

The escalator that led to the aviary had been turned off for the night so Ivan climbed the steps to the heavy flaps that separated the aviary from the outside world. He knew that his entrance would awaken some of the birds but they would soon calm down.

As he entered the aviary there was an immediate squawk from one of the birds near the entrance but that was it. The aviary was dark but not black. The moon and lights of the city shone through the dome and there were exit lights and reflections from the dome on the rocks and streamlets, so it was easy to find the place he had chosen without using the light from his phone.

He had picked a spot in the midst of a clump of bushes off the main pathways but which gave him an unimpeded view of the pavilion and the areas nearby. Unfortunately, the area was marshy and he resigned himself to being wet for the next hour or so.

He knew there was a Broad Billed nest not far from the pavilion but it would take an expert to see it. It looked like a bump on the branch in the daytime and at night it was almost invisible. He could see a spectacular Tufted Croquette who appeared to be dead. When hummingbirds sleep, they go into a kind of hibernation, where their metabolism, their body temperature and heart beat lowers drastically. They don't seem to be breathing but they're really sleeping.

Scanning the area, Ivan was horrified to see a rare Leucistic Hummingbird hanging upside down from a branch, within easy reach of the pavilion. It was solid white, except for its black eyes, bill and feet (which distinguished it from a true albino, which had a pink eyes, bill and feet) and often slept hanging from a branch.

That's the one that Omar will go for thought Ivan. He wondered if he should move it while there was still time. But that might jeopardize the whole operation, as the bird would awaken in a fury and go dive bombing after anyone nearby. Of course, it was possible to move it without awakening it – most hummingbirds were deep sleepers – but he couldn't take the chance.

The aviary wasn't entirely quiet. He was thankful that the hum of the HUAC system, and the occasional squawks and rustlings, would mask any noise that he would make taking the video and moving about for a better view. There were also noises from the city, sirens, horns, planes flying overhead that would make it even less likely to be overheard.

He settled in, not at all enjoying the moisture seeping through his jeans and socks, into his shoes. The lights in the pavilion were turned off. He looked at his watch and wondered how long he would have to wait. 9:35. This was going to be an ordeal.

He let his mind wander, first to Kimberly. How could he have been so wrong about her? How could he have not seen it, seen an inclination, seen anything? He must be the innocent everybody thought he was.

What must Kimberly's parents have thought? What did his own parents think? Did they know about it? And why was Kimberly so stupid to get herself pregnant in the first place? Unless she wanted it.

Or perhaps she fell in love with somebody and wanted to show her commitment. She never mentioned this over the phone.

But for a man, why was it so important to remain a virgin before marriage? Why was it so important for *him*? He could sleep with a woman in a heartbeat. Katie offered. Annie wanted his soul as well as his body. There were others in the building who had made no secret of wanting to deflower him. His status as an eligible virgin was well known.

But although he found both the Moran sisters attractive, he didn't want to be tutored by an expert. He wanted somebody who shared his values, somebody *pure*. Why was purity so important? He didn't know, it just was. Why go out of his way to make himself uncomfortable – just to feel *with it*, macho, popular? He was never going to be an alpha male and didn't want to be. If he was going to have a passion, let it be for God, or hummingbirds.

Of course, hummingbird males were utterly promiscuous. They'd find a willing female, have sex and then fly off to find another female. Come to think of it, the females might have several partners themselves.

The time passed agonizingly slowly. His mind shifted to the hymns he loved, and the teachings that gave his life meaning. The stories of Jacob and Daniel, David and Noah, the Sermon on the Mount, the Passion. What did it matter if the stories didn't happen exactly as the Bible chronicled them? The important thing was they were *his* myths, *his* culture, they were part of him. In this respect, faith was more important than reason.

What about love? Could he fall in love with a woman of experience? Well, he supposed it was possible. But what he wanted was Kimberly before her fall. Did that exist? Was he to be fooled every time?

He went on and on in this vein until he sensed, rather than saw, a new presence in the aviary. Instantly, he went on the alert.

He switched on his phone, hit camera mode and focused on the pavilion. Soon two people came out slowly, stealthily and Ivan set his camera phone to video. He found his hand was shaking and he willed it to stop. He had never seen Omar or Tero before but Alice had told him what to look for, a stocky, swarthy man of 30 with short, red hair leading a blind blond boy of 10.

This was not exactly what he saw. The man, presumably Omar, was closer to his height and he was not leading the boy, presumably Tero, who looked older than 10. The boy was coming out to the pavilion on his own but shakily, as if he wasn't quite sure where he was going. They were whispering but Ivan couldn't make out what they were saying given the hum of the HUAC system.

They reached the end of the pavilion, where it met one of the pathways into the aviary proper. As Ivan videoed him, Omar searched around the perimeter of the aviary. Ivan prayed he wouldn't notice the Leucistic, which was on a branch not far from where Omar was looking, blatant, obvious, impossible to miss.

Ivan shuddered as he saw Omar grow taut and his eyes hone in on the tiny white hummingbird, hanging upside down. Omar was smiling and said something to Tero. The blond boy reached back and offered Omar a butterfly net but Omar refused. Ivan thought he could see Omar mouthing the words, "I don't need it."

Ivan knew the Leucistic had no chance. Its deep sleep left it vulnerable to any predator who could reach it. Omar crept up to it like a villain in an old-time melodrama, with slow, silent steps, and his arms outstretched. Ever so slowly, he reached the branch and cupped his hands around the snowy white hummingbird, who remained in deep hibernation.

Ivan cringed and had to make every effort to still his hands as Omar plucked the bird from its perch and held it within his cupped hands. The Leucistic never stirred; it was still asleep.

Quickly but carefully, Omar moved back to the pavilion, holding his prize. So far, Ivan had a perfect view for his camera phone.

Omar handed the bird to Tero who held it in his hands for less than a second and suddenly, in one horrifying gesture, shoved the bird in his mouth, feet first, and clamped his teeth down on the bird's head, crushing its skull.

Rivulets of blood appeared at both sides of Tero's mouth as he continued to mash down on the bird's skull. He pulled out the beak, chewed the rest of the Leucistic to a pulp and swallowed it in stages, spitting out bits of feather as he went.

Even Omar was horrified at the sight, although he must have seen it many times before. To Ivan the scene was utterly unreal, like a slash of nightmare severing his mind. Even though he knew it was going to happen, it was so unexpected that it was impossible to compute at first. When his mind adjusted, he was relieved to see that he had kept his camera trained on the sight. He zoomed in slightly on Tero's face.

Within a few seconds, Tero had eaten the bird and wiped the blood away. He gave a shudder and pulled the bird's black feet from his mouth. He tossed them into the aviary and wrinkled his face to show how disgusting it was. Ivan caught every nuance.

Ivan kept the camera on them until they had left the pavilion. He crept out of his hiding place, moved toward the pavilion and focused the camera on the two black feet Tero had pulled out of his mouth. Evidently, he had taken the beak with him.

67

32nd, 61st and 85th Floors

BY 11 O'CLOCK that evening, Ivan had given his phone to Billy Moran to transfer the video to a permanent file and also onto a CD that could be viewed in a larger format.

At 11:30, the group that normally met in the cafeteria – Ivan, Alice, the Moran sisters, José from Security, Sophie and Alan from the hospital, with the addition of Billy – convened in Katie and Annie's apartment on 32 to view the video on their 65" monitor.

As could have been predicted, there was universal horror at the scene, particularly at the closeup of Tero's face while chewing the hummingbird. It was made even more horrifying by the audio component, which had captured the faint mash mash of Tero's chewing.

When the video was done and everybody's breathing had returned to normal, they viewed it a second time.

"How could he stand it?" asked Annie.

"How could he get it down?" said Sophie. "The feathers ..."

"And why didn't he throw up?" added Katie.

"You'd be surprised what people can swallow," said Alan. "When I was a resident, we once had a teenager who'd swallowed a flash drive because he thought he'd remember everything on the drive. Course, he was high at the time."

"I have to get this to Captain Martin," said José.

"Have her meet us at Faoud's," said Alice. "I'm supposed to report directly to Faoud."

"Will anybody be reachable at this hour?" asked Katie.

They got Faoud out of bed. He'd been nursing a cold and had retired early, with the help of a Nyquil, so he was groggy when he came to the phone. But when he learned what the call was about, his torpor faded. "Meet me at my office in 10 minutes."

Captain Martin was reached at her apartment on 32, which she shared with a woman who worked at the nursing home on 59. She was awake but slightly tipsy. However, when she was told they had definite proof of who had stolen the Woodstar and what had happened to it, she sobered up immediately.

Alice and Ivan, José and Captain Martin waited outside Faoud's office on 61 for the Head Butler to appear. He showed up in a heavy sweater with a scarf around his neck.

He was completely quiet as he viewed the tape. He showed no horror or discomfort and wrapped his scarf around him with a shiver. "Well done," he said to Alice and Ivan.

"How many people know about this?" asked Captain Martin.

"Just us, Katie Moran, the greeter in the lobby, her sister, Annie, Dr. Benjamin's receptionist, Sophie, the librarian, and Alan Graff, a doctor at the hospital. Oh, and Billy Moran, who downloaded the tape. He works part time in the IT Center on 8. They've all been told to keep it under wraps."

"That's 10 in all," said Captain Martin. "Even if no one speaks, people will know about late night meetings."

"I'll have to report another hummingbird missing to Dr. Benjamin." said Ivan "Actually, not just another hummingbird, but a Leucistic, one of the star attractions of our collection. I don't know about dollar value but I think it's just as rare as the Woodstar."

"So everyone who works in the aviary will know it's missing first thing in the morning," said Captain Martin. "It'll be all over the building by noon."

Faoud nodded but his mind was elsewhere. "So it's not just the brains but it could be somewhere else in the bird," he mused.

"What?"

"The reason Tero's beginning to see. It's possible we've been on the wrong track."

"Is it worth waking up Dr. Nikkanen?" asked Captain Martin.

Faoud looked as his watch. "I suppose so," he said, sleepily.

It was nearly 2 in the morning when the group gathered at Dr. Nikkanen's office on 85. Surprisingly, Silje was with him, and Apollonia. The lights of the city, the street lamps punctuating the vast darkness of Central Park, the sparkling crisscross of streets and avenues up to the purple lights outlining the George Washington Bridge were still bewitching at this hour.

Alice ran the video, with Apollonia describing it to Silje in a semi-whisper.

Paavo viewed it with a wry smile on his face and a grunt, seemingly in approval. He turned to Silje. "So we were right about Tero," he said.

"So it seems," she replied.

"I'm just sorry it had to be a Leucistic – that's a major loss. Can it be replaced?"

"We had the only pair in captivity," said Ivan. "There was another for sale on the internet but it looked sickly, and it might have been a fake."

"I was thinking of the research on hummingbird brains," said Faoud. "We may have to expand the search."

"Yes, of course, let's do that," said Paavo.

Silje turned to Apollonia. "Maybe you'll be out of a job," she said, gently.

"I hope," said Apollonia.

"Where is the hummingbird keeper?" asked Silje.

"Right here," said Ivan. "My name is Ivan Anderson."

"Well, Ivan, it doesn't seem to matter what kind of hummingbird Tero eats. It's whatever Omar can catch, and he hasn't the slightest idea of what's valuable."

"We think Omar's girlfriend came up with a chemical that made them easier to catch," said Ivan.

"Mustafa," she addressed Faoud, to the surprise of everyone who never realized Faoud had a first name, "let's keep Tero supplied with cheap hummingbirds until we can synthesize the cure."

"Dr. Benjamin has a good source," said Faoud.

Ivan was aghast. "Are we just going to let him eat hummingbirds? They're some of nature's most magical creatures."

"Are you saying I should accept being blind when there's a cure available?" asked Silje, sharply.

"Of course not," Ivan answered, chastened.

"I don't have the stomach to do what Tero does, but if there's a way out of my blindness, I'm going to take it."

What struck everybody more and more forcefully was that Silje, the soft, ethereal blonde, was actually in control of the meeting. Even Dr. Nikkanen and Faoud deferred to her. In body language alone, they sat back in their chairs while Silje leaned forward with absolute assurance.

"Since there's no way we can keep this secret," Silje continued. "we might as well be open about it and if any blind person wants to emulate Tero, we'll give them however many hummingbirds they need. We don't want a run on the aviary. Meanwhile, we'll continue with our research."

Everyone nodded in agreement, whether they agreed or not. The meeting was over. Alice said she'd make a copy of the tape for Silje. Faoud went back to his cold. As the group were leaving, Silje called out, "Is Ivan still here?"

"Yes, ma'am."

"It couldn't have been easy to lie in wait without moving and take a video of someone eating one of nature's most magical creatures. You did well."

As Ivan and the rest of the group left, Alice heard Dr. Nikkanen sigh.

"I'm so tired of this," he said to Silje.

"I know, papa."

68

7th and 85th Floors

O N WEDNESDAY MORNING, before the lunch hour rush but when many workers were taking a coffee break, a man whom nobody had ever seen before entered the cafeteria on 7. He was very blond, handsome, probably in his late 50's and looked a little lost. He picked a donut from the bakery case and seemed to have trouble pouring himself a paper cup of coffee, as if he had never before used the machine and had to figure out how it worked. He paid with the transponder implanted in his hand.

He took a table for two on one side of the room, took a sip of his coffee and got up to search for the sugar station. Back at his table, he stirred in a packet of sugar, sipped his coffee and took small bites of his donut, as if he was trying to draw out his break as long as possible. He seemed to be engaged in serious people watching.

He was a striking man but people were too polite to pay much attention to him. The cafeteria was not the venue of choice for people who were likely to know him.

A group of Bosnian men from housekeeping were taking an early lunch and, as they passed by the man's table, one of them stopped and stared for a fraction of a second, then moved on.

Shortly before noon, the lunch crowd began in earnest, but the man hadn't even finished his coffee, which was surely cold. He seemed fascinated by the onrush of people, listening intently to snippets of conversation and occasionally smiling to himself.

Ivan entered the cafeteria, loaded up his tray and set out looking for a friendly table. He spotted one of the interns at the aviary and headed in his direction when he passed the blond man's table and stopped. "Dr. Nikkanen?"

Paavo refocused his gaze from the general to the particular. "Yes?"

"I'm Ivan Anderson, from the aviary."

"Oh yes, you're the one who took the video of my son. I met you last night."

Ivan nodded and wasn't sure whether to smile and stay or move on. After a moment's pause, he said, "Did you want to be alone?"

Paavo pointed to the chair on the other side of the table. They sat for a moment in silence. Ivan felt diffident about taking a bite of his sandwich before Dr. Nikkanen had taken another bite of his donut.

"I've never been here before," said Paavo. "I helped plan it, I okayed the blueprints, I paid for it, but I've never seen it."

"As cafeterias go, it's pretty good," said Ivan.

"Is it?"

The tables were beginning to fill up. The cafeteria crowd were mostly lower level or part time workers, people in a hurry, or people like Ivan who didn't really want to mix with his peers at the moment.

"All these people work for me," Paavo mused. "I feed them, clothe them, give them shelter and I was hoping to give them more."

"More?" Ivan finally took a bite of his sandwich.

"It doesn't matter now."

Paavo gazed around the room, creating an awkward silence.

"I could tell everybody in the room, "you're fired" and they would have to go off somewhere, their lives would be upended, they'd be scrambling to find work, some would get sick, some would die, and it'd all be from my whim. I could do it right now."

"I hope you don't," said Ivan, not sure whether Dr. Nikkanen was serious.

"My wife would have done it," he said. "Did you know her?"

"She wanted my help in leaving the building. We were caught in the lobby."

Paavo smiled. "I remember hearing about that. I didn't know it was you."

"She was desperate to get away."

"She was desperate to get away from *me*."

"She told me something awful was going on in this building."

Paavo smiled again. "Well, she had a point."

There were so many things Ivan wanted to ask Dr. Nikkanen, about the building, the company, the vision that went into the building, the aviary and insect garden, the farms and small businesses, the virus and especially, the hummingbirds. Should he voice his strong dissent on killing them for science? But how were they different from laboratory rats and animals used routinely for experiments? Could he argue for the beauty and specialness of hummingbirds as opposed to rats? Would Dr. Nikkanen view him as some kind of an animal rights nut?

Unfortunately, Ivan never got a chance to ask anything at all as Paavo took a last sip of his coffee, stood up and said, "Time to go."

Ivan rose as well and was about to say something like *nice talking to you* when Paavo interrupted his intent. "Perhaps this will stay," he said, perhaps indicating the cafeteria, the building or the world.

69

85th Floor

THAT WEDNESDAY, WHEN Paavo was in the cafeteria chatting with Ivan, Silje was in her father's office on 85, sitting at his desk. She had been at her school for the blind in the morning and returned to the building for a lunch with Faoud, in her father's office.

In the waiting room outside Paavo's office, a group of candidates for various building positions was assembled. The most critical at the moment was the replacement for Aaron Houdi, the building manager.

Heejoo Kim, Aaron's assistant, had taken over the job while Aaron was in the hospital, but she was pregnant with her second child and didn't think she could handle it. She had several candidates of her own and was invited to sit in on the auditions, along with Wally Keypers, the head of HR for the building, Chrystal's boss.

After several hours, 15 candidates had been interviewed, and the four of them conferred and selected 3 possibilities, who would be re-interviewed by Heejoo and Wally. Their recommendation would have to be approved by Silje and Faoud and that was by no means a rubber stamp.

That round over with, they repeated the process for several other key positions and, by the end of the day, were down to a few personal choices for Silje. She summoned Alice to her office, just before dinner, when Alice was in her waitress uniform.

This came as a complete surprise to Alice, who had been told only that dinner would be delayed for an hour. It was slightly annoying to be pulled from her job just as she was setting up the motif for the evening, a Southwestern Desert scene, enlivened by distant lightning and the occasional slither of a Gila monster or rattle of a snake, chosen by Mika. It was Naziha who pulled her aside and escorted her down to Dr. Nikkanen's office on the 85th Floor.

"What's this about?" Alice asked.

"No idea. She hasn't confided in me since I was 12."

"When she lost her sight."

"Well, maybe a few years after."

They waited for the elevator in silence. Alice had never spent much time with Naziha. She was Silje's age and had been part of the family since her adoption at age 5 from Tunisia but she had always seemed apart from the family. Although she was quite attractive, she was short and dark, the exact opposite of the Nikkanens. She was also completely unaffected by the virus.

"Do you remember the time before you lived with Dr. Nikkanen?" Alice asked, to break the silence, but also out of curiosity, although this might have been too personal a question.

"I still speak Arabic," said Naziha.

"A 5-year old's Arabic?"

"No, I've taken Arabic classes. I can read and write. The Nikkanen's encouraged me."

"That should come in handy these days."

Naziha nodded. "I guess. Although at school, they kid me about being a terrorist, one step away from Al Qaeda."

"Really?"

"They *think* they're kidding," Naziha shrugged.

They reached the waiting room of Dr. Nikkanen's office, a comfortable antechamber with easy chairs as well as benches, a coffee machine, a rack of magazines – somewhat on the order of a doctor's office – with a cheerful, well-groomed Somali receptionist named Trudy, whom Alice had seen occasionally in the cafeteria and liked immediately. "Go right in," she said. "There's nobody else waiting."

Silje, Apollonia and Faoud were pouring over a chart as they entered. Silje was wearing the glasses that *read* written material but Apollonia still had to summarize the chart and take notes. "Who is this?" asked Silje as they approached the desk. "I recognize Naziha's step but I'm not sure of the other. Are you Alice?"

"Right."

"You can really recognize my step?" asked Naziha.

"You take short steps and one foot's heavier than the other. But more than that, there's a personal kind of music when people walk, a kind of unique rhythm – it's hard to explain."

"You never told me that before," said Naziha.

"I thought it would've freaked you out," said Silje, smiling.

"You're right, it would've."

"So why am I here?" asked Alice.

Silje, Apollonia and Faoud looked up, almost startled by what could have been Alice's abruptness, or lack of a hello or just Alice's way of announcing her presence.

"I need an assistant," said Silje. "From the time you waitressed at Tay's and put on a Southern accent to the time you kept your cool when Tero insulted you and made racist remarks, to the way you dealt with my mother when she wanted you to kill my father, to the way you carried out Mr. Faoud's assignment and befriended the kids to the way you solved the Woodstar theft, you've proven to be capable, resourceful, flexible, unflappable and able to get things done with a minimum of fuss."

"You've been keeping tabs on me all this time?"

"Please," said Silje.

"Why do you need an assistant?" asked Alice, who knew only that something major was happening.

"I need someone to interface with all the departments in the building, someone who can explain my decisions and, if necessary, enforce them."

"A hit man?"

"Not literally, but yes."

Alice stepped back, confused. This wasn't what she had expected at all. "What about your father?"

Silje was about to respond when Faoud stopped her. "I think we owe her an explanation." Silje nodded.

"Dr. Nikkanen has given control of the company, including the building, to Silje. I will be legally in control until Silje comes of age."

"Aren't you just 16?" Alice asked Silje.

"17 now."

"What about college?"

"Naziha and I will be attending Columbia next year, if Columbia cooperates, so we'll be close by. Meanwhile, Mr. Faoud is like a second father to us and we trust him completely."

"Wow, can I sit down?" said Alice, who had been standing at Silje's desk. "Let me get this straight. Dr. Nikkanen is handing control of a company worth billions to … how to put it …"

"A blind teenager," said Silje. "That's how inheritance works. But until I come of age, everything I do will have to be approved by Mr. Faoud. Your concern is just the building."

"Thinking of that, I'm not the best person for the job. Katie Moran knows the building inside and out."

"She's doing her Ph.D. thesis and having an affair with the manager of the garage. Besides, she's too nice, she's not an enforcer. You have the right mentality. I especially liked the way you said you'd beat the shit out of Mika and Tero. That was well done."

Alice smiled and essentially accepted the position, which started on the 1st of the year. Faoud explained the benefits, the salary increase, which was substantial, the right to a larger apartment, and access to virtually every nook and cranny of the building, dependent, of course, on her getting an implant in her hand.

"No fuckin way," said Alice.

But eventually, she was convinced that the benefits were worth the possibility of being controlled. "You're part of the establishment now," said Faoud.

"*Jesus*," said Alice, as she left to prepare for dinner.

70

54ᵗʰ and 40ᵗʰ Floors

MARY CHEN, THE director of a chemistry lab on 54, was the lead scientist on the hummingbird project. She felt she was not qualified for the position, as her expertise had nothing to do with what was essentially a pharmaceutical search. When she voiced her reluctance to Faoud, he simply said, "You're a great organizer. I need you to assemble a team that can solve this problem. You have *carte blanche*, an unlimited budget and no specific timetable."

"Meaning ASAP," said Mary.

"Of course," answered Faoud.

The goal was entirely pragmatic: find a cure for the blindness caused by the virus. Or, if not a cure, something that might help, that might bring back an approximation of vision. It was not important to identify the virus and describe the mechanism by which it inhibited vision, except as it would have practical results. So far, the only promising clue was Tero.

She had been briefed on Tero. Alice had showed her the tape. She had been told that Tero's sight was improving but that was not evidence. There was no way to determine how much he was improving without testing Tero personally. And no way to link that improvement with some feature of a hummingbird without some kind of scientific assessment. Unfortunately, she had been told that Tero was off limits. He would be supplied with hummingbirds through Omar, who would now pretend to have caught them.

Putting scientific method aside, Mary decided to assume that something in the body of the hummingbirds was responsible for Tero's improvement and proceed on that basis. It might be the whole bird; it might be the brain, for which there was homespun but highly questionable knowledge; it might be the heart or lungs or tongue or even the feathers. Or even the blood.

Once she had been assured by Dr. Benjamin of a steady supply of hummingbirds, she split the investigation into 5 subgroups. The first was to crush the entire bird into small capsules that could be swallowed by a patient. The other groups would mash various parts of a hummingbird into capsules and feed them to blind subjects.

Since no animals had been blinded by the virus, the only subjects were blind humans, such as Silje and Tero and the people still in the hospital. She would also test the various pills on subjects who were not completely blind but visually impaired.

Mary was diffident about the highly disagreeable task of killing and crushing some of the most beautiful creatures on earth. But everything about the task was distasteful. It was simplistic, for one. There was no attempt to isolate and analyze the chemicals responsible for combatting the virus. Because of this, there was no attempt to synthesize a cure that didn't involve hummingbirds. That would come later, Mary hoped.

The worst was the process of killing the birds and squeezing them into capsules made of gelatin. There was no alternative to pithing their brains with a needle. Gassing them might interfere with the solution. Drowning them, like the French delicacy, ortolans, drowned in Armagnac, seemed unnecessarily cruel. Pithing them was best but it had to be done by hand. At first, it was thought that they could be killed by electric shock, but that didn't always kill them. It was used to stun them before they were pithed.

The gruesome part was next. The beak and claws were removed and the corpse was put into a blender and pulverized until it was nothing but a heavy paste. The problem was there was too much liquid and they didn't want to drain the blood because the blood itself might have restorative properties. Mary's team devised a way to compress the paste of one bird into three large capsules, which should have all the properties of eating a whole hummingbird. The other teams had it easier but it was still a gruesome process.

Mary brought in specialized equipment to fashion the capsules and test them for purity. Her section on the 54th Floor was not set up to handle an operation of this magnitude, so she took over 50, one of the formerly forbidden floors, which had been used to manufacture one of the toxic gases. A sign of how important the process was that she had been able to commandeer an elevator that went only between 50 and 55. She was able to bypass any bureaucratic red tape that the government sometimes imposed on the scientific process. Her wishes seemed like laws, to be instantly complied with.

It didn't feel like science to Mary, but she wasn't complaining. If she could cure the hundred or so people who were blind or partially blind, that would make it all worthwhile.

There was only one thing that worried her, aside from not finding the cure. By executive fiat, the first patient to be given the first capsule of the whole bird would be Silje. There was no room for error.

71

The Fuller ICU Center

I T WAS MONDAY, December 4, the date Paavo had chosen to pull the plug on Tuuli. It had been a busy week, with a steady stream of mourners and the almost constant presence of Tuuli's mother, Pirkko, with or without Tuuli's father, Jari. Mika, Minna and Naziha came daily for perhaps half an hour, Silje and Tero showed up to hold their mother's hand or touch her face, both of which had been reconstructed to feel almost normal, actually slightly better than normal.

Most of the professionals in the building showed up at least once, whether they wanted to or not. For people like Dr. Benjamin or Dr. Chen, who had little to do with Tuuli, it was a professional courtesy. Dr. Aniashvili, the director of the insect garden, who had often tried to protect his charges from Tuuli, came because he had genuinely liked her, despite her craziness. Dr. Kavanaugh, the family doctor, came even though he disapproved of keeping Tuuli alive artificially when she had no chance of recovery.

Throughout the week, friends, associates and domestics showed up in a steady stream, like mourners at the body of Lenin.

Toward the end of the week, when most of the family was there, Father Pekonen gave a blessing, which Silje and Dr. Nikkanen appreciated and Tero and Mika found excruciating. Alice was there to support the family. She had no patience with religion but found the ceremony sort of quaint, so unlike the uninhibited rapture of some of her relatives who were into gospel and ecstatic Baptist sacraments.

Sophie, Katie and Annie showed up out of curiosity. They wanted to see what Mrs. Nikkanen looked like in her semi-embalmed state.

"She looks pretty good," said Katie.

"No expense spared," said Sophie.

This was correct. A team of plastic surgeons, aided by an embalmer, had done a bang-up job, not only on her face but over her entire body, including her hands and feet. What was presented to the public was her face, nestled against a cushion with her luxurious platinum hair splayed out on the pillow and over her neck, shoulders and arms, which seemed normal, and over the breathing tube in her neck, held in place by a blue cuff. The rest was covered by a sheet and thin blanket.

Ivan came on his own. He had vivid memories of trying to escape the building with Tuuli, and her request to stay with him in his room on 54th St. and share his bed. Would she really have slept with me? he wondered. Not that he would have agreed to it, but the thought intrigued him. She looked quite beautiful lying in state, especially since her eyelids were shut and she seemed almost peaceful. Several other people were in the room when Ivan arrived but when they left, and he was alone with the body, he did something that he would never have dreamed of doing even a few months ago. He looked around to make sure he was alone and then reached out, touched one of her eyes, and raised the lid.

Immediately, he stepped back. Her exposed eye was a blazing red, almost glowing with intensity, like a live coal. It seemed ferocious, laser sharp, and it was almost impossible to believe it emanated from a comatose body. Ivan left quickly.

On the day before Paavo was to pull the plug, Tuuli's parents spent most of the day there, a line formed outside Tuuli's room, including two people who had travelled from Finland for the occasion, and a group of people from the building who had just realized that they'd put off going all week and this was their last chance. Most of the kitchen and security staff were in this category. Several doctors from the hospital showed up, many of them curious about the results of the plastic surgery, but by early evening, people had been turned away.

At midnight, Father Pekonen read a service for the dead to the family in Finnish and to Faoud and Alice in English. Apollonia led both Silje and Tero to the body to kiss their mother on the forehead (Omar refused to attend) and the ones with sight did the same.

Through it all, Paavo remained standing stiffly, a study in anguish. The blood seemed to have drained from his face. His mother, Sanni, was alarmed and approached Faoud. "Do you think he's all right?" she asked.

"No, I don't," said Faoud. "But I don't think there's much we can do about it."

When everyone was through with their goodbyes, Silje went up to her father, guided by Apollonia.

"Do you want me to stay?" she asked.

"No, Kani, this is something I have to do myself."

The group slowly filed out. Sanni kissed her son and Silje took his hand for a moment. Paavo acknowledged both but it was clear he wanted to be alone.

When everyone had left, Paavo closed the door and wedged a chair under the handle, so the door couldn't be easily opened.

He returned to Tuuli, stared for a moment and then took hold of the sheet and blanket covering her and slowly pulled them away, which seemed like peeling a ripe fruit.

Underneath, she was naked. Although she was 51 when she jumped off the ramp in the aviary, she had an astonishingly youthful body. Aside from the various corrections made by the doctors and the tricks of the plastic surgeon's trade, her body was still shapely and athletic, although her muscles were soft from disuse. Her skin was fair, as one might expect from a Nordic blonde, and almost unblemished, the skin of a young woman, not that of a mother of four. Her breasts were still firm and the nipples hardening from having her covers removed. She had never breastfed her children so her nipples were, so to speak, virginal.

What Paavo hadn't expected was the familiar aroma of Tuuli's body, which evoked a host of memories, starting from their first kiss, in the library of the University of Turku, and continuing through the whole trajectory of their togetherness.

Despite having the cuff around her neck, holding the tracheostomy tube in place, and two tubes in her arms, the figure she presented on the bed was unquestionably erotic. Her long legs and thin feet, the dark blond bush between her legs and the vagina within, seemed unquestionably inviting.

Certainly, Paavo thought so. After pulling out her feeding and emergency tubes, which bled slightly, he ran his hands over her body, caressing her breasts and pulling her legs apart to finger her vagina. He stopped to undress himself and take out a plastic container of water and a small pillbox containing two iridescent black spheres. He folded his clothing and placed them on a chair near the bed. When he was completely naked, he hesitated for perhaps a minute while he stared at Tuuli's body, then downed the black pills with the bottle of water, which he threw in a wastebasket near the bed.

He bent over to feast on her body, savoring the familiar taste of her, until he was fully aroused and prepared for the final act of union.

He was about to mount her when, almost as an afterthought, he reached over to turn off the breathing machine. He pressed the *off* button and a prompt came on giving him a chance to change his mind. He pressed the *off* button again and the machine shut down.

After a few moments, Tuuli's chest stopped moving; the color began to drain from her cheeks, the machines flatlined; he assumed she was dead. He left the tracheostomy cuff in place around her neck because he didn't know how much she'd bleed if he took it out.

He pulled her legs apart and mounted her, pressing himself against her, when the black pills began to take effect. He was kissing her and imagined that she was responding to his tongue. He found himself in a kind of fog of lust, perhaps pressing his penis inside of her, or perhaps not.

Perhaps her legs were wrapped around him, or he was dreaming that her legs were wrapped around him. He felt that he was way up inside her, higher than he had ever been, and he could feel an orgasm building up in his mind or body, or dreamed he could feel it.

The tracheostomy cuff disappeared and her face smoothed out. Her tongue darted out to meet his and at the same time, he said, or mouthed, or thought, "Goodbye, Tuuli," in Finnish, or perhaps she said, Goodbye, Paavo," in Finnish, or English, or perhaps somebody else said something final.

The black spheres worked rapidly. Paavo began to fade out. He seemed to be merging with the flesh beneath him. He went higher inside her, not just his penis but his entire torso. He reached around her to clasp her buttocks and pull their torsos together, not just their genitals but the entire torso, continuing to merge the rest of their bodies. Their stomachs combined, their intestines, then their lungs and hearts.

When their tongues had merged and their faces were about to melt into one another, and they breathed as one, Paavo felt himself go completely limp, as if he'd had an orgasm. Perhaps, he'd had; perhaps he'd dreamed it. Perhaps he had orgasmed into himself.

Except that there was no longer any self, no Paavo to orgasm, no Tuuli to receive one. There didn't seem to be anything at all, not even a lump of love.

—————————

72

61st Floor

THE DEATH OF Tuuli and the bizarre suicide of Paavo sent shockwaves through the building. Although the deaths had occurred outside the building, at the Fuller ICU center on East 61st St., discovered by a nurse who had jimmied open the door, it was not something that could be kept secret. For one, there were tapes. Paavo of all people should have been aware of this, he who had taped almost every aspect of life in the building, but either he was not, or chose to ignore it. Probably the former, given his mental state at the time. It was not a death that anyone would want to capture for posterity.

Faoud viewed it alone, wondering if his wife, Aisha's, death would affect him so desperately. Now he had to decide who else would see the tape, and how to announce the death of Paavo. This was the one time he was glad that Silje was blind. He described the tape to her and together they decided not to let anyone else view it, even the immediate family.

To no avail. An IT functionary at the ICU center posted it online and within two days, everyone in the building had either seen it or heard of it. It made its way to porn sites under the category: necrophilia. (Subsequently, the functionary was fired and the center was sued.)

To her credit, Silje acknowledged the tape in her email on the building's intranet, crafted by Silje and Faoud together. It took 15 minutes to get the right tone and the result was terse and corporate:

> It is with great sadness that we announce the death of our mother, Tuuli, and father, Paavo, at the Fuller ICU Center last Monday, December 4th. A tape of the event, which is circulating on the internet, is an unwarranted invasion of privacy and we deeply regret its existence. There will be

funeral services in both New York and Finland but the date has not been set. We will let you know as soon as possible.

The Nikkanen Family

A press release gave brief biographies of Tuuli and Paavo, with only a spare suggestion of Paavo's role as head of a huge international empire. The names of the surviving relatives were given but Silje's future role was omitted.

Given almost no official commentary but a highly prurient tape, the press sensationalized the deaths as much as possible but they never once mentioned the experiments with toxic gases and the virus that had struck the Nikkanen community. They must have been aware of it. There must have been some sort of leak. There were thousands of ways the public would have known about it. Yet the press focused single mindedly on the necrophiliac ending.

What was even more bizarre was that social media had nothing to say about Paavo's company, his military connections, or Tuuli's suicidal leap from the top of the aviary, which should have been fuel for malicious gossip. It was almost as if there had been a blackout of news, or a conspiracy to hush up details of Paavo's company and clamp down on any incriminating information.

Katie certainly thought so. She discussed it with her brother, Billy, who was closely attuned to the universe of the internet. "It's highly suspicious," she said. "Here we have a major scandal with a company making toxic gas in the middle of New York which blinds or sickens hundreds of people and leads the wife of the industrialist to throw herself to her death and … nothing. It's gotta be a huge coverup."

"Well, I can uncover it if you like," said Billy.

"I don't know," Katie temporized. "With the kids losing both their parents – they don't need that."

With Joe, her suspicions of a major hush-up came to the fore. They had never been an official couple and now they slept together infrequently, whenever the mood took one of them. Both had other outlets as well. But they had developed a friendship and enjoyed one another's company. "Why does everything have to be so fucking mysterious?" she complained. "I could see a reason while they were still making a death gas ..."

"The government would insist on it," Joe offered.

"But why now?"

"Because maybe they're still making it, in another country," said Joe.

"I hadn't thought of that."

No doubt similar conversations were going on throughout the building but the habit of secrecy was so ingrained that nobody was surprised at the lack of a media explosion.

73

81ˢᵗ Floor

A MONTH AFTER PAAVO and Tuuli's death, after the American funeral, attended by a high-level throng of friends and relatives, denizens of the corporate world, high and low-ranking government officials, representatives of the military, the arts and sciences, and a passel of celebrities, and after the Finnish funeral outside of Oulu, where they were buried in the family plot, Silje was officially and legally installed as the Chairwoman of all the Nikkanen enterprises, with Faoud as President. By that time, Silje could tell the difference between light and dark and see shadows. The test subjects who had taken the full body capsules and the brain capsules noted similar improvement.

By that time, Katie had almost finished her Ph.D. dissertation, provisionally titled, *The Aesthetics of Ugliness.* There were a few things she needed to wrap up, especially checking out a classic work of the same title by a German philosopher in the 19ᵗʰ Century, which had recently been translated into English and may have given ugliness a moral dimension. Columbia had a copy but they were way uptown on 116ᵗʰ Street and the building library had its own copy. In fact, the building could connect to a whole literature of ugliness, which was easier to access than Columbia.

She had agreed to meet with Sophie on her lunch break but when the elevator opened to the 81ˢᵗ Floor, she almost didn't recognize the library. It was packed. There were lines at the information desk, the tables and chairs were taken, people were exploring the stacks and there were clumps of readers on the floor, their backs against a wall.

Katie knew many of them or recognized most and greeted or nodded to them as she made her way to Sophie's office. "What's going on?" she asked.

"Didn't you get the email from last week?" asked Sophie.

"Yes, but I didn't think it'd matter to anyone."

"The email said the library was now open to everyone and look what happened."

"Amazing," said Katie. "Is that Silje's doing?"

"I hear she's opening up the gyms and pools, there's even a rumor that we'll be able to see the aviary," said Sophie.

"I never would have expected this," said Katie. As they spoke, Katie noticed something even more unexpected: the absence of any sexual tension between them. Normally, Sophie's hunger was always in the air, if not overt – she had been out to seduce Katie since they met. Normally, Katie enjoyed the tension, though she had no interest in being seduced by a woman, even one as attractive and ravenous as Sophie. Her sister, Annie, would have been a better candidate. But for now, sexual tension wasn't in the air at all. It was gone.

"Oh, I have your *Aesthetics of Ugliness* by Rosenkrantz," said Sophie. "A new translation came out in '15 by Pop and Widrich. Is your thesis almost done?"

"I was just doing references and a bibliography but your book may make me rethink one part of it."

"And then?"

"I finish and turn it in to my mentor; he asks for major revisions; I make them; he wants more; we do one more round; finally he decides when I'm ready to appear before a committee of sadistic inquisitors who attempt to demolish my arguments and humiliate me."

"Actually, my experience was totally different," Sophie smiled. "Two of my committee members were friends and the outside member couldn't have been nicer."

"That's library science. There are no friends in philosophy," said Katie.

"So what happens after your Ph.D.?"

"I join a committee of sadistic inquisitors and try to humiliate other Ph.D. candidates."

"Sounds like an interesting life," said Sophie.

"Katie?" A woman who could have been 30, 40 or 50 approached her, assisted by a white cane with a red bottom segment, which indicated partial blindness rather than total blindness. She obviously wasn't comfortable with the cane and tapped it ahead of her gingerly, as if she wasn't quite sure how to use it.

"Chrystal?" said Katie.

"I recognized your voice," said Chrystal. She was dressed not in her normal blue business suit, suitable for her role in HR, but in jeans and a sports shirt that looked almost too big for her. In fact, she seemed to have shrunk and the light had gone out of her eyes, which were now a deep violet, like Minna's, only darker, almost purple.

"I knew you were in the hospital ..."

"Yes, you went looking for me."

"Isha's been keeping me up to date since then. I know you moved in with him."

Both Katie and Sophie were obviously mesmerized by Chrystal's eyes and caught themselves looking away out of simple politeness.

"It's alright," said Chrystal. "I'm used to it."

"But you can see a *little*," said Katie.

"I can see patterns," said Chrystal. "I can see light and dark and amorphous shapes, movement, near and far, but everything is out of focus. I get headaches from it."

"I'm so sorry," said Katie.

"Don't be. I woke up completely blind and this is better."

She had come for a lesson in Braille, which was in a small reading room that had been made over into a classroom. There were also magnification machines in the library and sight readers for the survivors of the virus who were blind or almost blind. Chrystal wasn't sure her sight would return and wanted to be prepared in case it didn't. She went off to join her class with a date to meet at Finnegan's later that week.

Katie and Sophie stared after her, wondering if her life would ever again be normal, if she'd regain her HR job and especially if she would ever marry Isha, who gave no clues.

But the feeling that stayed with them long after Sophie had returned to her desk and Katie had grabbed a quick bite at the cafeteria and returned to her post in the lobby was how lucky they were. The virus hadn't touched them personally. They had survived.

74

90th Floor

I T WAS THE first Saturday in February. Dr. Benjamin had spent most of the morning in the aviary, preparing his staff for the events of the day.

Dr. Lefkowitz, the head gardener, Dr. Aniashvili, director of the insect garden, and Dr. Sonam, head of the aquarium, did the same.

Coffee, tea and snacks would be served at the pavilion in the aviary, but Emile Lazarus had prepared a buffet in the family dining room on 87, including dishes by Tay Reneau, who could now see the outside world through a prism of little blue squares or rectangles, an awful way to see but better than blindness. The ambient theme of the buffet was the aviary, taken directly from the real one on the 90th floor, with its caws and cackles and the happy tones of birdsong.

Ivan had prepared a brief introduction to the hummingbird collection but his mind was taken up by a woman he had invited to the opening, with whom he had been corresponding on a Christian Singles site. Like Ivan, she was an orthodox Baptist from the Southwest, from a church he had heard of in Albuquerque. She also had been betrayed by a fiancé who had professed premarital celibacy and cheated shamelessly. She was a flautist, studying at Julliard and they were about to meet for the first time, although they had exchanged pictures, emails and texts, and spoken on the phone.

At 11 o'clock, Alice appeared and conferred with the directors of the various departments to make sure there were no disasters in the making. There was also a new escalator between the aviary on 90 and the insect gardens and aquariums on 88, bypassing the labs and work areas on 89. That seemed to be in working order. "The first visitors will be arriving at 11:30," she announced, "and Silje and Mr. Faoud will give say hello to everyone later on, down at the buffet on 87 I think."

Alice and her family had moved into a 3-bedroom professional apartment on 69. Although she could now afford a private school, she kept her children in the building school, mostly out of loyalty to the building, of which she was now a major force. Essentially, she was the gatekeeper to Silje, who relied on her common sense, basic unsentimentality and street smarts. She had almost singlehandedly organized today's opening of the aviary and in doing so consolidated her power within the building. She could tell people what she wanted and it was taken as the will of Silje or Faoud. She was also more or less in charge of Captain Martin and the security detail, the cleaning crews and housekeeping staff, among others.

The power never went to her head mainly because Alice couldn't believe she had it. It still seemed like some unlikely dream. She acted quickly, her advice was down to earth, people listened to her and, amazingly, regarded her as the voice of the establishment. It was hard to get over the fact that a year ago, she was living in a tenement in the Bronx, an unhireable ex-model with two young children, an elderly mother and no prospects. Or that three months ago, she was a waitress.

She took a moment to speak with Ivan, with whom she had developed some kind of rapport. "Are your hummingbirds ready for today?"

"One of our Rufouses has two eggs that could hatch today. Of course, the mother won't let us get near them."

"How big are the eggs?"

"About the size of a jellybean."

Alice smiled. "And I hear you have a special guest today?"

Ivan shook his head. "Is that all over the building now?"

"Well, you invited her."

"I should have known better. Does she like me?"

Alice laughed. "I wouldn't want to spoil the surprise."

What a thoroughly nice man, Alice thought. A year ago, she would have thought he was just another crazy white man, but now, she could appreciate his gentleness and strong religious feeling.

"Am I still the official 211A West 57th Street virgin?" he asked, as Alice was about to move on to the escalator to the 88th Floor."

"I'm afraid so," Alice smiled. "But you may not be after today." She left, wondering when her own social life would take off. Or rather start.

Today's activity was fairly straightforward. The guests would assemble in the aviary, be given a tour by the aviary and botanical garden staff, and then proceed by escalator to the insect and aquarium for another brief tour. They would then take a stairway to 87 for the buffet. The feeling was that it would be better if everyone ate *after* the tours, to avoid sleepiness and littering.

The first guests arrived slightly before 11:30. Many of them had attended Paavo and Tuuli's funeral, business associates, high level executives, a few celebrities, a large contingent from aviaries and zoos across the country, including Ivan's former boss at the Desert Museum in Tucson, ornithologists and entomologists, botanists and landscape architects, and scientists from the building.

Drs. Benjamin and Lefkowitz guided the visitors and made sure to keep them moving along to make room for others. Ivan was one of the docents, in case someone had questions about the hummingbirds, although he was now conversant with many of the other species. He had a long, happy chat with his former boss, pointing out the hummingbirds that were not in the Desert Museum, especially the one remaining Woodstar, which made a surprise appearance not far from the walkway. "There's a Rufous sitting on two eggs, back there in the bush," said Ivan. He handed his ex-boss a pair of binoculars. "Can you see it through there? They could emerge at any time."

A lot of the visitors had the same question. "Where did Mrs. Nikkanen jump from?" No one had been directed to hide the truth and so they pointed to the catwalk at the top of the aviary and down to the stone bridge where she fell. For many visitors, that was more interesting than the birds or flowers.

Coffee, tea and soft drinks were served at the pavilion but not allowed in the aviary itself, although he was hard to stop say, the Director of the Smithsonian Institution, from looking at the Blue-crowned Motmot coffee-cup in hand.

Ivan had just pointed out the Tufted Coquette to a corpulent industrialist and his almost anorexic wife, when a fresh-faced girl of 20 appeared before him. She had an athletic build, her hair was light brown and short, she wore no makeup and she gave the impression of being healthy and happy. "I'm Mary Day," she said, in a bland, Midwestern voice that Ivan found intoxicating.

Ivan was entirely flustered. He could barely squeak out a hello when she said she recognized him from his internet profile. "You look exactly like your picture," she said.

"So do you," he answered.

It took perhaps 20 seconds before he decided this was the woman he wanted to spend the rest of his life with. The attraction was so strong that he felt almost chemically bonded. He had never felt anything remotely like this with Kimberly. Mary seemed equally entranced, or at least stationary as she listened to Ivan explaining the difference between a Black-chinned Hummingbird and a Purple-throated Mountain Gem to a well-groomed couple and their young daughter.

"Are you staying for the buffet?" he asked, as the couple moved on.

"My teacher's playing at 7 at Julliard – I can stay till then. Would you like to come?"

"I should be done here around 4 – can I meet you then?"

"I could stay around," said Mary.

This was more than Ivan could hope for. "If you won't be too bored."

The first group passed down the escalator to the insect gardens as a new group arrived at the aviary. Mary never left Ivan's side while a third and fourth group arrived and left.

After an hour or so, Ivan took Mary down to the aquarium and insect garden and then to the buffet on 87, introducing her to various people along the way. By that time, Mary had decided 1) that he was not dangerous, 2) that everything he said about himself online was the truth, including his membership in the Tanque Verde Baptist Church and his aborted engagement, 3) that he was a lovely man – any man who loved hummingbirds that much couldn't be anything else, 4) that he seemed to be in love with her, and 5) that it was possible, barely possible since she had never experienced the like before, that she was in love with him.

The family dining room was not quite large enough for a crowd this size but it was a magical space none the less. The ceiling and walls projected a live broadcast of the aviary in full color, with the clutters and squawks, screeches and coos as they happened. The guests could see waiters cleaning up the tables in the pavilion and carting away the tables. They could see a bright sky overhead and hear the hum of the ventilation and heating systems. They could see everything as it happened. The music was the birds.

Emile Lazarus had created a magnificent buffet, with soul food by Tay for people who didn't appreciate such magnificence. It was an odd combination of caviar, truffles and cassoulet with collard greens and fried chicken, all consumed greedily and completely.

Faoud rose from his table and welcomed the guests to the official opening of the Aviary, the Insect Garden and Aquarium, all made possible by the generosity of the daughter of the late Dr. and Mrs. Nikkanen, Silje Nikkanen, and her brothers and sisters.

Silje stood up at a table in the front of the room. Behind her was a pond in which Scarlet Ibises were wading and rare Micronesian kingfishers floated on the surface. Silje was dressed in a black silk tunic, rimmed with iridescent lavender, her long hair falling over her shoulders and down the front of the tunic. She had the look of a fairy tale princess, magical and medieval.

Her sight was better than it was but still not close to normal. Still, she had given up the dark glasses she had worn when she was completely blind and looked out at the world with her own two eyes, which everyone could see were cobalt and penetrating. More out of habit than of necessity, Apollonia sat next to her and then Minna, Mika, Tero and Naziha. Omar was not present, as he had been fired. Completing the table were Paavo's mother, Sanni, Tuuli's parents, Chitra Shivaji, Silje's classmate and lover, and Alice.

"This is a big day for us at 211A West 57th Street," Silje said in a soft voice that she raised when she could see people straining to hear her. "The opening of the aviary to the public. The opening of the library, the gyms, the pools and most other facilities to all the residents of the building and their guests."

"Our chemical operations have been moved out of the city and the building has now been officially cleared by the Department of Health."

"And the chemical responsible for all our problems has been isolated and an antidote is in the works."

She looked over at Sanni. "On a personal note, our grandmother, Sanni Nikkanen, has graciously agreed to be our legal guardian until I come of age next year.

"And contrary to rumors, we are not selling the building. Our building, our company and our people are in better shape than ever. So let's celebrate."

At that signal, all the doors opened and a flood of hummingbirds was released into the room. They buzzed about randomly, filling the room with a pandemonium of iridescence, giving off flecks of emerald, copper, gold and topaz, and delighting the visitors, except for Ivan.

"This is insane," he said to Mary. "Where are they supposed to go? What are they supposed to do?"

Mary took his hand, which sent a shockwave through him and made him momentarily forget the plight of the hummingbirds. "They'll figure it out," she said.

"No, it'll be up to me," he said.

"What are they?" asked Mary.

"I see mostly Rufous, some Costas, Annas, up there a Calliope … the images on the walls are confusing them."

"Can't you just enjoy them?"

The question stopped Ivan for a moment, and he felt a wave a happiness wash over him, as they watched the hummingbirds zooming for position, divebombing for dominance, hovering over food and exploring the room at breakneck starts and stops.

"Yes, I can," he said, pressing Mary's hand. "They're magnificent."

The End.

Printed in the United States
By Bookmasters